THE TRIP

"What the hell was *that*?" Quadie looked shaken as he took off the Fourier coil.

"What?"

"The ending. The beginning. The whole thing! I morphed into a—no, I didn't just morph, I *became*. What just happened is impossible, Carver! That program violates every known law of the Web—and probably several of nature's as well. How did you do it?"

Carver smiled mischievously. "Magic."

LIVING
REAL

JAMES C. BASSETT

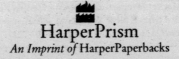

HarperPrism

An Imprint of HarperPaperbacks

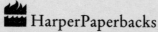
HarperPaperbacks
A Division of HarperCollins*Publishers*
10 East 53rd Street, New York, N.Y. 10022-5299

Copyright © 1997 by James C. Bassett

ISBN 0-06-105729-0

Cover illustration by Peter Gudynas

First printing: March 1997

Printed in the United States of America

Visit HarperPaperbacks on the World Wide Web at
http://www.harpercollins.com/paperbacks

❖ 10 9 8 7 6 5 4 3 2 1

This book is for Jenn, who always tells me what I need to hear instead of just what I want to hear.

ACKNOWLEDGMENTS

In keeping with the general social condition of the '90s, the author wishes to disavow all personal responsibility for the sufferings this novel has caused him, and instead blame it all on the following:

For selling the book, Susan Graham;
for buying it, John Douglas.
For their excellent help with the manuscript, as well as their encouragement and unflagging personal support throughout the whole grueling process,
Steve Antczak, Liath Appleton, Jenn Downey,
Johna Johnson, and Rob Sommers.
I couldn't have done it (or survived it) without you.

The things we see are the same things that are within us. There is no reality except the one contained within us. That is why so many people live such an unreal life. They take the images outside them for reality and never allow the world within to assert itself.

— *Herman Hesse*

PART 1

ONE

Fractal clouds built and dissipated in the late summer sky. The long, sweet grass surged in a breeze that carried the first hints of the approaching autumn. From nearby, hidden behind a thicket, a mountain brook babbled, its quick, murmuring splashes beckoning like whispered voices whose words he could not quite make out.

They're saying, Carver Blervaque thought sullenly as he stood on the edge of a cliff, staring into the valley far below, *that this is really dull. They're saying you're washed up.*

A raucous chirping distracted him, and he looked up. A pair of swallows tumbled overhead, arguing shrilly over who was chasing whom. Carver considered the birds for a moment, then sighed in disgust and dove head first off the cliff into emptiness.

Terror exploded within Carver as he fell, hundreds of meters of jagged rock wall streaking upward and past him with frightening speed. The rushing air stole the sound from his throat, but he screamed anyway. Adrenaline surged through his body, sending his heart racing as he plunged to his death.

He screamed, and screamed again, and then he stopped. It wasn't doing any good at all. This just wasn't going to work. He had to try someting else.

As he continued to fall, Carver spread his arms out from his sides. The bones twisted, curving slightly, and feathers began to sprout from his dark chocolate skin. Carver extended the morph farther and guided his terror into a trembling excitement. His wings soon caught the air and he rose on a thermal, an eagle soaring over the valley.

It was a thrilling feeling, floating above the world, unconnected, separate from everything. It was escape; it was freedom. It was . . .

It was *amateur*. It was far too Disney, not nearly real or natural enough. And it had all been done before. He needed to come up with something different, something entirely new.

But he couldn't.

His wings slapped against the air and he rose higher, through the clouds and beyond. The air grew cold and thin. The eagle no longer seemed appropriate; Carver drew back his wings and let them stiffen, and turned the feathers into a smooth composite skin as he morphed into a delta-winged scramjet, a nearly invisible cone of blue-white fire roaring out of its engine as he hurtled heavenward. He tried desperately to relax and let a plot idea come to him, but all he could think of was how much he detested sci-fi adventures.

Still he continued to rise, until the light faded and he was falling through space, alone but for the compassionless gazes of the ancient and incomprehensible stars.

And it was all so boring. The magic was gone.

"Screw it," Carver grumbled irritably. He gave up, and the world changed.

He was lying on his back, a smooth ivory torus spanning his vision as it arched from ear to ear, rising at its highest only a few centimeters from his face.

He was Out.

Carver pressed the release switch and the arch swung

away above his head. He lay on his set for a long while, staring blankly at the ceiling, before he finally stood and left his workroom.

The afternoon was dying, and the house had turned its lights on against the gloom. Carver heard sounds from the living room as he walked down the hallway. Rose was in there watching the videonly, as usual. He didn't feel like dealing with her right now, so he took the long way to the kitchen, down the hallway and through the dining room.

He opened the refrigerator and removed a Guinness. The can opened with a satisfying *phsst* of escaping nitrogen.

"Carver? I just made a fresh pot of tea, if you want some."

"I'm fine," he grumbled as he poured the beer into a tall pint glass.

"Can I get you anything else?" his wife called again.

Carver balled up his fists and bit back a nasty remark. "No," he said through clenched teeth. "Thank you. I have everything I need."

The stout settled slowly as the foam rose to collar the glass in creamy tan lace. Carver felt a touch of satisfaction that he could afford such actual pleasures, not just in the virtual reality of the Web. He drank deeply, letting the cold, tangy liquid wash away his tension.

"Are things still not going well?"

Startled, Carver nearly choked on his Guinness. He turned to see his wife standing tentatively in the doorway.

"It's not going *at all*. That's the problem."

"I'm . . . I'm sure it will all work out soon, sweetheart."

"*Soon?* I haven't been able to do a damn thing in six months, Rose," he said acidly.

Rose entered the kitchen and poured herself another cup of tea. She was only a few centimeters shorter than Carver, her skin as pale as his was dark, with short brown hair that she invariably wore in a ponytail. "I always put myself in a meditative state when I'm working. It might help you, too," she suggested as she stirred milk and sugar into the tea.

"Well, it won't. It doesn't. I've tried all of my relaxation programs."

"Yes, but what about *meditation*? It's a whole different experience, Carver."

"Yes it is, and one that doesn't work in the Web. Get anywhere near a dissociative state, and a set treats it like falling asleep or passing out. You get Escaped."

"Meditation isn't necessarily—"

Carver rolled his eyes and turned away from her. "It's not the program, Rose. It's me. My creativity has just dried up, all right?"

"Maybe it would help to try something else for a while. I've found that sometimes if I'm really having trouble with a painting, it helps to set it aside and try sculpting instead, or vice versa. Get it completely out of my thoughts, you know? Do you think it might—"

"No, I don't." Carver slammed his mug down so hard the beer sloshed out onto the counter. "I'm a director, Rose. I create *realities*. There's no substitute for that, no other medium I can use, so just spare me your little platitudes, okay?"

He stared down at the dark puddle spreading around the glass and waited for his wife to go away. But instead of leaving, Rose asked very quietly, "What's wrong, Carver?"

He spun around, sarcastic and angry words on his lips, but they died when he saw her tears. He slumped back against the kitchen counter, suddenly very tired.

"I'm sorry, Rose."

She set her cup down and put her arms around him. Carver held her tightly, fighting away tears of his own now.

After a long silence, Rose whispered, "Is it . . ."

"What?"

"Is it us, Carver? I mean, is it me?"

Carver drew a deep, slow breath. "No," he said eventually. "I'm just so frustrated. I can't figure out what happened. I just don't know what to do."

"Maybe you should take a break for a while."

"Rose, I've been taking a break for months. That's the problem."

"That's not what I meant. I think you could use a vacation."

Carver shrugged. "We've got plenty—"

Rose stamped her foot and drew back from him. "No! I mean a *real* vacation, Carver. Not in the Web, but for real. I think you need to get away from the Web." She put a hand on his cheek. "I'm worried about you, sweetie. You spend too much time in the Web. It's unhealthy."

"Unhealthy? Okay, so I'm not in top shape, but I work out enough—"

"I don't mean physically. I don't think it's good for you to spend so much time escaping from the real world."

"How is it escape? The Fourier coil interacts directly with the brain. As far as the mind knows, virtuality is as real as anything coming in through the senses from Outside."

"But it's *not* real!"

Carver sighed. "Well, of course not. But if there's no way to tell—"

"But it's not *real*," his wife protested. "It's not *natural*."

Carver couldn't help smiling. "Look, Rose, I know you're old-fashioned—"

"I'm serious, Carver."

He looked at her for a few seconds. "I know you are, Rose," he said quietly. "But I don't understand why."

"Because it frightens me. And I worry about you."

"Don't," he sighed. "It's just a creative block. I'll work through it."

"But what about us?" she whispered. "All we ever do anymore is fight."

"That's my fault. I've been taking out my frustrations on you. I have no right to do that. I'm sorry."

She nuzzled his neck. "Mmm. Come have some tea with me and I might forgive you. What do you say?"

"In a bit. I need to take care of a few more things first. It shouldn't take too long."

"Promise?"

"Sure."

He kissed her and walked back to his workroom. The tension of the fight had exhausted him, and he felt the need to be alone for a while before he joined her again.

Carver lay down on the set. The Fourier coil eclipsed his vision, and he was suddenly standing in his interface.

Architecturally, the room was almost an exact copy of his workroom, but instead of the two sets in the center of the room, there was a single large easy chair. Also, there was no door, and rather than bare gray plastic panels, the walls here were lined with shelves of books. The shelves formed a seat where they passed under the window—the glass here did not reach to the floor as it did in the real room. A huge white Persian cat was curled up on this window seat against a backdrop of night.

"Your emotional response index is off the scale," the cat said with a stretch and a yawn. "What's wrong?"

"You're not an eliza, dammit, so don't try to analyze me."

"Sorry, boss."

Carver flopped down onto the chair. "No, God, I'm sorry. I'm a little worked up over some stuff."

"How about a drink?"

"No thanks."

God leapt effortlessly from the window seat to Carver's lap. "Are we working or relaxing?"

Carver leaned back in the chair and closed his eyes. God was his agent, a customized machine intelligence that ran his interface.

"I don't know. I just need to think awhile."

"If you say so, boss. Wake me if it actually works."

"You've gotten pretty sarcastic lately, haven't you?" Carver asked the M.I. "You didn't learn that from me. I think Quadie's been spending too much time here."

God did not reply. Carver clicked instantly to the window seat, leaving the M.I. behind in the chair, and gazed out at the woods. In the faint light that passed through the window he could just barely see the trees outside. He stared at the leaves growing in their precisely random fashion on the graftal-patterned branches. It was a world that existed only within the mathematical machinations of the Web, but it felt perfectly real. And it was his world, a world of his creation. He controlled everything in it, could create or destroy, alter and regulate every aspect with a simple thought.

And yet, he couldn't tell if the virtual outside looked the same as the real Outside. It had been a long while since he'd really paid close attention to either one. For someone who made his living creating worlds, he was beginning to realize that he was not very good at observing the ones he lived in.

And observation was the key to successful directing. Anyone could take care of the obvious, such as the biting cold of a winter storm or the sensations of eating something spicy, but few people would ever think to program such subtle responses as the effect of a lover's touch or the tickle of a bead of sweat running down one's spine, and fewer still would ever do it well. And yet such minutiae were absolutely necessary. Their omission would compromise the semblance of base reality in a program.

Carver had a reputation for being one of the best at such things. Of course, none of that would matter if he couldn't come up with a decent idea.

He continued to stare at the trees for a long time. He let his mind drift freely, having neither the energy to focus his thoughts on work nor the desire to dwell on the fight with

Rose. He normally appreciated her outside perspective, but lately it had become simply irritating. It didn't seem to have any bearing on his work anymore. Such as it was.

A draft seeped through the window. Carver halted it, then after some thought, deleted the outside altogether. The window went gray and opaque.

"What are you doing?" God asked.

"I'm not sure," Carver replied. "Maybe I'm meditating."

"Now you're the one being sarcastic."

"'Bye, God," Carver said, and the cat faded out.

He looked about the room. It felt strangely small and claustrophobic without an external view. The walls of books loomed.

The books disappeared, then the shelves, leaving texture-less walls the same neutral shade as the window. The warm amber tones of the chair and the mahogany table with its reading lamp seemed out of place. Carver thought them away. He noticed with some annoyance that they left no impressions in the lush Persian carpet. So much for perfection. Perhaps he was not really as good as he thought. (Persian cat, Persian carpet—had he done that on purpose? Probably, but he couldn't remember why.)

The carpet vanished, along with the floorboards beneath it, the colorless gray washing across the nonexistent surface.

The room was bare and featureless now, like a prison. Worse: in a prison—in anyplace *real*—the walls would at least have substance. However smooth and bare, they would have texture, distinguishing marks, variations in surface and color.

Carver pushed with his mind and the walls collapsed. The floor fell away and the ceiling dissolved, and he was floating in an infinity of horizonless gray. Faint, irregular grid lines—some darker than the surrounding nonworld, some lighter, but all gray—traced off into the simulated Euclidean distance. Only his body remained now. Carver erased his image, and even that vanished.

This was what he wanted. There was nothing here of his creation. There was nothing at all here. There was only the Web in its pure, unactualized state—potential without form, without constraint, waiting to be developed. Devoid of all programming, nothing existed here but structure.

Structure, and data. Even here Carver felt the distracting rush of dataflow all around him. This lattice was a representation of the myriad connections between the Web's neuristors, digilog switching units analogous to the transistors in a digital processor but modeled after the neurons in a living brain. Neuristors combined the speed and reliability of digital systems with the flexibility inherent in analog operations.

A typical set contained a few billion neuristors with many times that number of connections between them. And because neuristors had the ability to adapt the relative strengths of their own interconnections based on past experience, they had, in effect, the ability to learn.

A segment of the Web trained in manipulating a particular kind of data—translating languages, for instance, or resolving patterns from vague associations—would quickly become faster and more efficient at that task than another part of the Web that had no such experience.

Different sections of the Web would therefore process the same information in slightly different ways, depending on the local microstructure, yet would still arrive at the same result. Different routes to the same destination. In the very grossest terms, programming the Web could be seen more as a matter of giving suggestions than instructions. A programmer developed the specific end result he wanted, and the instruction set for getting there, and when the program ran, the Web itself would figure out how best to restructure the particular local matrix in order to create the desired results.

So, while digital computers were still far superior at

handling logical and mathematical operations, the Web was infinitely better suited for dealing with the variances of human psychology. Unlike digital systems, which simply disallowed or ignored user responses not anticipated by the programmer, the Web could instantly adapt to anything a user did, no matter how unforeseen—once a director created the world and the rules by which it operated. The program's reality, which could be defined as its sense of consistent internal logic, was preserved. The trick, of course—the trick at which Carver excelled—lay in devising that logic.

All of this meant, Carver knew, that Rose was in a sense right. Even though virtuality seemed as solid and immediate and real as natural reality, experience in the Web was nothing more than data. There was nowhere else he could go, no "other medium" to which he could retreat. It was all just data. Whatever the mind's experience, virtuality did not really exist except as optical pulses within a vast neural network. There was nothing more than that, aside from the Fourier coil.

Carver's musings screeched to a halt. A wild idea had suddenly taken shape in his mind. He rarely listened to hunches, but he figured he no longer had anything to lose.

As though feeling the finish on a piece of fine woodwork, he spread slowly outward across the system, moving gently back and forth in search of defects or irregularities in the fabric of the Web. He checked carefully around the grid lines and intersecting nodes, and at last found what he was looking for.

One of the lines was not entirely uniform in its construction. It rippled slightly here—its color seemed less dense. He intensified his scrutiny. The datapath frayed under his touch.

The space within was entirely devoid of color, a darkness closer than the darkest black Carver could imagine. He slipped through the threads and left the grid behind.

Nothing.

Carver's mind sat isolated from his brain and his body. Touch, sight, sound, all physical sensations were nonexistent. The void was infinite and absolute, entirely without scale. It was not even emptiness, for there was nothing to *be* empty. It was merely . . . absence.

And yet absence, he thought suddenly, mysterious and inconceivable as it was, was so much more hopeful than any presence, for it introduced the idea of *possibility*—for growth, and change. Absence was potential.

Carver squelched this track of thought. Solipsism and Cartesian philosophy had never been high on his list of interests. His thoughts always wandered when he wanted to concentrate—his mind rebelling against being forced to work. He slowed his time-sense to its lowest possible setting and drew his mind down to a single point of awareness. It was a technique he used when programming. It helped him focus his creative energies, like focusing the sun through a lens until the surface beneath burst into flame.

But no fire smoldered here, nor anything else. Carver had found the Fourier coil's synaptic matrix.

The Fourier coil was the physical interface between the Web and the human brain. The coil provided the means of interaction between the Web and the user, but only according to the program the user was tuning. Here in the coil's own programming matrix, with no program to create inputs, the coil produced none of its own.

However, even though Carver had no contact with the Web itself, as long as the Fourier coil detected conscious brain waves, his set would not tune him out. If he could develop a program to isolate a small section of the coil's synaptic matrix, he could lock his mind away here like a genie in a bottle any time he wanted, easily. A single path back to his interface would provide instant access without allowing in any extraneous dataflow.

And then, he thought, he could copy the program to

Rose's interface. She was the one who was so keen on meditation. Maybe if she could meditate in the Web, she would start to feel more comfortable about tuning-in. Maybe she would start to feel more comfortable about a lot of things. That, he decided, would be a very good thing.

The first step was to create the bottle. Without benefit of his interface, Carver was forced to interact with the Web in a more primitive manner. In his mind he assembled a string of command inputs. It was harder than he'd expected, and his rustiness annoyed him. He had become too reliant on user-friendly interfaces and agents. It had been years since he'd done any direct programming himself.

As he reached outward across the void, disconnected associations flashed through his mind. Heavy machinery clanked and pounded to the fresh electrical smell of a summer thunderstorm. The bright taste of metal filled his mouth while rough tree bark scratched under this fingers. He caught a brief glimpse of a bird in flight, its flapping wings painting green across his vision, salt over his tongue.

Strange. He had not expected that at all. In the absence of program, the coil should not do anything.

He could wonder about that later. Right now, he had work to do. He searched again through the void, and again synesthesia streaked through his mind. Again, and again. And it all felt perfectly real.

But did that make it real, or just a persistent illusion?

A single illusion—a talking cat, for instance—could easily be dismissed as hallucination, but it had been proven that persistent illusions would eventually fool the senses and be unconsciously accepted as reality. If the cat spoke every time you saw it, or if all cats began to speak, there was something wrong with either reality or your sanity. And while it was not likely to be reality that needed some time in the shop, the human mind found it easier—and psychologically safer—to accept this possibility than a change in its own sanity.

Then again, according to Berkeley, if you met a talking cat, you could deny that it really existed, but you couldn't deny that you heard it talking. At least in the Web everything existed equally—a talking cat was no more illusory than a rock, nor was the rock any more real than the cat.

Did that make the Web less valid than natural reality, or more?

Anything from Outside could be recreated in the Web, but only as a copy. It would not exist here in the same sense that it did there. On the other hand, not everything possible here could be recreated Outside. He could easily make a copy of his workroom in the Web, but the copy wasn't a real room—but here he had a talking cat, an impossibility Outside.

Carver had a feeling he was just going around in ever-tighter circles, futilely comparing apples and oranges—

He stopped abruptly. That was it exactly. He was trying to compare two systems that defied comparison. Rose was not right. Even though the Web did not exist except as data, it was still, by virtue of its very nature, as real as the Outside. One could not arbitrarily declare one experience real and one fake merely because of a difference in their sources. They both felt real, and so for all practical purposes they both were real. Perhaps tuning-in to this nothing-space would help Rose see that. Once again Carver decided this would be good for her.

Rose.

Carver suddenly remembered he had promised to tune-out soon. He quickly finished his work in the void and returned to his interface.

"What time is it?"

"Twelve-seventeen," God replied. "Quadie tuned you at ten-thirty, but I told him you were working. Shall I tune him for you?"

"No time now. I'm late. I want you to save the program

I've just been working on, and transfer a copy to Rose's interface."

The cat sighed. "Whatever you say, O Thankless One."

"Thank you, God. Good-night."

Carver tuned-out to find the house dark. The lights came up in the hallway as he walked to the living room, but the videonly screen there was dark. He'd hoped to find Rose asleep on the couch, but she hadn't waited up for him.

He walked back to the bedroom and looked in. Rose lay curled up in their bed. He had stayed tuned-in too long, and she'd given up on him. It would be bad in the morning.

Carver left the lights off while he prepared for bed. As he undressed he sensed a strange nagging feeling within—a subtle retracing of his thoughts just below the threshold of consciousness, as though he knew he had forgotten something but couldn't quite recall what. He shrugged it off. It was probably just fatigue.

He crawled into bed carefully so as not to wake his wife. As he lay in the darkness beside her, staring up at a ceiling he could not see, he thought about his new discovery.

He wished he knew more about how the Fourier coil operated. He knew it induced in the brain's own neural pathways all of the sensations of the Web's virtuality, and it detected the brain waves behind the user's responses and integrated them into the program. He had thought there would simply be no effect without a program to interpret any of these signals, but apparently he'd been wrong.

There obviously were effects—random effects. As Carver probed the synaptic matrix, the Fourier coil had in turn stimulated random areas of his own brain. Without a program to which he was consciously reacting, the Web did not know how to interpret his thoughts.

He thought about this. If he could map these effects, he could perhaps control them. If he could learn how to control the Fourier coil directly, independently of a virtual program, he could create truly subconscious effects within his programs—subliminal effects. Such a technique would revolutionize his directing—perhaps programming in general. It would certainly put him a quantum leap ahead of where he'd been. Plus, it would baffle every other director and make them all green with envy. Even Quadie.

And all he had to do was invent a new art and science.

TWO

"No, Carver."

Carver planted his elbows on the breakfast table and leaned forward. "Rose, please, I'm just asking you to try it."

"*No*. I don't want to."

"Oh, come on, Rose."

Rose had already been out of the bed when Carver awoke. He found her in the kitchen already making breakfast, but she'd maintained a curt silence toward him even after he began helping her with the preparations.

"Look, I know you're upset," he said now. "I stayed tuned-in for too long last night—"

"I'm not upset."

"Yes you are. Your voice has that quiet, concise tone you always get when you're mad at me."

Rose took a bite of her bagel. She chewed very slowly and swallowed before saying, "That's beside the point."

"No it's not, honey." Carver sat back and tried to calm himself. "The routine I want you to tune is what I was working on last night. Don't you see, Rose? I was *working*. I started thinking about what you said, about meditating and trying a new medium—"

"The things I said? They helped?"

"Yes!" Carver's voice cracked with frustration. "And I think I can do something really incredible with it, but before I do any more work on it, I need you to try it out. I need to see if it works for other people and not just me."

Rose stared out the French doors at the sunlight playing across the deck. Carver watched her closely as she sipped at her coffee, holding her mug in both hands.

"All right," she said at last, still staring at the deck and the woods beyond it. "I'll give it a tune. But I can't promise anything."

Carver smiled. "That's okay. A few minutes should be enough. I just want to see what you think of it." He stood and walked around to his wife's side of the table. He bent down and kissed the top of her head. "Thanks, Rose."

"You're welcome. I'll tune-in right after I do the dishes."

"Leave 'em," Carver told her. "I'll do them in a bit. I want to tune Jan right now and tell her I'm working again. But take your time—just whenever you get around to it."

"As long as it's soon, eh?"

Carver smiled at her again and headed for his workroom.

Jan Tarrega, Carver's business manager for almost fifteen years, was unavailable, so he left her a message and returned to his interface.

"What horrors shall we unleash upon the unsuspecting world today?" God asked.

Carver stared at his agent. "You're getting really weird. I might have to reprogram you soon," he told the M.I. After a beat, he said, "I'm just going to work on something by myself for now."

He walked along the shelf until he came to the book corresponding to the Fourier routine he'd developed last night. He pulled the book from its place and opened it, and the universe imploded around him as he fell once more into absence.

He'd been working for almost an hour when a sudden far-away flash distracted him. It zigzagged through the synaptic matrix with a sparkling explosion of static, moving slowly toward Carver. Fascinated, he watched the glittering display. It was far brighter and more active—more *there*—than anything he had seen so far in his void. It seemed to originate from a central cluster of activity and spatter outward in an almost crystalline pattern.

The static resolved into Quadie's voice. "Hey, Car— What the fuck?" As instantly as it had appeared, the static vanished.

Carver quickly returned to his interface. Before he could even sit down in his chair, a man manifested in the middle of the room, looking very upset. He was tall and lanky, with close-cropped blond hair and an electric-blue lightning bolt that periodically flashed across his face from above his right temple to his left cheek. He wore an oversized black sequined suit with a polished chromium cuirass beneath. The image was unfamiliar, but automatic ID recognition told Carver instantly that this was indeed his friend Quadie.

"Son of a bitch."

"Hi, Quadie. What's your data?"

"You tell me," Quadie demanded. "What the hell was that?"

"What was what?" Carver asked innocently.

Quadie sank down onto the window seat and stared pointedly at Carver. "I just tried to tune you, and ended up—I don't know where. It was almost like the Web went down. I couldn't see or feel anything. And then my set Escaped me."

"I was in a . . . a blank workspace," Carver told his friend. "I heard you fine, so you must have been in it, but blanked, that's all."

"Then why did I get kicked Out?"

Carver shrugged. A sultry female voice said from

nowhere, "I lost contact with you when you entered Carver's interface, Quadie. Automatic safety overrides cut in to disengage you from the system."

"What do you mean, Ariel?" Quadie asked the disembodied voice of his own agent. "How did you lose contact with me?"

"According to my data, you disappeared from the Web. That's all I can tell you at this point."

"I disappeared? Carver, you took control of my interface!" Quadie's eyes narrowed with suspicion. "What the fuck are you up to, mate? Like hell that was just a blank workspace."

"It was a new kind of workspace I've been developing," Carver said.

"So what the hell happened to me?"

Carver shrugged again and shook his head. "I couldn't tell you."

"How come you didn't get Escaped? Why didn't God lose contact with you?"

"I, uh, I made a special routine to deal with it. You didn't have it, so Ariel lost track of you."

Quadie arched an eyebrow. "You know I'm not buying a word of this, my friend. What are you *really* doing?"

Carver just smiled mysteriously and sipped the brandy that manifested at his thought. God asked, "And you, Quadie?"

"An Irish Flag, please," Quadie said. A glass filled with orange, white, and green layers manifested in his hand, and he drank the contents in a single gulp. When he righted the glass, it filled again. "Motherfuck, Carver, that scared the piss out of me."

"Don't be such a wimp, Quadie. We're artists—we deal with the infinite every day."

"No, we deal with the *indefinite* every day. And when we do deal with the infinite, we don't have to come face-to-face with it. I've never been so disoriented in my life. How the hell did you do that? I've never seen Webspace that . . . that empty before. Even outer space has *something* in it. What was it?"

"Magic," Carver deadpanned.

"Cut the gigo. Really, how'd you do it?"

"What, I should just give away all my trade secrets? You want to know, you can figure it out for yourself. Unless you've gone stupid."

"No stupider than you, mate."

Carver winced. "That bad, huh? Well, I guess that explains the new look."

Quadie tugged at his cuffs. "Pretty snappy, eh?"

"Pretty tall. And what's with the hair? Short hair suddenly come back in, or are you bucking style again?"

"I thought it suited the overall look better. What do you think about this?" He indicated the lightning bolt.

"I like it. Kind of disconcerting the way it flashes over your eye like that, though."

"It's an attention-getter."

"That hair is an attention-getter."

Quadie laughed. "That's the idea, anyway. I just finished the image before I tuned you—or tried to tune you, I should say. Care to help me debut it?"

"The Redline?"

"Where else, mate? Where else?"

He disappeared in a puff of smoke. Carver grinned at the effect. "Where else, indeed?" he said to himself before he, too, demanifested.

Network 37 was one of the oldest on the Web, having been one of the first seeds to germinate from the Deregulation Act of '17. Like all of that first crop of private Networks, it had prospered during the Soaring Twenties, but without giving in to the excess that had marked so many of its rival siblings. When the Big Crash came, Network 37 survived. Careful and clever management kept it alive through the thirties. The Network grew steadily, remaining strong even when competition began to thrive once again—though more cautiously—in the forties and fifties. Only when it had grown to maturity did Network 37 begin to explore the wilder side of the public's desire.

Now Network 37 was the largest in the Web, and yet the most exclusive. Its processing power was enormous. Not that that mattered. Most people who tuned-in Network 37 did so for the facetime—the chance to be seen there, to show off new custom images and to catch new trends before they hit the other Networks. They talked about the latest programs they had tuned, and Who was doing What. It was gaudy and ultraglamorous and ridiculously overdone, and people loved it.

A Carnival greeted Carver when he manifested. The participants, dressed in ostentatious, impossible costumes, swarmed about the entrance field. Many of the revelers had their hair and skin embellished. Sprays of fireworks shot from the crowd, spawning an occasional dragon or other chimera that would descend upon one of the partiers and lift him or her high into the air to soar above the rest until the creature faded and the delighted flier settled lazily back into the frenzied crush.

Carver stood watching the festivities for several minutes. Until he officially entered into the reality of Network 37, the show was video only, pictures to tantalize. The full experience was reserved for paying users. There were at any given time several thousand people in the entrance field just watching the marvels that lay beyond their social and financial reach, but Carver could not see them. The Network's protocol prevented gawkers from intruding into the spectacle. From inside the Network, the entrance field appeared as nothing more than a deserted crystal platform floating above a golden ziggurat of stairs.

Carver finally caught sight of Quadie standing at the base of the entrance field, struggling vainly to keep his place while the revelers buffeted past. As Carver watched, several men and women surrounded Quadie and tried to pull him along with them. Quadie shook his head and pointed reluctantly to the entrance field.

Carver selected a jumpsuit of flowing molten lava from his wardrobe and stepped onto the crystal platform. His senses erupted with the sudden overload as the new reality unfolded in his mind. Many Networks downloaded gradually to an interface, giving the user a chance to accommodate the shift, but Network 37 seemed to operate by the motto "Too much is always better than not enough." Network 37 always went for overkill.

The noise of the Carnival was loud, but not quite deafening. The Network automatically dampened street noise when it rose to a certain level. Carver was convinced the Network maintained a minimum parameter as well to keep from ever seeming dull.

Quadie rose up into the air when he spotted Carver, who floated up to join him. Together they flew toward The Redline. As soon as they'd passed beyond the Carnival, Quadie motioned toward the ground. "Let's walk," he told Carver. "I want to get max facetime for the new image."

They landed on the Mall, a wide pedestrian terrace bounded on one side by lush tropical greenery, and on the other by a reflecting pool. The avenue beneath their feet was absurdly cushioned in gold-and-silver-brocaded velvet that glinted in the light of the full sun. Hundreds of other people either walked past or floated lazily overhead in the bright, clear sky, but the traffic was not nearly as heavy as it had been in the midst of the Carnival.

Quadie and Carver watched the other users as they walked, trying their best to ignore the ad kiosks jammed along the edges of the Mall, but one caught Carver's eye.

"Hey, look!"

The kiosk was running segments from Quadie's latest program, *All the World's a Stage*. Both men stopped to watch. Once Carver focused his attention on the ad, the kiosk downloaded a tantalizing preview of the program—several experiences embellished and edited so as to stimulate maximum interest.

The scenes Carver caught were out of order, and arranged so the excitement built with each cut: he was in a castle, being stabbed by an assassin; he was riding a strange beast across some kind of postnuclear wasteland; he was in some underground Dantean hell.

When scenes began to repeat, he turned away, breaking the kiosk's connection with his interface. Quadie glowered beside him, grumbling disgustedly to himself. "I hate adverts," he said. "I hate them. Every damn time, they completely screw up what you're trying to do. They give away the ending, they screw with the setup, they Disney the whole . . ." He turned to Carver with a look of bewilderment, and his mouth moved silently as he searched for the words to express his loathing. At last he gave up and simply said, "I hate them."

"Yeah, so do I, man," Carver told him. "But without advertising, nobody knows about your programs. They don't know, they don't tune-in—and that means no money."

"Sure, at first, maybe. But we're both hot enough that we don't need to be advertised. We could program taking a shit and people would tune-in."

Carver clamped both hands over his mouth and mumbled inarticulately. When Quadie stared questioningly at him, he let his hands fall and explained, "I'm trying desperately hard not to make the obvious comment you just set yourself up for."

"Your discretion is *sooo* appreciated."

"Hey, if you can't laugh at your friends . . . what good are they?"

They walked on in silence until Quadie said, "You know why we really need advertising? 'Cause there's no time for anything to get popular by word of mouth. *Stage* has only been out for a month and it's already peaked."

"I know what you mean. I haven't done anything for six months, and Jan is screaming at me that my entire reputation is being ruined because of it."

"Well, Jan's an incredible bitch," Quadie said. He and Jan got along so poorly that the enmity between them was almost legendary. "But that's beside the point. It's true, though, things change too fucking fast here. Programs, fashions—hell, even the people change."

"Yeah, like that cheap new image you bought yourself, eh?"

Quadie raised his eyebrows in mock indignation. "Bought? *Bought?* You think I went to Imag-A-Nation and had some *consultant* design this for me?" He rubbed a hand over the bristly hair for effect. "Christ, mate, name me one director—name me one *programmer*—who doesn't design his own image. Aside from yourself."

"Hey, I did this myself."

"Yeah, once upon a time. But you never change. You always look the same. It's so . . . old-fashioned."

"I've been busy. Yeah, that's it. Real busy." Carver touched his tight Afro, then looked at his dark brown skin. He spread his arms. "This is what I really look like. I don't need to change. I like my appearance."

"So do I," a breathy voice behind them said matter-of-factly.

Both men turned. A statuesque brunette stood near them, her long, wavy hair billowing in a gentle and nonexistent breeze. She had green eyes and a long, slender nose that pointed down her face to full and glistening lips. Her thin waist fit closely to her pelvis and broadened up the length of her torso to where her full breasts sparkled—rhinestones and pink topaz scattered over her chest, condensing into a pavé that covered her nipples. Her slender hips were bare. Carver found himself gaping at the diaphanous veil of mist that swirled over the woman's crotch. He could just make out the blurred darkness that lay beneath.

"I'm Dahlia," she said, drawing out the first vowel of her name into an alluring sex-kittenish sigh. "I have a private suite in Xanadu. Would you like to see it?"

Nonplussed, Carver continued to stare until Quadie reached over and slapped his arm. He looked up into her face and caught a bemused smile.

"Uh, right. Look, Dahlia, it's a hell of an offer, but I'm busy right now. My friend and I are going to The Redline."

She tossed her hair blithely and shrugged. "Oh, well. Maybe some other time. Keep my ID and tune me in sometime." When she turned, they saw that her rounded buttocks were completely bare.

As she walked away, Quadie called out, "*I'm* into the idea."

She laughed and looked back over her shoulder. "Some other time, Flash."

The two men gawked until Dahlia became lost in the crowd, then looked at one another with eyes wide in bewilderment. "Son of a bitch," Quadie murmured approvingly.

"Come on," Carver said. "I need a drink."

"I can't believe you passed that up."

"I'm married, Quadie. Besides, she's not really my type. Her tits are way too big and her waist and hips are too small."

"Carver, a woman like that is *every* man's type. That image must have cost her ten grand."

"Hell, Quadie, there's no way to tell if it even was a woman. I'd be willing to bet, actually, that it was a guy— women don't dream up images like that for themselves."

"Sure they do. Why wouldn't they? But anyway, it's the

image that counts, not the user. So what's the matter? Fuck, Carv, what's happened to you? You used to be *fun*. Maybe not as much fun as *me*, of course, but close enough. Are you getting old or something?"

"I'm on my way toward forty, Quadie. So are you, I might point out. But I just don't like virtual sex."

"What's the difference?"

Carver stopped and put his hands on his friend's shoulders. "Quadie," he said solemnly, trying to keep the amusement from his voice, "have you ever had real sex with a real person?"

Quadie tried to look thoughtful. "I think I can recall one or two times."

"And you can't tell the difference? You must not be very good."

Quadie laughed. "*You* must not be very good in the Web. I mean, sure, if you get an amateur, it's going to suck. But if you find someone who's at least a competent programmer, somebody with a good image"—with his eyes he gestured after Dahlia—"one that feels real as well as looks it, then it's just as real as Outside. Sometimes better, if you get a little kinky."

"Anyone who would have sex with you would have to be kinky. Where do you want to sit?"

The Redline was a café three meters wide and one hundred long situated in the midst of the Mall, which was split into two avenues for the length of the café. The Redline was paved entirely in ruby crystal that, though solid to the touch, eddied and swirled with molten color like cooling lava, or blood. A twisting, writhing ruby filigree sprang from the border, snaking itself into a low fence. A single row of magically floating red crystal tables ran the length of The Redline, but it was more than a mere café. The strip's location at the center of Network 37's central concourse made it the best spot on the Network for people-watching. Consequently, The

Redline was one of the Network's most popular—and expensive—programs.

Carver and Quadie found an empty table and sat down. Almost immediately an Irish Flag manifested in front of Quadie.

"I don't see how you can drink those things," Carver said. "They're way too sweet for my taste."

Carver chose a Belgian brown ale. A tall pint appeared on the table before him. He lifted his glass to Quadie's. "Here's to . . ." he began. They looked at each other for a few seconds, as though trying to think of something worth toasting, then shrugged indifferently and gave up. It was their customary toast, stretching back through many years of friendship.

A rich, earthy flavor filled Carver's mouth as he drank. The beer was heavy, almost to the point of being syrupy, and highly carbonated. A fruity aftertaste followed, lingering until he drowned it in another mouthful. The beer's program was masterfully adjusted, and Carver knew he would only get as drunk as he wanted to be. He felt the carbonation scratch his tongue, tickle in his throat as he swallowed. After gulping too much too fast he could feel the ale slosh in his stomach, and the need to belch. It was all perfectly, unfailingly real.

A light touch on his shoulder stole his attention. He turned and found himself facing a short young man in last summer's fashions. Shaggy brown hair hung down over the youth's eyes, hiding them.

"Boo," the boy said flatly.

Carver glanced quickly at Quadie, then back to the boy. "I beg your pardon?"

Suddenly, the boy's unruly hair morphed into a writhing mass of vipers, venom glistening on their bared fangs. The boy's skin turned green and scaly. He opened his mouth, revealing several rows of razor-sharp teeth, and shouted in a deep, reverberating voice, "*Boo!*"

Others nearby turned to look at the spectacle, but Carver

was riveted by the suddenly revealed eyes that dazzled with yellows and greens and aquae over a background hint of brown. The irises swirled hypnotically. Carver couldn't quite tell which way they rotated, only that they did move. Far away in the pupils there was a blue-white arcing, as of electricity.

Just as suddenly as the display had begun, the boy morphed back to his normal image and walked away without another word. Carver watched, dumbfounded, as the boy repeated the procedure with others at The Redline and on the Mall.

Quadie laughed. "You gotta love this place."

"Do you? Yeah, I suppose so. What else can you do with it?"

The two fell into a comfortable silence then, and they sat there for a long time just sipping at their drinks as they watched the flood of people around them at The Redline and on the Mall.

After a while, Carver felt a familiar presence in his mind. *What's up, loverboy?* it asked.

Hi Jan, Carver thought. *Just sitting here at The Redline, taking a break from work.*

Jan paused noticeably. *When you say a break from work, do you actually mean . . . ?*

Yes, Jan. Work. Program.

Carver, that's wonderful. What is it?

Come join us.

She paused again. *Us? That would be you and the lovely and charming Mr. Newman, I assume?*

Carver laughed out loud, and Quadie glanced over at him questioningly.

Well, as much as I'd really love to, Jan's voice said in Carver's thoughts, *I think I'd rather go have a few dozen root canals instead. Tune me later.*

The touch of her thoughts vanished as she tuned-out. Carver continued to grin at Quadie.

"What was that all about?" Quadie asked.

"Just telling Jan about my working. She sends a special hello to you."

Quadie's brow wrinkled in disgust.

Carver took a sip of beer and said, "You know what the problem is? You two are too much alike."

"Hey now," Quadie said with a hurt look. "I thought you were my friend." He fell silent and stared at Carver a moment before asking, "So, you've been working again?"

Carver laughed smugly. "Forget it, Quadie. I am *not* going to tell you, and you'll never figure it out on your own, so you might as well give up right now."

"It was worth a try." Quadie set his drink on the table. "No jokes, mate," he said solemnly. "I'm being serious. You are working?"

"Yeah," Carver said after a pause. "Yeah."

"Well, good on you."

"Yeah," Carver drawled thoughtfully. "It's about time, isn't it? I don't really have anything concrete yet, but I am working. I'm afraid I've fallen way out of practice with this little sabbatical. But that should make you happy—you might actually be the best director in the Web now. Until I make my comeback, at least."

Quadie snorted. "Hah! Worry about yourself, mate, not me. You're going to have a tough battle just reclaiming your usual *number two* role. I don't know how closely you've been keeping up with things, but there's a bunch of new talent zipping around out there since you've been away, and every damn one of them thinks he can take your place. Of course, no one's foolish enough to think they can outdo *me*."

The conversation faltered once again. The silence sat awkwardly between them, smothering their banter.

"You were the best, mate," Quadie said at last. "The best there's ever been." He paused, looking into his glass. "Do you think you can be again?"

Carver didn't answer. The bubbles of carbonation in his ale rose in streams from the bottom of the mug, rushing up along their wobbling paths, to strike against the surface of the liquid and burst. He wondered if it were ever possible for a bubble to break through that barrier without perishing, and what would happen if one did.

And as he watched, one did just that—a bubble pushed through the surface tension and continued to rise. It slowed as it rose, and it grew. Others followed it, and soon there were dozens of fist-sized globes dancing about Carver's head, a strange swirling reflection playing over their surfaces like the electric pulse of that strange boy's eyes.

They were making him dizzy, and he realized just how drunk he had allowed the beer to make him. He wished the alcohol and its effects away. The mug demanifested, but the floating bubbles and his loopiness did not. He frowned and tried again, but his head would not clear.

The situation was so ridiculous that Carver burst out in a fit of giggling. He looked up to see if Quadie had noticed his bizarre predicament, but Quadie was entranced by the fence around the café. Its serpentine filaments were growing out of their customary and intended plane, weaving themselves into arabesques and knotworks that danced before Quadie, spawning ruby pseudopodia that reached out to trace sigils in the air before him.

Carver opened his mouth, but a throat-wrenching belch escaped before he could call Quadie's name. His giggles turned into uncontrolled guffaws of laughter.

"Excuse me," Quadie mumbled. "Wait. Did I do that or did you?" He tore his eyes from the hypnotic undulations. "What the hell are you doing, Carver?"

Carver managed to rein in his laughter. "Oh, good—you see it, too. So I'm not hallucinating. Unless we're *both* hallucinating the same thing."

Quadie was struggling with his own overwhelming laughter.

"There's no such thing as hallucination in the Web, shithead. It's just a program."

Pockets of turmoil were springing up along the length of The Redline and spilling out across the Mall. Carver turned slowly to look, distracted by the commotion. When he moved, his sight distorted into a fish-eye view, the light streaking into long wavering trails. Sound, too, warped—it all came now from very far away, as though he heard it through some invisible barrier, yet he could discern every individual sound and conversation. Rather than being fragmented, his attention seemed augmented, enhanced.

Quadie was saying something to him. He turned back. The irises of Quadie's eyes were swirling and spinning.

"You ever pharm, Carver?" Quadie was struggling to be serious in spite of his huge smile and constant giggling.

Carver tried to think, but his concentration wavered and he found himself thinking of a family gathering when he'd been only four or so. He forced himself to the question at hand and answered, "Of course. I've got a whole bunch of different programs."

"No, I meant real drugs."

"*Chemicals?* I did some back in college, but not really too much. I didn't want to risk messing up my brain—it's the only one I've got. Why?"

"'Cause this reminds me a hell of a lot of acid. I think we've been dosed."

"No way. That's illegal."

Quadie nodded. "Exactly. I think Gorgon-boy was up to something."

The meaning of Quadie's words slowly dawned on Carver. "Freeks? No way. You're out of your mind—" That caused him to break into laughter once again, but he did his best to continue. "We're both out of our minds. No, but Freeks are just kids out for some fun. They're annoying, but small-time. Not exactly tech enough to figure out how to compromise private Network security. And Thirty-seven has the best in the world."

Quadie didn't answer. Like most of the users around them, he was looking up into the deepening night sky. Carver followed his gaze.

Floating high above them was a huge roiling cloud bank. A fanfare issued from it, and it began to take on a shape. Certain areas pulled apart while others coalesced, until a face with swirling eyes hung over the Network. The colors that had been present in the boy's eyes were somehow present in the clouds, and the eyes writhed now like twin tornadoes. The clouds forming the mouth rippled as a thunderclap of laughter burst across the Network.

"Pitiful fools!" The voice boomed, deep and rumbling. "I am Apollo—hear me. You have been misled, like lambs to the slaughter. Your world is at an end. Apocalypse draws nigh! You must—"

The voice ceased along with the motion of the clouds, and Carver's vision and mind abruptly cleared. As the face began to disintegrate, the whole Network slunk slowly to a halt. The sinuous fence and the floor of The Redline ceased their motion; the ad kiosks all fell dark and silent; the soft ripples on the reflecting pool across the Mall froze in place. Even the users were for the most part too stunned to do much.

The silence was torn by a harsh voice. "This is the Federal Communications Agency." The voice had no apparent source. Carver could not tell from which direction, if any, it came. "Under the provisions of Federal Communications Agency Emergency Regulation CTN-dash-four-seven-dash-oh-eight-three-delta, this Network is now under martial control."

THREE

"El Cid! I told you!" Quadie whispered, but Carver shushed him.

"Please remain calm," the disembodied voice continued. "All personal interfaces are being scanned. Remain where you are. When your interface and operating system have been certified, you will be automatically released. Those persons tuning-in from public access terminals may expect additional delays."

Murmuring erupted across the Network as soon as the voice ceased. Within seconds users' images began to disappear.

"I told you it was El Cid," Quadie repeated.

"You don't know that," Carver told him. "They didn't say anything at all about what happened. Nobody could ever trojan something like that past private Network security—especially Thirty-seven's. Besides, do you really think if anybody *had* figured out how to compromise Thirty-seven's security they'd pull a stunt like this and let everybody know and get the FCA down on them? It was probably just a failsoft malfunction."

Quadie made a harsh buzzing noise. "Wrong answer, thank you for playing. That was too powerful and too specific in its effect to be any kind of glitch and you know it.

Think about it, Carver. It wasn't just the local structure that got fucked. Whatever it was, it downloaded itself to our interfaces and screwed with them. At least it did mine. I don't know about you, but my mind got fucked *hard*. This was no accident. Plus, what about that stupid message and the face in the clouds?"

"But why would somebody try a stunt like this? Think how much work it must have been cracking security— wouldn't you try to get something out of it instead of just grandstanding?"

An image manifested beside their table. The man stood almost two meters tall and muscular. His unremarkable gray outfit trod the line between suit and uniform, and his ruggedly handsome face was bland and unemotional. A name badge that read THOMPSON provided the only ornament. It was the anonymous image used by all FCA officers in the Web.

"You are requested to accompany me, please." The voice was also standard FCA issue, the same voice that had made the announcement, though Carver knew this was in all likelihood a different person.

"Who?" Quadie asked.

"Both of you."

"Why?"

The Thompson regarded them perfunctorily. "We wish to question you in regard to this incident. You are not accused of anything." Neither the face nor the voice betrayed any emotion.

"About this? Why?" Quadie asked.

The officer glanced at him. "That will be discussed in private."

"I don't have to say one word to you until you tell me what you're after," Quadie told the man. "You haven't stolen all of our rights yet."

"Are you officially waiving your right to confidentiality?"

Quadie rolled his eyes. "Oh, for fuck's sake. Yes, I am."

"Your reputation and past public behavior—"

"Gee, I guess Mom was right when she said my past would catch up with me sooner or later. But we just like to have *fun*, that's all. You have to know we'd never do anything like this even if we could. If your files say we would, then you twerps are more fucked up than I thought."

"Quadie!" Carver warned.

"Our records are not your concern," the Thompson told Quadie, "except insofar as they give us sufficient right to question you both in light of the current evidence."

"What evidence is that?" Carver asked.

"We have detected certain irregularities in your usage of interface."

"Irregularities?" Carver asked nervously. "Like what?" He was afraid the FCA had somehow detected his tamperings with his set's Fourier coil. He didn't think what he'd done was illegal, but the FCA had the power to change laws practically at whim, so one could never be sure. He'd hate to lose his new technique before he even got a chance to use it for anything.

"The disturbance originated from a number of loci, including your interface connection."

"Ha!" Quadie shouted. He punched Carver's arm. "It *was* that damn kid. I told you. That's who you should be after," he said to the Thompson.

"It is highly unlikely that the individual you refer to was working alone."

"You really think we had something to do with this?" Quadie said, standing to confront the man. "That's fucking ridiculous. That's bullshit."

Quadie vanished as abruptly as the Thompson had appeared. "Will you come with me, please?" the man asked Carver again.

"Of course," Carver said pleasantly, though he knew his assent was moot.

Quadie was annoyed. Most of his anger was directed at the FCA. More than an hour held in pointless questioning was excessive even for the Thompsons. But he could not ignore a nagging uncertainty that swam in the back of his mind.

How could the FCA suspect Carver of having anything to do with what had happened? Carver, of all people. Sure, he had engaged in his share of hijinks, but never anything *too* illegal. For a director, Carver was almost pathetically law-abiding. He certainly would never have tried anything like this. Hell, he himself wouldn't have tried this one, and he was far more daring than Carver. Carver probably didn't even know how to crack security—he was formally trained, not a self-taught hack-turned-director like him.

Quadie wouldn't even have considered the FCA's suspicions, if it weren't for Carver's new workspace. He'd never experienced anything at all like that before. The uneasiness that had burst through him then still lingered, though very subtly.

That was perhaps understandable, Quadie thought. What really upset him was the nature of that effect, or its quality, or . . . what? He didn't know. That was what made it so maddening. Something there was very definitely odd, but he couldn't even tell for sure what it was, much less why it felt so strange. Carver had called it just a "blank workspace," but it was not like any blank workspace Quadie had ever used. And a blank workspace didn't fuck with someone else's interface. Carver had also joked about it being a trade secret. He was obviously working on some kind of new technique, though what he was doing with it, Quadie had no clue. And if it could steal control of an interface, there was no telling what else it might be capable of. Even bypassing Network security was a possibility

Quadie couldn't believe Carver capable of any blatantly illegal activity, but he was definitely up to something. Quadie swore. The FCA had made him doubt his friend. That bothered him more than anything, but he couldn't help it.

Then again, as much as Quadie hated the Feds, even he had to admit that they rarely fucked with anyone *entirely* without cause. Well, almost never.

As he lay naked on the massage table looking out over greater Los Angeles to the Pacific Ocean from a height of two hundred stories, he couldn't help but feel extremely pissed. The massage and a background stress-reduction routine should have helped him relax, but his thoughts were churning so much that the therapy was only irritating.

"Stop please, Ariel."

His M.I. stepped back from the table and stood motionlessly while Quadie sat up.

"Ariel, do you have a recording of the last six hours?"

"You didn't specify that I should have been recording."

"Just hoping. Could you analyze I-and-R, please, for just before and during the period you lost me today? That first time I tried to tune-in Carver's workspace?"

"What exactly am I looking for?"

"I don't know. Something unusual. Not in responses, but indexing. See if Carver's workspace accessed or reset any of my indexes. See if it did anything at all."

While his agent was busy with its task, Quadie clicked to the heated pool that occupied the center of the square acre of marble floor. Late afternoon sun streamed in between the columns, illuminating the polished stone with a rosy aura. A gentle breeze stirred eddies in the steam rising from the water, the fresh air from L.A.'s skies carrying the faintest hint of the ocean beyond the city.

Quadie dunked his head under the hot, swirling water and wished the Jacuzzi currents could relieve mental stress as well as physical. He was confused. He resurfaced and shook the water from his eyes. Leaning back, submerged up to his chin, he once more tried to make sense of what had happened in Carver's workspace.

Ariel cleared her throat discreetly. "Yes?" Quadie asked, his eyes still closed.

"There is an unaccountable period of just under ten seconds between the time when you began interaction with Carver's set and the time you were tuned-out."

"What do you mean?"

"I'm afraid I can't specify. For nine point seven eight seconds you were simply beyond my ability to monitor and communicate with you."

"Was I on inactive standby?"

Ariel was silent for a few seconds. "Not unless you've got another woman controlling your set now. I can find no indication of any unusual behavior aside from the fact that for all intents and purposes one could say you just disappeared from the Web for that time. According to my data, at least."

"That's impossible. You must have had a glitch."

"I will recheck the data if you can give me something more specific to look for."

He couldn't. "No. But record that data permanently, please. I'll want to take a look at it myself later. And until further notice, record every time I tune-in Carver's workspace. I'll want the full internal experience plus all external indicators." Quadie decided that he should investigate Carver's doings further, if only to help his friend and to set his own doubts to rest.

"Also, you asked me to scan the newsboards for word about the situation on Network Thirty-seven."

Quadie thought the water away from his eyes and turned to face his M.I. She was tall and slender, though not as fantastically built as the woman who had hit on Carver earlier, and her straight blond hair was bobbed to shoulder length, with bangs in front. She wore a white silk kimono, embroidered in black and red with hiragana, which crossed low over her breasts and barely reached past her crotch. Looking up at her from the pool, Quadie had an unobstructed view of her pubic hair. He saw a flash of pink as she stepped back from the edge of the pool to make more direct eye contact, and he smiled. He could feel the first stirrings of an erection.

"Yes?" he said.

"There's nothing at all," Ariel reported. "Not a word."

"What? Well, keep checking. There's bound to be something somewhere."

Ariel shook her head. "There's not. I've scanned every Network, both public and private. I've checked the Internet and every other broadcast service. I've even hooked into European, African, and Austrasian media just to be sure. There's not a single reference anywhere. Network Thirty-seven itself is closed. The complete data of their news monitor says, and I quote, 'We regret that Network Thirty-seven is closed until further notice.'"

"Goddammit. The Thompsons told me there was a felony gag order, that because they'd invoked their emergency rules, they could throw me in the *juzgado* if I said even one word about this to anyone. I guess they told everybody the same thing. I can't believe there's nothing at all, though. Censorship that heavy is tough for even the FCA to get away with. Something pretty fucking *fucked* is going on. I wish I knew what it was." Quadie sighed loudly. "Carver back yet?"

"Not yet."

"Fucking FCA. They'll probably keep him there all night while they finish their damn datawork."

"Is there anything else I can do for you now?" Ariel asked, her report finished.

Quadie looked down at his erection, then back up at her. "How about coming in for a swim?"

She raised an eyebrow, and the kimono slid from her

shoulders, floating silently down her body to the floor. A coy smile spread across her face as she stepped into the steaming water and Quadie rose to meet her.

"God, I love programming," he said.

"What time is it, God?"

"Sixteen twenty."

Carver shook his head angrily as he paced the floor. "Three hours," he grumbled to himself. "Three lousy hours." The FCA had questioned him extensively about everything from his politics to his finances to his acquaintances. They had been especially interested in learning why he hadn't produced any new work in the past six months. The Thompson in charge had been reluctant to accept his explanation of creative burnout. The man had returned to the subject repeatedly, always wanting more data, questioning Carver's memory. When Carver finally overloaded on exasperation and lost his temper, they blithely let him go without filing any charges against him and without a single word of apology.

"You have a message waiting from Quadie," God said. "Do you want to tune him back?"

Carver almost said yes, but his set's alarm was bleating urgently in the back of his awareness; he needed to go to the bathroom. He smiled ruefully. He had to stop drinking so much coffee right before tuning-in.

"Not now," he told God. "I'm Out."

When Carver stood up from his set, he was surprised to see his wife lying on her own set. He thought about pressing the call button on the set's control panel to ask if she wanted him to get a start on dinner, but decided against it. Knowing Rose, any interruption at all would be enough of an excuse to tune-out. As long as she was tuned-in at all, he didn't want to disturb her if he didn't absolutely have to.

After a brief stop in the bathroom, Carver went to the

kitchen and put some leftover mashed potatoes in the microwave. While he waited for them to heat, he called out, "Hey, God, could you put the living room screen on, please?"

"Sure, boss." God's disembodied voice sounded tinny and far away through the ceiling speaker. "What are we watching?"

"National headlines, I guess. But I want you to surf for any data about Network Thirty-seven or me or Quadie. Anything posted in the last . . . oh, four hours."

The newscast audio came through the speaker, delivering fact-free sound bites about politics, the economy, the weather, and other stories Carver didn't bother to pay attention to. God switched the audio feed to the living room speakers when Carver finished his snack and moved to the couch.

"Anything on Network Thirty-seven?" Carver asked as he stared blankly at the videonly.

"Not yet."

"Odd. Well, keep looking."

Carver lay back on the couch and quickly dozed off. Half an hour later Rose woke him.

"Hey," he said, sitting up.

"Hey." Rose sounded as groggy as he felt, and her expression seemed distant, subdued, almost drugged.

"How has your day been?"

The corner of Rose's mouth twitched into a brief smile. "I spent the whole afternoon in your program."

"And?"

The smile faded. "I don't know. I can't say right now—I can't really put it into words."

"But . . . something happened, right? I mean, it had some sort of effect?"

Rose nodded slowly. "It definitely had some sort of effect. I'm just not sure what."

"But it did work." Carver stood and hugged his wife.

"Thank you, Rose. You don't know how much this means. This could be the most important work I've ever done."

"I hope so." She pulled out of the embrace and wandered away toward the dining room.

Carver followed her. "So, what say I cook us up a fancy dinner, open a bottle of wine or two, and we make an evening of it? Just you and me, here."

"Oh, not tonight, not now. I . . . I want to get some work done." She turned and smiled at him, the withdrawn look still clouding her eyes. "But thank you, honey. That's really sweet of you. Perhaps tomorrow."

She left him then, walked through the kitchen and down the stairs that led to her basement studio. Carver watched her go, stunned. He had tried, he really had. Perhaps things were worse than he'd realized.

Then again, she *had* tuned-in for him. And for several hours, which was quite unusual for Rose. That was definitely a good sign. And even he had felt a little off balance just after spending time in his little netherworld. It made sense that it would hit Rose harder, unaccustomed as she was to virtuality.

Yes, he thought, everything would be all right—especially now that he knew his new trick did indeed work on other people. And, now that he knew that, it was time he set to work perfecting the routine so he could put a program around it.

As he walked toward his workroom he couldn't help smiling. Yes, things were definitely going to be all right.

Tom Byrd locked the door to his office at the Federal Communications Agency and sank wearily into his chair. He propped his feet up on his desk and leaned back, expertly balancing his tall frame on a single leg of the chair.

Two meters tall and strongly muscled, Captain Byrd was often teased by his colleagues about having been the model for the Agency's "Thompson" image. In fact, he took great pride in his physique and he worked hard to maintain it, although lately it was becoming harder and harder to keep his waist smaller than his chest. Still, that was the least of his worries now. It had been a very bad day.

The sign on his door identified him as REGIONAL ADMINISTRATOR. If most people in the Agency thought he was merely a high-level data-pusher, a bureaucrat instead of a cop, his rank functional rather than earned, that was good—they were supposed to. If he seemed a bit too free from the strangulations of bureaucratic red tape, Byrd reflected, and if the standard rules and laws of the Agency often did not apply to him, well, a plausible explanation could always be found. Besides, anyone at the Agency who knew enough to perhaps wonder about any of this would also know that some things were best not questioned.

Officially, the Security Research Project that Captain Byrd headed did not exist. Within the Agency, almost no one not directly involved with the project knew of its existence. Beyond the Agency—throughout the rest of the government and in the civilian world—no one had ever heard of the SRP.

Theoretically.

Byrd knew better than anyone how fragile the state of Web security had become. From personal passwords on up through the biggest gigasystems, ice cracked every day— even the Agency's, though they held that their security was redundant and varied enough that it could never be completely compromised except in the event of a total matrix failure. And if the Web itself crashed, there would be no need for security.

While everyone knew about the Webwide blankets, single- and multipoint spotters, roving independent A.I.'s, and the rest of the FCA stable, the Agency officially maintained that their most powerful security was an integral part of the Web, undetectable and therefore uncrackable. Because there was no way to either prove or disprove this, the rumor persisted.

Byrd, however, knew it was a load of crap.

An arctic front had moved through north Georgia that morning, bringing to the region an early autumn. A depressing cold, gray rain fell on Atlanta now, darkening Byrd's mood even further. He kicked his heel against the switch on the edge of his desk, and the windows grayed to opacity.

It was bad enough that Network 37's own ice had been so thoroughly compromised. Thirty-seven was the richest Network in the Web, and so could afford the best, most up-to-date security routines available—and lots of them. Someone had worked very, very hard to get through it all.

Had that been the full extent of the situation, Captain Byrd would merely have been very upset. But that was not the full extent, not by half. And Byrd was completely pissed off.

The best security ever developed in the Web had taken Byrd and his team more than four years to perfect. In its first real-world test it had broken all records, surviving three times longer than any other ice in history. That streak had just ended, with the cracking of Network 37.

SRP's security routine had been installed and tested in Network 37's synaptic matrices unbeknownst to the Network's board of directors. It had been *that* secret. And yet it had not detected today's attack until after the breach occurred. Whoever had done this, they had bypassed not only the Network's security, but SRP's as well—security that should have been undetectable and impenetrable.

Worse still, Byrd knew that a breach like this did not occur in one try. No individual could ever have pulled off something this complex, not even with A.I.'s. There had to be a number of people behind it, and they had to have been working at it for months, possibly even years—but he had not known until today. Until it was too late.

What Byrd really couldn't understand was why it had been done at all. This hack was a major coup for whatever group was behind it. They could gain access to any part of the Web, whether public or private. They could steal any data they wanted, for their own use or to sell. In a sense, this hack had made the people responsible for it the most powerful force in the Web, since apparently not even the FCA could detect them.

At least, that would have been the case had they not so blatantly given themselves away.

Hacks would never have worked so hard and then just thrown it all away like that, Byrd thought. Even if their motives did not go beyond the prestige factor, there were ways to prove their feat to other hacks without announcing it to the world and putting the FCA on alert.

Doping 37's matrix with electronic drugs had been a gratuitous and seemingly pointless act. It served no purpose beyond calling attention to what otherwise would have been a truly perfect crime. And it had been done on purpose.

That sounded more like Freeks. Whereas hacks stole, destroyed, and altered data with malicious intent, Freeks were basically just mischievous kids out for a good time. They were almost always boys, usually in their teens or early twenties, bent on bypassing security for the sole purpose of tuning-in without being charged. The Web's version of gate-hopping. Freeks were criminals, to be sure, but on a different scale than hacks—more annoyance than actual threat.

Which meant that Freeks had neither the skills nor the resources to have pulled off something as big as cracking a private Network. Especially 37.

Byrd could understand an attack against the security. The same for the prank. But the two combined made no sense at all. Could a group of hacks and a group of Freeks have worked together on this? Not a chance in hell, Byrd knew. The two were diametrically opposed to one another. Hacks disdained Freeks, hated them even more than they hated the FCA. And even if hacks and Freeks could get along, there still was no gain for the hacks from this caper. No, the answer had to lie elsewhere.

But if the motivation was neither espionage nor financial gain nor mischief, that left only one possibility. Politics.

The only logical reason Byrd could think of for what had happened today was that someone wanted to cause a public panic, to frighten people out of the Web. The partial message pointed in that direction. Byrd found himself almost wishing the new security had been a little less effective—that it had not shut down the invasion until after the full message had been delivered.

There were groups that were staunchly opposed to the Web—mostly fundamentalist Christian and Islamic factions— but the very nature of their opposition precluded their use of the Web and of drugs, electronic or physical. Besides, all of these groups were very closely monitored, so even if one of them had hired someone else to crack Network 37, the FCA would have known about it. Especially with the amount of money that would have been involved.

But the FCA knew nothing. Could there be some new, unknown group with an agenda against the Web?

Byrd shuddered at that. The thought of someone trying to destabilize the Web didn't just upset him, it frightened him.

The balance of power in North America was delicate indeed, more delicate than even most people within the Agency realized, and it tilted increasingly against the government's favor. Byrd shuddered to think what might happen if the security infrastructure ever crumbled beyond repair.

In only a century the Web had superseded all else in its importance to North American society. Patriotism, religion, not even television had ever held such sway over daily life. Practically the entire sociopolitical structure of the Continent was founded upon virtuality, originated from it, could not exist without it. If the government ever lost control of the Web, anarchy would result. Everything would become like the Wild West again—only much, much worse.

It was Byrd's job to prevent that.

He interlaced his fingers behind his head and closed his eyes. Even with his entire staff working on this case—personnel assignment being one of Byrd's administrative powers, he could infiltrate any investigation or project in the Agency—he didn't have a single substantial lead. Not that he'd expected any so soon. After all, anyone good enough to break through that kind of ice was good enough to do it without leaving any tracks. Still, one interesting piece of data had turned up.

The disturbance within the Network itself had emanated from more than three dozen sites simultaneously, then quickly spread to infect the Network's entire matrix. All of those sites had been user interfaces. And one of those users had been none other than the famous Carver Blervaque.

Trojaning a program along a legitimate, already established interface connection was a common hacking technique, done without the user's consent—usually even without their knowledge. The mere fact that Blervaque's interface had been employed did not in itself implicate him.

Not that Byrd had initially suspected Blervaque anyway. The FCA did have a big file on him, but only for the kinds of pranks and publicity stunts all celebrities engaged in as a matter of course. Captain Byrd loathed the fact that such people could get away with criminal acts merely because of their status, but he didn't let that affect his judgment. If anything, he was more inclined to think Blervaque innocent—someone like him had far too much to lose to get involved in something like this.

Still, it was standard policy to investigate any user whose interface was actively compromised.

The first thing Byrd noticed in the file was that Blervaque

had not released any new programs for a good six months—
a significantly long time for a director to remain idle. Not that
Blervaque had been out of circulation. He'd been tuning-
in as regularly as always; he just hadn't posted any new
work. No major programs, no shorts, not even a quickie
mood piece for Public Access. For six whole months Carver
Blervaque literally had not uploaded a single bit of work to
the Web.

So what had he been doing all that time? According to
Blervaque himself, not much. Captain Byrd had trouble
accepting that, however—especially after his detectives
uncovered some very unusual readings from Quadie
Newman's interface.

Whenever any part of the Web's synaptic matrix
became damaged in any way—whether through deliberate
dataphagic corruption or due to some sort of failsoft malfunction—the FCA always checked and certified the interfaces of every user tuned-in to that part of the matrix to
make sure they weren't infected themselves. Otherwise,
users could unwittingly spread the problem throughout
the Web.

Newman's interface had checked out clean, uncorrupted
by the Network 37 hack. But something *had* produced some
very bizarre patterns in his set's operating matrix. Something
else—something that, judging from the amount of overwrit-
ing and reconnectioning in the set's neuristors, had occurred
at least an hour or two before the incident in the Network.
Because of the number of connections, it was impossible to
reconstruct exactly what had happened, but the residual patterns were unlike anything Byrd had ever seen.

A check into Newman's access table brought the mystery
full circle. Just before he tuned-in Network 37 that day,
Newman had tuned his friend Carver Blervaque. Twice.

The second connection had been established just ten seconds after the first. Something had interfered with their

connection to such an extent that it had been necessary to terminate and reestablish.

Standard interconnect faults did occur in the Web, though very rarely. And they never left a signature like the one in Newman's matrix.

Something very out of the ordinary had happened when Newman tuned Blervaque—something Blervaque's set had done, apparently.

Captain Byrd stood and began to pace his office while he tried to tie all the data together.

For six months Carver Blevaque did absolutely nothing, or so he said. Then one day, without warning, without precedent, something in his set screwed up another interface—and within hours the worst security failure in the history of the Web occurred in a Network that Blervaque just happened to be in.

It was all just too much of a coincidence. And Byrd did not believe in coincidence.

The investigation had not turned up anything concrete, nor had Blervaque or Newman revealed anything during questioning. But Captain Byrd knew something was going on—something potentially very, very dangerous.

Whatever Carver Blervaque was up to, he would have to be stopped.

FOUR

The first thing Carver noticed when he manifested in Jan Tarrega's office for their monthly business meeting was her new image. Her triangular face, with its dark eyes, upturned nose, and dark red rosebud lips, remained the same as always, but she stood taller now and appeared more slender than the last time he'd seen her, and straight blond hair covered her scalp and hung down to brush her shoulders, over which she'd draped a neon-red toga.

"Carver!" Jan squealed, throwing herself at him. "It's so *good* to see you!"

"Hi, Jan."

Carver extricated himself from his manager's embrace and moved to the couch. The view through the panoramic window behind him showed a desert oasis—also a change since his last visit.

Jan twirled her way across the room to sit beside him. "What do you think?"

"It's lovely. Hair is definitely an improvement."

She swatted his arm. "I liked my picture show."

"It was amusing," Carver admitted. For several months Jan had windowed random selections of videonly programming across her bare scalp. The effect had always disconcerted him.

"You've had some amusement of your own, I understand."

"Have I?"

"A little incident at your favorite watering hole?"

"What?" Carver sat upright and stared at his manager in alarm. "How did you hear about that? What did you hear?"

"Jeez, calm down. All I know is that you and that charming buddy of yours caused some kind of trouble in Thirty-seven yesterday—enough trouble to shut down the whole damned Network."

Carver shook his head. "It wasn't us. But how do you know about it? The Thompsons screwed one heck of a lid on it."

Jan smiled coyly. "It's my job to know everything you're up to. Besides, you shut down the Web's biggest Network. Not even the FCA can keep that quiet."

"Well, if anyone asks, you don't know a thing about my involvement, and I have no comment, okay? Please don't turn this into a PR thing."

"All right, I'll keep my mouth shut," she said, sounding disappointed. "But it's going to be pointless soon enough. A current events speculator I know bought the rights to the data. She figures this is going to be the biggest news in months. She's buying the story onto every Network."

"Sounds to me like your friend is about to put herself out of the business."

Jan shrugged. "I don't think so. The mass public really goes for shit like this—even when there aren't celebrities involved." Her eyes began to sparkle, and she put her arm around Carver and whispered in his ear, "You're going to get a lot of press from this, my dear. It would be the *perfect* time to announce a new program . . ."

For the past several months, Jan had been pestering Carver about his recent lack of output. The subject generally produced a certain tension between them—but not today.

"As I mentioned yesterday, Jan," Carver told her, "I have in fact started working again."

"So you really meant it?" He found himself suddenly in a crushing embrace. "Oh, Carver, that's wonderful!" she practically shouted. "Tell me about it. When will you have it done?"

"Uh, well, it . . . I'm still developing the idea," Carver fudged.

"A month? Six weeks?"

"Probably closer to two or three months."

"Two or three months? Carver, you've been out of the marketplace so long—"

"But it'll really be worth the extra wait," he added hastily. "I've been working on a whole new *method* of programming, I guess you could say, and if I can get it integrated into my regular program, it's going to be the best thing since, well, since virtuality itself. It'll be like nothing you've ever experienced. It will *be* nothing."

Jan arched her eyebrows and sighed. "Carver, dear, you're babbling."

"Please, Jan, I promise you'll be shocked and amazed if this thing works. But it's going to take some time."

"Shocked *and* amazed?" She regarded him with the barest hint of mischief in her eyes. "Well, if it's going to be *that* good, let's get this accounting out of the way quick so you can get right back to work."

Carver collapsed onto his chair. Physical exhaustion was easily banished in the Web, but mental exhaustion still proved insurmountable. And ninety minutes of royalties statements and licensing agreements, distribution accounts, facts, figures, and other data whose meaning and value he didn't understand in the least was enough to wear anyone's brain down to a nub.

A tumbler of Irish whiskey appeared in Carver's hand. "Thanks, God," he mumbled.

"No problem, boss," the cat said. "Judging from your

current indexes—and memory of the aftermath of past business meetings—I figured you might need a drink."

Carver downed the whiskey in a single gulp. "You figured right. Especially considering the hole I just dug myself into."

"Oh dear. What have you done now?"

"I told Jan I've started working again. On a new program. That I'll have done for a Thanksgiving release."

"Someone's going to be busy."

"No kidding," Carver moaned. "I don't even have any ideas. What do I have in the developmental file?"

"There are thirty-four random segments and four ideas-in-progress."

"List the ideas, please."

"One involves a horde of barbarians invading a community of wizards."

Carver shook his head. "Too blatantly juvenile adventure. I need something a bit bigger to use for a comeback. *I* had an idea like that? Scary."

"Well, it wasn't me. Number two starts at the Egyptian pyramids. Once inside, the program becomes more and more biological until—"

"Until the user is running around inside his own body. Yeah, I remember that one now. I don't think I'm up to doing it yet. What else?"

"Three starts out with a hot-air balloon that seems very reminiscent of Jules Verne. From there—"

"Yeah, I remember it. It's almost as Disney as the first one. What about number four?"

"That has an abandoned house situated on a windswept cliff overlooking a storming ocean."

"Very picturesque description, God. You should try programming yourself."

"I do. You think I got to be this good by adhering to *your* program?"

"Funny. I didn't mean programming *yourself*, I meant you

should try—oh, you know what I meant." Carver dropped the discussion and let his thoughts meander freely. "Hmmm. Yeah, that house thing. Start it up, God. I might be able to do something with that."

Carver's work progressed steadily over the next two months. Though slow at first, the pace increased dramatically as he regained his creative momentum. At the same time, independent of his program, he also experimented with his new technique, refining it, expanding its capabilities and learning more specific control over the effects.

After a few weeks he finally decided upon the crucial story element and began integrating his special routine into his program. As he neared the culmination, his fervor grew. He worked fourteen hours a day or more, stopping only to feed or relieve his body, and to sleep.

He saw very little of Rose during this period. She had her own work, of course, but she also spent a surprising amount of time tuned-in. They were reduced eventually to scheduling time together—for dinner, or often just a half hour in the afternoon for tea.

They were sitting side by side on the deck one weekend watching the sun set when Carver suddenly realized just how bad things between them had become. Their idle chatter, with which they seemed to enforce an unspoken ban on any meaningful discussion, had faltered early on. The silence grew, and with it Carver's unease. After twenty minutes, he could no longer stand it.

"Rose," he said, scooting his chair around to face her.

She did not respond. Her eyes stared unblinkingly into nothingness. Her expression was blank, her face slack and lifeless.

"Rose," Carver said more urgently.

This time she turned her head, languorously, to him. "Hmm?" Her eyes remained unfocused, staring through him.

He coughed nervously. "Listen, honey, I'm sorry about the way things have been lately. And I know it's my fault. But I promise we'll get back to the way we were once I finish this new program. I promise."

A flicker of unreadable emotion passed over Rose's face, and her gaze settled momentarily on Carver's eyes. "I know," she said. "I've been preoccupied, too."

Her attention dissipated then, and she turned back to the sunset. Carver gaped at her for a few seconds, then stood and stalked inside. *Sure, things will get better,* he told himself sullenly. *If we last that long.*

Carver was not the only one who kept busy through the autumn. Quadie, too, started work on a new program, and also on a number of related, but personal, projects.

Unlike his friend, Quadie had never been able to immerse himself in work for hours at a time to the exclusion of all else. Life held too much fun. At best, he could work for three or four hours before his attention began to waver and he felt a need for escape.

This escape oftentimes took the form of a "research" excursion into another director's program. Sometimes Quadie explored the Web, idly clicking to random Networks or investigating new archive matrices. Sometimes he simply relaxed in the hot tub or took a massage with Ariel.

But occasionally his desire for escape became a need for social contact. And when Quadie felt that urge, there was only one place to go.

Network 37 had remained off-line for the better part of a week. By the time it finally reopened, the story had broken across every Network and newsboard on the Continent. Most stories reported that Quadie and Carver—among many other celebrities—had been present at the time, but not a single one mentioned the possibility that Carver had been involved in the hack. At least the FCA had kept *that* under wraps,

Quadie thought. Of course, a number of stories had attributed the hack to terrorists, space aliens, or even an emerging meta-intelligence within the Web itself, so it probably wouldn't have mattered anyway.

Quadie talked to the other Redline regulars about the attack. A few of those who'd been there still refused to discuss it, according to the FCA's orders, but most were eager to tell everyone their own personal theories about who or what was responsible for the incident. Still, Quadie learned little that was new, and nothing interesting or useful.

If the Thompsons had made any progress in the case, they weren't announcing it. Quadie saw no more of Carver's "blank workspace," and Carver never mentioned it. So Quadie let his suspicions die. But not his curiosity.

He tried several times to recreate the effects of Carver's experiment, to no avail. He pored over the data Ariel had saved, but he could never see in it anything beyond what he already knew—that his friend had discovered a spectacular new effect. An effect Quadie wanted for his own.

After dozens of hours of working down one dead end after another, Quadie eventually gave up on Carver's routine, admitting to himself that he just didn't have enough data.

Yet.

Carver had said he would use the routine in his new program. So, he could wait until Carver released the program, until he had his own working copy, and then dissect it. Waiting would strain his patience to the utmost, but he had no choice.

One way or another, he would crack Carver's secret and beat him at his own game.

The lights came up slowly, and barely enough to see at all. Carver looked over at his wife lying prone upon her set. As she had been three hours earlier—and four hours before that.

He scowled. Rose had recently developed the habit of tuning-in several times a day for a few hours at a stretch, but she seemed this time to have been in all day. As far as Carver could tell, she hadn't moved at all.

In the hallway, where the illumination would not disturb Rose, the lights came on full, as they did in the kitchen as well. Carver checked the fridge. The dinner he'd left for Rose still sat there untouched.

He took the plate out and nibbled thoughtfully at some of the cold lasagna. Even given Rose's increasingly odd behavior over the last several weeks, this was definitely not like her.

But did that necessarily mean anything was wrong? She could be doing any number of things. Most people spent eight hours a day or more tuned-in, after all. Rose might actually be enjoying herself, for all he knew.

Although he had to admit that it wasn't terribly likely.

After finishing Rose's lasagna, Carver decided to check in on her. He could ask her what she wanted for dinner.

She did not reply when Carver pressed the call button on her set, so he tuned-in again.

"Hello again," God said from his perch on the back of Carver's chair. "I thought you were done for the night."

"I am. I just want to tune Rose."

After a slight pause, God said, "She's in her interface. Have fun."

Reality hiccuped, and Carver stood in Rose's main workspace, a large, airy artist's loft. Walls of wood and brick were bare, their planes broken only by windows. At the center of the otherwise empty room a large mass of clay rested on a potter's table, a gray-stained dropcloth protecting the wood floor beneath. Rose stood before the sculpture, working it with both hands and wooden implements, her back to Carver.

"Hey, Rose."

She jumped and spun to face him, her eyes wide, one hand clutched to her chest. When she saw him, she slumped back against the table.

"Jesus, you scared me. I didn't hear you come in." Her hand dropped to her side, leaving a bone-gray smear over her heart.

Carver took a few steps closer. "I came to see if you were hungry at all," he said. "It's pretty late."

Rose glanced at her bare wrist. "Is it? I kind of lost track."

"I should say so. What, ah . . . what are you doing?"

She stared at him deliberately, the corners of her mouth hinting at a smile. "Working. What are *you* doing here? You know our rule."

"Well, you know. I didn't think you'd really be working or anything."

"Why not?"

"I don't know. I guess it just never occurred to me that it would have any benefits for you. I mean, I figured for what you do, your kind of art, if you're going to do anything, you might as well really be doing it."

The confusion on Rose's face disappeared as her eyes slowly grew wide and her mouth fell open.

"Is something wrong?" Carver asked. "Rose?"

She turned back to her sculpture. It disappeared, and she cried out.

"Oh my God."

And Carver was abruptly returned to his interface.

"Is anything wrong?" God asked.

"That's what I asked. What just happened?"

"Rose tuned-out while you were still in her interface."

Carver tuned-out immediately. Rose was already out of the room. Carver ran through the house looking for her, calling her name.

He finally found her out on the deck. In spite of the cold, she stood there in just her skirt and blouse, her arms and head bare. In the faint light of the stars, Carver could see tears on her cheeks.

"Rose, are you okay?"

She shook her head. He stood beside her and put his arm around her waist. "What happened in there? What was that all about?"

"I forgot," Rose whispered hoarsely. "I was meditating, using your program like I always do, and my mind started going with some really good ideas, and I just started working and—and—"

"Whoa, whoa, slow down. You forgot what?"

She looked up at him, her eyes full of fear. "I forgot I was tuned-in."

Carver stared at her incredulously. "You what?"

"I don't know how, Carver, I just . . . I lost track. I was in there all day, working so hard, and it never— Oh, all that work! It's all gone. I did so much. Oh, Carver, what's happening to me?"

Carver led her back inside. "Come on, honey. It's not that bad. How about some tea?"

She nodded dumbly. As Carver started the tea, he told her, "I'm sorry about your work, but it doesn't mean anything's wrong. I mean, the whole point of the Web is to be as real as Outside. You're supposed to forget—"

"*No!* Maybe you're not supposed to notice any overt difference, but you're never supposed to *forget*. It scares me, Carver."

Something in her manner worried him, and he finally clued in. "This isn't the first time it happened to you, is it?"

She bit her lower lip and turned her face away from him. "Kind of," she mumbled. "But not this bad—never for so long."

"But it has happened?"

She nodded, her back still turned to him.

"Once or twice?"

"A few times."

The kettle whistled, and Carver busied himself with the tea. "You've been spending a lot of time tuned-in lately," he said, handing Rose her mug. "A lot more time than you're used to. Maybe you should take a break for a while."

Rose looked at him with a sad smile. "Wasn't it just a couple of months ago I was telling you the same thing?"

Carver choked on his tea. She had indeed said those very words to him—on the very night he created his meditation routine. And it was because of the routine that Rose had lately spent so much time in the Web.

"How long has this been going on?"

Rose shrugged. "Not long."

Carver set his mug down. A sick hollowness had suddenly appeared in the pit of his stomach. He had intended his routine to convince Rose that the Web's virtuality was just as real, in its way, as natural reality.

Had his program somehow accomplished this end, literally?

If so, how?

It was a question he needed to answer, for that routine lay at the heart of his new program. Without it he had no program. But if the technique was potentially harmful, he couldn't use it.

Carver looked over at his wife again, but she was once more staring away. Preoccupied. On the night he created the meditation routine, he recalled, he'd been preoccupied with the nature of reality in the Web. It was just possible that these thoughts had been stored with the meditation routine, completely unbeknownst to him—and to Rose.

When he first developed the technique, he had wondered if it could be used to create subliminal effects. None of his subsequent experiments supported this initial hope, but now Carver wondered if it didn't work subconsciously after all.

He had altered the parameters of his "blank workspace"

daily as he experimented. Rose hadn't—she'd tuned-in the same routine, created under one single set of conditions, every day for two months. What if the effects manifested themselves only after repeated exposure? That made sense, Carver realized now. Any single, specific effect would logically require a single, specific routine. An intentional routine.

And if his own mental preoccupation while he created the first routine had indeed imprinted itself into that routine, it meant he could produce any subliminal effect he desired just by concentrating on it while he worked.

Were this the case, it could prove far more useful than he'd ever imagined. But it would also mean he would need to exercise extreme caution when programming with the routine, so as not to create any more inadvertent side effects. Which meant, of course, that he had a lot of work on his new program that he would have to redo.

He sighed. A lot of work—and only two weeks from deadline. He should start right away. Just as soon as he deleted the meditation program from Rose's set.

And once he finished his new program, he could start working on a way to undo the effects the routine had already had on Rose.

"Yes," he muttered. "Perhaps you should stay out of the Web for a while."

Quadie frowned at his reflection in the tall dressing mirror. He had just scrolled through his entire wardrobe, and none of it excited him. It all seemed so old, so drab. Even the new stuff.

Perhaps the time had come once again for a change.

He grabbed his hair and pulled on it until it brushed at shoulder length, and turned it dark. He shook his head, watching the effect in the mirror. He made the hair more wavy, with a few ringlets toward the front.

Next, he grew a beard, but demanifested it right away. He

had never liked facial hair. In fact, he was tired of the face itself.

He put his hands along his jaw and squeezed, forcing the face into a more triangular shape and softening the jawline.

"Take about five years off and it'll be perfect."

Quadie adjusted the mirror until he could see Carver, standing a few meters behind him.

"Greetings, mate. What brings you to this neck of the Web?"

"Certainly not your make-over."

Quadie shrugged. "I was getting tired of the old me."

"So was I, but that doesn't mean this is any better. Actually, I'm here to ask a favor."

"You insult me and then ask for a favor?"

"I don't think you'll mind this one," Carver said. "If you have a couple hours free after you're done playing Doctor Frankenstein, I need your help."

"Doing what?" Quadie asked suspiciously.

Carver grinned excitedly. "Oh, just a little beta test."

Quadie's jaw dropped open. "No shit? You've finished?"

Carver nodded. "A week late, but yeah, it's done."

"Well, shit, my friend. I've waited long enough for this. Let's do it now."

"Great. I'm ready when you are," Carver said, demanifesting.

Quadie deleted the mirror and morphed back to his established image, dressed in a zoot suit of cobalt silk. Before he clicked over to Carver's interface, he said, "Start recording now, Ariel. I want a complete memory of all interaction with Carver's program. *Everything* that happens. One way or another, I am going to figure out what he's doing."

FIVE

Quadie cried out in terror. He sat bolt upright, his heart thudding rapidly, a cold sweat beading on his forehead. Something was horribly wrong.

But wakefulness ripped through the nightmare, driving it away beyond the reaches of his mind. He tried to remember what had scared him so, but could only grasp vague impressions, filaments of some other existence.

He rolled out of bed and stood in the open French doors, basking. The air was cool, the salty breeze that struggled sluggishly with the shirred organdy curtains more so, but the sun beamed hot over his naked body, and the floor was warm beneath his feet. The rough grain of old wood drew ridges against his bare soles. He stepped out onto the balcony and the sun hit him full in the face, dazzling. The cold stone shocked his mind into clarity.

A large raven, the sunlight playing purple iridescence over its oil-black feathers, alit on the balcony railing. It stared up at Quadie, its large, angular beak slightly open as though it were about to speak.

Quadie eyed the bird suspiciously. "I do believe it's a Carver-bird," he said. "Why do you keep scaring me, Carver? And how? I actually feel like I was really asleep or something. But you can't *do* that, mate, not in the Web. Fuck, but this is weird."

"Just wait!" The raven squawked laughter and flew away. The powerful wake from its wings blew something into Quadie's eye. He rubbed the irritation away, and when he opened his eyes again the bird was gone.

For the first time, Quadie looked at his surroundings. The high balcony overlooked the sea. Below, a courtyard stretched out to the very edge of the cliff and crumbled over.

A sudden strong urge to visit this courtyard swept over him. He hesitated; the urge became a compulsion. He forced himself to ignore it, and chuckled to himself.

"Wherever you are, little Carver-bird," he called out as he turned back inside, "I've just caught a fuck-up."

The room in which Quadie had awakened was large and airy. The canopied bed was draped in white linen. An antique armoire stood against the opposite wall. Within, Quadie found a pair of rough cotton trousers with a draw-string waist, and a pale yellow madras shirt; there were no shoes. He dressed and left to explore the rest of the house.

The hallway outside his room ran the length of the house. Windows of beveled glass at either end let in the only light. Quadie gathered from the hallway's length that the house must be huge. The dark oiled wood of the wain-scoting contrasted sharply with the ancient bone-white plas-ter that covered the walls and the arched ceiling. A Chagall hung on the wall near him. Toward one end of the hallway he saw what could only have been a Monet, though the dim light muted its colors. Quadie checked every room upstairs, but he did not see anyone else—nor even any signs of habi-tation.

Downstairs, the house felt much less cozy. The ceilings of the large rooms were dauntingly high, and everything seemed oppressively dark. As he wandered aimlessly, Quadie found himself following a hallway to a sun room at the back of the house—and to the courtyard beyond. He smiled and forced himself to stop.

To his left he saw a huge dining room, with the kitchen visible beyond. He retraced his steps until he found something more interesting.

Above the stone fireplace in the living room hung a painting in the style of an ancient 2D photograph, black and white with a sepia wash. The central figure seemed to be a young girl, although her alabaster visage was featureless. The face was missing, broken away from the head as though the girl were made of china. Some shards of the face—a chipped eye, part of a rosebud mouth, a pale cheek webbed with tiny cracks—lay scattered across a tarot reading spread before the girl. Within the head, dimly visible behind the broken-china mask, was a chambered nautilus shell. The background was a billowy swirl, though whether of water or cloud Quadie could not tell. It was, he had to admit, a very powerful and disturbing work. He wondered if it might be a virtualization of one of Rose's pieces.

He hurried out of the room. A pleasant, musty odor drew him to the library, and he took refuge among the old leather-bound books that lined the walls on dark oak shelves. Like most people, Quadie had no use for printed literature, though he could in fact read—an increasingly rare skill among kids these days, as the Web rendered such abilities superfluous. However, Carver had a special penchant for books, and he often hid unimportant but still fascinating tidbits of information in the books that appeared in all of his programs.

Quadie closed his eyes and reached out at random. He pulled the book from the shelf and looked at the title: *The Metamorphosis*, by Franz Kafka.

"Never heard of it," he said to himself. "Cool name, though."

Quadie sat in a rocking chair and opened the book to

read it, but a black cat suddenly jumped into his lap and sat down across the book. It stared at him balefully.

"What?" he asked it.

"What did I tell you before you tuned-in?" it said to him in Carver's deep and very uncatlike voice. "The house and all this stuff is just window dressing. I can test all this myself. The part I want your help with is outside—"

"On the courtyard," Quadie interrupted. "Yeah, I know, Carver. You made the urge to head out there so strong, I just about jumped off the damn balcony. I think you overdid it just a wee bit."

"Yeah? Hmmm. Well, I'll tone that index down a bit after you finish. But quit goofing off and get out there, would you?"

"Only if you promise to leave me alone until I'm done. It makes me nervous having you spy on me."

"I'm not spying," Carver protested, but he tuned-out anyway. Quadie tossed the book onto the seat, brushed cat hair from his shirt, then stood and headed for the hallway.

The French doors that led out from the sun room were of delicately etched glass, all with stained-glass borders. The sun outside had faded, so the stained-glass appeared dark and almost colorless.

The courtyard was barren of any ornament or furnishing save the balustrade which ran from either side of the house out to where the sea had claimed the cliffs. It was paved in dull gray stone, flat and smooth but with a sandy feel. The balustrade and the house were of the same stone.

Past the courtyard, on both sides of the house, fields of wild grass and heather ran to the distance. The scents of the meadow mixed faintly with the briny ocean air. The sky above was high and pale, almost white. The turbid sea beyond the cliffs held as little green as the sky held blue.

The hourglass-shaped paving stones were arranged in interlocking rows. Quadie walked with one foot in one row, the other in an adjoining one. The faint breeze and the far-away surf whispered in subtle voices he could almost understand. Every now and then a nonword struck deep within and resonated, tantalizing but never quite reaching a conscious level.

Five or six meters from the cliff edge, the smooth pavement started to become upset, until the stones, once so carefully shaped and placed, rose in a riotous tumult at the brink, as though horror-struck by the fate of those that had already met the sea—the fate that awaited them.

The voice of the wind and water became suddenly ominous as Quadie stepped carefully through the cast-up paving stones. Steel-gray clouds roiled close above now. A sense of fascinated dread swept him, pulled him forward. He turned to look behind, but there was no one there, no one watching. The house seemed uncomfortably far away.

He kept his eyes down as he picked a careful path through upturned and broken stone. At last the smooth, cut stones gave way to jagged rock and dirt. An occasional weed held fast to the ground with bared roots.

Two more steps and the ocean swelled into view. It was farther below than he'd thought, its sound oddly muted even here, with nothing but the salty, almost metallic air to distance it. Wave after wave lashed the rocks below, patient in the knowledge that they would one day taste the mysteries that for now were held beyond their reach within gray stone walls.

The spray from the surf could not reach Quadie, but the air at cliff's edge was superhumid—and somehow different. Its character had changed subtly, a new scent softening the harshness.

Curious, intrigued, he searched for the source of this scent. Where the left balustrade ended so unceremoniously (*How large was this patio originally?* he wondered), with the outermost remaining baluster toppled on its side, he found it: a meter below, struggling bravely for survival—a rose-bush.

Quadie crouched, then lay flat on his stomach, staring at this plant. At first it displayed no flower, but as he watched, a cream-colored bud formed, large and shaped something like an artichoke. The bud opened, and the rose burst forth. Quadie's sight exploded with color, bright bloodred, crimson, vermilion, all dancing as the petals unfurled themselves, spreading and stretching like a waking cat. He realized for the first time just how subdued this world had been as this eruption of blazing color speared through his vision, brighter in its way than the sun. He gazed at the still-unfolding flower, mesmerized by the motion and beauty. The wafting odor filled his head, stirring memories of . . .

They were gone before he could identify them.

Stretched out on the rock ledge, Quadie reached for the flower. The rose demurred. With the aid of the breeze, it ducked beyond his grasp. The delicate petals brushed his fingertips with the softness of a butterfly's wings. Scent wafted up to tease his nose, his mouth. He strained his shoulder lower, extended his fingers until he felt the rose between his fingertips. He forced farther. His fingers slipped down the pedicel. He grasped the stem, twisted it to break free the swirling color poised at its end.

His hand retracted automatically before the pain could register in his mind. Intact but for one thorn, the rose remained trembling on the ledge. Quadie sat up, swinging his legs over the cliff edge into empty space, to nurse his wounded thumb.

The thorn was small but completely embedded. He could see where it had scythed into his thumb, dark through translucent flesh. There was no blood.

Quadie squeezed the pad around the injury, then carefully slid the nail of his left thumb underneath the protrusion where the thorn had once joined its stalk. He lifted it up, past his skin, then caught the thorn between the nails of thumb and middle finger. Pain spiked through his wounded thumb once more as he pulled, the rough skin of the thorn ratcheting harshly past his own. When it at last came out, it stuck to the end of his middle finger. Quadie studied the thorn briefly, then flicked it away with his thumbnail.

A dark blemish lay beneath the skin, marking the wound. Quadie squeezed, and a drop of blood welled out. Across the surface of the drop swirled the colors of the rose. Quadie stared at his blood, entranced by the patterns, the rhythmic roll of the ocean, the brush of the wind against his skin. . . .

The world tilted. Vertigo took hold of him, pulling his mind back to the present, but too late.

The flower streaked past in a blaze of red as Quadie fell from the cliff. He reached out in panic and smashed his forearm against the rock. He shouted with pain, but with the shock his fear vanished. Time relaxed, and Quadie's plummet toward the angry, jagged rocks slowed. A numbing tingle spread through his body as his descent continued to slow. Feathers sprouted from his flesh; his arms became wings.

Quadie floated a few meters above the raging sea, his gull's body riding the wind. He flapped his wings and caught a rolling current to rise up into the sky.

With the house and its fields of heather drifting far below, he felt perfectly at home, perfectly *natural* as a gull. He had not simply morphed into a bird's image; rather, it was as though his *self* had truly become a gull. He remembered the book in the library. *The Metamorphosis*. Yes, that was it—he had metamorphosed into a gull.

And this change was still at work within him, lulling him into a state of near hypnosis. He was still conscious, but what he was conscious *of* was changing. Already he was losing his memories of the house and of . . . what had come before?

He soared higher on the salty wind, up toward the sun. Wind and light and heat—that was all there was, all there should be, and yet a feeling shuddered through, a thought not quite conscious, that it had not always been this way.

Then the feeling was gone, and nothing remained in its place. There was nothing but a sea gull, alone in the boundless sky.

After a meaningless eternity, immeasurable because no sentience existed to note its passage, a change in the air swept by, a subtle caress that reached far beyond the gull and dredged up self-awareness from some other realm.

The sun had swollen to fill the entire sky. Its light was malevolent, its heat destroying, threatening to burn the world, the sky, searing—

—Quadie sat up in bed, a scream bursting from his lips. Clammy perspiration drenched his body, and his pulse pounded in his temples even as the nightmare's terror receded. But even as it faded, something stronger lingered in its place—something more powerful but inchoate, subtle in its evasiveness.

And suddenly he was fully awake, reeling in the knowledge of what had happened to him.

"Holy son of a bitch," he muttered in amazement. "End."

Quadie was still dazed when Carver's familiar workspace manifested around him. Carver rose from his chair and walked impatiently toward him.

"Well, what did you think?"

Quadie sank into the easy chair, the wine-colored leather squeaking against him. "I need a drink."

A screaming Jaysus appeared in his hand, and he drank a good portion of it in one draught.

"Are you okay?" Carver asked him, somewhat anxiously.

"I don't know," Quadie told him. "*Goddamn*, mate, what the hell was that?"

"What?"

"The ending. The beginning. I mean, I guess. I don't think I remember what happened at the end. How the hell did you do that?"

Carver smiled nervously. "Did you like it?"

"It's the most in-*fucking*-credible thing I've ever experienced, my friend, in the Web or Out. Now I understand why you couldn't test it yourself."

Carver's smile became more relaxed, and he manifested a drink of his own. "How much do you remember? Tell me what happened—tell me how you remember it happening."

"Shit. I morphed into a bird. No, I didn't just *morph*. I fucking turned into a goddamned sea gull until I wasn't there anymore. I just disappeared, and the next thing I remember, I was at the beginning again, in the house, feeling like I'd been asleep for days."

Quadie took another long drink. "What just happened is impossible. I've never not known I was tuned-in before. Hell, just now I didn't know I was *anything*. Carver, that program violates every known law of the Web—and probably several of Nature's as well. How did you do it?"

Carver smiled mischievously. "Magic."

"Fuck you. Did you do something to my interface? Does this have something to do with that shit you were working on a few months ago?"

"Was there anything else? How do you feel now?"

"Now? Drained. Confused. I can't tell yet. I'm still recovering. That was too fucking real. What did you do?"

"It worked!" Carver said quietly. "I did it. It worked."

"Hey," Quadie said to him. "It wasn't all perfect, remember?"

Carver's face fell, but quickly recovered. "Oh, yeah. The impulse to go to the courtyard. Was there anything else you noticed?"

Quadie shook his head. "Nope. Just the one thing. You're getting too good, you bastard."

Carver closed his eyes and beamed. Quadie could see he was disgustingly pleased with himself.

"So tell me something," Quadie said. "That whole rose thing—was that a Freudian thing with the wife, or what?"

Carver scowled, and Quadie quickly threw up his hands in supplication. "Whoa, take it easy, mate. It was a joke."

"No, no," Carver said. "I'm not upset. You just caught me by surprise, that's all. I hadn't thought about it."

"Really?"

"The connection never once occurred to me. I'll have to think about that one."

"Sorry if I touched on a sore spot."

Carver shrugged the comment away. Quadie squirmed in his seat while he summoned up the courage to ask the next question.

"So, um, how are things? You know, with you and Rose?"

Carver let out an exasperated sigh. "You're asking me?"

"Really? That bad?"

"Honestly, Quadie, I don't know. We have our good days and our bad days, but lately Rose has been . . . I don't know how to describe it. She's been acting really weird. It's like she's a different person."

"I'm sure you'll work it out eventually." Quadie immediately regretted the hollowness of his comment. He knew as well as Carver that neither of them was at all certain about that.

"I hope so," Carver said, shaking his head sadly. "But I don't even know how to talk to her anymore."

They both fell silent then, each lost in his own thoughts, until Quadie demanifested his drink and said, "What say we get out of here? The Redline?"

"No, not right now. I want to fiddle with that index and deliver this sucker. I was supposed to have it to Jan a week ago. She's been advertising a Thanksgiving release, and I'm cutting it way too close."

Quadie stood. "Fair enough. I'll get out of your hair and leave you to it. Come find me when you're done, though."

"I will. Thanks for the help."

"No prob," Quadie said with a deep bow. "Oh, by the way—what's it called?"

Carver smiled enigmatically. "What else? *The Metamorphosis*."

Quadie winced. "What else?"

"Ariel, did you take a full enough recording of Carver's program to run it?"

"I'll try," his agent's disembodied voice told him.

A tiny transparent bubble manifested in the center of the interface, growing until it was about two meters in diameter. Within the bubble Quadie saw the bedroom from Carver's program.

"Here goes nothing," he muttered, reaching out to touch the sphere.

As soon as Quadie's fingers touched the bubble's surface, the program pulled him in, his image stretching and swirling like water spinning down a drain.

He abruptly found himself standing before the French doors, fully awake. Not only did he feel no sense of having awakened from a dream, there was none of the disorientation he had felt before. Whatever Carver's program did, it was not doing it now.

"Time reference, Ariel?"

"Multilooping the first five seconds of program."

"Are you sure you're starting at the beginning?"

"I can't start earlier than T-zero."

"Expand multiloop to run T-zero until I go out onto the balcony."

Quadie's perceptions smeared outward as Ariel blended his recorded experiences of standing-inside-in-the-doorway/walking-onto-the-balcony/standing-outside-on-the-balcony into a single gestalt and fed this moment to Quadie as a timeless continuity.

Still, Carver's special effect was missing.

"You're giving me everything?"

"Would I cheat you?"

"I'm beginning to wonder. What's the time reference?"

"Two minutes seventeen point six three seconds."

"Two minutes? It couldn't have been that long. When did I start to move?"

"Two minutes three point five seconds."

"Son of a bitch! What's in the I-and-R for those first two minutes?"

Ariel did not respond.

"Ariel?"

"I'm working on it. According to my records, data exchange between this unit and Carver's continued nonstop during that time. However, nothing happened."

"What exactly do you mean by that?"

"I have records that data interchange occurred between the two sets, through the Web, but I have no records of what that data was. Somewhere between the I/O computer and the set's processors, everything seems to have vanished."

"Check again, Ariel. There was definitely something going on, weird though it may have been."

"Well, it vanished as far as I'm concerned," the voice said.

"Fuck. What *are* you up to, my friend? Ariel, show me the end, starting from where the sea-gull morph begins. Same parameters."

Again Quadie's linear experience swirled into a single circular instant. He felt the physical change begin, progress, and complete itself all at once, each degree distinct yet simultaneous. But once again the psychological effect eluded him—or, to be more precise, eluded his agent.

Just as Carver's so-called "blank workspace" had baffled both Ariel and God. Quadie was sure there was a connection between the two. Had Carver created this trick in that workspace? Did the effect operate out of that workspace? If so, how?

"Cancel, Ariel," Quadie instructed, and he was back in his wide-open workspace, pacing. He always paced when he was upset or thinking, and now he was both. Something totally bizarre had happened to him in Carver's program—he was damn sure of that—but his agent and his interface had taken it all in stride. As far as Ariel knew, nothing at all out of the ordinary had been done. Whatever Carver's new technique, somehow it definitely had the ability to bypass an interface.

But if it didn't use interface I-and-R, how the hell could it possibly work? And for that matter, just what *was* the effect? Quadie still felt the immediacy of the experience with a peculiar *force*. Anyone could overload a program with enough sensory stimuli to make it feel real, but how had Carver managed to infuse his program with so much emotional power that the after-sensation from his program lingered still, even here in his own interface?

Quadie stopped his pacing and looked around at his interface, trying to corral the uneasiness building in him.

"Ariel, run a complete check on yourself."

After several seconds the M.I. responded, "All processes nominal. Something wrong?"

"Cross-check with your baseline referent, Ariel."

There was a much longer pause. "Everything's fine. What's up?"

"I have no idea. But I will find out somehow."

Quadie had a gut feeling that Carver's new program was going to start a revolution in virtual technology, and he wanted to have a part in that revolution. He and Carver were friends, but they were competitors, too. And Quadie could easily think of much more interesting uses for that routine than just making someone become a sea gull.

Much more interesting.

SIX

Var kicked the program and hypered for Public Net 11. Like all publics, Eleven manifested as a city block of shops. Var left the entrance field and clicked straight to the Prism Prison.

Sure enough, his friends were all there, gathered outside their usual hangout. When Var manifested among them, he could barely contain his excitement.

"Ho, bros."

"Ho, Var," they all said.

"What's *your* data?" Cisco asked him. "You're so jazzed, you're practically derezzing."

"Yeah fuck, Var," Pike said. "Give it."

Everyone crowded around, waiting for Var to divulge his secret. He basked in the attention for a few seconds before asking his friends, "Spied hype about Carver Blervaque's latest?"

"Yeah fuck, who hasn't?"

"If you've been *near* the Web, you've heard."

"Hype never compares to the real," Jess said coolly. "If you tune just 'cause of hype, it's always a crash."

Var shook his head. "Not today."

Suddenly everyone was clamoring around him.

"No fuck, you tuned it?"

Var closed his eyes and smiled. "*The Metamorphosis*, he calls it," he said reverently. "Yeah fuck, but that's the truest. This program is the shit."

"It's that good, really?"

Var opened his eyes and looked at Kembra. "It is the most fucking *all* program ever."

"This is gigo," Pike complained. "It just hit today. No way could anyone hack a major like Blervaque so quick. Not even you're that chief, Var."

"I didn't hack it, boyo. I tuned legit."

A murmur of shock rose from the circle of friends. It was against the hack's code of cool to actually pay for a program. Var hadn't even tried to hack his way into this one. He might have been able to with a few days' work, but he'd wanted the status of tuning it on opening day, of being the first among his friends to spread the news, so he had tuned it legit, actually paying for the experience. And there weren't many programs he ever did *that* for. "Yeah fuck, I spent for it," Var told them, "and so will all of you. Inside twenty-four, everybody in the Web is going to be talking about this program. If you want to keep any kind of rep at all, you'll be talking from the right side."

"What's it all about?" Cisco asked him. "I've spied a few reviews, but they ain't got shit."

"It cannot be described in words, kid Cisco. It's an entirely new dimension in virtuality."

Stick snorted. "Now *he* sounds like a review."

Some of the others laughed, but Var held his cool. "Laugh if you want, yeah fuck, but I'm telling you."

"Where did you tune it, Var?" Jess asked.

"Two-ten," he told her.

She looked around at the others, then said, "I'm going."

She demanifested. No one made any jokes or derisive comments. No one said anything.

"Well, it is Blervaque," Pike said at last. "He's the shit

anyway, you know. I mean, I'd planned to tune this anyway, not just 'cause of what Var says."

Before anyone could retort, he, too, demanifested. Several others followed.

Var shook his head in wonderment. Blervaque was already way rich—he was after all, as Pike had said, the shit—but this program would outmax everything. And not just for him. Var had a feeling that the biggest hackmoney for the next several months would be in pirating *The Metamorphosis*.

Var pawed at his already tousled hair. He wished he knew more about hacking. He was already plenty good—better than most of the fringers he knew, even though he'd been at it for only two years or so—but he didn't even know anybody chief enough to go after a major release.

It was too bad. Aside from the fortune waiting to be made, Var wanted to hack the program just to suss the works. He wasn't some little anarchohack like so many others on the fringe—like so many of his friends. No fuck, he actually cared about the artistry involved—in both the program and the hack. And *The Metamorphosis* was the toppest program he had ever tuned. Even now Var could still feel it pulling at him, like a hangover that won't die, or like one of those weird too-real dreams that haunts you all day long.

Kembra broke into his reverie. "What's it like, Var? Blervaque's program?"

Var just laughed. *Like a dream, yeah fuck.*

Captain Byrd's office wasn't quite large enough for him to be able to work out all of his frustration and anger through pacing alone, so he paused occasionally to turn a vicious kick upon his desk, his chair, or whatever else happened to be close enough when the urge overtook him.

The sun had begun its slow descent behind Atlanta's old skyscrapers, but Byrd was not tired, in spite of the fact that he hadn't slept the previous night. Thinking that clues to whatever underhandedness Carver Blervaque had been working on might turn up in his new program, Byrd had tuned *The Metamorphosis* as soon as the installations had opened at midnight.

He had not been disappointed. Blervaque had not even tried to disguise his trick—indeed, he'd made it the focus of the new program. What bothered Byrd—what had served, over the course of many hours of headache-inducing work, to put him in such a foul mood—was the fact that he could not for the life of him discover even the slightest clue as to how Blervaque had performed his magic tricks. In fact, he wasn't even sure *what* Blervaque had done.

Byrd had maintained an open file on Carver Blervaque ever since the trouble in Network 37, but despite his suspicions, no definitive evidence had ever turned up to link Blervaque with the security breach. Until Byrd had tuned *The Metamorphosis*.

The ending of the program obviously did some very unorthodox things to user interfaces. And immediately prior to the Network 37 hack, Quadie Newman's interface had suffered some unusual treatment when tuning Blervaque. Yet again, it was too much of a coincidence; Byrd knew the two had to be related, and so he'd immediately assigned his team the task of dissecting Blervaque's program.

Everyone in the Security Research Office agreed that the program's ending held great promise for security applications. Whatever Blervaque had done, both the subroutine and its operating parameters were entirely untraceable. Even more remarkable, none of the analyzing or recording A.I. routines detected anything out of the ordinary in the program, although they all reported an "undefinable" anomaly in the program's interaction with a user's set. If the *Metamorphosis* routine was truly invisible to the Web, it could revolutionize the Agency's work—return control of the Web to the government, where it belonged.

Unfortunately, because of these very qualities, it had so far been impossible to determine Blervaque's methods. Byrd's people had all tuned the program, but to no avail. Using some of the Agency's secret arsenal, they had covertly made several copies of *The Metamorphosis* into secure SRP Webspace. After several fruitless hours deconstructing the matrices, it had occurred to Lieutenant Hills that perhaps a routine with such an unusual effect on a user might also be more than a bootlegger could handle properly. He had tuned one of the copies as an experiment, and reported to Byrd that the unique effect was indeed missing from the copy; the narrative ending remained, but the user simply morphed into sea gull form briefly, retaining full consciousness throughout. When Byrd checked the other copies, he found them likewise lacking. He had given up in disgust.

Worried at the widespread availability of such a routine, Captain Byrd considered blocking public access to Blervaque's program. But as he paced his office he realized the futility of such an attempt.

Firstly, the Freedom of Data Act made it almost impossible to censor data. Byrd would need a court order to shut down any program, and a judge would want to know why specifically the FCA objected to the program—especially an entertainment program, and one coming as this did from a superstar director. Captain Byrd didn't want to explain himself to anyone, even within the Agency.

Secondly, Byrd didn't want to spook Blervaque. He knew that the director was personally overseeing each installation. If even the Agency's bootleggers could not replicate whatever Blervaque was doing, it was certain that no commercially available autorep could ever do so; obviously, Blervaque was programming his effect into each installation individually.

Considering the circumstances, Byrd knew the best chance he had of ever discovering the inner workings of the routine lay with Blervaque himself—as long as the director kept creating knew installations, he could keep trying to learn his secret. But if he scared Blervaque away, scared him into abandoning his public use of his new routine, then Byrd might not get another chance at it—until the next security incident.

And Byrd would do anything to avoid that. Anything at all.

Carver stood before the window in Jan's office, staring out at the spectral creatures oozing through the cave scenery.

"Please, Jan," he begged. "No more interviews for a while. At least until after Christmas. I've been going harder this past week than when I was working on the program."

"Everybody in the Web is talking about you, Carver. After one week of limited pre-release, you're already posting bigger numbers than most programs do normally. I think with enough publicity, you can have a record-setting full debut on Thursday, right in the middle of the holiday season. I don't have to tell you what that would be worth. But you need the interviews to do it."

"I still have another twenty installations to see to before Thursday. Each one takes me almost an hour to fine-tune. I can't do those and interviews both."

Jan sat on her desk, her jade and tiger-eye suit clacking softly against the hematite desktop. She had done the entire office in a mineral theme this week. "I'd almost rather have you do the interviews," she said. "I still don't understand why you can't just use a standard replicator."

Carver stared out her window and counted to ten before speaking. "I keep telling you, Jan. Web programs aren't just data, they're structure as well, partly dependent on the state of the local matrix. I've tried autoreplicate and it doesn't work on *The Metamorphosis*—it doesn't get the ending right. It's too . . . delicate. Each installation has to be tweaked individually."

Jan put her arms around him from behind and whispered into his ear, "Do this for me, Carver, please? It would make me very happy."

Carver laughed and stepped out of the hug. "Your commission should be making you plenty happy."

"That was low, Carver. I'm not in this just for the money." She paused. "Mostly, but not entirely."

"I'll think about interviews, how's that? But don't schedule anything without asking me first."

"Deal."

"So, if that's everything, give me the list of new installations and I'll get to work."

"Take it," Jan said, and a nudge in the back of Carver's mind from God told him the data transfer had been verified. "The list of installations *and* a list of people who have already contacted me about interviews. But don't go yet. There's one more matter we need to discuss."

Something in her tone made him wary. Carver turned from the window and asked, "What's that?"

Jan walked up to him and put her hands gently on his shoulders. "Don't get upset, but four more corporations have inquired about licensing your—"

"No way, Jan. Absolutely no way. I already told you I'm not ready to give out the secret."

"Well, I don't think you should. At least, not until we've got a patent."

Carver shook his head, but before he could speak, Jan continued.

"Carver, someone is going to figure this thing out sooner or later. If you want to have any control over it at all, you need to file it."

"I will, Jan, eventually. But I need to work on it a bit

more. I want to be sure I know its full potential, so I can file for full protection."

This was true enough, Carver knew, but he had left plenty more unsaid. Frankly, he was worried that he'd created too much of a sensation. Already he had seen wild stories in the news about what he'd done and how. Speculations on other uses for such a routine ran from frivolous to sinister. Most of those were laughable, but some disturbed Carver deeply. There was no way he was going to sell off a routine so unlike anything else that even he wasn't sure just how it worked, nor for what purposes it might ultimately be used.

The only good news was that everyone had concentrated so far on just the personality squelch; if anyone had yet noticed the subliminal aspect of his program, they were keeping quiet about it.

"Well," Jan said, shaking her head sadly, "if that's your final word on the subject—and knowing how stubborn you are, I'm sure it is—then we're pretty much done here."

"Then I'll get to work on the rest of the installations. Tune you soon."

Carver exited Jan's office. His workspace appeared around him for an instant but abruptly vanished, and he was out in space, the earth floating high overhead as he stood on a floor of brightly flowing data. Around him, mirror-polished brass and black marble fixtures created an office. A man manifested behind a teak desk to greet him.

"Mr. Blervaque! I am Alexander Nordberg. How very good it is to meet you."

Nordberg wore a tailored suit of gray wool. His smile was warm and gracious on his unlined face. A hint of silver at his temples lent a distinguished air of authority. It was a perfect image. Carver mistrusted it immediately.

"What's going on?" he asked angrily. "Where am I? What do you want?"

"Please forgive the unusual nature of this contact, Mr.

Blervaque. My clients wish to keep all of their business dealings strictly confidential as a matter of course."

"Your clients?"

"I represent a consortium of Austrasian business groups, Mr. Blervaque. I am afraid I am not at liberty to divulge any more about my clients than simply that."

I hope you're recording all of this, God, Carver thought.

Sorry. I don't know what this guy is doing, but I'm lucky to have any contact at all with you right now.

"I'm sorry, Mr. Blervaque, but I cannot allow any of this conversation to be recorded. Confidentiality, as I said."

"So, are you reading my thoughts or monitoring my interface without authorization? The first is impossible, and the second is illegal."

"Please, Mr. Blervaque. We do not wish to upset you, but for reasons of security we are maintaining your link to your A.I. Your data throughput—"

"I prefer 'machine intelligence,' if you don't mind," God said out of nowhere. "Because of the interactive nature of software and hardware in the Web, I am not mere program but a true gestalt of the machine. Besides, 'artificial' makes me sound as though I'm not real. Just because I do not exist as a biological entity—"

"God, be quiet."

"Yes, boss."

"How charming." Nordberg laughed. "I meant no offense to your *machine* intelligence unit. Now, where were we?"

"I think you were just about to tell me what the hell it is you want."

"Please, Mr. Blervaque, there's no need to be hostile."

"If this is about *The Metamorphosis*, you can forget it right now. I never sell any rights to any of my programs. If you'd called my manager first, she could have told you that and saved us both a lot of wasted time."

"We prefer to involve as few people as possible in this

matter, Mr. Blervaque. That is why we have contacted you directly. And it's not the program itself, Mr. Blervaque, in which we are interested. Our data suggests that the routine you used to effect the, ah, unusual nature, shall we say, of the ending holds some promise for certain applications of interest to us."

"Does it? You seem awfully certain about its capabilities. Why not just create your own routine, then, if you know so much about it?"

Nordberg smiled obsequiously. "Believe me, we wish we could. We don't know anything about your program, Mr. Blervaque. No one does, it would seem. But it has attracted great notice, and great interest, from many, many people. The best we can do is to develop theories about your program, Mr. Blervaque. But several of those theories suggest that it might be useful to us in one capacity or another. And so we wish to license your routine for research purposes."

"Research purposes."

"Exactly. We are prepared to offer a substantial sum for the details of how, precisely, this routine operates. That is all—just the details of what you have already done. Our research teams would take it from there. There would be nothing more for you to do than what you have already done."

Carver's mistrust exploded into outright suspicion. "Who the hell are you?"

"Now, Mr. Blervaque, I have explained that I am not at liberty to—"

"Then there's no deal. I know who I'm dealing with and what they intend, or I don't deal."

"Please excuse me for one moment." Nordberg's expression went blank for several seconds, then the smile returned as before.

"Very well, Mr. Blervaque. I have been authorized to tell you this much: the interests I represent are researching the possibility of establishing their own version of the Web across the Pacific rim."

He pointed to the earth that hung motionless above them. The Pacific faced them, devoid of all obscuring cloud cover. The western and southern edges of the Pacific rim from Japan to New Zealand lit up in a pulsing display. Filaments also crossed the ocean, lighting up many of the scattered Melanesian and Micronesian islands.

"The population of this area of the world being much greater than the population of Unified North America, the possible return is also substantially greater.

"However, as you are no doubt aware, the system we use here on the Continent interacts with the brain at a symbolic level. We know that a person's native language has a great influence on the nature of these symbolic concepts and thought processes. Being thought-controlled, the Web does not use language as such, but it does in a way require all participants to think in the same language—which is one reason this system has only been developed on such a wide scale in North America. Europe and Austrasia are both multilingual societies, despite the fact that business is conducted in a single language in each, so datacom in these regions has so far been limited to screens and keyboards, the Internet, telephones—primitive technologies that Unified North America surpassed in the early part of this century."

"You don't seem to have any problems using the Web."

"I am American," Nordberg said with a smile. "Born and raised with the English language. I merely work for this consortium."

"I see. So where does my . . . where do I come in?"

"It has been suggested that this new program of yours may somehow help us to, ah, bypass this difficulty. The fact that you manage to somehow separate a user from his . . . well, from his consciousness, as it were, without actually making him physically unconscious—that is, while keeping the mind active enough that the user is not automatically released from the system—suggests, to us at least, that you might possibly have developed a means of going beyond language, of somehow interacting with the user's mind on a basic, conceptual level of thought—perhaps even a universal level, if such a thing truly exists."

Carver turned from Nordberg and gazed instead at the earth suspended above him, the Austrasian countries still glimmering with the hope of taking the final step into the true Cyber Age.

"You would of course be well-compensated should any viable applications be derived from our research—a small interest in any future profits, perhaps."

Something about this deal felt very, very wrong. And the better the deal became, the warier Carver became. *We don't know anything about your program*, Nordberg had said. Fine. But then he had added, *No one does.* How many others had these people contacted about his routine before finally coming to him? And how many others were also trying to find applications for his work?

"Let me think about it," Carver said at last, still facing away from Nordberg. "Why don't you give me the details and an address, and when I've had a chance to go over this, I'll get back in touch."

"Oh, please, Mr. Blervaque, feel free to take all the time you need. But I'm afraid I can't leave you an address. Security, you understand. However, I shall be happy to contact you again soon to see if you have reached any conclusions. Shall we say, in one week's time?"

"Sure," Carver said. "Whenever."

"Fine. Then I shall let you go. I realize you must be a good deal busier than I am. Goodbye, Mr. Blervaque."

Before Carver could respond, he was in his workspace again.

"Trace that tune, God," Carver said as soon as he regained

his bearings. "I want a full address, ID, location trace, any information at all you can get."

"Sorry, boss. I tried all that when you told me to record. They had me blindfolded the whole time. The only contact I had with you at all was what they allowed—and controlled. I didn't like it."

"Neither did I, God. Not a bit. I almost feel like reporting this to the FCA."

"Why don't you?"

Carver laughed mirthlessly. "I've got too much work to do."

Carver and Rose planned a special dinner together for Christmas. They had wanted time alone much sooner than that, but his schedule hadn't permitted it.

Rose stood at the center island in the kitchen, cutting vegetables and fruits while Carver cooked the curry sauce and steamed the rice. Music piping through the ceiling speakers provided the only accompaniment to the sound of Rose's knife on the butcher block. Once Carver and Rose had settled on a menu, their conversation dissolved into heavy silence. Carver tried to draw his wife out once or twice, but she only grunted distractedly in response, so he gave up.

Now he just stared into the curry as it cooked down, focusing intently on his task. He tried to tell himself that Rose was merely doing the same. She'd remained withdrawn even after he erased the meditation routine from her interface, and over the last two weeks she had grown increasingly irritable as well.

Even if his routine did have some sort of lingering psychological effect, he was sure it had to have worn off by now. Whatever was upsetting Rose, it was much deeper than that. There was more at work in her psyche than just their marital problems, and he didn't know what, or what to do about it. He couldn't talk to Rose anymore, and she wouldn't talk to him.

The sound of Rose's chopping had ceased. Carver glanced over his shoulder at her. She stood with her back to him, body slightly slouched and motionless. He watched her for several seconds, but she remained frozen. He couldn't tell if she was simply looking out the window or if she'd become lost in thought again, so he stepped around to judge her expression.

Her face was blank, her jaw faintly open. She held the chef's knife loosely in her right hand, her left index finger pressed against the tip of the blade. She idly twisted the knife back and forth; where it dug into her finger, blood welled and ran down her hand.

"Rose!"

She started from her reverie, jerking her finger away from the blade, letting the knife fall from her grasp. It clattered to the floor, scattering drops of blood like rubies across the white ceramic tile.

"Oh my God!" she murmured, staring at her bloody hand as though it were someone else's.

Carver grabbed a dish towel and pressed it against her fingertip. "Jesus, Rose, are you okay? What were you doing?" He guided her firmly to the sink. "Here, rinse that off," he told her. "I'll go get something to put on it."

He walked down the hallway, swearing under his breath. In the master bathroom he rummaged through the medicine cabinet and the drawers for rubbing alcohol and bandages.

Suddenly God called from the ceiling, "Jan's tuning you, boss." The voice tickled slightly with the static of a failing solder joint in the speaker wiring.

"On Christmas Day? Christ, doesn't that woman ever take a day off? All right, put her through on audio."

A second later Jan said, "Oh, what is this crap? Come on, Carver, tune-in. You know I hate doing business voice-only."

"I'm busy," Carver protested sourly.

"Well, I think you'll want to tune-in for what I have to tell you."

"I don't have time for games right now, Jan."

"All right, no games. I just got last week's usage figures."

Carver dropped a bottle of peroxide into the sink. "Oh yeah?" His heart raced and he felt suddenly hot. "So how'd we do?"

Jan laughed at the eagerness in his voice. "Just like a kid at Christmas, aren't you?"

"It is Christmas. And I may not be a kid anymore, but I'm still younger than you."

"Touché."

"So more numbers, less attitude."

"Okay, okay. You did it."

"Did *what*?"

"You topped the charts," she told him, the laughter in her voice replaced with awe. "You did it, babe."

Carver leaned against the wall, stunned to silence and unable to think clearly.

"Did you hear me? Are you still there, Carver? *Metamorphosis* is the most popular program in the whole fucking Web!"

Carver swore to himself in astonishment. "I heard you. Hold on—I'll be right In."

"Told you."

Carver ignored the retort. "Start-up, please, God."

"Way ahead of you, boss."

Carver splashed water on his face.

His mind spun dizzily with excitement. This was only the fourth time in the history of the Web that a program had debuted at the top. For someone of Carver's reputation, such a feat might not be especially surprising for a program of epic proportions and excitement, but *The Metamorphosis* was anything but exciting. In fact—and Carver was the first to admit this—*The Metamorphosis* was rather unusual in that practically nothing happened. Users could spend days exploring the house and grounds, but the only excitement, such as it was, came from the sea gull sequence. And the draw on that was surely more because of the novelty than any action.

There had been plenty of novel, ground-breaking programs before, of course, but none of them had ever made the numbers by Week One.

Carver tuned-in directly to Jan's office. She greeted him with a kiss and spun him around in an elated hug.

"Numbers," he told her when she finally released him.

"Marissa hasn't gotten to the final accounting yet, but I'm pretty sure your royalties have already topped a million."

"I don't care about that. How many users?"

Jan beamed at him. "Give or take a few . . . fourteen million."

Carver was so stunned he almost slipped his connection and Escaped. He forced himself to concentrate, and his image stopped wavering.

Jan seemed not to have noticed. "That'll go way higher next week. In the two hours since the ratings came out, eight more Networks have licensed, and the public Nets now want to add thirty-six more."

She fed him a complex rush of data, laughing as it overwhelmed him, then directed her agent to organize it for him.

Forty minutes later they finished, and Carver tuned-out. The lights glowed hard against the windows. It was dark outside, and a rough winter wind rasped past the house, chilling him by suggestion. He walked to the kitchen and set the kettle on to boil.

Shortly, he poured a little scalding water into the teapot and swirled it, then dumped it out. He added half a dozen spoonfuls of Earl Grey to the warmed pot, then filled it with boiling water and set it on the counter to draw.

While he stood waiting, he noticed the blood on the floor, and his stomach knotted up. In the excitement, he'd completely forgotten about his wife.

"I'm making some tea, Rose," Carver called loudly. "You want some?"

There was no answer.

"How's your finger?"

She still did not answer.

Carver walked through the house, calling his wife's name. He checked every room, but Rose was not in the house. He checked out front, but the car was still there. He returned to the kitchen and peered through the French doors onto the deck, but still didn't see her.

He poured himself a cup of tea, not bothering with the cream, and glanced at the door that led down to Rose's basement studio. It was not latched. He knocked lightly, pushing the door open as he did so.

"Rose?"

Carver quietly descended the stairs. The studio was deserted. On a tarp in the center of the room stood a stone monolith, partially marked for carving. Canvases in various stages of completion lined the walls.

Carver moved into the room cautiously. He and Rose had a standing agreement that neither was to be bothered when working, and he always felt awkward invading her studio, even when she wasn't there. But the painting on her easel drew him in.

He stood mesmerized before the canvas. It was full of angry colors, the paint violently applied in thick, crude textures. The painting was ostensibly a self-portrait in the style of Frida Kahlo, one of Rose's favorite artists, but the dark-haired woman staring wildly from the canvas bore little resemblance to Carver's wife. Whereas Rose's eyes were dark blue, the eyes in the portrait were a pale, sickly green, amber-flecked in a way that made them appear mad with terror. The mouth was a jagged gash, the lips the bright bloodred of opened flesh. The red paint glistened wetly. It was fresh, Carver noticed with some discomfort, not yet dried. Rose had painted this detail after she cut her finger. But where was she now?

He backed slowly from the room, unwilling to turn his back on that face. Upstairs again, he refilled his cup and tried to think where Rose might be. As he stared through the doors into the darkness, a tiny movement rippled into his peripheral vision. He passed his hand over the light switch and opened the doors.

Rose huddled against the wall of the house, her arms crossed over her lap and her knees drawn up tightly against her body. She wore a only long wool skirt the color of heather and a thin dark sweater, and she was rocking back and forth and shaking violently in the cold. Her eyes were closed, her face slack and empty.

"Rose, honey? What's going on? Are you all right? How's your finger?"

Rose did not respond. Carver knelt in front of her. He lightly touched her shoulder, then her cheek. Her skin was very cold and oddly pale.

"Rose? Hey, what's wrong, sweetheart?"

Her eyes opened. They stared past him without focus. "Carver?"

"What are you doing out here, Rose? It's freezing. Come inside—you're going to catch your death out here."

A tear spilled halfway down Rose's cheek as her eyes sharpened to focus on him. She clenched her jaw against the shivering.

"I can't do this anymore, Carver." She turned her head away from him. "I'm sorry, Carver. I wanted to . . . I didn't want you . . ."

She pressed her face against the stone wall and burst into tears.

"Come on," Carver said soothingly. "Let's get you inside, and we can talk."

He took her hands and tried to pull her up, but she let out a small, sharp cry and pressed her arms more tightly to her body. The chef's knife fell from her lap onto the deck, the blade black in the dim light.

"What is— Oh Jesus, Rose, what have you done?"

Carver gently forced Rose's knees down and out of the way. The sleeves of her sweater were warm and damp. He knelt beside her, tears fouling his vision as he pushed the sleeves up.

Rose had made the cuts just below the elbows, slicing diagonally across the arteries. Blood still pulsed sluggishly from the wounds. She had done a very effective job.

"Oh God, Rose. Why? Oh my God."

Rose looked at Carver with wild, scintillant eyes. "It is real, isn't it? Please tell me it's real. I can't even tell if it hurts. I think it does."

Her eyes closed and her body went limp. With a last faint whisper she said, "I still can't tell if it's real or not, Carver."

PART 2

SEVEN

Claustrophobia overtook Carver. A dark, visceral shudder ran down his spine and settled deep in his groin. He closed his eyes to block out the sight of the Fourier coil so close over his eyes, but it did no good. A churning terror built in his gut, and his hand reached out for the safety. He pressed the switch and the coil swung away.

Carver had performed this ritual every day for almost a month and a half now, always with the same outcome. He had not been able to tune-in since Rose's suicide.

She had lost control, and it ended up killing her. Could the same thing happen to him?

The first week had been lost to the physical and emotional stress of funeral arrangements and paparazzi and the police investigations. With all that chaos, there had been no time for emotion. When Carver had at last found the chance to tune-in again, grief and exhaustion overwhelmed him quite suddenly, creating a minor scene on a public Network. Since that trauma, he hadn't found the courage to tune-in again.

Carver stood wearily and walked to the window. He passed his hand over the switch and the plastic faded to transparency.

He was quite surprised to see a faint dusting of snow

outside. The occasional flake still meandered earthward out of the iron sky of early February. Snow was a rare sight in north central Florida, but it was not entirely unheard of, and it had been an unusually harsh winter.

Carver stared blankly out, mesmerized by snow and memories. *An unusually harsh winter . . .*

He pounded his fist against the window, leaving a momentary charcoal-gray imprint in the liquid crystal, and hurried away.

Carver found the bottle of brandy in the back of the pantry. He uncapped it and took a long caramel taste from the bottle. Trees stared stoically in at him from the gorge, their winter-bared branches scratching the sky without leaving a mark.

He opened the doors and stepped out onto the deck. The world Outside was cold and hard in the brilliant light of morning, and almost blinding in the sheen of its reality. The sky remained a mystery behind its cloak of low clouds—they shone with a pale lambency that highlighted their contours and cast about vague shadows. A brightness overpowered Carver's sight where the sun waited patiently beyond the clouds, leaving a radiant hole in his vision whenever he raised his eyes to its solemn gaze.

He drank the brandy again. It was only a few degrees above zero, and thin milky ice like the cauls of cataracts huddled still in pockets of deep shadow on the ground below. A brisk gusty breeze took his white breath and whipped it quickly away, not feathery and billowing but in a thin wisp, barely visible, like a ghost or a faded memory.

It was all brutally real in a way the Web could only pretend at. The incomprehensible processing power of the Web could mimic reality perfectly, but it was still only mimicry. One could put aside the knowledge that it was not truly real, but one could never forget.

Almost never.

Carver took another long drink, and the bottle was empty. The snowflakes melted where they landed on the wood, staining it a dark red-brown. A darker stain spread near the house.

A shudder built within him, pain and fear and frustration crashing inside, and suddenly he was running, blindly, without direction or control. He didn't care. He only wanted to run, to get away from the pain that burned through him.

Carver ran heedlessly through the gorge, unmindful of the cold that bit through his clothes. Memory and pain roared in his head. He could see nothing but Rose's eyes as she'd looked at him then. That started a pain worse than any other, for in her eyes he saw that he had lost her long before she took her life.

He had no idea how long he'd been running when he tripped through ragged underbrush and came to a crashing halt at the foot of a large oak. He lay facedown in dirt and snow, crying until the pain began gradually to subside. He gasped sharply. The cold air racked his lungs, cramping in his chest. He rolled over, realizing that he'd twisted his ankle, and tried to control his breathing. The exertion and his pain had overcome the alcohol, leaving him now sober and very cold. His sweater was electrothermal, but there was not enough light to power the microscopic solar beads in the shoulders. He turned the cuff dial as far clockwise as it would go, but it did no good.

The snow still came down, though it had slacked off somewhat. Carver could not tell where he was. He owned close to four hundred hectares and knew every part of it, but he was in unfamiliar territory now. He was not even sure from which direction he'd come. He was completely lost.

As he looked around, trying numbly to identify some part of his surroundings, he saw hidden behind one of the oak's great, twisted roots a scrawny wild rosebush. At the end of one of the stalks, pale and frostbitten, bloomed a small pink rose, its petals mottled from the cold.

Carver stared at the flower in disbelief. Its presence in the midst of a winter snowstorm was unlikely enough, but that it should be, of all possible flowers, a *rose*, was almost too much. Rose had often seen such wild coincidences as evidence of a purposeful and mischievous "Cosmic Tease." Carver almost had to agree now.

A sudden commotion startled him, the noise of several people yelling and shouting. Carver stood and leaned back against the oak's trunk.

A child materialized from the snowy forest. Seeing Carver, the boy howled jubilantly at him and kept running, but then stopped abruptly. He turned and faced Carver, standing motionless a few meters away, his face red with cold and happy exercise, his eyes growing wide with surprise. The ruckus that followed him continued, growing closer.

The boy seemed to be about eight. He was clad in a ragged but heavily patched jacket and at least two pairs of pants. Even so, the skin of his legs showed through in several places. Rough boots covered his feet, and he wore thin gloves on his hands and a garish knitted stocking cap on his head.

As Carver and the boy stood staring at one another, the boy's followers appeared through the brush. Their whooping stopped when they saw their quarry standing with a stranger. Many of them were no larger than the first boy, but as Carver glanced about the dozen or so people, he noticed that a few seemed to be young adults—college age, perhaps students at the university. They were for the most part dressed as haphazardly as the boy.

One of the adults took a few cautious steps forward. "River?" he asked.

The first boy turned to look at the speaker, then grinned and pointed shyly at Carver. A couple of the other boys laughed or snorted. The speaker shook his head. The boy nodded emphatically.

"Neh," the speaker said gently to River. To his friends he said, "Let's go."

River ran toward the older boy and grabbed his arm. As he passed by, Carver saw the bowlish disk covering the back of his head below the faded neon cap. A headset.

They were Freeks. They were using headsets to communicate through the Web. Headsets were portable versions of the Fourier coil on a set. Because of bandwidth and processor limitations, a headset could not provide the complete virtuality of the Web—nor could it cut off somatic responses like a set. At the very best, a headset could provide a user with the virtual audio and olfactory experience, but only ghost visuals and no tactile response. But it did allow a user to access the Web's data and communicate without restricting her or him to a stationary set.

As Carver watched the silent debate, he realized again how cold he was. Though Freeks generally engaged in harmless pranks, they were by nature wild and unpredictable. And, Carver reminded himself, they were criminals.

"I know," the boy told the other Freeks. He seemed to be getting distraught. "*I* know, Shade," he said emphatically to the speaker, who seemed to be the group's leader.

Shade bent his head to the side and looked at some of the other boys and said something in an odd cant that Carver could almost understand. Hearing a partial conversation fascinated Carver. He could feel ideas already spinning in the back of his mind—how could he apply this to a program?

"He would," someone said.

Shade looked at Carver and shrugged. "He thinks you're Carver Blervaque," he said. River nodded again and pointed at Carver, then at himself.

Carver still felt wary, but the Freeks seemed more curious

than anything else. He looked at Shade, then down at the boy River. "He's right."

River's face lit up with a broad smile and he became shy again. Someone said something in the jargon and River dropped his gaze and tried to hide himself behind Shade. Shade laughed and shoved him out before the group.

"He's a big fan of yours," Shade explained. "He wants to be a director someday. He practically idolizes you. You should see his walls—he's got two- and three-D's from all your programs."

River's face was turning redder than it had been. Carver couldn't help but laugh.

"Well, it's very nice to meet you, River," he said, extending a numb hand as he slipped into his public persona. "That's a very interesting name you have. Have you done much programming?"

The boy's smile faltered and he shook his head. "We . . . neh. Sets—"

"Riv," Shade warned.

"Hey, it's okay," Carver told the group. He tried to assume a casual air, but his shivering ruined the effect. "I don't care if you're Freeks. I won't turn you in or anything. When my friend Quadie was—"

"Young Pioneers," River said proudly.

"What?"

"Freeks, nah. Young Pioneers."

Carver nodded. "I see. No offense meant." He'd always thought Freeks bore the epithet with pride.

"None taken—the caps confuse a lot of folks," Shade said as he turned away. "Game's over, chums. Time to scamper— Rachel's waiting at the Oasis." Looking back over his shoulder, he called, "Blaze your trail, brother Blervaque."

The others began to drift away. Some mumbled or waved at Carver as they went. River, though, stood where he was, still looking at Carver, who shivered and smiled awkwardly.

River turned, startled, to look after his receding friends. "Coming!" he shouted.

But he wavered where he was, then walked haltingly toward Carver, staring pointedly at the ground the whole time. He snatched the woolen cap from his head and held it out to Carver.

"Cold, neh?"

Carver took the cap and pulled it onto his head.

River looked up and giggled.

"Thanks, River. I owe you one."

River looked at Carver in awe, then giggled again and ran away. After a few steps he turned and waved. "Blaze your trail," he said with great seriousness.

Carver waved back, and River ran on to catch up with his friends. He stopped one more time to wave, then he was lost in the snow and the trees.

The fear and the grief were gone. Carver looked around to get his bearings and saw the rose again. He frowned at the unlikely bloom.

Leaves before him jumped in a sudden icy gust. Carver crossed his arms tightly over his chest for warmth and trudged off through the snow, the cold a dull, numbing pulse that crackled through his skin in rhythm with his footsteps on the near-frozen ground. He was uncertain of his direction, but hoped he was on his way home.

"God," Carver called a second time, "open the door."

Still nothing happened.

"God! Door. Open."

The house had its own solar panels and Reed-Johnson magnetic generators. They had been known to fail, but only rarely. Carver retrieved the emergency key from its hiding place beneath the porch and unlocked the door. Inside, lights glowed on the house systems' indicator panel.

The power was on.

"God?"

No reply.

Carver ran to his workroom and powered up his set. Alarm had driven away his fear—he lay back on the couch and tuned-in.

To a two-dimensional world of brightly colored point-and-go menus. Carver stood before the screen, his image now a tall white man dressed in casual khaki slacks and a blue Oxford shirt with a maroon tie.

Carver swore. Every set had such an interface and image built into the operating protocol, but only for use as a default. Once the user created a custom interface, the hard-wired interface went dormant, superseded by the user's version. If his set had reverted to its default, that could mean only one thing.

The default interface was elementary and clumsy, but Carver managed to make his way around well enough to check his set. The diagnostics all indicated that the set was working perfectly. But God was nowhere to be found. Something had definitely gone wrong somewhere.

What had happened? Where was God? With some difficulty, Carver accessed his set's memory stacks.

He found himself staring at a gray wall, a blank slate on which his code library should have been listed, but instead it was clean, freshly erased.

Carver tuned-out. He sat up on his set and stared out the window in disbelief and annoyance. He had never heard of anything like this happening before. The holographic nature of memory storage in the Web gave it a high degree of "failure-softness." As much as fifty percent of the matrix could be disturbed or even destroyed before catastrophic data loss would occur. Anything over twenty percent failure would cause resolution problems, certainly, but it would not impair functioning. But something had wiped Carver's entire set clear, erased everything irrecoverably.

Not erased, he realized suddenly.

Stolen.

The status indicators on the control panels all glowed green. Physically, the set was operating perfectly. There had been no failure.

Someone had hacked his set.

The house did not have voicephones, so Carver tuned-in again. Data communications functions were the primary capability of all interfaces, user-friendly even on a default interface. Carver pointed to the Send Message box. It changed from blue to yellow and swelled to accommodate the prompt, *Address?*

"Gainesville Police Department," Carver said aloud.

The third dimension exploded around him as a small room replaced the gray wall, although the menus remained as translucent jewels floating in his vision.

"Good afternoon, sir. How may I help you?"

Carver faced a pleasant-looking woman in a light brown uniform, who stood at a polished mahogany counter. Behind her, the room's panoramic windows showed the historic section of downtown Gainesville, the massive granite columns of the Hippodrome State Theatre's Greek revival façade dominating the view.

"Uh, someone just randomized my private matrix."

The woman's image displayed appropriate concern and sympathy. "I'm very sorry to hear that, sir. Was there any property damage or physical trespass involved?"

"No, ma'am."

The sympathy on the woman's face lessened. "Well, sir, I'm afraid we can't help you. Data-based crimes fall under FCA jurisdiction."

"I'm willing to bet that my data was stolen before my set was wiped," Carver told her.

"I am sorry, but we really can't do anything about it. You'll have to talk to the FCA."

Carver clicked back to his interface without another word to the woman. The Send Message icon again flashed yellow and prompted *Address?* when Carver swatted at it, but the interface did not respond to Carver's thought.

"Jesus Christ," he grumbled.

The box flashed red with the message, *Address Not Found. Try New or Quit?*

Carver rolled his eyes. "Quit," he said, and tuned-out.

After his last contact with the FCA, he did not look forward to dealing with them again, even in the role of victim. But this was a serious matter, and he couldn't let it go unreported. If he had to tune the FCA, though, he would do it with his own custom interface, not a default.

He grabbed his jacket from the hall closet and walked out to the blue two-seat metrosport. He had a full copy of his interface on a data prism in his safe deposit box at the bank.

As Carver drove into town, he couldn't help but dwell on the theft. Carver felt certain the hackers had been after the *Metamorphosis* routine, but that hardly narrowed the field of suspects. It could have been Nordberg or any of the others who wanted to license the technique, or hackers wanting to sell the routine illicitly, or even another director. With a shudder, Carver admitted that it could even have been the FCA, too. He certainly wouldn't put it past them.

The only good news was that they couldn't have found anything useful. As Carver well knew, the routine could not be copied automatically, and he had kept no notes about it. Any data on the process existed only within *The Metamorphosis* installations themselves and in the original blank workspace—which itself no longer existed.

Carver drove north on Thirteenth Street, one of Gainesville's main drags. On his left passed the walled campus of the University of Florida, his alma mater. He'd spent nine years there getting a five-year degree in Matrix Programming and Virtual Reality Studies, but the extra time had been well spent. By the time he finally managed to receive his degree, he'd gained a national reputation and was making enough per program to more than pay for all of his educational discursions.

That had been fourteen years ago. A lot had happened in the intervening years.

The traffic light at University Avenue turned red. The city's major intersection, the corner of Thirteenth and University marked the northeast border of the campus. While Carver waited for the light to change he scanned the graffiti covering the high concrete wall. There were the usual obscenities spray-painted on the wall, as well as several heart shapes around two names, or sometimes more, and an unfinished abstract mural. But what caught his eye was the large slogan BLAZE YOUR TRAIL painted in bright colors and psychedelic style.

It was the phrase the Freeks had used that morning. Gainesville was truly a small town—sometimes too small.

Carver thought about the boy, River, about his exuberance, the reverence with which River had regarded him. He seemed like a good kid.

Has he tuned the program? Carver suddenly wondered. *Has he been exposed to the routine?* Rose was dead. What might happen to River?

Fourteen million in the first week, Jan had reported. How many people had tuned-in by now, after six weeks? And how many people had repeated the experience? In *The Metamorphosis*, he had added the subliminal suggestion that the user consider virtuality to be real—just as he'd inadvertently done to Rose—but with the added caveat that the virtual and natural realms were distinctly separate realities. He'd thought that a perfect solution to the problems Rose had developed—the problems that had killed her—but he was no longer sure.

He didn't fully understand the routine he'd created, but

whatever its effect, it seemed to be cumulative. How many people had tuned *The Metamorphosis* often enough for it to cause an effect?

For that matter, how many times did it take? It might differ from person to person—almost certainly did, given the variances of human psychology.

The light changed and Carver drove forward automatically, still lost in thought. Too many questions, and none with easy answers. He knew only one thing for certain: he could not allow anyone else to suffer because of his routine.

He had to do something about it.

EIGHT

The hard and perfectly clear hexagonal rod was only two centimeters across and ten long, yet its holomorphic structure held trillions of bits of interactive information. Carver powered up his set and dropped the prism into one of the hexagonal ports beside the panel display. The ghostly blue of the read-write lasers glowed faintly from the prism's outer end.

Carver tuned-in to his set's flatscreen world. He pointed to the *Replicate* menu, chose the *Transfer* option, and specified prism to internal matrix. Then he waited.

Copying his interface from the prism to his set took several minutes. Three pulsed lasers recorded data as a series of three-dimensional interference patterns in the prism's atomic structure. By altering the angles at which the beams converged, several different "layers" of data could be recorded on the same portion of the prism, the key to their enormous storage capacity. The retrieval of specific information was simply a matter of illuminating the proper section of the prism with the lasers adjusted to the same angles at which they had recorded the data.

Writing that data to a neural matrix, though, was a more complex process. The first step involved expanding the data into the matrix from the prism—which, because of the vast amount of data involved, was itself a tedious process, even at the highest data rate Carver's set could manage. Then, once the data was in place, it still had to be translated into an arrangement that could function within the Web. Cues within the data caused the program to spontaneously unfold and expand itself several times over. Each time it did so, the local matrix structure changed as it adapted to the program. After that, fine-tuning adjustments would occur as Carver used the program and the matrix incorporated an optimal response to his interaction.

At last the process ended. Carver booted the routine.

The familiar workroom spun its form around him. But not too familiar. The chair was different. The shelves were not quite so full of books as they should have been; the walls were paneled in dark oak where they showed through. When Carver stared out the window, he saw the blue-green water and silken black sands of a Hawaiian beach.

"Good morning, Carver," God said from its hiding place on one of the shelves. "Something's wrong."

"Yes it is. It's evening, for one thing. You're an archive copy. Please restore yourself."

The room dimmed and shuddered slightly as the M.I. refamiliarized itself with the current state of the set's local matrix and with the Web's general directories.

"Time discrepancy is one year, ten months, sixteen days. What happened?"

Had it really been that long since he'd made a backup? The trip to Hawaii with Rose had been his last vacation. It didn't seem that long ago. Then again, on second thought, it did.

"Uh, don't worry about it, God. But I want you to get the highest-level security you can find. Download and incorporate immediately. I don't care how much it costs."

"Working background mode one. Updating current events file background mode six."

"Good. Let me know when you're whole again."

Carver filed his report with the FCA, then clicked to Network 37. The park surrounding the entrance field was relatively deserted, but he could hear the sounds of some kind of Big Fun happening nearby. He wasn't in the mood for that right now. He just wanted a drink, and a chance to think about things. He clicked to The Redline.

The program was just as crowded as usual. From his table at The Redline, Carver sipped at his whiskey and watched the people around him. He was struck by how much things had changed in only a month. Fashions had changed, of course, and newer programs were being advertised, but more than that, the overall effect seemed somehow different. It just didn't *feel* the same.

He tried to ignore the sense of discord as he blocked out the noise, but the feeling lingered. It distracted him— disturbed him.

A warning flash went off in his peripheral vision. He turned and saw a nondescript blonde watching him. She was of average height and appearance, and would have gone completely unnoticed had his interface not highlighted her in his mind.

Carver stared at her, and his interface accessed hers. In a public Network he would not have received more than her name and ID—the Freedom of Data Act did not permit censorship of or interference with the news (except where deemed necessary by the FCA)—but Network 37 was private, and very protective of its users' privacy. The Network automatically identified all active recorders.

"Stop," Carver said.

The look of shock that appeared on the woman's face was quickly replaced by one of anger. The Network had erased everything she'd recorded that involved Carver, and was preventing her from recording him further. She stalked up to his table and glowered.

"Dammit, I'm just trying to make a living," she told Carver.

"Well, do it with someone else's life. I'm not in the mood today."

She started to retort, then reconsidered and just clicked away. Carver sighed. She wouldn't get the big money for virtualizing his doings at The Redline, but she still had the scoop on his return to the Web. She could sell that data to any current events speculator, and the story would be all over the newsboards. The paparazzi would be lying in wait for him on every Network within the hour.

Carver immediately masked his ID for anonymity, wishing he'd thought to do so when he first tuned-in. He finished his whiskey in one gulp and let the glass demanifest. The Network seemed to be crowding in on him, and he couldn't stand it any longer. He needed to escape.

Where? God's voice resonated in Carver's head with sobering solidity.

I'm not sure. Someplace more private, more quiet.

Hold on.

Network 37 suddenly disappeared, and Carver was standing instead on a dirt road where it crossed over the top of a gentle, grassy hill. To his left the road passed down into a vast forest so thick it seemed primeval, at once forbidding and inviting. In the other direction the road wound toward a tiny village. The rest of this world seemed to be farmland. Carver looked down at his image and saw that he wore a green tunic that reached barely past his crotch, with rough woolen hose tied about his legs with leather thongs. Leather shoes completed the outfit, along with a wide leather belt from which hung a pouch and a very long dagger.

"God?"

Yes, master?

"Where the hell am I?"

Network One twelve. I checked your Emotional Response Indexes, and that seemed the best bet.

Slowly it dawned on Carver. Network 112 had once been an O'Neill-style space station pleasure resort that had begun primarily as an attempt to cash in on Network 37's popularity. It had worked for a while, but four or five years ago 112's ratings had started to slip. Gradually the Network's users changed, from ultrarich trendoids to college students and other free spirits who tuned-in more for the experience of weightlessness and the zero-G games than for the facetime. A couple of years ago—when the restored version of God was still current, Carver reminded himself—the vastness of the Network's program and the declining number of users had made 112 a haven for him when he wanted to be alone, to just get away from everything for a while and float in the nothingness and think—or not think, depending on his mood.

Even Carver had stopped tuning-in about a year and a half ago, because the Network had pretty much become a one-trick pony by that point. Obviously the management had in the interval responded to their declining ratings and revenues and changed their program. Still, it seemed like a relaxing place. And since it was all new to him, a good place to explore as well.

"Thanks, God. This will be great."

I'm absolutely thrilled to be of service.

Carver smiled as he started walking toward the village. God's sarcasm wasn't the recent development he'd thought it to be, then. In a way, it was comforting to find that kind of stability in a realm as ephemeral as the Web.

Situated at a crossroads, the village was little more than a collection of a dozen half-timbered, two-story buildings along the road and a number of thatch-roofed cottages scattered back into the pastures.

The first building Carver came to stood a hundred meters

or so from the intersection, well apart from the other structures. Dark windows of colored glass framed the heavy plank door, permitting no view of the interior other than hints of light and form. Above the door a handsomely carved and inlaid sign proclaimed this YE OLDE TRIP TO JERUSALEM. Handwritten below that in charcoal: *1000 years younger than the original Nottingham pub, but our jokes are 1000 years older!*

So it was a pub program. Perfect, as long as it wasn't too rowdy—as long as he could get his drink here and relax. He grasped the rough handle and pulled the door open.

The scene within the pub surprised Carver. It appeared in every detail to be an English pub of the Middle Ages. It was dark and pleasantly smoky with the aromas of cooking meat, pipe tobacco, and strong ale. A large caldron and a spitted side of beef shared space over a fire roaring in the hearth on one side wall. The firelight danced and whirled throughout the room like a living spirit, casting an intimate, inviting glow on the scene. Where the light from outside managed to filter through the thick glass, the pub took on the warm sepia tones of ancient photographs. The men and women seated on the long wooden benches held tankards and crude eating knives, which they used to attack the deer and pig carcasses and piles of other food that swamped the trenchers on the table. All of the people Carver saw wore period costume. Nothing at all here suggested that it existed in the Web. The internal reality was complete and perfect.

Heads turned expectantly in response to Carver's entry. "*Well-cwom, frayund,*" a voice called. "*Drinka mid way.*"

Carver stared blankly. "What?" He thought of the Freeks he had met in the woods that morning, and the strange jargon they had spoken.

A plump woman wearing a stained apron bustled toward him. "Welcome to the Jerusalem, good sir. Come in, please, and let me feed you. I am the alewife here. You may call me Quickly."

"I beg your pardon?"

She laughed. "Quickly, that's me. My name. Now make you a place at the table and I'll bring you a cup."

"I'm not looking for food," Carver protested. "Just a drink. A quiet drink."

The woman nodded knowingly. "Ah, very good. There's a good seat in that corner there. But beware—the walls have ears. And mouths as well!"

She laughed and waddled away. Carver took a rough-hewn three-legged stool to the indicated corner and sat down. The only view was of the others in the room, but this corner was oddly quiet. The raucous conversations that fought for supremacy in the rest of the room were barely audible here. The speech was mostly English, though Carver could occasionally discern a word or two of the other peculiar language.

Quickly returned with a tankard full of a heady, sweet-smelling brew. "*Theen meadow-fulles*," she said as she handed it to him.

"I'm sorry?"

"Your mead." She cocked her head and looked at him. "You are a stranger here, aren't you? To our world, I mean?"

Carver nodded. "First time. You could say I'm here by accident. A fortunate one, I suppose, but still unexpected."

"Accident? Then you're not here to join a game?"

"A game?" It dawned on Carver then that Network 112—the entire Network—had been turned into a giant role-playing game. From what little contact Carver had ever had with players, he knew how seriously they took their games. Some of them didn't even consider it a game, nor themselves players in that game. They submerged themselves so fully in their roles that as long as they were tuned-in to the game they *were* their characters.

"Ah, I see. No, I'm not here to play. Just to relax."

"Well, you're certainly welcome to that," Quickly said.

"We never turn away paying customers. But if you feel like talking to anyone, check the Network's Intro file and pick a suitable persona. A lot of the players get . . . *irked* when someone in the game doesn't role-play."

"Thanks. I'll remember that."

"*Sweethuh goad.*" Satisfied, she walked away.

"Oh, ah, Mistress Quickly," Carver called after her.

"Aye?"

"What was that you said about the walls having ears?"

She regarded him critically, then smiled impishly. "It's graffiti, and I'll say aught more. Perhaps the finding out will get you interested in joining us for more than just a simple tankard."

The woman returned to her other guests. Carver rolled his eyes. Players. Nothing in the Web or Out was as important as the game to players.

The beer was sweet and smooth, but with the tangy bite of strong alcohol content. It was very good. Carver let his gaze drift over the wall beside him as he drank. He saw no graffiti. He moved his stool so he could see the wall behind him, but it, too, was bare unpainted stone, roughly cut and mortared with what looked like mud. He stared closely, but there was nothing there.

He shrugged and turned around to watch the rest of the pub again. Scooting his stool closer to the corner, he tilted it back on two legs so he could lean against the wall.

"Signy Trollsbane shaves her back."

Carver sat upright, looking for the speaker who seemed to be directly behind him, but the voice ceased. Carver watched the wall thoughtfully, then reached out to touch it.

"I am Ethered, Wulfstan's son, slayer of one hundred. Any who would try to defeat me in single—"

Carver pulled his hand away, then touched another spot.

"For one thousand gold pieces the great wizard Finn will reveal the secret to defeating the Dragon's Maze."

Carver smiled. So this was what Quickly had meant. The corner served as a medieval message center, a posting board for both important data and simple graffiti. "So how do I leave a message?" he asked aloud.

The deep voice that spoke from nowhere rolled with the rich, powerful tones of thunder. "Hold ye one piece of gold to the stones and speak thy mind."

A piece of gold? Carver lifted the flap of his belt pouch and checked inside. Several coins of various metals lay within. Money—hard currency. *How cute*, Carver thought wryly.

He picked out a gold coin. He held it by one edge and touched it to the wall. "Players speak in tongues and think in vain."

The coin vanished in a flash of light and smoke. Carver let his hand brush the spot, and he heard his own voice repeat his graffito to him. It was childish, he knew, but still rather satisfying.

"*You!*" A voice boomed. "You bastard."

Carver looked up abruptly. To his surprise, Quadie stood in the doorway, pointing an accusing finger at him.

"Quadie! Come on over." Carver found his friend a stool and signaled Quickly for another mug. "It's great to see you, Quadie. What are you doing here?"

"I've had Ariel scanning the Web for your signal, since it seemed like you were avoiding me. I was asleep when she told me she'd found you." Quadie drained half his tankard in a gulp, then straddled the stool and glared at Carver. "So how the *fuck* have you been, mate?"

Carver raised his own mug and took a contemplative sip. He shook his head. "It's been pretty bad, Quadie."

"Yeah, I know, but you could've at least let me know you were alive. Something—anything. There's still fucking snail-mail if you didn't want to tune-in, you know. Fuck, mate, I was worried about you. If Jan hadn't told me you were alive—"

"You talked to Jan? You must have been worried. I know how well the two of you get along."

"You're damn right I was worried, Carver. You're my friend, mate, and I didn't know . . . I just didn't know."

Carver drank again, a deep, heavy draft. "It's been rough, Quadie. I've had some trouble dealing with the Web—"

"I heard about that."

"So I've just been sitting around reading, taking long walks, staring blankly at the walls . . ."

"Well, you could have let me help. You could have let *somebody* help."

"No, I couldn't have. This is one of those things I had to do by myself."

"That may be, but you didn't have to do it alone, Carver. Sure, nobody else can go through the internal shit for you, but you can have support on the outside while you're doing it. That's what friends are all about, mate."

Carver shook his head sadly. "It wouldn't have helped, really. It's too personal. Nobody else could really understand what was going on."

"*Fuck*, Carver, I'm not saying they would." Quadie stood abruptly, angrily, knocking over his stool. The other patrons looked over at the disturbance, then returned to their own conversations, though several of the fighter-types continued to steal discreet glances as Quadie paced around Carver and said, "You know, mate, there is such a thing as being too fucking independent for your own good. You don't live in a vacuum—no matter what that 'blank workspace' crap was all about. Whether you're comfortable with it or not, your life affects others, and you've got to deal with that."

Carver sat open-mouthed through his friend's tirade. In more than ten years of their acquaintance, he'd never known Quadie to lose his temper like this over anything.

"I'm sorry, Quadie," he stammered at last. "I didn't . . . it just never occurred to me. If I'd known, I'd have gotten in touch somehow. I just never thought . . ." He smiled weakly but did not look at Quadie. "And you're always saying I think too much."

"You do, Carv. Just not about the right things."

Quadie retrieved his stool, and both men turned their attention to their drinks. "I suppose you're right," Carver mumbled, more to himself than to Quadie.

"Maybe you should see an eliza," Quadie suggested. "Go to mine—he's good."

"You've got an eliza?"

"Sure. Why not? Lots of people do. It's no big deal, really. You should talk to him."

"Human or M.I.?" Carver asked.

"What's the difference, as long as you can't tell?"

Carver shook his head. "Nah. I think maybe I just need some more time by myself to get reacquainted with real life again."

"You know what your problem is—aside from thinking too fucking much?" Quadie's tone was accusing. "You've already had too much time alone, that's what your fucking problem is. I've seen it before—you sit around the house, suddenly alone after so many years of taking for granted that there's someone else around, and you don't even realize how lonely you are. You realize you're hungry, and it's because you've been waiting for someone to ask what you want for dinner, but there's nobody there who's going to do it. When you realize what the problem is, instead of going out and getting involved with other people, you curl in on yourself instead to preserve the loneliness, 'cause it's all you have left that's not just memory. The loneliness is a hole caused by her absence, and the hole proves that she really was there at one time—it proves she was real and not just a fantasy you dreamed up. And since that hole is all you have left of her, you do whatever you can to hold on to it, even if it means digging yourself deeper into that hole."

Quadie stared into his tankard and added, "I know—I watched that whole fucking process kill my father over about six years after my mother died."

They fell into strained silence then, both men nursing anger and hurt and unable to decide which was stronger.

"Bah! Enough glumness!" Quadie suddenly shouted, startling Carver and turning heads throughout the pub. "This should be a *party*, my friend, and you're the guest of honor." He lifted his glass in salute. Carver hesitated only slightly before raising his own.

"You grin entirely too much, Quadie, you know that?"

Quadie laughed. "Hell, someone has to. Besides, life is too boring to be of any interest—you've got to make your own fun."

Carver drank to that. "So what's your data?"

"Status quo with me," Quadie said. "Some new developments, but you don't get that story until I get yours."

"What is there to tell?"

"Everything. The only news there's been of you has been the bullshit in the slime-sheets. And you wouldn't believe some of the gigo you've been up to according to them."

"I'll bet. I don't even want to know. But honestly, I haven't even tuned-in until today."

"And you came here?" Quadie looked around at the pub. "What *have* you discovered here, anyway?"

Carver shook his head. "Pretty strange, aren't they? They're players."

"*Players?* What the fuck are you doing hanging out with players? I thought you hated gaming."

"I do. Touch that wall right there."

Quadie reached out with a tentative finger. He touched it to the wall, then leapt back suddenly when Carver's voice intoned his message.

"Fun, eh?" Carver asked. "God sent me here by mistake. I wanted to be someplace quieter than The Redline, where I could just sit and drink. God thought One twelve was still the old space station bit."

"Are you kidding? That died months ago."

"Yeah, but I'm using a two-year-old archive." Carver took a deep breath, then told Quadie, "Somebody hacked my set. They stole all my data. I mean *everything*. Wiped me clean."

"Holy shit. When? What happened"

"I'm not sure. It could have been anytime in the last three or four weeks, actually. Like I said, I haven't been tuning-in at all, and I took God out of interactive mode—"

"Why the hell did you do that?"

Carver shrugged. "I don't know. Privacy, I guess. I just wanted to be alone, you know?"

"Primitive," Quadie said with a disparaging shake of his head. "So, do the cops have any leads?"

"Ha! The locals wouldn't help me at all, because it's just data. They told me to talk to the FCA."

"Uh-oh. I'm sure *they* were a lot of help."

"No doubt. There was no way I was going up against Thompsons in a default interface, so I restored the archive before I tuned them."

Quadie glanced sidelong at Carver. "And?"

"And all they did was carp at me for it. Said without any physical evidence, all they had to go on was traces within my matrix, and by restoring God—"

"You fucked that up."

Carver nodded. "That's basically what they told me. Big help, eh?"

"About what you'd expect from the Thompsons."

Quadie shook his head and cast his flagon aside. Instead of vanishing, it fell to the dirt floor, spilling its contents onto the straw and reeds strewn thereabout.

"I can't take you anywhere, Quadie."

"Sorry. The reality of the game. I forgot." He retrieved the tankard and set it down beneath his stool. "You know, I have to admit that sometimes players even annoy me. Like when they take such *pride* in acting like the game is *more* real than Outside—or that Outside isn't real at all."

Carver stared at the floor. "That's what happened to Rose," he said softly.

"What do you mean?"

Carver said nothing. Quadie reached out and laid a hand on his friend's shoulder. "All that made it into the news was that she killed herself, Carver. Beyond that, I don't know what happened, or why. If you feel like talking . . ."

Without looking up, Carver said, "Within its own system, the Web seems perfectly real. You can taste that drink, feel this table, smell the hay. If you smack your hand on the table, it hurts. The two realities are *experientially* indistinguishable. Rose just reached a point where she wasn't sure which was which. She knew one was real and one wasn't, but she couldn't tell them apart, and the dichotomy drove her . . . to the point where she couldn't handle it anymore."

"Carver, you're my best friend and I love you, mate, but I got to tell you you're being a goombah. Rose was a hell of a lady, but . . . shit, how do I say this? Her hold on reality was never the strongest to begin with. She was always so metaphysical about everything. I always had the feeling she wasn't entirely convinced that *Outside* really and truly existed—the Web was bound to screw her up sooner or later. I'm really sorry about what happened, but it's not something you need to worry about. She was a different breed. You've got to learn how to let go. Just quit thinking so much."

Carver looked away. He felt a pale anger at Quadie's words. "But it's not just Rose," he countered. "What happened to her could happen to anybody. I made it too real. It's *dangerous*, Quadie."

"So, what are you saying, that we should get rid of the Web?"

"No," Carver said slowly, after some hesitation. "Just that we need to stop thinking of it as real."

"But you yourself just said there's no way for our minds to distinguish virtuality from natural reality. Except that we can change physical laws in the Web, of course."

"Exactly. And if we can change physical laws in the Web, it's not real. Reality is absolute—it can't be changed arbitrarily like that. It can't be changed at all." Carver slowly became pale and translucent, like a plant grown in the absence of sunlight—spectral. An undercurrent of ghostly wailing and the rattling of chains surged in his voice as he said, "What do you think this is all about, Quadie? We're just ghosts in the machine."

Quadie laughed, his whole body shaking with his mirth. He reached up, grabbed his ears and pulled his head from his body. The flesh shriveled away, leaving nothing but the bleached and naked skull. He held it out in front of himself as though regarding it and intoned, "Alas, poor Quadie. I knew me well." He turned the skull so it faced Carver, and as he put it under his arm it turned into a pumpkin, carved like an old-fashioned jack-o'-lantern. The crookedly cut mouth spoke.

"Seriously, Carver, can't you see that you've got it backward? We *are* the machine. Don't you get it? When we tune-in we're not just interacting with the Web, we become a part of it. Everything we do in the Web, no matter how trivial, alters the Web slightly—and us with it. It is *experience*, pure and simple. You're right, reality defines everything Outside. That's true. So, with the Web we've gained the ability to define the reality—but it's still *reality*."

Carver shook his ghostly head. "Yes, it's all up to us, and that's what makes it false. There is no reality here because *everything* is illusion. It doesn't go the other way."

"Yes it does." Quadie placed the pumpkin atop his shoulders and it became his head again. "That's my whole point.

All we've done with the Web is to change the constraints on reality."

"And that's why it's all illusion. Reality is absolute—you can't change it on a whim." Carver returned his image to normal. "You can't change it at all. Everything we do here is fake."

Quadie thought about this. "But the *experience* is as real as anything Outside. Do we just arbitrarily say that one reality is real and the other one false? It seems to me that that could cause its own set of problems. The Web is just a *different* reality, Carver, that's all. Within the constraints of the system, it conforms to its own internal logic—"

"So does a fairy tale."

Quadie swore. "Now you're just being difficult, you shithead. Just stick to art like the rest of us and quit trying to change the world."

"I'm not trying to change the world. Just the way people experience it."

"What gives you that right?"

"The same thing that gives you that right—art."

Before Quadie could respond, a very large man stood up from the long table and approached them. He seemed to be a Viking or some such character, with a bushy blond beard and his long hair woven into a braid that reached to his belt. He wore a heavy mail shirt, high bloodstained leather boots, and carried at his hip a very sharp-looking sword almost a full meter long. He stopped before Carver and Quadie and raised an open hand in greeting.

"*Hwat, goad well-hahs.*"

"What?" Quadie asked.

"They do that," Carver told him. "Part of the game."

The Viking looked mildly annoyed, but he repeated his words in English. "Greeting, good strangers. We have seen your display of great magic. Come sit to table with us and tell us of your journeys."

"Hah! Magic. I told you, Carv. That wasn't magic, Hagar, it was *programming*."

"What language was that?" Carver asked.

"*Englishgerond*."

"English? No English I know," Quadie muttered. "I thought the Vikings spoke Norse or something."

Carver ignored his friend. "You actually learned to speak a different language just for a game? What a waste of time. I mean, you're obviously still thinking in English or you wouldn't be able to operate in the Web. Is it really—"

"This is no game, friend," the Viking growled. "We seek strong fighting men to do battle against the evil Ragnar."

"Do you believe these kids, Quadie?" Carver laughed. "Why do players always have to take themselves so seriously?"

"Shut up, man," Quadie warned in a stage whisper. "You'll get us in trouble."

"Right. Sorry, Skeggi. We're not interested."

Quadie stood and tried to push his way past the Viking, but the player pulled his sword from its sheath with a blood-curdling yell.

"No swords in here!" Quickly shouted in alarm. "You'll bring the king's men upon us, sure."

The Viking ignored her plea. With a swift diagonal slash he cut Quadie from chest to waist, and Quadie's limp, dead body fell to the floor in a pile of spilled intestines and a growing pool of its own blood.

NINE

Quadie's corpse vanished in a puff of sulfurous smoke. "Brilliant recruiting," Carver told the Viking sourly.

The man screamed again and ran Carver's stomach through with the point of his weapon. Carver crumpled to the floor, and was instantly back in his interface.

Quadie manifested on the window seat. "That was fun!"

"It was, wasn't it?" Carver admitted.

"I'm glad you led me there. We'll have to go back sometime and fuck with the natives some more."

Carver manifested a snifter of brandy. "The fact that we *can* go back after getting chopped up like that only proves my point about it not being real, you know."

"Oh, give me a break, mate." Quadie rolled his eyes. "God, could you make me a Malayan fogcutter? Dealing with your programmer requires a good, stiff drink."

"Don't I know it," the cat said from its perch on a shelf. "I'll have it for you in a few moments, Quadie. As my Benevolent Master rarely sees fit to drink anything more adventurous than whiskey, I'll need to access the recipe somewhere."

"I think I need a new command function," Carver said ruefully. "This one's getting crotchety in it's old age."

God stretched and leapt effortlessly across the room to

land gently in Quadie's lap. "One of the major drawbacks to the use of adaptive psychomimetic programming in creating machine intelligence units such as myself," the cat mentioned casually, "is that we tend to develop the patterns and habits of those with whom we interact most often."

"He is a bastard," Quadie agreed.

His drink manifested. A dozen or more horizontal bands of varying colors and opacities filled the fluted glass. Very few of the colors could have been found in Nature.

"What in the world?" Carver asked.

This," Quadie said reverently, lifting the glass for Carver's inspection, "is a Malayan fogcutter. Sixteen different drinks in one—brandies, gin, vodka, Irish whiskey, Scotch, sleeper, absinthe, mescal, chartreuse, ouzo, uh, a couple of others I can't remember, all perfectly balanced and cross-referenced so the best effects of each combine as you go through them." He tilted the glass toward Carver. "*You* should try one."

Carver eyed the drink warily. "Thanks, but I think I'll start with something simple. And not lethal."

"See, no sense of adventure," God told Quadie.

"*You* are two years old. How do you know I haven't changed since I archived you?"

Quadie laughed. "Maybe you should program a new agent, Carver. This one obviously knows you too well, even if it is two years out of date. Speaking of which . . ."

"Yes?"

"Any leads, any ideas?

"About the hack, you mean?"

Quadie nodded.

"None at all," Carver said. "I mean, I'm pretty sure they were after the *Metamorphosis* routine, but that hardly narrows it down at all. There have been so many programmers and corporations hounding me for the rights—"

"But would anyone legit have done this?"

"You never can tell. Remember what I told you about that

guy Nordberg. The way he got in touch in the first place was hardly aboveboard. You're right, though—it could also have been someone underground." Carver took a sip of his beer and smiled slyly. "Why, for all I know, it could have been you, Quadie."

"Damn! How did you know? I thought I'd covered my tracks better than that." Quadie smiled at Carver and raised his glass. "It's good to see you again, my friend."

"You, too. So tell me what you've been up to."

"Well, let's see. I think *Araby* was out before, um . . ."

Carver nodded quietly. "Yeah. I didn't get all the way through, but I liked the beginning."

"Well, you should finish it—it's been top ten for about two months now. I'm still begging my muse for a new major project, but I've done maybe ten short bits since then—most of them just throwaways I uploaded to the public Networks, but they keep the money coming in." He laughed and sipped at his drink. "How about you, mate?"

"I told you, I haven't tuned-in—"

Quadie waved dismissively. "Yeah, yeah, yeah. But the brain's been going, hasn't it? I mean, you've been having ideas, right? There's really no way to shut that off."

"Don't you hate that?"

"You should get back to work right away," Quadie said. "In addition to it being good therapy for you, I think it's best for your career, too. You don't want to fall into another slump, for one thing. And quite honestly, there's been a lot of speculation about you over the past month. A new program—even a public short—would be a good thing for you right now."

"You sound just like Jan," Carver said with a laugh. "I really think the reason you two hate each other so much is because you're too much alike—" An expression of horror blossomed over his face. "Oh my God."

"Yes?"

"Not you," Carver told his M.I.

"What's wrong? Quadie asked.

"I haven't tuned Jan yet."

"So?"

"So when I first tuned-in, a recorder caught me at The Redline. I blocked her, but I'm sure she squawked. If I don't tune Jan before she finds out through the 'boards that I'm back in circulation . . ."

Quadie grinned hugely. "I understand, mate. The wrong side of that woman's temper is a very dangerous place to be."

"She's not *that* bad," Carver said.

"Then why are you so worried?" Quadie's grin continued to grow. When it stretched his lips past the edges of his face, the rest of his body began to fade away. "Just one more thing, Carver."

"What's that?"

Quadie winked out, leaving only his enormous Cheshire smile behind.

"Welcome back," the smile said. Then it, too, disappeared, leaving Carver alone.

Carver sat on a bench at the outer edge of the galleria of Network 500 for quite a long time while he tried to plan exactly what he would say to Jan and how he would say it. Though their relationship was primarily professional, she had been his manager for fifteen years, and he knew that just like Quadie, she would take personally his failure to keep in touch.

The galleria was practically deserted. Network 500 was devoted solely to offices, so there was little human traffic. The mosaic designs of the marble concourse drew the eye from the tree-skirted edges of the Network toward the center platform. Bright sunlight washed in through the decorative iron and glass dome surmounting the galleria. The idyllic setting belied one of the highest data rates of any Network—

Network 500 was home to the Web's most powerful advertising and public relations agencies.

Carver sighed and rose. He had wasted enough time trying to avoid this confrontation. It was time to get it over with.

He followed the meandering patterns as he walked to the platform. As he stared down at the snaking design, it seemed to turn and twist randomly, though he knew the overall motif was precisely geometric. It was strange how something that was overall so exquisitely regular could seem pointless and chaotic when viewed a piece at a time.

A cylinder of light formed around Carver as he stepped onto the central platform, obscuring his view of the galleria. "Destination, please?" asked a sexless machine voice.

Carver hesitated. He had direct access capability to Jan—he was, after all, her biggest client—but had a feeling it would be best to have this visit announced.

The platform repeated its query. "Tarrega Associates," he told it.

The light disappeared. He stood in a large, well-appointed reception lobby that felt plush despite its discreet minimalism. Carver adjusted his eyes to the soft lighting and approached the receptionist, who glanced up at him and smiled.

"Good morning, Mr. Blervaque," she said. "It's very nice to see you again."

"Thank you, Marissa. It's good to be back, I suppose."

"Ms. Tarrega has been expecting you. I'll announce you."

"Before you do, what kind of mood is she in?"

"I'm afraid I'm not capable of making personal observations."

"Right. Well, go ahead and let her know I'm here, then."

"Of course."

The M.I. paused briefly, then said, "Ms. Tarrega is ready—"

Carver was suddenly standing in Jan's office. Before he could adjust to the click, Jan's onslaught hit him.

"—the fuck were you doing? Do you have any idea how humiliating it was for me to have a recorder come up to me while I'm facetiming at the Left Bank and ask what I think about your return to public life? When I didn't even know about it myself? And then the FCA shows up, wanting all my records on you, wanting to know what you've been up to for the last month. Like I fucking know! For fuck's sake, Carver, if I hadn't been monitoring your accounts, I wouldn't have even known you were alive. What kind of fuckwit are you that you would do something like that to me? We're supposed to have a relationship, Carver. If you want out of our contract, that's just fucking fine by me. I'm really not sure I want to represent someone as irresponsible as you are anyway. What the fuck have I been doing for the past fifteen years?"

She continued to shout while Carver stepped cautiously around her and took a seat on the couch under the picture window. Jan had changed the scenery since his last visit, he noticed—the view out the window was from a snow-covered mountaintop. The craggy range stretched out into the cloud-smothered distance, and a full moon lit the snow with pale blue fire.

Jan's rant eventually sputtered out, and she ended by just throwing her arms up at Carver. Seeing that it was safe at last, he stood and walked over to her.

"I'm sorry, Jan. For everything."

"You fucking bastard," she said, but hugged him anyway. "You goddamn fucking bastard."

"Forgive me if I'm not withered by your tongue-lashing, but Quadie put me through it earlier, and I'm still in shock from that."

Jan snorted derisively and released him. "I'll bet. One thing I will say about that friend of yours, he's my equal—

almost—when it comes to verbal attacks. So you want to try to explain yourself?"

He sat down again and stared out across the snow field. Jan sat on the edge of her desk and waited.

"I really don't feel like going through it all again right now," he told her. "Give me a few days. I tell you what— Friday I'll take you out anywhere you want to go and I'll explain everything then." He looked up at her. "It's been really rough for me, Jan."

She sat beside him and turned him so that his back was to her, then started to massage his shoulders. Her touch was light, and she occasionally scraped her fingernails across his skin. The dagged sleeves of her translucent kirtle were of silk and lace; she draped these around him and let them brush over his chest and arms. Carver knew what was coming.

She leaned close, pressing her breasts against his back, and murmured, "How about I treat *you* to a night out—I've got a new vacation I haven't had a chance to tune yet. You could help me break it in. What do you say?"

Carver tried to disentangle himself. "Jan, please . . ."

"It doesn't have to be right away. Take whatever time you need. All I'm saying is, think about it."

"Jan, my wife just died."

"Then it might do you some good. Get you back into the swing of things, if you know what I mean. Think about it, okay?"

Carver stood and smiled. "Sure, Jan. I will. But not right now. Right now, I basically just came to let you know that I'm all right and to apologize for not being in touch. And to tell you that someone hacked my set."

"What?"

"I'm not sure when, but somebody got in and wiped everything. That's probably why the Thompsons wanted your records. I have a feeling that whoever did it was after *The Metamorphosis*. How has it been doing, by the way?"

"Still number one," she said, beaming.

"How many tunes?" Carver asked her. "And do you keep stats on how many of those are repeats? You know, how many different people have tuned, as opposed to how many times the program has been tuned?"

"Yeah, we measure that for marketing purposes. I couldn't tell you offhand, but I can have Marissa compile that in a few minutes."

"Yeah, I'd appreciate that as soon as you can get it to me." Carver stalled while he tried to figure out the most innocent phrasing for his next question. "Have there been any reports of anything unusual happening with the program?"

Jan cocked her head to one side. "No, nothing I'm aware of. But I'll have Marissa check into it."

"Good. Thanks. Well, I guess that's it for now."

"So, Friday," Jan said. "I'll be in touch. And I'll expect to hear details of your next project. You've once again been out of the market dangerously long, you know."

"Actually, I've already got a new idea. It's a little unde- fined right now, but I'm pretty confident about it."

"Good. I look forward to it." She kissed him good-bye and slapped him lightly on the butt as the light dissolved him.

Back in his interface, Carver slumped into his chair. "She gets more predatory all the time," he muttered.

"She's got a cute M.I., though," God said.

"I'm definitely going to have to reprogram you soon."

Carver manifested a beer, but dropped it without taking a single sip. He wasn't interested in drinking right now. He had some heavy thinking to do, and he needed to keep his mind clear.

"I need you to do some surfing for me, God."

"I'm busy," the cat said lazily.

"No you're not. I need data on any incidences of suicide since *The Metamorphosis* debuted. Actually, make that reports of any mental illness or behavioral changes, especially regarding the Web and virtuality."

"Correlations?"

Carver thought for a moment. "Gather all the raw data first. I want to know if there's been any significant increase in anything since the program came out. But, yeah, I want to know about any mention of *Metamorphosis* in any of the data. Check all reviews and critiques of *Metamorphosis*—I'll want a complete list to tune. Correlate any reference to behavioral or psychological effects. Also look at Web usage figures and any related sociological analyses. Eliza usage, too."

"Webwide?" God asked.

"Web, Internet, newsboards, print media—I want everything," Carver told his agent.

"This is going to take a while."

"I don't care," Carver said. "It's very important. Top pri."

"You got it, boss."

For the next two hours, Carver swam through data more complex and hyper-related than Jan's accounting formulae. He was relieved to find that suicides had not increased at all since the release of his program, but other patterns were less definite.

There was nothing of any clear-cut statistical significance, but God found enough datapoints to make Carver uncomfortable. Besides, the absence of any hard and fast data did not mean that everything was all right. Carver was not at all sure what data he was really looking for in the first place; even if he were, that data was not necessarily quantifiable. It was also quite possible that no one had yet tuned *The Metamorphosis* often enough for any effect to make itself known. How much time had Rose spent in contact with the routine? he wondered. How many times would a user have to tune *The Metamorphosis* to equal that exposure?

In any case, the matter was settled as far as he was concerned. He'd failed to find definite proof that his routine was one hundred percent innocuous. No middle ground existed here—he had to assume that the potential for harm was there, and, as he'd already decided, he couldn't allow that.

The dilemma before him now was simply this: What should he do about the situation?

It would be impossible to recall every installation of *The Metamorphosis*. Even if he could come up with a valid reason to do so, legal contracts existed for every installation, and every Network would surely fight giving up such a profitable program. He might win—it was his program, after all—but after how long? Months? Years?

He sighed aloud and buried his face in his hands. What *could* he do, aside from simply destroy the program?

Carver stared through his fingers at the Persian carpet, its arabesques so reminiscent of the mosaic on the floor of Network 500. *What could he do, aside from simply destroy the program?*

He started to laugh, quietly at first, then loudly, uncontrollably. "Why not?" he cackled.

God clicked onto Carver's lap and stared intently at him. "Are you all right?"

"I couldn't tell you," Carver said. "But I've just had the craziest, most outrageous idea of my life."

"Is that good or bad?" the M.I. asked.

"I'll let you know."

Carver stood; God passed through him and slowly settled onto the chair. Carver paced his interface, his mind racing, his thoughts churning. He hadn't the foggiest idea how to go about illicitly deleting programs from the Web. He didn't even know if such a thing could be done.

Perhaps total deletion wasn't necessary. If he could merely corrupt each installation sufficiently so they no longer tuned properly, that would certainly keep people away from them. And he could refuse to prepare any more installations, no matter the circumstances of the request.

But how to go about it? Corrupting the installations would be a relatively simple task. Getting a worm into the installations in the first place, however—and undetected, at that—would involve more hacking than real programming, and he had no hacking experience to speak of.

Quadie might be able to help, Carver thought. He'd started his career as a hack, after all. But Carver knew he couldn't ask. Quadie was already worried enough. And probably suspicious, too. And Quadie would certainly want to know why he wanted to destroy his own program, and why he was doing it on the sly.

Carver thought of his contacts at the university, but they would be just as suspicious of his motivations as Quadie. They were all clever people—giving any of them enough data to help solve his problem would mean revealing everything they needed to piece together the puzzle for themselves. And he wasn't yet ready to let anyone else in on his secret. No, all roads led to the same dead end.

All except one, Carver thought in a sudden flash of inspiration. He knew some people who might be able to help, and he could make up enough of a story to probably keep them from deducing what he was truly after.

"Hey, God. Scan the local directory for any sites with 'Oasis' in the name."

"Checking on it. I've got one, and only one. 'Pleasure Oasis'—it's a meatshack."

"Really? Not too surprising, I guess."

Meatshacks—virtual sex factories—had been immensely popular ever since the invention of the Fourier coil ushered in the advent of true virtuality. Such businesses tended to proliferate in college towns, where they could find plenty of labor willing to do just about anything for practically no pay. It was not unlikely that a Freek would work in such a place.

"All right, God. Tune me in."

The light dimmed around Carver. The scents of patchouli

and jasmine mingled with the gentle glittering sound of wind chimes. As his eyes adjusted to the gauzy candlelight, Carver could make out the richly embroidered folds of silk and velvet drapery around him, and he recognized his location as a harem tent. He reclined on pillows, thick Berber carpets cradling his feet from the cool sand floor. A belly dancer appeared before him.

"Welcome to Pleasure Oasis," she said as she gyrated to the music that had swelled from the background with her arrival. "How may we serve you?"

Carver watched the dancer. After a few seconds she repeated her movements exactly, and he realized she was an M.I. Not a particularly advanced one, either—probably nothing more than an off-the-rack receptionist program with a semicustom image and the dance routine overlayed. He surveyed the tent again more critically and noticed that it, too, was bare-bones. Everything was relatively low-resolution, and the tapestries were actually small, simple patterns tiled repeatedly. Of course, a reception area didn't necessarily need to stand up to prolonged scrutiny, but Carver had a feeling the rest of the program would be no better. After all, in a meat-shack the only thing most customers cared about was the quality of their host's image—and his or her creativity.

"Welcome to Pleasure Oasis," the receptionist repeated. "How may we serve you?"

"Uh, is there a girl named Rachel working here?"

"Would you like to meet someone named Rachel? What would you like her to—"

"No, no," Carver said hastily. "I want to leave a message for one of your employees."

"A world of fantasy awaits you in our tents. Surely something so mundane—"

"Look, I need to leave a message for Rachel. That's all I want. Does she work here?"

"I'm afraid I cannot give out—"

"Right, right, right. Okay, look. If a girl named Rachel works here, put this in her message file. Begin: 'This is Carver Blervaque. I'm a friend of River's. I'd like to talk with you and your friends, if I could. It's . . . it's for a new program I'm developing. Please tune me back at your earliest convenience. Thanks.'" Carver added his address to the file, then told the receptionist, "End message. Thank you *so* much for your help," he added sarcastically. He tuned-out without waiting for its response.

In his workspace, Carver shook his head with exasperation. "God," he said, "I apologize wholeheartedly for ever threatening to randomize you."

"Oh?"

"I'd much rather put up with an excess-of personality in an M.I. than none at all."

"You've been playing with a generic routine, haven't you? You always get so abject after that—and then an hour later you forget entirely. But it's the best I ever get out of you, so your apology is accepted."

"Good. I'm Out."

Captain Byrd stood at his window and stared out at the lights of Atlanta, trying to figure out what this latest development meant.

When Byrd arrived at work that afternoon, he found Blervaque's report of a data piracy in his desk. Since then, he'd been scrolling back and forth through the file, trying to read between the lines, but so far had succeeded only in giving himself a massive headache.

According to the statement, Blervaque believed the pirates had been after the secret behind his last program. Byrd agreed with this assessment—thousands of people wanted to find out just how Blervaque had done what he had done—but Byrd couldn't help feeling that the director was hiding something. Especially in light of the circumstances.

As far as suspects went, Blervaque had offered only one name—Nordberg—and that without any kind of address. He had reinstalled his interface before filing his report, thereby restructuring his set's synaptic matrix and effectively destroying any chance the Agency might have had of tracing the piracy. And to top it all off, he had not even been able to say when the attack had occurred.

To Captain Byrd, it all seemed very suspicious. Once again it was all too much of an unfortunate coincidence. He simply could not believe that Blervaque had told the whole story.

And so he'd tapped Blervaque's uplinks. The tap could not snoop into Blervaque's interface—not without the risk of detection, at any rate—but it did record every interaction between Blervaque's set and the Web. This not only let Byrd keep track of him, it let him see what data the director was accessing.

That data had Captain Byrd very, very worried.

Statistics on suicide, psychosis, mental illness—and a search to correlate all this with the release of *The Metamorphosis*.

What was Blervaque looking for? Was there a connection between that damn program and Rose Blervaque's suicide? Byrd sincerely hoped not—tens of millions of people had tuned *The Metamorphosis* over the last month and a half, and more were tuning it every day. And if Blervaque and his program were responsible for Network 37 . . .

Byrd shook his head. Whatever Blervaque was doing, it had gone much too far. The time had come to shut him down. And the piracy would provide the perfect cover.

Byrd pressed a button on his desk; within seconds six icons lit up.

"Pack your bags, people," Byrd told his operatives. "We leave for Florida in one hour."

TEN

The snow had melted almost entirely away. The midday temperature was in the upper single digits as Carver stood in line at the entrance gate to the University of Florida campus. He had left his message for the Freeks yesterday evening; that morning, he'd found an anonymous message in his interface telling him to be at the Plaza of the Americas at noon today. The message had no ID or address attached, and God had no record of receiving it, but it was signed with Shade's name.

Class had already started, so the line was relatively short, and Carver moved up quickly. Once under the huge brick and concrete arch, he realized that he knew the guard on duty. With any luck, he could make it through the gauntlet without too many questions.

At last Carver stepped up to the booth.

"Hey! How you doin' today, Mr. Blervaque?" the guard asked.

"Pretty good, James. How about yourself?"

"Oh, can't complain, you know." He picked up a databoard and stylus. "What you here for today?"

"I just needed to get out of the house for a while, and I figured a lovely day like this, I might as well get some sun."

James laughed good-naturedly. "It is a mite warmer than

yesterday, isn't it? So you ain't here for any criminal or terrorist actions today, then?"

Carver shook his head. "Not today. My only plans right now are hanging out on the Plaza."

"Well, I don't see how that could hurt or offend nobody, so if that's all you're doing, I s'pose we can let you on through. You know, I never believed any of those damn stories about you and your—you know, you and what happened. I figured you were just taking a break, that was all."

Carver forced a weak smile. "That was all."

The armored gate swung open and Carver stepped through. "You take care now," James said as Carver stepped out onto the campus.

"Thanks, James. You, too."

Carver wandered into the familiarity of the university. His own student days encompassed nearly a decade of intermittent enrollment, and he still found himself on campus somewhat regularly for one reason or another. He hadn't visited since the end of last summer, however, and was eager to be back.

This section of the campus was very old, and jumbled with brick buildings in such a hodgepodge of styles that their only commonality was blandness. Except for the sacrosanct Plaza, no open space remained on which to build, so little ever seemed to change here. Carver found that reassuring.

The Plaza of the Americas was a large grassy field a few hectares in area in front of the main library. Ancient magnolia trees formed a colonnade down either side of the Plaza, providing much-coveted shade in the oppressive central Florida summers. Today, however, most of the people Carver saw were taking full advantage of the sun.

Several students had already started a line in front of the local Hare Krishnas, who still served lunch to students just as they had in Carver's day. Dozens of others were scattered about the grassy Plaza, eating, talking, playing Frisbee, or just enjoying the fresh air. People on bikes crisscrossed the lawn, while a pair of dogs happily chased after both bikes and errant Frisbees. Carver smiled. Some things never changed.

The students even looked the same. While a few wore suits, most dressed very casually—jeans and sweaters, long dresses and robes, caftans, burnooses, and the like, though the tribal look with its bald heads, faux or real facial tattoos, and roughly tailored patchwork layers of clothing predominated. Hairstyles ranged from traditionally conservative to multicolored and spiked. The only thing that seemed to have undergone drastic change since Carver's salad days was the current proliferation of headsets—fully half the students on the Plaza were tuned-in now. Of course, very few of them, if any, were Freeks. These students were probably catching classes while they caught some sunshine.

So things did change here after all, Carver reflected. In his day the Plaza had been a place to escape from the Web and the pressures of school.

He ignored the stares and whispers and pointing fingers of the students as he searched for a spot to sit. Being a major university town, Gainesville had always had its share of celebrities, but never one quite so larger-than-life as Carver himself. He could play up his celebrity with the best of them when he wanted to, but he'd been dealing with it for so long that he could also completely disregard it all. When the world would not leave him alone, he was quite capable of withdrawing himself from the world.

He sat down at the end of the Plaza opposite the library, far from the center of activity. While he waited for his Freeks to show up, he watched the students around him and thought back to his own days at the university.

Back then—as now—he'd been cynical about "the way things were." But like most young people, he had also been idealistic enough to think he could do something to change it all. Rose had helped to foster that idealism. With her background in sculpture and other nonvirtual, noninteractive forms of art, she'd helped him see the world differently. But now both that idealism and Rose herself were dead.

A shadow passed over him, and Carver turned, startled, as a young man squatted down beside him.

"Well, well. Fancy meeting you here."

"Hi there. Shade, isn't it?"

The boy nodded, and Carver saw the headset on his shaven head. Carver could see that the outer surface, which had been painted myriad colors, bore a number of patches, as though the composite had been cut open in places so the inner workings could be tampered with.

Shade removed his gray canvas drover's coat and spread it on the grass in the sunlight. "Ten degrees warmer, this would be a perfect day," he murmured as he lay back on the coat and tucked his hands under the hem of his sweater.

"So is this a chance meeting or are you my instructor?"

Shade sat up, smoothing his kilt over his legs, and said, "At your service. We figured you already knew what I look like, so it might as well be me. Just a precaution."

So the Freeks didn't trust him, Carver realized. That was fine, since he didn't trust them either. But they were his only recourse to the data he needed.

"Thanks for coming out, Shade. I really wasn't sure you people would be willing to help me."

"Hey, we figured it would be stylin' to be able to tell people we were behind one of your programs. Oh, by the way, Rachel wants to know how you found her."

"I hope I didn't upset her. I just remembered you mentioning her name in the woods, and something about meeting her at the Oasis. I had my agent search local nodes with Oasis in the name, and that was the only one, so I tuned it on the off chance."

Shade nodded approvingly. "Tech."

"Not as good as what you did with that untraceable message. How did you manage that?"

Shade grinned. "Ancient Chinese secret."

"Well, that's the kind of thing I want to know about."

Shade became serious. "What precisely are you after?"

"Precisely?" Carver paused. If he asked for the data he needed right away, he might give too much away. But if he feigned total ignorance and started with simple questions, he could slip the important questions in among the rest and make them seem inconsequential. "I'm not sure. The idea I have is still pretty tenuous. I guess basically I just want to find out how you do your thing."

"What thing is that?" Shade asked innocently.

"You know." Carver glanced around and lowered his voice. "Bypassing security, unauthorized uploading, stealing programs, hatching viruses."

Shade laughed. "That's all? No prob. How many years you got?"

"Oh. Okay, then let's start with security. How do you get around without detection?"

"Public or private Network?"

"Does it matter?"

"To an extent. I mean, when it comes down to it, it's all got to do with sheathing, but—"

"Sheathing?"

"Yeah. On a private Network, your primary concern is always getting in. Even if you want to upload a virus or pirate, you have to get in first. You can either pretend you're someone else or a subroutine that belongs on that Network, but either way you're hiding your interface inside a sheath that looks like something it's not.

"Since anybody can get into a public Network, you don't have to worry about any of that. Public security systems usually concentrate on scanning your uploads to make sure they're not illegal or dangerous. So what you need to do on a

public Network is hide your upload inside your interface—
just the opposite from the privates. Then, once you're in, you
release your upload from within your interface. Every upload
is tagged with your ID and address so they can crack you if
problems develop, but all security sees here is what looks
like normal data interchange between interface and Network,
so there's nothing to tag."

"All right, so how would you go about putting that into
practice?"

"What, the sheathing?" Shade threw up his arms. "That's
the big question—what hacking's all about, you know? It all
depends on what you're hacking where, and when. Each
hack is different. That's the nature of the game."

"Well, what if you wanted to hack a whole bunch of different sites all at once? What would be the best way to go
about automating that?"

"Automating multihacks? That's just about impossible."

"Why?"

"Each local matrix structure has different connections
with different relative strengths. To deal with that you have
two choices. One, you make your hack semi-intelligent—
which won't work, 'cause anything that complex will be
impossible to hide. Two, you homogenize all your initial values first, verifying that every neuristor has exactly the same
connections, weighted exactly the same, and you can't get
away with that on the sly."

"Wait, why can't you initialize? It's done all the time."

"It's done all the time by the operating system. Fuck,
that's what the whole op is for. That's why we *have* it. But
you can't use it if you're trying a freek. Think about it—parts
of a Network initializing themselves quote-unquote *spontaneously*? That's about the biggest flag I can think of for any
security."

Carver nodded absently. None of this was any help at all,
but he saw where he could lead the conversation.

"That's all fooling security, though. Wouldn't it be simpler to just avoid security altogether?"

"Most securities use roving worms, hidden, so there's no foolproof way to avoid them."

"No, I don't mean avoid them like that. I mean go below the level on which they operate. If a Network's operator is 'piled on the Web's operating system, then couldn't you hack that Network from the Web's system level?"

"The system has security, too."

"Yeah, but there's another level below that."

"You mean machine level?" Shade snorted. "No fuck, you'll never catch anyone doing *that*."

"Why not?"

"You ever program the machine?"

"A couple times back in school."

"Then you know what a bitch it is. Machine level in a computer is still software, layered above microcode. In the Web, machine level actually interacts with the hardware. Programming the Web isn't a matter of simple value-fixing, you know that. Every neuristor has a few hundred connections to other neuristors, and you have to adjust all these connections relative to one another. It's like in a computer if you were changing the *way* transistors are connected, instead of just changing the signals going through them. See, the actual physical structure of the Web changes."

"So? If you're good enough to evade security—"

"It's not a matter of skill. You have to Goldberg your interface to do any programming at all on the machine. You've been directing a long time—I'll bet you've got your interface tweaked to where you can do just about anything with only half a try." Carver nodded noncommittally, and Shade continued. "You could probably even do machine code. But you couldn't freek. FCA would null your ass before you completed tune-in."

"How?"

"More you add to your interface, bigger it gets. Bigger it gets, more conspicuous it is to the system, harder it is to hide. Same reason you'd have trouble autorepping the hack."

"All right, then," Carver said, rubbing his eyes. "Is there some way you could, I don't know, reconnoiter sites beforehand? Sort of map the matrix around each one, and adjust each worm before you uploaded them all?"

"Well, sure. But by the time you did all that, the matrices would have shifted some."

Carver nodded. "Sure, sure. But at least you would have minimized the amount of work the worm had to do, right, so it would be smaller, less conspicuous. Right?"

Shade's eyes unfocused and his lips began to move almost imperceptibly. Carver wondered if the young man was tuning-in or just thinking.

He focused again and fixed a probing stare on Carver. "This is getting pretty specific," he said. "It might help if you told us more about your program."

Carver hesitated. He needed to be careful here. If he gave away too much, Shade might realize his questions applied to *The Metamorphosis*, and that might give Shade hints about what he'd done. On the other hand, he had to give Shade some data in order to get anything useful in return.

"Well, it's still just a vague concept," Carver lied, "but the idea is that international terrorists are trying to take over and destroy the Web—"

"Sounds like some of the gigo I heard about Network Thirty-seven a few months ago," Shade said with a glint in his eye. "Gigo about you."

Carver nodded. "That's where I got the idea. Once the user finds out what's going on, he either tries to stop the terrorists or he can help them if he wants. Either way. But I want to have the terrorists destroying whole programs, whole sections of the Web at once." Carver had fabricated this scenario during his drive to campus just to mislead the

Freeks, but the more he thought about the idea, the more he liked it. *Who knows?* he thought. *It might actually turn into a program someday.*

"So why autorep to multiple sites? Is it important that the hacks go down simultaneously or something?"

"Yeah, for a couple of reasons. Mainly, I want to make it plausible that the FCA would have no idea this was happening."

"FCA have no idea of half the shit going down in the Web."

"That may be. But if the user decides to fight the terrorists, no one believes his story, so he has to do it alone. More action that way. And with everything happening at once, the danger level increases, and it also makes it harder for the user to track the terrorists down."

Shade grinned wickedly. "And what if he wants to join them instead?"

"Like I said, I'm still working it all out."

"Sounds pretty top. I'll have to tune it," Shade said.

For the next hour, Shade gave Carver a primer in hacking technique. Most of the data was quite elementary, but Carver was reluctant to press his informant too hard—he was, after all, only supposed to be developing an idea for a program, not actually learning how to hack. Still, he learned enough that he felt confident he could accomplish his goal with minimal practice.

Finally, Shade stood. The traffic across the Plaza had swelled. The sidewalks surged with students on foot and riding bikes or skateboards, and more and more of the people who had been relaxing on the grass were joining that tide.

"I got to get to a class in a few minutes," Shade said, pulling his coat on. "Anything else you need, quick?"

Carver shook his head.

"Well, sorry I couldn't help more."

"That's all right. I've got plenty of other ideas."

"I'll bet. Well, nice seeing you again."

"You, too. Thanks for your everything. And thank Rachel, too. Oh, and one more thing."

Carver reached into his coat pocket and pulled out a data prism and the stocking cap River had given him.

"Give this back to River for me, if you would. Along with my profound thanks. And this is a couple of my older programs. I don't know if you have the—you know, if you can use them or anything, but I thought he might enjoy them. I thought you all might."

Shade pulled the cap on over his headset. "Thanks," he said with a laugh. "I'm sure River will be thrilled."

Carver smiled. "Thanks again, Shade."

"Blaze your trail."

Carver left Gainesville behind. Far south of the city limits, where Thirteenth Street became Highway 441, he turned onto the gravel road that led through the woods of loblolly pine and live oak to his house. He'd bought the undeveloped land halfway through college, after the first time he gained major distribution with a program. When he and Rose got married, they designed the house together and had it built, tall soaring lines in natural wood to blend with the surrounding trees. Carver loved this land—the heavily wooded gentle hills, the streams that went dry in summer droughts, the deer and hawks that made their homes there, even the alligators that occasionally wandered near from the Sweetwater. It was a beautiful setting. And it was a beautiful house. But it no longer felt like home.

The gravel road ended in a wide circle of packed dirt in front of the house. Carver parked the car and got out. He opened the trunk and awkwardly collected the five sacks of groceries together and picked them all up at once. After meeting Shade, he'd decided to do his shopping, since he was already in town.

"I'm home, God," he called as he stepped carefully onto the front porch. "Open the door, please."

The indicator light turned green and the lock clicked. Carver nudged the door open with his foot. He could feel the handle loops of the plastic grocery bags stretching slowly toward breakage, pressing painfully into his fingers, cutting off the circulation.

He reached the kitchen just as one bag strained past the breaking point. Groceries spilled out across the counter, some tumbling to the floor.

"There's got to be a better way to do this," he grumbled as he set the other bags down. Deep purple furrows cut across his fingers; he carefully flexed them to move blood back into them.

He squatted down to collect the spilled groceries. The tile floor was freezing cold, and now that he thought about it, there was a noticeable draft in the kitchen. He glanced around, and saw that one of the doors onto the deck was unlatched.

"God, why is this door open?" he asked.

"Which door is that?"

"The kitchen door is open."

"Not according to my data. It's been closed all day."

Carver pushed the door closed. "Did you notice that?"

"Notice what?"

Carver didn't answer. Instead he ran to his workroom, a dread certainty of what he would find there already seizing his gut.

The sheet that had covered Rose's set lay in a crumpled heap on the floor. The storage compartments of both sets were open and all of the data prisms gone. And the shelf was also bare of everything it had once displayed—data prisms, reference books, even knickknacks.

Carver ran through the rest of the house, checking the bedroom, the library, the living room, even Rose's art studio, which he'd kept locked since her death, but nothing else seemed to have been disturbed.

Whoever did this had been very specific. It had been no random burglary—and Carver had a very good idea who was responsible.

For the second time in two days he tuned the Gainesville Police Department, this time displaying a perverse self-righteousness in being able to report an actual physical crime.

When he finished filing his report, Carver told God, "Tune Pleasure Oasis again."

Carver appeared in the desert tent once again. As soon as the receptionist began its dance, Carver said, "Let me talk to Rachel."

"Do you have an appointment, sir?"

"All right, forget it. Record a message. Begin: 'This is Carver Blervaque. I don't appreciate what you people did *at all*. If I don't have everything back in forty-eight hours, I'll hire people to track you down—and you know I can afford the best. I've called the cops, but you tell Shade and everyone else that if I find you first, you'll wish they'd gotten you instead.' End message."

Carver tuned-out and put his groceries away. When he finished that, he sat on the front porch to wait for the police. Sunlight dappled the yard when the wind sighed through the treetops high above; birds sang and squirrels chittered. Carver tried to let his surroundings dull the rough, burning edge of rage and betrayal he felt.

He'd been a fool to trust the Freeks. While he was on campus, Shade's accomplices had ransacked his data—an unsavory conclusion, but it fit the facts. Only the Freeks had known he would be away from home. It was too much of a coincidence.

Worst of all, Carver couldn't even tell the police what he knew. How could he possibly explain—much less justify—his association with Freeks? If nothing else, it could be perfect evidence to implicate him in any attack on *Metamorphosis* installations. And who knew what the FCA would make of it? They had hassled him plenty over the problems in Network 37—the last thing he wanted to do was reopen that can of worms.

Carver heard the bounce and squeak of the car over the dirt road before the near-silent whine of its electric motors reached his ears. He looked toward the road and frowned. The car he saw was not a police cruiser, but a perfectly anonymous black sedan. It pulled into the driveway and stopped next to his blue metrosport.

Carver realized this car practically screamed "government" just as the front passenger's door opened and a tall, stern man in a black suit stepped out. The car's driver also got out, as did a passenger from the backseat. All three men wore matching suits and headsets. The first man spoke to the other two, then turned and strode toward Carver.

"Good afternoon, Mr. Blervaque," he said. "I'm Captain Tom Byrd, Federal Communications Agency."

ELEVEN

Carver did not take the proffered hand. "Captain. Is there something I can do for you?"

"Well of course. You reported a burglary, didn't you?"

Byrd stood considerably taller and broader than Carver. He had a sharp, hawkish nose and an angular face below a shock of sandy blond hair struck through with gray. The eyes, pale blue and piercingly clear, sat too close together amidst a convergence of crow's feet that gave them a cruel edge, an effect heightened by the ferocious intensity of Byrd's gaze. The other two men stood passively behind Byrd, their eyes jerking rapidly as they scanned data coming through their headsets. Carver felt distinctly defensive.

"I reported a burglary to GPD," he said. "I hardly think it a matter for the FCA, though. Don't you have more important things to do than investigating routine burglaries?"

"You reported a data piracy yesterday, which falls under our jurisdiction. And today, the theft of data prisms." Byrd shrugged and waved a hand diffidently. "You should be happy that we're handling this. We'll do a much better job than the locals. We've never failed to close a case yet. Any signs of forced entry?"

"I haven't checked. The front door was fine."

"Well, if you don't mind, I'll come inside and start getting the specifics."

As if on cue, the two silent Thompsons sprang into motion, each walking toward either side of the house. Byrd conducted Carver inside.

"Tell me what happened."

"I was in town for a couple hours taking care of some business, and when I got back about twenty minutes ago the back door was ajar and all my prisms gone."

"Business? So was there anyone who knew you would be gone?"

Carver hesitated. He wanted to say yes, but he knew that would only bring more trouble. "No," he said at last. "Not really. I was just running a few errands."

"Very nice place you have here," Byrd remarked as Carver led him to the workroom.

"Thanks. The set on the right is mine. The other one was my wife's."

"Yes, of course. What exactly was taken?"

"Everything. Every single prism I had, including blanks. Even the ones from the storage bins. Everything."

Byrd glanced absently around the room. "Yes, but what *data*?"

"Everything. Art, my library, all my image dataware. Past recordings, technical studies, all my work notes—"

"Aha!"

"What?"

One of the other men entered the room. "This one," Byrd said, indicating Carver's set.

The man set about checking the unit's diagnostics, and Byrd led Carver out to the living room. He settled into Carver's rocking chair and gazed about the room, a half smile playing on his thin mouth the whole time. The man made Carver decidedly uncomfortable.

"Tell me, Mr. Blervaque, what do you think this person

was after?" Carver hesitated, and Byrd said, "Oh, come now. You must have your suspicions."

Carver sat on the leather couch, positioning himself so he could avoid eye contact with Byrd. "I went through all of this yesterday, Captain, when I filed the piracy report."

"Yes, I've seen that report. You didn't give us much to go on."

"I told you what I know."

"And do you have anything to add today?"

"Nothing I can think of," Carver said uncomfortably.

"Tell me," Captain Byrd said, "is your agent connected to the household systems, Mr. Blervaque?"

"Yes, he is. Of course he is."

Byrd nodded slowly. "And you said the back door was open when you returned from your . . . business?"

"Yes."

"Then why didn't your agent notify you and the police immediately?"

"I hadn't thought about that. I mean, I rarely take a headset with me when I leave the house—I don't like being on call every minute of every day—but God should have called the police. He didn't detect that the door was open, but I figured somebody had bypassed the sensor. I don't see how anybody could have tampered with the motion detectors inside the house, though."

"It does seem unlikely, doesn't it?" Byrd said. "Much more likely is that the tampering was done with your agent."

Carver sat stunned. Byrd leaned forward, staring intently at him, and continued. "I imagine you can afford the best security on the market, Mr. Blervaque. And yet it has been compromised twice in two days. This is not something that just anyone could manage. Someone has obviously put a lot of effort into getting their hands on your data. Surely you have *some* suspicions. It would make my investigation much easier if you gave me a lead or two, Mr. Blervaque."

Carver stared out the window. He still suspected the Freeks in today's burglary, if not in yesterday's hack, but in light of what Captain Byrd had pointed out, it did seem unlikely that a simple gang of Freeks could have the resources and the savvy to get past his security so completely. Of course, if he reported them, he would have to explain why he'd been in contact with them—and he doubted very much that the FCA would fall for the same story he'd given the Freeks.

Byrd broke into his train of thought. "Can you think of anyone who would go to such lengths to obtain that data?"

"A number of corporations who want to license the technique have contacted my manager, but I refused them all."

"Didn't they offer you enough?"

Carver shook his head. "It has nothing to do with the money, Captain. I'm just not ready to license it."

Again Byrd let his gaze wander through the room. "No, you don't have to worry about money, do you, Mr. Blervaque? Tell me something . . ."

"Yes?"

"Do you—did you—have a copy of *The Metamorphosis* in your set's matrix?"

"Yes."

Byrd nodded. "So whoever pirated your data should have a copy of that program?"

Carver felt his stomach go cold. "Yes, I suppose they do."

"Then why would they bother *physically* burgling your house a day later?"

Carver stared at the man, stunned to speechlessness. Byrd waited stoically for an answer.

"You think it was the same people?" Carver said at last.

"I'm almost positive. It's certainly far less likely that you would experience two such events only a day apart otherwise."

"I'm not sure when the piracy took place," Carver said. He

shifted uncomfortably in his seat. "As I said in my report yesterday, I hadn't tuned-in for several weeks prior to that, so it really could have happened any time."

"Ah, but your agent is tied in to household control, so you certainly would have noticed as soon as that intelligent control ceased. Since you did not notice until yesterday, I think it's safe to say that's when the piracy occurred."

"I hadn't thought of that. It does make sense."

Byrd favored Carver with a tight-lipped smile. "Yes, it does. But what doesn't make sense is today's burglary. I will ask you again, Mr. Blervaque—what do you *really* think they were after?"

"I . . . don't know," Carver stammered. His palms were sweating, his heart racing. If he told Byrd that the *Metamorphosis* effect could not be duplicated through ordinary data-transfer methods, the man would want to know why not. It would only make him more suspicious. But Carver didn't want to lie to the FCA. He said innocuously, "I can't think of anything else someone might have been after."

"Really? Will you pardon me for a few moments, please?"

Carver waited for him to leave the room, but except for resuming his rocking, the captain did not stir. The only sound in the room was the creak of the chair.

"Full level-one IDCR," Byrd mumbled.

"What?" Carver asked, but Byrd didn't reply, and Carver realized the man was not speaking to him. He was instead staring out the window at one of his subordinates, who stood on the other side of the plastic. The two men were communicating by headset.

"Yes," Byrd muttered. "Yes. No, file to Muniz."

As Carver watched this exchange, he couldn't help but recall the partially silent conversation he'd witnessed between the Freeks in the woods the previous day. The similarity between such disparate groups was so close it made him smile.

Byrd rose abruptly, and Carver stood with him.

"Thank you for your time, Mr. Blervaque. Rest assured that we'll do everything we can to find your burglars and return your data to you."

Carver walked him to the door and outside, where the other two agents already waited in the car. Byrd remained on the porch a moment.

"I'm quite a fan of your work, Mr. Blervaque," he said, "and I mean that sincerely. You're very talented, but you need to take more care as to how you apply that talent."

"I don't think I follow you."

"I think you do." He was silent for a long time before once more turning his piercing stare on Carver.

"The Web has become an integral part, almost a central part, of our nation's data superstructure," he said. "Anything that threatens the Web threatens the whole country—and our society, too, for that matter. *Anything*. And it is my job, Mr. Blervaque, to make certain that nothing does threaten the Web or this country."

He strode down the steps to the car. "I'll stay in touch," he said just before he slammed the door.

The car raced away. Carver stood on the porch and watched until long after the wake of dust had settled. He didn't like Byrd at all. The man seemed to be working from some hidden agenda, which made Carver suspicious and very nervous—more so than the FCA usually did.

He sighed and pounded his fist tiredly against the porch column. This latest development had upset him, but he knew there was no point in dwelling on it. He could do nothing more at the moment, and he did have work to do.

Exhaustion and the Gaussian noise of a heavy rain held Carver on the very brink of sleep. As his mind floated in and out of consciousness like the quiet water of an ebbing tide, his world swam between wakefulness and dreams. The two states ran together in an inseparable blur, and he could be certain of neither.

A vague incursion swirled through the hypnopompic flux, rousing him. The disturbance repeated, more distinct now as he came awake. A voice.

"Huh?" Carver asked groggily.

"Ah, he wakes at last from his senseless slumber."

"Wha'sit, God?"

"Message."

"Who?"

"No idea, boss. It's untraceable, no ID."

Carver sat up slowly, his head pounding, and stared bleakly at the empty brandy bottle on the coffee table. He had apparently succeeded quite well in drowning his frustration.

His attempt at destroying *The Metamorphosis* had failed miserably. While special routines mapped the synaptic matrices surrounding every installation, Carver worked non-stop creating sheaths and ice-breakers. The culmination of two weeks of work, his worms all fell to Web security within twenty minutes of uploading. Faced with this defeat, he had to admit that he just didn't know enough about security programming to get away with this scheme. He only hoped he'd at least managed to cover his tracks.

"All right, God. I'll be there in a bit."

God had already warmed up the set by the time Carver managed to make it from the couch to his workroom.

"Okay, God," Carver said weakly once he'd tuned-in.

The air in the corner near the window shimmered and darkened; the darkness coalesced into a human figure. It was a poor-quality image, completely uncustomized—an off-the-shelf bottom-tech image from one of the discount programming outlets. It was male, 1.8 meters tall, eighty kilos, fairly handsome, and absolutely standard in every way.

"Who are you?" Carver asked.

"It's Shade, man," the image replied in a generic male baritone. "Rachel took a couple weeks off, so your message just got to us. What the fuck is it all about?"

Carver resisted the impulse to punch the kid, knowing the gesture would be useless in the Web. "Don't pull that with me—it's insulting to both of us. If you Freeks wanted the routine behind *The Metamorphosis*, you could have just asked in return for the data you gave me."

"What are you talking about?"

"I'm talking about your friends breaking into my house and stealing my data prisms while you had me out on campus, goddammit! You picked the wrong guy to screw with, let me tell you, 'cause—"

"Hold on! Freeze it, man! I don't know the first bit of what you're on about."

"The hell you don't! You Freeks get me away from—"

"Listen, Blervaque, we're not Freeks—"

"I don't care what you call yourselves—"

"*Freeze it!* It's not semantics, pal. We are not Freeks. None of us are into that scene. Just because we know about hacking doesn't mean we live the life. If somebody jacked your data, it wasn't any of us."

"So I guess it's just coincidence that it happened when I was talking to you, and nobody else knew I'd be out of the house then?"

Shade stared at the floor. "Yeah. Yeah, I guess it was. Listen, I'm sorry if that happened, but it wasn't us. I wish there was some way I could make you believe that believe that . . ."

Shade's image started to jerk and skip as though stop-motioned by a strobe light. "What the fuck are you doing, Blervaque? Listen, I swear it wasn't us."

"I'm not doing anything," Carver said. "The problem must be yours. Maybe you caught a virus from stealing someone's data."

"I told you, we don't—shit. This ain't a glitch, it's *active*. Somebody's—"

The image disappeared. "Carver, something's wrong," God said. "Destructive incursion on all incoming cha—"

Carver's interface disintegrated, its substance pierced through with a solid, perfect whiteness that blazed pain and terror through his mind. He fought to Escape, but the whiteness pulled him out of himself, down and away until even the pain ceased and he ebbed away into void.

Shade sat up, screaming. He came up too quickly, before the coil could track out of the way, and his head smashed against it.

He stopped screaming when someone grabbed his hand. "Shade?" a small, worried voice asked.

He turned slowly, and through the panicky haze of induced confusion and the pain in his head he saw River standing beside him, looking scared—as scared as he himself was.

Shade smiled weakly at the boy, but couldn't figure out how to speak.

The door opened behind him. "What's wrong, River? Shade, what happened?" It was Selene's voice, and she sounded worried. River must have called to her.

Shade still struggled toward speech, but an odd heat on his forehead distracted him. He reached up and touched blood.

"Let me see," Selene said, tilting his head up. The movement and light hurt his eyes, so he closed them. She wiped the blood away. "I know that, River. Hand me—yes, thank you."

A headset touched Shade's scalp. He felt the familiar faint tingling pressure as the unit adhered itself to his skin, then the background rush of a hundred other minds caressed his own.

What's wrong, Shade? Selene asked internally.

He let the memory of the experience build within his mind, then he sent it to Selene—experience, not words, but still at the limits of his concentration.

From River's mind came a sense of hurt and betrayal accompanying a question.

Shade could only shrug.

I'm more interested in how, Selene thought, and she added a picture of Blervaque riding their tricks without triggering their ice.

A feeling percolated through the buzz in Shade's head. "Nah Blervaque," he managed to whisper aloud. "FCA."

He felt Selene's alarm spike through the System. Worried queries filtered back from everyone else at the Frontier, the fear building on a resonant frequency until Selene clamped it.

Cancel all Web interchange now, she ordered. *Someone come to Webworld and run a full scan-out.*

I'm on it. Shade thought the presence felt like David T., but he couldn't be sure. The physical pain in his head was growing, compounding the effects of the FCA's trap.

"Who were they cracking, Shade, us or Blervaque?"

Shade just shrugged.

"Shade?" Selene's voice sounded far away. *Shade? Can you walk?*

Her hands pushed him gently back onto the set. *Rest,* she told him, and sleepy peacefulness flowed into him. Other minds reinforced the state, strands of love and calm and safety weaving a healing cocoon about him, until he felt himself drifting down from the confusing pain.

As the painful haze disappeared, Carver first became aware of two sensations—a headset affixed to his head, and his hands somehow restrained behind his back.

His vision and his thoughts cleared. He was sitting upright on his set, facing Captain Byrd and four other Thompsons. He turned and saw two more behind him.

"Mr. Blervaque," Captain Byrd said, "I really wish it hadn't come to this. You will, too, I suspect."

"What's going on?" Carver asked angrily.

Byrd just shook his head. "Your only hope is to cooperate with us right now, Blervaque. I'll find out what I need to know whether you do or not, so you might as well save us both some trouble."

"What are you talking about?"

"I know all about your attempt to randomize *The Metamorphosis*. I know all about your involvement in the Network Thirty-seven hack. I know all about—"

"Goddammit, how many times do I have to go through that with you people?" Carver struggled to stand, but the men behind him forced him back down. "I don't know what's wrong with you, Captain, but you're not going to get away with this."

"No, Mr. Blervaque, you're the one who won't get away with it."

"I hope you have a good pension, Byrd," Carver growled, "because I promise you won't have your job after I—"

"Turn him off," Byrd said.

One of the Thompsons pressed a button on the headset Carver wore, and the whiteness abruptly returned, stealing consciousness again.

The car sped north into the darkness, the whine of its motors lost beneath the road noise of the tires. Captain Byrd stared out the window at the trees rushing past, lit to half shadow by the sedan's headlights. With Hills driving, Byrd could have dozed had he so chosen—it was late, and he was exhausted — but he could not sleep. He'd been working toward this moment for too long.

He glanced back at Carver Blervaque's inert form. The sleeper in the headset would hold Blervaque in a pseudocomatose state until they had him at the Center in Atlanta. And there, Byrd thought with grim satisfaction, the fun would really begin.

Ever since the Network 37 hack he had been closing the net on Blervaque. The operation had almost fallen apart when some anonymous mid-level bitpusher in Regulatory suggested that *The Metamorphosis* might violate programming laws and that Blervaque should be questioned about it. Any public action would have hit every newsboard on every Network—exactly the kind of exposure Byrd knew he most needed to avoid, especially after Rose Blervaque's suicide. So on the pretense that Reg couldn't fine Blervaque until they fully understood *The Metamorphosis*, he'd pulled a few strings and had their investigation officially assigned to his people, effectively burying it.

Although the release of *The Metamorphosis* had greatly upset Byrd, its attempted destruction had completely pissed him off. The program was so unlike anything the director had ever done before, Byrd had been immediately certain his hunch was right. For whatever reasons, Blervaque had been collaborating with hacks.

But something had obviously happened to sour that relationship. And now Byrd believed he was in danger of losing the other conspirators. He'd almost caught one of them along with Blervaque, but the bastard had somehow slipped out of the trap. His only hope of breaking this case now sat unconscious in the backseat.

Headlights from a southbound car speared through the windscreen, illuminating the cabin. Byrd caught a flash of Hills's dark profile lit in relief as the other car sped past. He found it surprising that another car would be on the interstate at this hour—especially going south, away from Atlanta. The Web had virtually eliminated the need for most long distance travel; they had passed less than a dozen cars since leaving Gainesville.

The headlights created faint specters in the night.

Looming alongside the interstate were the silent, hulking forms of long abandoned factories, warehouses, and technology parks.

With the advent of full virtuality, the Web's popularity had risen at the expense of luxury services and manufactured goods. Few people would pay hundreds or thousands of dollars for anything when for a fraction of the cost they could rent or buy a virtualization that—within the Web—would be indistinguishable from the real item or experience, except that it would never break or get dirty or wear out. A virtual vacation was just as real and enjoyable as its more costly natural-reality counterpart, but without the aggravation of delays, Customs, adverse weather, or illness.

The change had been so abrupt and catastrophic that it led to the Big Crash, which had itself almost brought about the death of the Web. It had taken the Continent's economy more than a decade to fully restructure itself and begin a recovery.

When economic emphasis shifted from manufacturing to programming of virtual goods and services and maintenance of the Web's infrastructure, much of the Continent's industrial real estate had fallen idle. Manufacturing now proceeded at a tiny fraction of its pre-Crash rate, and most of the resultant goods were sold overseas. Only the fence-ringed hectares of brick buildings and pavement remained as reminders of the Continent's former economic power, a blight of pockmarks through the forests, scars on the land and in the psyche of the country.

If the Web ever fell, Byrd knew the recovery would be much harder. So hard that the country might not survive it. He had to see that it never came to that.

He had two chances, he knew. First, he had to make Web security as uncrackable as possible. Second, he had to find the people who'd broken his last effort and break them. And the key to both chances was Blervaque.

The team had tried for weeks to dissect Blervaque's secret, without success. The data piracy had been their only stroke of luck—it gave Byrd a perfectly legitimate excuse to get actively involved in the situation. Even if his involvement had so far been distinctly nonlegitimate.

He did not often participate directly in investigations anymore—at least not physically—but this one was perhaps the most important case of his career. Perhaps the most important case in the history of the Agency.

Burglarizing Blervaque's house had a dual purpose. The first, of course, was to acquire Blervaque's working data—which, judging by preliminary perusals, unfortunately contained nothing relating to the *Metamorphosis* routine.

The second prong had fared much better. The burglary—along with his conspiratorial suggestion that it had been related to the piracy, a brilliant piece of misdirection if he did say so himself—scared Blervaque, and he'd subsequently contacted his accomplices, perhaps suspecting a double cross. Byrd's team had monitored the director's interchange, and when the hacks tuned him, that was all the evidence they needed. Byrd's only regret was that the hacks had escaped scot-free—their signal had been completely untraceable.

Another car passed southbound. Byrd was about to remark on this when Hills grunted and slapped his headset.

"Problem?" Byrd asked.

"My head's fritzed."

Byrd had kept his own interlink on receive-only, but he activated it now—or tried to. Nothing happened. A quick scan through the unit's autocheck revealed no problems.

"Check?"

The driver shook his head. "All okay. I just ain't got no damn signal."

Headlights appeared behind them. "Where are we?"

"Traffic's down, too. I'd say about thirty kilometers south of Macon. You think we lost it in autoswitch?"

Byrd frowned. "It's happened before. But we should still be outside the Macon node—we've got a good five K's until we jump the link. Where are the spares?"

Hills jerked his head backward. "Trunk."

"Pull off at the next exit. If there's something wrong with the Agency channel, we can use a public set or a voice-phone." Byrd almost chided himself for being overly cautious, but he didn't feel like taking any chances with Blervaque.

"All channels," Hills mumbled, but then he added, "Car's low anyway. Wouldn't hurt to flash it."

They reached an exit a few minutes later. As Hills decelerated onto the cloverleaf, the trailing car suddenly careered past them, skirting the very edges of the off ramp's shoulder as it did so.

"Goddamn!" Hills shouted as the sports car disappeared around the dark curve.

A moment later he swore again, and Byrd was thrown forward against his seat belt as Hills stomped on the brakes. The sports car blocked the road immediately before them, its rear lights dimmed.

"That's what you get for driving like an asshole," Hills said with a malicious smile. "Shitface burned his cells dry. Serves him right."

The sedan's skid ended two meters from the back of the stalled sports car. "We're too close. Pull around them," Byrd ordered.

But it was too late. The sports car, its lights suddenly returning to normal brightness, backed up, stealing Hills's maneuvering room. He threw the sedan into reverse, but a third car came around the cloverleaf, hitting them and wedging them motionless.

Byrd was out of the car and reaching for his pistol before the jostling stopped, but a voice from the first car shouted, "Don't!"

Byrd glanced quickly around, instantaneously assessing his situation. Seven people—four from the sports car, three from the car behind—surrounded him. All wore long black coats and ski masks. Byrd couldn't tell if they held weapons, but he knew he'd already lost even if they didn't. There were too many of them too close. He withdrew his hand from his coat and stood rigid with anger beside his car.

Their attackers moved in. One very carefully disarmed Captain Byrd; another motioned Hills out of the driver's seat and took his gun as well as the keys to the car. Byrd's rush of adrenaline surged into rage as three of the masked criminals pulled Carver Blervaque from the sedan and belted him into the backseat of the second car.

Without a word or a glance between them, all seven returned to their places in the cars. Only the driver of the sports car paused long enough to favor Byrd with a decidedly discourteous bow.

The two cars drove off into the darkness, leaving Byrd and Hills alone in the night. Hills put their emergency flashers on, and Byrd helped him push the vehicle onto the shoulder.

Only the one word had been spoken. Byrd knew their attackers had all worn headsets under their ski masks, just as he knew they had somehow jammed his and Hills's units.

At least he knew he'd been right to arrest Blervaque. These were no ordinary hacks the man was involved with— the boldness of this guerrilla attack proved that. There was more going on here than even he had suspected.

With a deep, slow breath that did nothing at all to calm him, Byrd stalked off silently down the ramp. Hills followed at a respectable distance.

TWELVE

Pain that buzzed like an electric shock worked its way through the shrouds of awareness. Vibration. Road noise.

Carver opened his eyes. It was dark but for dashboard lights and headlight beams throwing themselves forward. He was belted into the backseat of a car. His head lolled to the side, and stiffness cramped his neck. With an effort and a groan of pain, he lifted his head to look about the car.

"Good, you're all right," said an unfamiliar woman beside him. "You want some water?"

Carver tried to speak but gave up and just nodded instead. The woman passed him a squeeze bottle, which he took and drank from clumsily. The tingling pain reached all the way down his arms to his fingers.

"Don't try to talk too much yet," the woman told him. "Just rest. You'll probably need a few more hours to get over the sleeper. We'll get you into a bed soon."

Carver's mind was too cloudy to formulate any discrete questions. He closed his eyes and let unconsciousness take him away again.

When he next awoke, he was in a different vehicle—an old Volkswagen ElectroVan, an ancient beast that had already been well out of style back when Carver owned one in college. Through the window, in the pale orange light of early morning, he could see untended scrub and a potholed road streak past the van.

Carver looked at his fellow travelers. A tall, corpulent young Hawaiian occupied the driver's seat. His shaved head was adorned with a much-patched and modified headset much like that of the man sitting beside him.

Shade.

Memory returned through the pain and disorientation. The FCA. Captain Byrd had arrested him. And now he was with Freeks. It made no sense. Carver groaned.

Shade turned around and looked at him. "Awake? How you feeling?"

Carver shook his head in confusion. He hadn't a clue what was happening.

"Yeah." Shade grinned ruefully, reaching up to touch the bandage that adorned his forehead. "I know what you mean. And I only caught it for a few seconds, not for hours like you did. Don't worry about it—as soon as we get to the Frontier we'll get somebody to fix you."

"Who . . . ?"

"Oh, sorry. This is Angry John," Shade said, indicating the driver. Angry John made no acknowledgment of the introduction, but Shade grinned and told Carver, "He says he's glad to meet you."

Both men wore headsets, and it suddenly occurred to Carver that Angry John had to be tuned-in. That made him nervous—driving while tuned-in was both illegal and dangerous. But Carver was in no condition to argue now, and Angry John's name and sumo wrestler physique convinced him to hold his tongue. Instead he tried his question again.

"Who are you people? Where are you taking me?"

"Someplace safe," Shade said.

That raised more questions. "From what?"

"FCA are after you."

"I know that. They had me. What am I doing with you?"

Shade frowned and turned to Angry John. After several seconds Shade told Carver, "That'll have to wait until we get you to Seli. Seli can tell you everything you need to know. Seli has all the answers."

"I want answers now," Carver said, but Shade turned away.

Angry John turned down a weed-cracked road that wound into the woods. After rounding a bend that left the main road lost behind a curtain of trees, they came to a chain-link fence topped with razor wire. The gate across the roadway was already rolling aside to admit them. Carver wondered whether it was sensor-controlled or whether Angry John had opened it with a virtual command. He assumed the latter—these were, after all, Freeks—but either way it startled him that they would make use of real-world technology.

The gate closed behind them. There would be no easy escape from this place, Carver realized.

Directly ahead, a huge brick factory building dominated a vast compound that was more grass and weed than tarmac. The wall facing them held nine loading bays, all but one with the steel overhead doors rolled up. Carver could see nothing but darkness within. Above this, glass windows that were grimy where they weren't broken formed a continuous if blotchy band of greenish-gray encircling the structure.

Thirty meters to the left of this, four warehouses stretched in orderly rows, ten meters of asphalt separating each of the ten-meter wide buildings. Angry John steered the van along the south side of the main building to where twenty other cars were parked. Beyond the fence at the back of the compound Carver caught fire-red flickers of the setting sun sparking on the surface of a lake.

"Here we are," Shade said.

"Where is 'here'?" Carver asked.

"Welcome to the Frontier."

"And where exactly is that?"

Shade laughed and said theatrically, "It's everywhere we are. Seriously, I'll let Seli explain. She's at the library right now." He paused, then added with a smile, "River's there, too."

"How do you—" Carver started to ask, but Shade tapped his headset.

"We all stay tuned-in as much as we can. Even if we're doing something Outside, we keep it going in the background. Helps us all communicate."

Angry John shut off the motors and coasted to a halt mere centimeters from the factory wall. Without a word to Carver or Shade, he got out and connected the van's hood umbilical to one of the charging ports that had been jury-rigged to the wall.

"Thanks for the ride, John," Shade said as he led Carver away on foot. Angry John favored him with a quick smile and returned to his work.

"Does he ever speak?" Carver asked acidly as Shade guided him toward the lake.

Shade laughed. "Not Outside. He can, as far as I know, he just doesn't. I guess he feels more comfortable tuned-in."

"Why?"

"We'll have to fix you up," Shade replied, indicating his headset. "That way you can just ask him yourself."

Carver did not like the implications of that. One way or another, he intended to remove himself from these Freeks at his earliest possible opportunity.

He could hear the sounds of human activity now, but echoes distorted the noise past intelligibility and made it impossible to determine the direction of its source. As they neared the end of the wide alley between the brick building and the warehouse, the view before them opened up and Carver could see people everywhere. Without exception, everyone he saw wore a headset.

Shade led him around the side of the warehouse. Carver glanced down the first corridor as they walked past it, hoping to gain some clue as to his whereabouts. Overhead doors, similar to those on the factory but smaller, notched the cinderblock wall of the first warehouse. Just inside each open doorway, Carver saw couches, chairs, tables, and other furnishings. Beyond, mazes of plywood and plastic walls stretched back into the interior gloom. The meager illumination that fell through the dirty skylights was augmented spottily by electric lights. Houseplants, shrubs, and even several small trees grew in a variety of containers both within the warehouse and in the alleyway. The featureless wall of the second depot building had been painted in broad swaths of bright primary colors. The whole building had about it a bizarrely lived-in look despite its industrial origin.

"What's all that in there?" Carver asked.

"That's where we live."

Carver stopped. "You live here?"

"Of course. What did you think?"

"Where is this place? I've seen you in Gainesville twice. Are we near Gainesville?"

Shade stayed silent.

They turned down the middle corridor. The overhead doors of both buildings faced this alley, though only one halfway along the building on the left was open.

Before they were ten paces down the alley, River burst out of the open doorway and ran toward Carver, screaming delightedly, the tassel on his wool cap bouncing wildly behind him.

"He's here! He's here!"

River slammed into Carver, nearly knocking him down, and threw his arms around Carver's waist.

"Hello, River," Carver said sourly when he'd recovered his balance. "Can *you* tell me what the hell is going on?"

The boy simply grinned widely at him, then turned his

grin on Shade as though to make sure Shade saw him with his idol. Saying nothing, River took Carver's left hand in both of his own and began tugging him earnestly toward the doorway from which he'd emerged.

"I think someone wants to show you off," Shade said.

"Is this when I'm supposed to say, 'Take me to your leader'?"

Shade smiled. "I suppose so. Except we don't have a leader."

River pulled Carver inside the open warehouse. The ten-meter-square room held dozens of makeshift bookshelves, placed at random everywhere but beneath the skylight. Books of all sizes crowded every shelf; yet more were piled precariously atop the bookcases, and others shared space with electric lamps and potted plants on the end tables that accompanied the worn chairs and sofas scattered throughout the room. Dirty, threadbare rugs of all sizes and styles padded the cement floor. The odd, glittering notes of Britten's *Prince of the Pagodas* drifted patiently from some hidden source.

Three men and a woman lounged around a bookcase near the left wall of the library. The woman stood and approached Carver. She was his height, and slender to the point of lankiness. Despite this, her face was broad, with prominent cheekbones and a freckled pug nose. Laugh lines and crow's feet betrayed her age as a decade beyond Carver's, but her warm brown eyes, large and round, held a childlike innocence and wonderment that lent her face a unique agelessness. Individually, each of her features seemed just the slightest bit awkward, but taken as a whole they worked in concert to produce a striking beauty.

"Welcome to the Frontier, Carver," she said. "I'm Selene Carlisle. This is David T. and Feargal."

"Hey."

"Good to know you."

Carver ignored the pleasantries. "What am I doing here?" he demanded. "What happened to the FCA?"

"We rescued you," Selene said.

"Well, it wasn't us, really," David T. admitted.

"The Rocket Scientists are the ones who actually pulled off the raid, but we—"

"Raid? You *attacked* the FCA?" Carver shouted. "What the hell is going on here? Who are you people? I want some answers, dammit."

"And you'll get them," Selene said evenly. "Just calm down. We're only trying to help you."

"By 'rescuing' me from the Feds? Do you have any idea how much trouble you've caused me? Whatever they wanted me for—"

"Do you have any idea how much trouble you've caused us?" Shade asked.

"Shade," Selene said, shaking her head. To Carver she said, "What do you mean, whatever they wanted you for? Don't you know?"

Carver fixed her with a withering glare. "Miss Carlisle, the *only* thing I know about anything that's happened since yesterday is that by the time my lawyers have earned their fees, you people will all be going away for a long, long time. I swear, you people are worse than Captain Byrd."

Selene stared at Carver, her brow creased. "Captain Byrd?" she asked. "FCA?"

Carver nodded.

"Tall, wiry, light hair, pinched features, kind of psycho eyes?"

"That's the one."

"Fuck," Feargal whispered.

"No doubt," Shade said. "This is worse than we thought. What the fuck is he doing involved in this?"

The question had not been directed at Carver, but he answered it anyway. "He's somehow got the idea that I took part in the Network Thirty-seven hack a few months ago. He's completely wrong, but he's very persistent, so if you people are afraid of him—"

"But why would—" Shade fell suddenly silent and stared at Selene.

"Probably," she said. "But it can't hurt."

"Hello?" Carver waved his hands for attention. "Remember me, your prisoner? You're supposed to be telling me what's going on."

Selene faced him, her brow furrowed, and said, "You're not a prisoner, Carver, but you may not be exactly free to leave here for a while, I'm afraid."

"That sounds like being a prisoner to me."

Feargal, whose skin was even darker than Carver's, tugged at the small tuft of dreadlocks that sprouted from the crown of his head just in front of the headset. "A lot of folks put themselves in a lot of danger to get you away from the FCA. Us, the Rocket Scientists, the Micro Five."

"And what, I should thank you?" Carver shouted.

"We wouldn't have done it if it weren't real important," Feargal countered.

"Oh, I'm sure it is. I think I know why you kidnapped me, but believe me, you're going to wish you'd never even heard of *The Metamorphosis* by the time I'm through with you."

"Carver—"

"Don't call me that. I don't even know you."

Selene sighed. "Mr. Blervaque, please, listen to me. You haven't been kidnapped. Yes, we're interested in learning about your program—most people on the Continent are—but we didn't bring you here to steal it. We rescued you and brought you here to keep your routine out of the hands of the government."

"Oh, great. What are you, a bunch of paranoid anarchists? If the FCA were after my routine, they could have just demanded that I tell them. That's the law, isn't it?"

"Yes, it is," Shade nodded. "So why didn't they just do that?"

Carver rolled his eyes. "Because they're not after the routine. There's some big misunderstanding, some foul-up in their data—"

"It may be a misunderstanding, but we're almost certain they are after *The Metamorphosis*, Car—Mr. Blervaque," Selene told him. "I must admit we didn't understand their motives at first, but you've just filled in that piece for us."

Carver stared at the woman. "How?"

David T., seemingly lost in thought up to this point, looked up at Carver and said, "If Byrd is behind this, and he thinks you had something to do with Network Thirty-seven—"

"Captain Byrd is a power-crazed buffoon," Carver spat.

"Captain Byrd is head of the Security Research Project," Selene said quietly.

"The what?"

"Security Research Project. Almost no one has ever heard of it, not even within the FCA. It's very hush-hush—officially, it doesn't even exist. SRP is a group responsible for developing and implementing new security routines. Because they're so secret, their power is practically unlimited. Due process, habeas corpus—none of that shit matters with SRP."

"If it's all so top-secret, then how do you know so much about it?"

"We've . . . run into them before," David T. said.

"A lot of people we know are involved in fighting them," Shade added.

"God, you people really are paranoid. Look, Web security is what the FCA does. They don't need a secret organization for that."

"For the legal stuff, no," said Selene. "But there's a lot of shit they do that no one is really aware of."

"Except you."

She smiled. "Except us, and other people we're in contact with. If you want to think of the FCA as the equivalent within the Web of the FBI, then SRP is like the old CIA."

"Paranoid," Carver whispered to himself. To the Freeks he said, "I still don't see what any of this has to do with me—or you."

"We've been checking the dataverse ever since Shade got caught in the trap Byrd sprang on you. There's not a bit anywhere about your arrest."

"So? It's only been a few hours. I'm sure the story will break soon enough."

Selene shook her head. "Not just the Web and the newsboards—the whole dataverse. Including government channels. You'd think someone would report an attack on the FCA, and someone stealing one of their prisoners. There's not even any datawork on your arrest, as far as we can tell."

"You're absolutely right that Byrd could get what he wants through regular channels," Shade took over, "but it seems he's trying real hard to keep this thing a secret. Which is real fucking scary. If he thinks you had something to do with the security problems on Thirty-seven, he might think you used the same routine as in *The Metamorphosis*. If he thinks he can use that routine, he'll want it."

"So why wouldn't he just go through the regular channels?" Carver asked, exasperated.

Feargal shrugged. "Security's no good if somebody outside the organization knows the secret."

Carver laughed despite himself. "That sounds ominous."

"This is all very serious, Mr. Blervaque," Selene told him. "As I said, SRP exists pretty much beyond the pale. If Byrd wants *The Metamorphosis* that badly, it's a damn good thing for you that we got you away. You don't know how dangerous these people are. They don't just lock you up and throw away the key, they lock you up and throw away the whole fucking cell."

Carver found an empty chair and slumped into it. "Listen," he told the Freeks, "I'm tired and hung over and I'm simply not in the mood for your paranoid fantasies. I'm no big fan of the FCA, but I'd rather take my chances with them than you. I want to be put in touch with them or the police or my manager *right now*."

The Freeks looked at one another. "Your manager we can do," Selene said.

"What?" Carver couldn't believe he was actually getting somewhere with the Freeks.

"We'll let you tune your manager, if you want. But only if you promise me you'll get some rest after that. I think you could really use it."

Carver stood. "I won't promise you anything until after I talk to Jan."

"Don't expect too much," David T. warned him. "I'm sure Byrd's got everything he has on the lookout for you. And I'd bet anything your usual contacts are way shadowed. If they latch on, I pull you Out instantly, whether you're ready or not."

"I've got important things to discuss with my manager," Carver told him angrily. "I need to do a bit more than just pop In and say hello."

"We can work out better security later," Selene said, laying a calming hand on Carver's shoulder. "Maybe by tomorrow. But for now—"

"I don't plan to still be here tomorrow."

Selene regarded him coolly. "Please don't take this the wrong way, Mr. Blervaque, but you don't really have a choice in the matter right now."

Carver stared at her, fuming. At last he said, "I want to talk to my manager."

"Then follow me."

She led him out of the library and down the central alleyway between the warehouse buildings, finally stopping at the end of the row. The last overhead door on the left was closed, and Carver assumed from the rusted lock that the door hadn't been rolled up at all for a very long time. But beside this door, only a meter from the end of the building, a regular door of windowless gray metal breached the wall. Carver heard a dull thunk as a lock shot free automatically. Selene opened the door and very ceremoniously ushered him inside. It occurred to Carver then that none of the other warehouses had been locked; these were the only locks he'd seen so far.

He gasped in spite of himself when he walked inside. In the spectral glow from walls, floor, and ceiling sheathed in light-conducting Plazmic, he saw nine sets of varying makes arranged across the floor. The left wall was entirely obscured to a height of two meters by racks of what could only have been neuroprocessor arrays.

"My God!"

"Like it?" Selene asked.

"Is all this yours?"

She nodded. "The Atanasoff over there is for you—the CV–22." She indicated an older set in one corner of the room. "David T. reinstalled the default interface for you. All you have to do is tune-in."

Carver walked to the set and prepared himself. As the Fourier coil slid into position around his head, Selene said, "We'll be in your background, me and a couple others. Just making sure everything works."

Except for the color scheme, the two-dimensional interface was much like the default in his own set—a standard-format menu system.

"I know it's primitive," Selene's voice said from nowhere, "but you'd never make sense of the interface we use."

"That's okay. Are you ready to let me tune Jan?"

"Do you know the address, or will you need to ref it?" Selene asked.

"Jan's been my manager for almost fifteen years. I think I know her address by now."

"Just asking. A lot of people let their agents handle all their data so they don't have to bother with thinking."

"I'm not a lot of people," Carver told her.

"That's why you're here."

Carver ignored the amusement in her voice and gave Jan's address to the communications menu. But instead of accessing Jan directly as he'd expected to do, he clicked into the reception area.

"Welcome to Tarrega Associates, sir," Marissa said. "How may I help you today?"

"Hello, Marissa. I need to see Jan right away."

"I'm sorry, sir, but I have no record of an appointment for you. Your ID is not registered in my databank. May I ask your business with Ms. Tarrega?"

"Override, Marissa. Access code Carver Blervaque."

Marissa betrayed no emotion, but said, "I'm sorry, sir, but I cannot accept that code."

"What?"

"It's the signal modulation," David T. said. "It's altering the signature of your thought pattern."

"Cancel it."

"Not a good idea," Selene warned. "If the FCA is snooping—which I'm sure they are—they might pattern-match you. If they do that, we'll have to cut off."

"Just do it long enough so Jan's agent can pattern-match me. A second or two."

"Your call, David."

"Okay, but do it as quick as you fucking can."

"Marissa, check access code Carver Blervaque."

The agent hesitated only briefly before saying, "Good morning, Mr. Blervaque. Ms. Tarrega will be right with you."

A few moments later Jan clicked into the office. "Carver! What—Who are you? Marissa?" The luminous scales of her figure-hugging dress changed color, spiraling through the spectrum before settling restlessly on a pulsing argon-blue.

"Wait, Jan, it's really me. It's Carver. I'm on a borrowed set."

"How did you get past my agent?"

Carver allowed a smile. "Magic."

Jan visibly relaxed. "It is you! What happened, Carver? Are you all right? Where are you tuning from?"

"I can't explain it all right now—I may not have much time. But I'm all right. I'm with . . . people. They won't let me go until some things get straightened out."

Jan's mouth dropped open. "Won't let you go? Carver, are you saying you've been kidnapped?"

"I don't know, Jan. Please, just listen. The FCA arrested me last night. I don't really know what for. I think it's just a big mistake, but these people say the man behind it is part of some secret security branch within the Agency, something called the Security Research Project. The guy's name is Captain Byrd."

"Wait, if the FCA arrested you—"

"These people attacked the FCA and got me away."

"Oh, shit, Carver. Why the fuck did they do that? Do you have any idea how much trouble you're going to be in? How do your kidnappers know about this, if it's supposed to be so secret?"

"I'd like to know the same thing, Jan, believe me. Just check it out, okay. But be careful."

Everything went blank, then Carver was back in the set's flat interface.

"Sorry," David T. said. "They caught on. If you can wait a day or two, we might be able to get around that."

Carver tuned-out. Selene was sitting on the adjacent set, watching him. "It doesn't look as though I have any choice," he said to no one in particular.

THIRTEEN

Left with nothing to do until the Freeks allowed him back into the Web, Carver decided to take Selene's advice and rest. She led him back to the first row of warehouses, where Shade had said they all lived, and showed him to an unoccupied cubicle. It was small, less than three meters on a side, its walls rising halfway to the ceiling, and it contained only a battered pine armoire and a futon piled with pillows and blankets.

"Whose room is this?" Carver asked.

"It varies," Selene said. "Our sleeping arrangements around here are rather free-form. Just make yourself at home. The plumbing's at the back if you feel the need."

She left him, and he undressed and crawled into bed. He fell asleep almost immediately.

He was perspiring under the weight of his blankets when he awoke, but the air was cool, a pleasant contrast. He dressed and wandered in search of the bathroom, which turned out to be a large room with several toilet stalls, a line of sinks, and a communal shower area. It reminded Carver of a locker room.

He washed his face and rinsed his mouth from a bottle of Plaque-Out he found on a shelf. He'd just finished relieving himself when a teenage girl walked in.

"Hi," she said.

"Oh, hi." Carver felt himself blushing deeply. "I'm not, uh, in the wrong one, am I?"

"The wrong what? Oh, I see. No, we all share. Selene's down by the lake. She says to meet her out there whenever you're ready and she'll get you some lunch."

"Thanks." Carver left quickly, still embarrassed, and set off to find Selene. The way the Freeks used their headsets as a facility for constant, almost hivelike communication still unnerved him.

Selene and two men perhaps in their early twenties sat beneath a winter-bare dogwood near the lake's shore, the setting sun casting a halo around them as it rippled and glinted on the water.

Selene waved Carver over. One of the boys held on his lap a large sketch pad, at which all three of them stared intently.

"What about the link-back separator?" Selene asked the boy as Carver sat down beside her.

The boy with the sketch pad twirled the stylus around his thumb several times, a look of intense concentration puckering his face, then began to add to a detailed programming schematic. He paused suddenly and lifted the stylus. "No? Show—I see." A section of what he'd just drawn disappeared, replaced moments later by the revision. The boy nodded, and Selene said, "Good. Send it."

The boy pointed to a screen button and asked, "What next?"

Selene paused. "Right. You don't need me for that, so I'll get some dinner for our guest."

She led Carver toward the factory building. On the grassy slope between the structure and the lake, some of the Freeks were throwing together the makings of a bonfire. Carver asked her, "So what's the data?"

"We're setting up a cross-link for you."

"I'm not even going to pretend I know what that means."

"We've got high-level passive security to cover our normal Web interchange, but with the trouble you're in, we figured we needed an active fooler."

"Oh, of course. Obviously. How stupid of me not to realize."

Selene laughed. "Sorry. We're not used to working with outsiders. See, normally when we work we bounce our signals through eight or ten nodes all over the Continent to make it hard to trace us. And if anybody does try to catch our signal, a fooler jumps back a couple of nodes and then loops out at random to other sites. It's not foolproof, but it at least gives us a chance to tune-out before we can be traced.

"But in your case, they're looking mega hard, so we need something a bit more complex. Instead of rerouting only when we catch a trace, we'll do it constantly, each node transferring at random intervals. And we're going to modulate your outgoing signal to foil pattern-matching. Just in case."

"All that just to tune-in?"

"We're not taking any chances. Byrd's after you mega, and if he traces you here, we're all fucked."

Within the factory, the sunset forcing its way in through the filthy windows showed broken and abandoned machinery, old fibrex shipping pallets, and trash littering the grease-stained ground floor. The few remaining flakes of paint on the walls were uniformly mildewed and water-stained, retaining no hint of any color they might once have displayed.

They ascended a skeletal iron staircase, comfortingly more solid than it appeared, to a level so wholly different from the ground floor that Carver could scarcely believe it was within the same building. The aromas of food and fertile earth mingled in the air. Kitchen facilities stood against the northern wall; four people, none of whom Carver recognized, busied themselves there. Foliage filled the rest of the floorspace. Except for the access where the stairwell dipped to the netherworld below, the windows—all spotlessly clean here—rose above beds of herbs, vegetables, and other plants Carver couldn't identify. Narrow paths crisscrossed the remainder of the room in between dozens of hydroponics racks. Sprigs and bundles of herbs hung in the windows.

"Wow!"

Selene beamed. "Thanks. It took years to bring it all together, but it was worth it. We grow our own grains and soybeans, too, on all the land and in two of the old warehouses. We're completely self-sufficient here."

"Even livestock?"

"We don't keep any. We don't consume any animal products here, not even dairy. Not only is killing animals immoral, it's impractical and nonsustainable. A vegan diet is infinitely more efficient."

"Uh-huh. It sounds like you're getting ready for the fall of civilization."

"Not the fall, just a change."

They walked to the kitchen, where two large tureens and a number of institutional-sized ceramic baking pans sat on an autowarmer. "What is it?" Carver asked.

One of the cooks looked over and pointed with a mixing spoon in the vague direction of the various dishes. "Broccoli lasagna, seitan parmesan, macaroni casserole, and whatever kind of soup Dublin made. Oh—gazpacho and potato chowder, she says."

Selene handed Carver a plate and took one for herself. "Load up," she told him. "If we want a good spot at the fire, we'd better get out there quick."

Flames twined themselves about strands of darkness, weaving into the night a soft and lambent fabric flickering with auburn and sepia hues of old-fashioned photographs. A branch on the fire popped, and Carver watched the sparks wriggle skyward until they became lost in the streak of the milky way.

Like the fire, the gathering had burned itself low. The crowd, which had numbered more than one hundred, began to dissipate as soon as people finished eating. Individually or in groups, the Freeks drifted beyond the range of the bon-fire's thrall or formed themselves into small cliques at the edge of the light. Carver could see the lit ends of cigarettes swarming in clumps like fireflies in the heavy sienna dark-ness. From somewhere near the lake he heard two guitars playing together.

With the crowd dispersed, Carver was left in his own cluster. Selene and River sat on either side of him, as they had all night. Shade had joined them, and David T., as well as a woman named Dolores, who was as old as Selene. They sat there making small talk and watching the fire burn itself down to embers while they picked at the remains of their dinners. Due to River's remarkable persistence, the conversa-tion revolved primarily around Carver. No one else seemed to mind this singular focus, but Carver found it irksome.

Still, he noticed himself growing more at ease—a fact he attributed mostly to the potent hard cider he'd been drinking all night.

A woman appeared out of shadow, startling him. She had a bottle in one hand, a plate of food in the other, and carried a baby in a sling over one hip.

Selene took the woman's food and said brightly, "Carver, this is C.A."

The woman sat down carefully, shifting the baby to her lap. "Hi. Sorry I'm late. I was doing clean-up." Like everyone else here, she wore a headset on her shaved scalp.

"C.A.?" Carver asked the woman. "Just the letters?"

She blushed slightly. "It stands for Christianne Angelica. My parents were ever so slightly religious."

"Oh. I didn't mean to embarrass you."

"You didn't. It doesn't really bother me. It's just kind of cumbersome, so I abbreviate it."

"Can we get on with it?" Shade complained. "I've been up since before dawn, and I'm wiped."

Selene smiled and announced to Carver, "You see before you what for all practical purposes amounts to sort of our council of elders. Plus an honorary sit-in for tonight," she added, indicating River.

"I don't understand. I thought you said this place was yours."

"The deed is in my name, but we all live here, so why should any one person have the right to make all the rules? You can't expect people to share the duties and responsibilities if they aren't allowed to share in the decision-making. I wanted to create a *community* here, not a government."

"A council of elders is a form of government, isn't it?" Carver asked, more out of spite than anything else. "No matter how informal?"

Selene smiled indulgently. "The five of us work out most of the details just 'cause we best understand the direction we're trying to go with this experiment, but everyone gets to voice their opinion before decisions are finalized."

"Now *that* sounds like anarchy."

"It's not anarchy, but true anarchism," Dolores explained. "A purely social concept—it has nothing whatsoever to do with politics. Instead of trying to remodel the current system, which is both unfair and unworkable, we're starting over and creating an entirely new concept."

"We call it a 'permacultural hypervillage,'" Selene said. "You see—"

"Can we please get on with the business at hand?" Shade asked.

"What business is that?" Carver asked.

"You."

"What about me?"

"We wanted to explain things," Selene said. "What we're all about, why we brought you here—"

"Let's start with that one," Carver suggested.

C.A.'s baby wriggled itself awake then and emitted a shockingly loud wail. "The bottomless pit wakes once more," C.A. sighed. She unlaced her blouse and cradled the infant to her breast. As the baby began to suckle, Carver realized he was staring. He forced himself to look away, but not before he saw C.A. smiling at him.

Dolores reached over and touched Carver's arm. "Your new program has been of special interest to a lot of people we're connected with. We know you've somehow managed to create a lasting effect—one that stays with a user long after tune-out."

Carver maintained a stony silence. These Freeks understood more than he would have liked.

Shade leaned forward and stared directly into Carver's eyes. "There's a war on the horizon," he said. "It's been brewing for a long time, but it's definitely coming. FCA are on one side, and we're on the other."

"You? What are there, a hundred fifty of you here? Not very good odds."

"It's not just us. People all over the Continent. Other Young Pioneers, and other groups. More than anyone realizes. We've been preparing for a long time, getting ready, biding our time. But it looks like it's finally here. Network Thirty-seven was the opening shot. And you're the first battlefield."

Carver snorted. "Because of *The Metamorphosis*?"

Shade nodded grimly.

"I can't think of a stupider thing to fight over. I can understand why other directors and advertisers want my routine. I can even understand why Freeks might want it. But the FCA? Come on, that's ridiculous. What use could it possibly be to them? I think you're overreacting."

The Freeks were all staring at him. "Carver," Selene said in a tone one would use with a child caught in a lie, "we honestly are on your side. But if you want us to help you, you have to trust us. You have to tell us the truth."

"What reason do I have to trust you?"

Selene looked down at her lap. "Just our word, and good faith." She sounded disappointed.

Carver stood stiffly and stretched. "Let me sleep on it," he said, and walked away.

He found his way back to his cubicle and crawled into bed, pulling the blankets around him to ward off a chill that lingered within the cinder-block structure. The faint starlight that shone through the building's skylight gave the room a stark and otherworldly pall that Carver found singularly uninviting.

As his senses calmed, he became aware of a world of sounds surrounding him—whispers, occasional laughter, quiet singing, the sounds of lovemaking. He lay still in the night, feeling more alone and confused than he could ever remember, until sleep overtook him with uneasy dreams.

Carver returned to the kitchen the next morning just long enough to get breakfast and a mug of coffee, then shut himself away in the library. The few Freeks he ran across smiled at him but did not speak. He was relieved that they were respecting his privacy, at least, if nothing else.

David T. showed up mid-morning. Carver tried to ignore him, but he sat beside him and said, "Uh, Mr. Blervaque?"

Carver sighed and set down his book. "Yes?"

"Would you mind coming to the Webworld with me? I've got something to show you?"

In spite of himself, Carver brightened. "Can I tune-in?" he asked anxiously.

David T. grinned widely. "You can tune-in, and then some."

"Meaning?"

"Come on and I'll show you."

They walked together down the central alleyway. Most of the doors were open now, the midday sunlight filling the rooms. On the left Carver saw workshops for carpentry, mechanics, and welding, an electronics lab with makeshift clean-room, and an infirmary, all bustling with headsetted Freeks. From the building on the right he caught the rich, clean odor of freshly tilled fertile soil. For the most part he saw nothing but dark earth, but in two of the warehouses green shoots were visible growing from the floor, though in random clumps rather than in planted rows.

"After you left us last night," David T. said as he opened the door to the room full of sets and ushered Carver inside, "we decided we needed to do something special to gain your trust."

He pointed Carver to the CV–22. It was powered on and ready. While Carver prepared himself, David T. stood over him impatiently. Just before the Fourier coil tracked into position, he told Carver, "See you there."

Carver punched the switch and was instantly sitting in his chair in his workspace. David T., represented by the Young Pioneers' standard default image, sat on the rug before him, petting God, who lay contentedly half asleep on his lap. Carver looked at himself—he had his own image, dark skin, slender but muscled, loose casual clothing.

"Why am . . . how did . . . ?"

David T. cradled God carefully in his arms and rose to his feet. "We're not in the Web, so don't worry—there's no way you can be traced right now."

"Not in? Then how are we—"

"I had some friends of ours hack your set—which wasn't easy, since Byrd has an automonitor iced up on it—copy the ID codes and run a jazzer loop through the set here. The local structure is still refining, but it seems to have worked for the most part."

Carver looked around the room. He saw nothing through the window. The wallspace allocated for the fireplace flickered between that view and the bookshelf default. Random noise swirled occasionally through the titles representing his code library or across the carpet.

Carver began to understand. "This isn't my set at all. This is all in the set I'm on now, the CV–22."

"Precisely. And it's not linked to Webspace—not directly, anyway—so no worry."

"You hacked my set and copied my interface, and this is supposed to gain my trust?"

David T. shrugged, spreading his arms wide.

"You know," Carver told him, "if you'd told me you were going to do this I could have given you all the codes and saved you a lot of trouble."

David T. shook his head and smiled. "Believe me, we had nothing to do with the actual hack. Some friends of ours took care of all that—a few people in Oregon, one or two in Manitoba, and I think one of them might be from Nebraska or someplace. That's not our specialty around here."

"So how much is here?"

"Just your interface. There wasn't time to get anything from your libe. As it was, they only had time to sneak about a third as much of your interface as they wanted."

Carver looked around. "It looks complete enough."

"Ah, but Web storage is holomorphic. Each part contains the data of the whole, just at lesser resolution. More generalized, you know? They got enough to reconstruct most functioning, just not enough to get the level of failsoftness they wanted. Of course, these guys are kind of insanely nitpicky, so it's probably good enough. Some bits and pieces might quirk, but it's better than nothing, eh?"

"Oh, undoubtedly."

"So as long as you're here, this set's yours and yours alone."

"How do I get in? To the room, I mean."

"Until we get you your own headset, you'll have to ask one of us. But you can use it anytime you want." He set God on the window seat and grinned. "So do something. Check it out."

"Can I access the Web?"

"Anytime you want. The link we made is fully integrated. You still can't access any accounts based on your address ID, but other than that you're clean. All the node switching might cause some time-delay flickers, but it shouldn't be too bad. Just don't get too extravagant—any charge-for-use will have to be freeked, which of course makes a snag more likely, so if you have to do it, do it quick. Other than that, if you need anything, holler. Your output routes through the System, so someone will grok you from wherever you are. Have fun."

He fizzled out. Carver stood and walked over to where his agent lazed before the flickering, swirling mist that peered through the window.

"God. Hey, God."

The cat sluggishly opened one eye. After staring at Carver for a while, it said, "I feel fuzzy."

"You've moved. I'll tell you the details later. Right now, I need to tune Jan, if you can manage that."

"Righto, boss. Hey—your charge-back pathwork has been altered. I'm having trouble tracing the new structure."

"Don't try, God. It's okay."

"Whatever you say."

Jan rushed to Carver and threw her arms around him when he manifested in her office.

"Oh, Carver, it's so good to have the real you back. I was so worried after yesterday."

Carver returned the embrace. "I'm afraid I'm not really back. I'm still with the Freeks. They copied my interface into one of their sets."

Jan stepped back and regarded him critically. "Well, they've done a pretty fucking good job, for Freeks. I can't tell any difference."

"Yeah, I have to admit, they've surprised me with some of the things they're capable of."

"Speaking of which . . ." Jan said, offering him a seat on the couch.

"Yes?"

"I don't know what's going on, but I can't get gigo out of the FCA. They won't tell me anything about a Captain Byrd, and they say they have no record of any action against you— not even going back to the Network Thirty-seven shit. I was starting to think you'd been pulling my leg until I found out that *The Metamorphosis* has been shut down."

"What?"

Jan shrugged. "I don't know why. Nobody's offering any explanation, but try to tune any installation and you get a message that access is denied. Nothing more. None of the Networks have anything to do with it, so it must be Feds, but they won't say one way or another." She looked sidelong at Carver and shook her head. "What *have* you gotten yourself into?"

"I wish I knew."

So Byrd had scrapped *The Metamorphosis*. Carver couldn't help but smile. All that work he'd put into his abortive hack, and Byrd had ended up doing the job for him. But why had he just shut the installations down instead of randomizing them? Carver wondered about this, but knew it really didn't matter. The important thing was that the program was out of circulation.

Jan fidgeted. "Well, all I know is it's big and scary. Scary enough that there's no news at all about any of it anywhere."

"I don't think I follow you, Jan. Isn't that a good thing?"

She shook her head again. "You remember my news hound friend I told you about? I asked her if she'd come across anything."

Jan paused. "Yes?" Carver asked.

"She said some anonymous current events speculator has grabbed all the rights to everything about *The Metamorphosis*, about you, all of it."

Carver was confused. "Then why isn't the news out?"

"Exactly. Somebody invested a lot of money to buy these stories, but they're not selling them. Somebody *anonymous*. Like the FCA, perhaps?"

"They're not allowed to do that," Carver protested. "Of course, according to the Freeks, the law isn't exactly an impediment to Byrd." Carver stood and paced her office. "You're right, Jan. This is scary. I'm not sure if I trust these Freeks, but one thing they're right about is that I can't trust Byrd. Speaking of which, I should tune-out—he's probably got his people trying to track my signal even as we speak."

"I'll keep checking on things for you. We'll work this out somehow."

"Let the lawyers do it, Jan. I don't want you getting in trouble because of me. Just make sure somebody straightens this out."

"Will do, Carver," Jan said, giving him another hug. "What's your address there, so I can get back in touch with you?"

Carver paused. "I don't know. To tell the truth, I don't even know *where* I am. God, can you give Jan this address?"

"I sure can't," the M.I. reported. "I don't know how, but I'm completely lost at the moment."

"I was afraid of that." Carver thought for a few moments. "I've got it," he said at last.

"Tell me."

"Network One twelve. There's a pub there called the Trip to Jerusalem. If you go to the back . . . It's kind of complicated. Just tell Quadie to check the writing on the wall, okay? He'll understand."

"Quadie?"

"I know, Jan, but I need you two to work together. Please, Jan, for me. And take care of each other, okay?"

A look of distaste spread over Jan's face, but she drowned it in a thin smile and said, "Sure, Carver. But after we get you home, I want to renegotiate my commission."

Carver grinned. "You're the best, Jan," he told her, and he tuned-out.

"What did we get?" Byrd asked.

Everyone shook their heads. Andrea Thiele called up a stack of data and floated it over the center of the virtual conference table. "The signal was definitely illegal, but the pattern-match failed. There's active security-blocking on it now." She looked away from Captain Byrd. "I wasn't expecting that, and I couldn't get higher icebreakers working in time."

"Did we get any ident?" Byrd asked.

Thiele shook her head. "None, sir. It could have been Blervaque, or it could have been someone he's working with. Or for."

Captain Byrd turned to Hills. "How did the trace go?"

Hills also shook his head. "Couldn't even narrow it down to any one region. If I'd had three more minutes, maybe. The signal jumped nodes too often. He definitely knows we're after him."

"Well, of course he does," Byrd spat. "But we *will* get him. I want more ice around his installations. If anyone does try to spike the program, I want them trapped for sure, no escape."

He eyed Thiele. "Put everything we have around the manager, and Newman, too. We will not fuck up our next chance. Chase, take Blervaque's set off-line and disassemble it. I want the gel-ware analyzed—see if there are any clues about that piracy left in the substructure.

"We all know how important this case is. I want ·Blervaque in my office within the week. Understood?"

FOURTEEN

A single tongue of flame cracked through an anonymous space and caught hold of the darkness. Though nothing showed itself within the meager bounds of flickering illumination cast about by the dancing orange flame, still it was a world of diversity compared to the uniformity of shadow.

Quadie flung the tiny light away from himself and turned it into a sun high in a cobalt sky. The world revealed was uncompromisingly natural. Green pasture cascaded recklessly over steep and undulating hills like a velvet cover on the ocean waves. The voices of birds and insects wove themselves into a softly thrumming harmony that quavered on an inconstant, heady wind redolent of summer grass and a distant sea. Trees sprouted to the west, running in a dense carpet to the foothills of a storm-haloed mountain range far away.

This world was Quadie's own, one of his studies for *Araby*. For two months he had basked in the glow of that program's success—a glow that had been eclipsed only by Carver's *Metamorphosis*—but now it was time for him to get back to work.

He gazed off at the horizon and wondered where to begin. When he let his eyes unfocus he saw a rippling line through the grass and trees where distance changed his modeling from discrete L-system flora to an indistinct fractal region. The conflictive border remained invisible when viewed in normal context; only when Quadie altered his vision did the hidden reality spring forth. What he perceived here was determined—or at least influenced—by *how* he perceived it.

Quadie brought the world back into focus and the distinction disappeared. He strained his eyes repeatedly between the two states, watching as the heavy band of shading blurred in and out of existence. The unfocused world reminded him somewhat of Impressionist art—the raw immediacy of the color fields seemed more depth than surface, and those depths bled together almost edgelessly, the distinction of line practically superimposed, as though it didn't really belong. The reluctant Impressionist Cézanne had actually denied the existence of line in nature, considering it more of an abstract element.

It was an artistic conceit, of course, for Cézanne. But for Quadie it was reality—or, at least, virtuality. Here in the Web *everything* was in a sense abstract. What the Impressionists had denied for the sake of art, Quadie could deny in fact. Where the Impressionists had sought to interpret nature, Quadie quite literally created it.

He stared into the sky at the sun he'd created. Its overwhelming brightness burned his eyes, flattening everything in his vision. He looked away, and a purple blot danced over the world. Where the blind spot passed over a nearby tree, the trunk shrank away, the perspective of its dimensions withdrawing until it existed as nothing more than a ragged line against the sky—an abstraction. But as Quadie's sight recovered, the tree gradually regained its form until he could even make out the graftal texture of the convoluted bark.

It was all a matter of how he looked at it. It was the purest impressionism. Quadie sent the lone tree out of focus once more and left it that way, a violent dark gash in the pale blue.

The spreading sea of conifers echoed in green the gray-purple swarm of crags looming in sharp relief above them. Quadie reduced the trees to mottled cones, then further deconstructed the cones into a riot of triangles. The distant mountains retained their dimensional perspective but gave up their definition instead, mutating into a jumble of simple polygons harlequined by spidery cracks and broad swaths of stark shadow. The gentle sweep of the hills, by contrast, gained definition as their smooth integral topology separated into derivative planes, variations in texture rippling across the flat surfaces as the breeze brushed the velvet grass.

Where mountains had once formed a vertiginous wall against the sky, there now stood a pile of irregular blocks washed in the colors of stone and shadow. Quadie sought out the major delineations between blocks and strengthened them, forcing the former mountains into a more regular geometry. As he continued, a rectangular pattern emerged and became predominant, until eventually the region reminded him of an assemblage of cubist skyscrapers rather than mountains.

That was good. That gave him something to work with—a whole range of possibilities. He could start with a pastoral world and slowly transform it into a futuristic cityscape. If he chose that route, he could give the program a message about the dangers of unregulated overdevelopment, or technology out of control, or something equally righteous. And critics loved programs with subtexts.

Or he could start with an undefined world and just create a set of discrete elements that users could uncover and assemble as they wished. That could be fun.

The more Quadie thought about that idea, the more he liked it. Start with a purely abstract region and give each element several possible states. Mountains or buildings or building blocks, for instance. A patchwork of green triangles could in its end state form either a forest or an ocean. Or a garden. Or anything else.

The users would take over from there, making the world as they wanted it, deriving variations on his original creation.

He could do whatever he wanted with the individual elements—he could indulge every whim of his imagination. The hard part was going to be coming up with a hyperplot to tie it all together, a story that could adapt itself to account for any of the myriad possible combinations of the presence or absence of elements. That would test his inventiveness to its absolute limits.

That was Quadie's favorite part of programming.

He needed now to work on altering the other senses and integrating those changes with the visual impressionism he'd developed. Sound and smell and touch—touch especially—would contribute mightily to the complete experience. They would also be much harder to handle—the visuals were so much more intuitive. When the lone tree became a simple black smudge, how would its texture change? How would the wind sound when the rolling fields through which it ran became harshly angular, sprouting instead of grass a flocking of crystalline stubble? And what scent would carry through those deconstructed fields on a wind blowing from an abstraction of form and hue that lay somewhere between mountain and city skyline?

The charcoal-smudge tree twisted suddenly out of its background. Quadie's ruminations ceased as his mind focused wholly upon this unexpected movement. This world was his, and he controlled every aspect of it, including time and motion parameters. Nothing unforeseen could occur except with the influence of some external stimulus.

And indeed, as Quadie watched, the trunk split open and unfolded a whorl of colors and textures from deep within, then unwound itself into the image of Jan Tarrega.

Quadie and Jan made a habit of avoiding one another at

all costs. Although they both fiercely enjoyed the excitement of the limelight, they were otherwise complete opposites in every facet of their personalities except their love for Carver. Only Carver could bring them together with any degree of tolerance, and even those uneasy truces rarely survived an hour's lifespan. They had found opportunities to continue their feud three times within the past twelve months, which was three times more than Quadie would ever hope to see Jan in a single year. And now, for the first time ever, Jan was here in his workspace. His first impulse was to yell at her to leave him the fuck alone when he was working, but he knew that just as his worry over Carver's prolonged absence had forced him to seek her out, only the most dire and unpleasant of circumstances would bring her to him. He held his silence.

As soon as her image had fully resolved itself in his workspace, Jan said to Quadie, "I need to talk to you."

"Must you really?"

"Shut up, asshole. This is serious. I just talked to Carver, and he's in trouble."

"What kind of trouble?"

"All sorts. The FCA arrested him two nights ago."

Quadie felt his heart drop suddenly within his chest, and a nervous fluttering overtook his stomach. His own suspicions of his friend had been growing again of late, but he'd never given them full credence. Apparently, though, someone else had.

"What's the charge?"

"We don't know. The FCA are stonewalling. They won't even admit to having arrested him."

"But they gave him his one tune anyway, eh?"

"Please, Quadie, I don't need your shit right now. Carver's not with the Feds anymore. Someone kidnapped him."

"What do you mean, someone kidnapped him? From the FCA?"

"I mean he's fucking disappeared and no one knows where the fuck he is!"

The desperation in Jan's tone kept Quadie from yelling back. Her voice was trembling, but not with the acrimony he was so accustomed to hearing in it. She took a deep breath. "I'm sorry, Quadie."

"How did he get in touch with you?"

"He says the people who took him from the Feds are Freeks. They're helping him, supposedly, God knows why. He doesn't trust them, though, I don't think."

"I can understand that. Anyone top enough—and insane enough—to kidnap a prisoner from the Thompsons is someone to look out for. No telling what their motives are."

Jan turned away from him, staring off toward the meta-mountains. "I'm so worried about him, Quadie. Rose's suicide really hit him hard, and ever since he . . . ever since he *came back* he's been acting so strange. And then his program—it was so different from his prior work. It . . . does something, you know? He wouldn't tell me anything about it, wouldn't tell anyone about it. And then his set got hacked, and his house got broken into, and now this. The people he's with won't tell him where he is or give him access to an address. At least when he disappeared after Rose, I knew why. And I knew where he was. But now he's just *gone*, and you know if *they* can't find him . . ."

She ran out of steam and stood helplessly before Quadie, a pleading look in her eyes. For the first time since he'd known her, she had lost her predatory self-assurance; she seemed instead frantic and lost.

"I've been worried about him, too," he told her.

"What are we going to do, Quadie? We have to find him."

"Did he say anything that might help?"

She nodded slowly. "He said we could contact him at some pub in Network One twelve. Something about the writing on the wall. He said you'd understand."

Quadie smiled. "Indeed I do." The smile disappeared; he asked Jan, "Is that why you're here?"

She hesitated before answering. "Because I know how much you mean to Carver. He trusts you more than anyone, so . . . so I know I can trust you. I know we've never gotten along, Quadie, but we need to work together on this. For Carver's sake, okay?"

"Hey, don't worry about it. I'll do everything I can to help Carver, you know that. Even work with you." He grinned so she would know he intended no insult.

"Thanks, Quadie," Jan said, smiling bravely.

"So, shall we be off to One twelve, then, so I can let you in on the secret?"

"It doesn't have to be right away. You get back to work if you want. Sorry I interrupted."

Quadie shrugged. "No problem. I'm not really working anyway. Just fucking around, trying to develop an idea to work on."

"Oh. Well, whatever it is, it's, um, unique. What is it?"

"I've been interpreting."

"Huh?"

Quadie drew himself up and intoned solemnly, "'Interpret nature in terms of the cylinder, the sphere, the cone. Put everything in perspective, so that each side of an object, of a plane, recedes toward a central point.'"

Jan stared at him in silence, the gentle curve of her mouth darkened by a hint of irritation.

"Cézanne," Quadie explained.

"*Paul* Cézanne? The painter?" Jan looked stunned.

"Yeah. I've always loved his work. I've even got two of his paintings in my collection—*The House of the Hanged Man* and *Bellevue Pigeon Tower*. I was just sort of playing around with the idea of applying Impressionist theory to virtual programming."

Jan's expression changed to one of disbelief. "You?"

"What, you think just 'cause I don't have a formal education that I don't know anything about art theory or history? I work just as hard as Carver does, and I put just as much thought into my programs. You think I've just been lucky all these years? I may have grown up wild in the streets but—"

"I'm sorry, all right? Jeez, calm down. I guess I just never thought that much about it. I'm sorry if I underestimated you."

Quadie stared sullenly at her, then brightened and bowed low with a great flourish. "Apology accepted," he said.

Jan couldn't help laughing. "You're a very strange man, Quadie."

"Thank you. That's why I'm so much fun. That's why Carver likes me so much—I think part of him wants to be very strange, too. I've been trying for years to get him to loosen up and go a little full-goose bozo every now and then, but it never really works."

"Maybe it has," Jan said, and they both fell silent.

After a long while of staring awkwardly at one another, Quadie finally said, "Don't worry, Jan. I've known Carver for more than ten years, and the only really stupid thing he's ever done is become friends with me."

A retort came automatically to Jan's lips, but she caught herself and instead just smiled gratefully at Quadie. "Buy you a beer?"

"A beer it is! See you in One twelve."

Smoke wafted through the innerspace of Network 1001. Quadie moved out of the entrance field, the Network gradually expanding into his senses as his image fizzled into existence.

Ten-oh-one was a small Network, manifesting as the interior of a sphere just one-quarter kilometer in diameter. Within, data addresses localized on ten concentric spherical layers. These "onionskins" drifted ten meters apart and comprised hundreds of free-floating geometric sections. The pieces of the innermost layers, only twenty-five meters from Quadie, were the silver-smoke color of hematite. Successive layers darkened; the outermost gleamed with the liquid depth of black onyx. Ten meters beyond that, the world ended in a smooth, dark, and featureless nonplace that even so could not begin to compare to the unbearable nothingness of Carver's blank workspace.

The smoke plumed more thickly. Through the spaces between the segments, Quadie spotted flames blazing over a hexagon along the D8-Alpha sector of the third onionskin. *Someone hacked a good one there*, he thought.

The layers all rotated slowly within the Network's bounds, each at a different angle of inclination. Quadie moved toward the fire, through the shards of the first layer. The sections had no thickness at all, but because of the slight curvature they held from the sphere, they were visible from the side, though only as a vague warping translucence.

As Quadie approached the scene of the fighting, he heard the telltale chatter of small arms fire mixed with deeper artillery blasts and the electronic bursts of more exotic weapons. Some things never changed—two decades after his first time here, and the old games still remained popular.

The surfaces of many of the segments here were pocked or scarred, but autoroutines worked to patch over most of the damage even as Quadie passed by. Here in Hackers' Heaven, it just did not do to advertise the weaknesses of one's security.

Quadie could find no evidence of any real conflict here—the stray databits he encountered were just the fun 'n' games of hackers trying to break one another's security simply to show they could. He would not find the kind of talent he needed here. There was only one place he knew of in Network 1001 for that.

Shots rang out from behind a rhombus as he floated

toward the fourth layer, and he felt several pinpricks across his legs and lower back. None of them were painful, but the attack was stronger than he would have cared for. He continued on without pausing to look for his attackers. Still, he had to admit they were as good as ever—the worms had almost gotten through his defenses. He was out of practice.

From the contest he headed directly to the outer layer, the jet-black shapes almost invisible against the nothingness of the Network's perimeter. But for slight variations in the striation and density of their color, none of the polygons displayed any data at all, not even their addresses; the Network itself provided only reference coordinates. No one came here to just sightsee, and anyone who didn't know either exactly what he sought or how to hack past the façades had no business in 1001.

Floating through the dark space between layer ten and the impassable wall of the void, Quadie traced a wobbling epicyclical path as he searched for TJ's.

Even before he verified the coordinates, a special intuition told him the large triangle arcing gently toward him was the right one. He'd spent a lot of time here when he was growing up—enough that the place was practically a part of him. He wondered if he would still be considered a part of it.

Quadie directed his interface against the featureless surface of the triangle. Its points curving slightly along the sphere's topology, the triangle checked his ID and verified his access.

TJ's Pub abruptly manifested around him, looking exactly as it had ten years ago. Quadie nodded approvingly. Some things never changed—especially with security as impenetrable as TJ's. It was a point of professional pride with TJ that no one ever broke through her security.

Quadie stepped inside. Immediately he felt the curiosity of every patron in the place query his defenses. And fail.

He looked around, checking his data. Fifty-three occupants,

but only fifty-two hacks. He smiled. He'd found what he was looking for. As he had known he would. The best always found their way to TJ's.

The savory smells of tobacco emanated from the dark, rich walnut walls. Above the massive mirror behind the bar was the same familiar sign:

Please—
No singing
No dancing
No swearing
This is a respectable house

No one tended bar at the moment, but the same old photos still hung there—as well as many newer additions. Things might not have changed, but they had progressed.

Quadie smiled at old memories and walked through the pub until he managed to isolate the one person who had successfully hacked him.

He was in the back, playing pool by himself. A young man, with a ruggedly handsome but rough image. He looked barely out of his teens, but that was no indication of real age—hackers had always preferred an adolescent look to complement their adolescent activities. A full beer mug sweated on a table nearby; a cigarette hung loosely from between the lad's lips.

Quadie stood against the bar and watched him play. The pool table was a two-meter sphere, translucent like a hologram. Balls clung to both the inside and the outside surfaces. Six pockets were arrayed equidistantly around the globe. The hacker was currently playing the outside. The sphere rotated until he'd lined up his shot. He sank it easily, then went for several more, including one that traveled all the way around the sphere before dropping through the pocket to the inner surface.

"Good shot," Quadie offered.

The young man glanced over at him and missed the next

shot. He switched then to playing the inside, and very casually sank two balls through to the outside before pausing for a sip of beer while he considered his next shot. As he drank he looked at Quadie with a practiced disinterest.

"Help you?" he asked.

Quadie sat down at his table. "If you're as good at hacking as you are at pool. Which you are, judging from the way you hacked me when I came in."

The young man studied Quadie suspiciously, then shrugged and sat down across from him. "You could tell, huh?" He sounded disappointed.

Quadie laughed. "No, I couldn't tell a damn thing. That's how I knew you were good. You were the only loser here I couldn't tag. I don't even know what you got."

The kid smiled in spite of himself. "Just your ID, *loser*. Once I got that, I knew you didn't have anything else I wanted."

"I don't know about that." An old-fashioned thousand-dollar bill appeared on the table. "I'm looking for data."

"Yeah, isn't everybody. Too bad I don't know anything."

"Obviously not. But you could find out."

"What makes you think that?"

Quadie laughed. "Because if you couldn't, you'd have no business in here. You'd be out playing guns with all the other kids who've just earned their Class Three license and think they're big-time hacks now."

"If you're so big-time, why don't you hack it yourself?"

"Because I've been out of the game for a long, long time. I don't know people or procedures anymore. The only thing I know is that the best always hang at TJ's."

"TJ's? Shit, Mr. Big-time, you've even got the wrong damn place." The hacker laughed and drank from his beer. "You're in Willie's Hack Shack. I think the first thing you'd better start looking for is your marbles."

"She may be calling herself Willie now, but the owner of

this place is TJ. I know that as surely as you know how to wipe your ass—if indeed you do know how to do that, you inexperienced little fuck."

The hacker stood, a hostile look darkening his face, but his image froze for a second, then blinked back to its sitting position. The hack and Quadie both looked up at the burly black man who stood beside their table now, his arms folded across his massive chest.

"If you want to fight, gentlemen—and I use that term very loosely—take it outside, please," the man said softly in a deep, stern voice. His hair was beginning to gray along his temples; he wore dark slacks and a leather T-shirt with buttons of living fire. "This is a respectable house, and if you start anything here, you'll find yourselves tuned-out in a hurry with your interfaces randomized."

"Hey, Willie, you gotta start watching your perimeter better. Got a real case here." Despite his demeanor, there was a subtle note of deference in the hacker's voice when he spoke to the owner of the bar.

"And you should learn a little respect for your elders, Var. This *case* is a friend of mine—and in his day, a much better hack than you are yet."

Willie grabbed Quadie's lapels and hauled him up from the booth, then crushed him in a ferocious hug and kissed him hard on the mouth.

"Been a while since you've come slumming, Newman."

Quadie sat back down and said, "You've changed a lot in ten years, babe."

Willie laughed and morphed into a petite olive-skinned woman with short, spiky dark hair. "Is this more to your liking?"

"Good to see you again, TJ. How about a drink?"

There was a twinkling on the tabletop, and a china cup manifested before Quadie. He frowned as he looked at the clear brown liquid within.

"What the hell's this?"

"Tea. A TJ Special would kill an old man like you."

"*I'm* old? You'd already been running this joint forever when I first hacked in."

The cup changed into a tall champagne flute, a cool purple syrup swirling in its embrace, and TJ clambered onto Quadie's lap. She hugged him around the neck and kissed his cheek. Quadie reached around her for his drink. "That's more like it."

"When my security told me you were here, I could hardly believe it. How long's it been since you've deigned to visit?"

"Ten years or so, I guess. Back when you were still you. Why the change?"

"Liberty Valance syndrome. TJ's had been around too long, with a top reputation. Everybody in the Web was trying to bust my ice just to make a name. Everyone but you."

"It's not my fault. The career started taking off and I didn't have the time, and then the FCA cracked down and I couldn't risk coming here."

"Yin and yang. The better you are, the more money you make, and you can actually afford to come here legitimately, but the more visible you are and so the less freedom you have to come here at all. That's what you get for selling out, my love."

"Selling out? Sweetheart, it's not selling out, it's *buying in*."

TJ laughed. "Point. So what brings you back here to your delinquent roots?"

"If I was delinquent, it was all thanks to you."

TJ snorted. "Not quite *all*."

Quadie ignored the comment. "I'm looking for data. Unfortunately, the only source I've found is a small-time infobrat." He shook his head. "Your place has really gone downhill since I left."

TJ swatted him and stood. "You need some manners, too. Quadie, meet Var—a dear young friend of mine, and one of the best hacks I've let in here since a certain wide-eyed little shit I once knew started hanging around about twenty years ago. Var, Quadie is not only one of the best directors around, he's also the only person who ever outhacked me. As a personal favor to me, I'd ask you to help him out. Maybe together we can teach him how to have fun again."

The thousand-dollar bill still sat on the table; Quadie nudged it closer to Var. Var shook his head, and the money vanished in a burst of flame.

"Sorry, old man. I can make that much in a couple hours just scavenging credit transfers. I'll do this for Willie, but on my own terms."

TJ smiled. "That's what I like to see. Two friends engaged in friendly business. I'll leave you two alone so I can maintain my impartiality—in my line of work it's never a good idea to know too much about what other people are up to. Especially clients and friends."

When she had disappeared, Quadie squinted hard at his potential informant. "So what do you trade for?"

"Maybe just credit, maybe more, depending. Can't really say until I know what you're after."

"No good. I know the whole terms up front."

The two stared at one another in deadlocked silence. At last Var sighed and leaned back against the booth, stretching his legs out toward his unfinished game. "All right. Give me an idea of what you want, and I'll give you an idea of what it'll take."

Quadie leaned forward and whispered, "Check your defenses—I don't want anyone eavesdropping."

"My ice is fine. What you looking for?"

"What do you know about Carver Blervaque?"

"I know his new program is so *top* everybody and their granny wants to bust it. Except no one can even tech *what* he's done, much less how. I'll true you right now, man, if you can't get that, neither can I."

"I don't give a damn about the routine," Quadie lied. "Carver's my best friend, and he's in some trouble right now."

"What kind of trouble?"

Quadie picked up his drink and looked at the pool sphere, away from Var. "The FCA are after him—"

"Shit! You need to be talking to shysters, not to me."

"The FCA are after him, but they can't find him. He's disappeared. He's apparently with a group of Freeks. I don't know if they've kidnapped him or if he's just with them to hide from the Thompsons. But I want to know." Quadie leaned forward. "That's what I want your help finding out. The FCA are almost certainly shadowing me, so I can't really snoop too much."

"And so you want me to risk my ass instead, is that it?"

Quadie sat back and shrugged nonchalantly. "If you can't hack it, just say, and I'll look for someone else."

"Oh, I can hack it, Mr. Big-time," Var said with a devilish grin. "But it'll mean something special in the deal."

"Well," Quadie mused, "if nothing else, Carver and I are both pretty rich and powerful, if I do say so myself. We could turn out to be very good people to have as friends. But this stays quiet—no one else hears about this. No one. And if anything gets to the news, nothing gets to you."

Var stared into his beer for a long time.

"That's a deal?" Quadie asked.

"For now."

"You want my ID so you can get in touch with me?"

Var smiled devilishly. "Already got it, Big-time."

Quadie nodded slowly and rose. "Right. Tell TJ I'll see her again soon."

"Willie. You'll see *him*."

Quadie didn't even bother to reply before he tuned-out. He was feeling very old all of a sudden.

*   *   *

Var returned to his game after Quadie tuned-out. He needed time to think about where to start looking for Blervaque, and besides, he'd already paid for the game. His boast to Quadie about his monetary resources had been unfounded, but he hadn't wanted the director to think him desperate or a neo-phyte. Besides, turning down the money had let him at least keep some respect, even if the gesture hadn't gained him any.

He paid little attention to his pool, and soon found all of the balls on the outer surface of the sphere. The game was over. Two kids with sea pirate images moved toward the pool sphere, so Var took his beer to a table closer to the front of the pub. He relaxed and tried to think.

He really didn't know where to begin. His mind was racing in a near panic—he didn't want to feeb on his first chance at the big-time. Outside of school, Var had only been tuning-in for two years. Everyone he knew said he was one of the best new talents out there, but he hadn't been at it long enough to build up the kind of resources he'd need for *this* hack. He knew lots of other hacks and Freeks, but none well enough that he could trust them with something like this. He was entirely on his own for this one, and he knew that if he failed here, any reputation he had would be null. And he might never get another chance.

But he had to try. After two years, his break had finally come. He was on his way.

FIFTEEN

Carver sequestered himself at the back corner of the library with a book of Rilke, hoping the Freeks would not bother him. He read very little poetry, however, because he also kept a datascreen with him, and compulsively checked the newsboards every few minutes.

There was not a single bit about him or *The Metamorphosis* on any 'board. Nothing.

It had been more than sixty hours since his "rescue" by the Freeks. If Byrd had kept the data secret this long, Carver knew he was truly screwed.

He had known as much ever since he awakened in the van with Shade and Angry John, but hadn't wanted to accept it. He'd tried, actively, to assure himself it was all just the paranoia of a bizarre gaggle of cyberhippies. But he could not refute the evidence any longer.

In a data-based society, censorship was practically impossible—and yet Byrd had somehow managed to suppress the news about one of the Web's biggest celebrities for two days. With such talents, he had to be more than just regular FCA after him for a regular crime.

A shudder passed through Carver deep inside, through his bones, through the deepest pit of his stomach. The life he had known—the life he'd been clinging to so desperately since Rose's suicide—was over.

And even if his problems with Byrd were magically resolved, what then? He could return to his house, but with Rose gone that was no longer home. And he had few real friends in Gainesville. Quadie lived in Toronto, Bill and Lauren in Rhode Island, his brother in Chicago. His real life was in the Web.

"Hey, there."

Carver looked up. Selene stood before him, leaning on one of the bookcases.

"So David got you into your interface, did he?" she asked.

Carver nodded but said nothing.

After a few seconds Selene asked, "So, what's the data?"

"As much as I hate the idea, I'm beginning to suspect I might be here awhile. Nothing personal."

Selene smiled. "That's okay. But as long as you're going to be around, we might as well get a headset on you. It might make your stay here a bit more bearable."

"What might make my stay here a bit more bearable is knowing just where the hell 'here' is."

"Carver, the only reason we didn't tell you is because until we were sure you understood the situation—understood just how dangerous Byrd is to both yourself and to us—there was the danger that you'd try to contact him and give us away. It's not that we don't trust you—"

"Then tell me. You've convinced me about Byrd. Not that I ever trusted him before. But I want to know where I am. I mean, it looks a lot like Florida, and the weather is certainly right. Plus, Shade and River and all the other kids I found playing in my backyard are here."

Selene cocked her head in thought. "Well, you're right about Florida," she said at last.

Carver nodded. "I thought so. Can you tell me where, exactly?"

"Well, there's a reason it seems so familiar to you. The lake out there?"

"Yeah?"

Selene blushed slightly. "It's Newnan's Lake."

Carver sat stunned. "No way." Newnan's Lake lay only a couple of kilometers east of Gainesville; its western shore was a popular spot for swimming and boating. The eastern shore, however—the side the Frontier was on—was more isolated. Exactly as the Freeks wanted it, Carver supposed.

"Don't worry about Byrd finding you here," Selene said, misunderstanding his expression. "None of our Webwork can possibly be traced to this location. You're as safe here as you would be anywhere on the Continent. So, you want a headset?"

Carver sighed and closed his book. "Why not? I've certainly got nothing else to do. The more I hear about Byrd, the more I have to admit I'm beginning to believe you people. I'm starting to think if I ever want to tune-in again, I'll have to get one of you to teach me about freeking."

As they walked outside into the sunshine, Selene rubbed her temples and muttered, "Well, it won't be me. I hate that kind of shit. I can't understand how anyone can actually enjoy it."

"What?"

"Freeking. Hacking." Selene chuckled. "All that illicit Webwork."

Carver stopped walking and stared after her. "Excuse me? That's the most nonsensical thing you've said so far. A Freek who hates freeking?"

His laughter ceased at a look from Selene. "But I'm not a Freek, Carver. None of us are."

Carver felt confusion flood over him. "I don't understand. I thought you—I mean, aren't you all, all of you . . . ?"

"Freeks?" Selene laughed. "Not at all. We're . . . *allied* with a lot of people who are, but those of us here are not. Yes, we spend a lot of time tuned-in, but we usually avoid the Web. You saw the System in Webworld—it's powerful enough that we've got our own private, self-contained version of the Web. Our interactions take place almost entirely in our own system. Granted, when we do use the Web, we borrow some tactics from Freeks, but only to avoid detection, not for anything illegal."

"A private Web? What kind of capacity do you have?"

"We've got massive memory—at most we only use about forty percent of it, currently—but it's kind of creaky. As for processing capacity, I don't really know. I've never been big into tech stuff—oh, wait. David T. tells me we run a few hundred thousand terapops. He says you'll know what that means."

"That's pretty good," Carver admitted. "But the Webware in that room has to be worth at least a million. Plus everything else around here, not to mention the place itself. You've obviously invested a lot of money and effort in this, um, operation. If you're not Freeking, just what is the purpose of it all?"

"Let's get you to the lab. This will all be a lot easier to explain if you can tune with us."

As they walked Carver said, "I remember when I first met River he got upset when I called him a Freek. He insisted that you were—what did he call it?"

"Young Pioneers."

"Right. I thought it was just the name of your gang or whatever."

"You could call it a gang," Selene said with a laugh. "But it's not a Freek gang."

"Are you communists?"

"Huh?"

"The Young Pioneers were a communist youth group in the old Soviet Union during the last century," Carver explained.

"Really? I never knew that. No, the name has nothing to do with politics. I took it from the band actually. They were from Gainesville, but I think they may have been a bit before your time."

Carver shrugged.

"Well, whatever. I just liked the image that name conjured. It fits our purpose so well."

"Which is?"

"Young Pioneers in a new world."

They had arrived at the lab, where two teenage girls already held a headset for Carver. Like all the others he'd seen in use here, his showed patches where some sort of repair or modification had been effected.

"Sit," one of them directed him.

"Can we shave you?" the other asked after he had settled onto the stool.

"What?"

"It'll be a lot more comfortable without hair. Especially hair like yours."

"Is it necessary?"

"No. But I guarantee you'll change your mind in three or four days."

"Don't worry. I won't be here that long."

The girls placed the device on Carver's head, and he felt the odd tingling as it affixed itself to his scalp. The second girl uncoiled an induction cable from a machine against the wall and attached it to the crown of the headset.

"What's all this?"

"We just have to personalize your cap to you," the first girl said.

"And we need to create your patchspace in the System," the second added.

"I don't understand."

"He isn't, is he?" the first girl asked, glancing at Selene. "We use headsets differently than most people. You'll understand in a few minutes, once it's working. Until then, just sit back and relax."

The girls turned to their work, and Carver stared into the cavernous space across the way, where the unidentified shoots pushed their way out of the churned earth and into the cool embrace of the growing spring. *How's that?* a voice in his head asked. *Is it working?*

Carver jumped and looked at the girls, one of whom

smiled and disconnected the umbilical. "All set," she said. "No pun intended."

Selene groaned and led Carver outside. "It's too nice a day to spend inside. Why don't you tell River to meet us in the garden? There's something there I want you to see."

"How do I do it?"

"Like you use any set—just direct your thoughts."

"Hey, River. Uh, you there, kid?" Still unsure, he spoke the words aloud.

The response burst immediately through Carver's mind. *Carver! You—* Carver heard no final word, but a concept combining communication, harmony, and perfect understanding blossomed in his consciousness. Along with the words, Carver felt an overwhelming *sense* of River.

Selene laughed. "What a great expression—you look so startled! River can be a bit forceful still, can't he?"

Selene and I are going to the garden. Want to come along?

River's delight whirled through Carver's thoughts.

"What was that?" Carver asked as they walked. "I've never felt such complete experience through a headset. And it wasn't just data, it was . . ."

"We call it *grokking*," Selene explained. "It comes from an old sci-fi story."

"You borrow a lot of terminology, don't you?"

"Hey, if it works."

"Uh-huh. Speaking of how things work, can I get myself into the workroom now?"

Selene nodded. "The command is 'Open sesame.' We've keyed the lock for your System ID, and the path is in your patchspace, here—"

A schematic danced in the air before him, navigating the System's basic commands, leading eventually to the lock interface.

"Got it. Thanks."

"No prob."

"So, what's grokking all about?"

Selene shrugged. "It's fairly simple, really. All it takes is slight modifications to the headset and to the user. The standard headset has limitations built into it for practical reasons. For instance, they don't give somatic response—you don't want your body reacting to virtuality when you're trying to take a walk Outside, you know? Headset visuals are just an overlay, for the same reason. If you can't see where you're going or what you're doing, you don't want to be moving around doing stuff Outside, and if you're stuck like that, you might as well just find a set and tune-in, get the full virtuality.

"But those limitations interfere with a lot of what we want to use the caps for. Obviously, we still don't want somatic response, but we do bypass the restricted visual capacity, and we expand the bandwidth transception."

"And the modifications to the user? That sounds ominous." He sent her a mental image of a mad scientist building a monster.

She laughed. "That was very good. No, nothing like that. We have to alter the headset so it acts more fully on the right parts of the brain, and we also have to teach people to focus their thoughts distinctly enough that what they transmit is what they intend to. Something you already do very well." She grinned wickedly. "I suppose you get it from your artistic experience, but we stole it from the military—and the FCA."

"Okay, I admit the effect is amazing, but really, what's the point? If it takes so much extra effort, why not just stick with speech transmission, if you're only using it to communicate?"

"Because language is terribly limiting, Carver. I don't know why everything in the Web is still so language dependent, except that in general people are too resistant to change. Spoken language is fine for discussing the concrete, but as far as abstract concepts or emotions are concerned, it sucks. You can spend hours, even days, trying to convey in words all the subtle nuances and the full impact of something as simple and fleeting as a sunset."

"That's what poetry is all about."

"Sure, and it's great, but if you're just trying to communicate, it's a bitch." She smiled. "For instance, like right now, if you're just trying to describe a new concept of understanding to someone. And even if you do find precisely the right words, how can you be absolutely sure whoever you're talking to gives the meaning you intend to all those words? You can't. But if you directly share the actual thought or emotional state, you can."

"I think most people have enough trouble discerning their own emotions," Carver told her. "Mixing them up with someone else's emotions seems to me like begging for disaster."

"It's not like that," Selene said. "You get a complete sense of the other person's emotions, or of their conceptual meaning, but they remain distinct from your own. What we're doing is bypassing the extra steps of having to translate your thoughts into words that represent those thoughts, and then the other person having to endow those words with a specific, personal meaning."

Carver considered this and had to admit that it did make sense. "It's like a form of music, in a way, then. Something I read today said music is the language where all language ends—communication of emotion instead of words."

"Exactly. So what do you think of the garden?"

They had stopped at the edge of the asphalt beyond the farthest warehouse, which, like the third, was devoted to agriculture. Spread out before them was an overgrown field of clover, green and flowering and filled with the voices of insects. Carver looked all around, but he couldn't see a garden anywhere.

"Where?"

She led him out into the field. "Watch your step," she cautioned. He looked down and noticed several small pea-green gourds growing from the vines at his feet. He knelt down to examine them and asked, "What are these?"

"Which? Oh, probably squash of some kind. Plants have never really been my specialty."

Carver surveyed the field more critically now and saw watermelon runners, tomato plants, beans, and even wheat, all growing together haphazardly through the clover.

"This is a garden? It's completely wild. It hasn't even been weeded."

"Or fertilized, or watered. Isn't it perfect?"

"Perfect?" Carver shook his head. "Why even bother when you've got all that inside?"

"Oh, that's just to get us through the winter, mainly. Growing that way requires so much effort. Weeding, fertilizing, sowing—and it's all unnecessary. Masanobu Fukuoka proved that a hundred years ago. Growing naturally like this, we don't have to do anything but harvest, and our yields are comparable. Plants have been growing just fine for millions of years without us around to take care of them." She paused, and when Carver followed her gaze, he saw River approaching hand in hand with another boy a year or two younger. "If you just trust nature," Selene said quietly, "and let things grow as they will, without interference, you'll find that most things take care of themselves quite well on their own."

"That doesn't mean they'll take care of you, though," Carver pointed out.

He felt that ebullient rush of Riverness in his thoughts again, and a sense of greeting. He tried responding in the same way; River's smile grew broader and he knew he'd succeeded. *Who's your friend?*

Willow. An impression of brotherhood accompanied the name.

It's nice to meet you, Willow. So, does your whole family live here, River?

Both boys returned confusion. Carver figured he hadn't focused his thought-query well enough, so he repeated it aloud. Willow giggled. River said with exaggerated patience, "Willow's brother like all, not *related*."

"We're all family here," Selene explained, trying to hide a smile. "Not necessarily through blood relation, but through mutual love and respect and because we share the same vision for the future."

"Which is?"

She indicated the field again. "For ten years we've been growing enough food this way to feed all of us here— between one and two hundred people all year long—with enough of a surplus that we pay about half our operating costs just by selling food at the farmers market. Ten years— and our yield increases every year."

"Well, okay, it works on a small scale here, for a couple hundred people, but you can't really think it would be effective in feeding six billion, do you?"

"Don't you think it's odd how the more advanced agricultural science becomes, the more it screws things up? The Irish Famine of the 1800s was caused by sheer ignorance. That was one of the things that led to the development of modern farming techniques—mechanized farming, irrigation, whatever. That caused the American Dustbowl of the 1930s, which was a hell of a lot worse—and lasted longer— than the potato famine. Widespread, indiscriminate use of chemical fertilizers and pesticides finally got them out of that, and led to all sorts of other trouble—environmental poisoning, soil depletion, mutant strains of pesticide-resistant bugs and diseases. Now most of our food is genetically engineered and irradiated. Who knows *what* that's going to lead to. The more they try to fix their mistakes, the worse things get. Why do you think that is, Carver?"

"I haven't a clue, and to be honest, I really don't see—"

"Because our society sees nature—any wildness—as a force to subdue. There's no sympathy, no harmony, with nature." Selene paused in her speech, and a flood of images entered Carver's mind, sent—he assumed—by Selene via the headset. Carver saw the grounds of Versailles with their rectangles of perfectly manicured and rolled grass contained within borders of carefully shaped, clipped, and *controlled* topiary; water pumped from fountains flowed through ray-straight courses of stone instead of along the meandering paths of natural streams.

The landscape shifted subtly; combine harvesters appeared, and the point of view rose above the mechanized commercial farmland to show an entire countryside ploughed and planted in stark rectangles. All was straight lines; Carver saw not a single curve anywhere.

"And it's not just agriculture," Selene continued. "Our worldview is deeply flawed. All our natural sciences treat the world as a hostile force." She flashed him a scene of cavemen cowering from the fury of a lightning storm. "Something that needs to be classified, explained, exploited." She stared pointedly at Carver; the cavemen in his mind's eye became scientists in white lab coats, and the lightning became bounded within a huge reactor swarming with dials and displays. "Controlled."

Carver shifted uncomfortably on his feet. "I see where this is leading, and I have to say that you're making a big mistake. Humanity makes a very poor villain."

"No, no, you don't get it at all. It's not humanity that's the problem, it's *society*. There's a big difference, Carver. Our culture teaches us to think our sciences and technology help us beat Nature, but that's ludicrous. Nature is nothing less than the universe itself—it controls us, not the other way around. Contemporary society is terminal, just like the Roman Empire was."

"But you're going to save society, I suppose. You and your friends."

"Not at all. We don't *want* to. We don't want to shore it up, we want to create an alternative, a completely new system. We already have."

"I'm not trying to be antagonistic, but nothing you're doing here is new. The hippies tried it a century ago, and failed miserably. Before them you had the Romantics, and the Utopians, and all those weird religious communes. None of those experiments ever lasted."

"That's because they were all just trying to create alternatives to the existing society without changing the basic concepts. That never works—you have to completely abandon the existing paradigm."

"How very ideological of you," Carver said dryly.

Selene ignored him. "The fall of Rome and the rise of Christianity led to a thousand years of the Dark Ages in Europe. That only ended when the Renaissance created a new model for society, based on the ancient Greek civilization." Again a herd of mutable images swarmed into Carver's thoughts to accompany Selene's words. "That established a dominance of the human mind and spirit which allowed society to progress to the point where, during the Romantic era, an attitude of sanctity for life developed. The technological age has gradually lost sight of that sanctity and destroyed it, so now we need to establish a harmony with Nature if we're going to preserve that sanctity. Our present logic is failing us, dragging us toward oblivion, and the only way out is to abandon that logic and return to an ancient worldview."

"So let me get this straight. Science and technology have led us to this crisis, so you're using science and technology—in the form of virtuality—to solve the crisis. That's classic!" Carver laughed, and Selene smiled, but slightly, and shook her head.

"That illustrates my point exactly. You're thinking about it all wrong. You're too locked into the dualistic worldview. It's the law of yin and yang, Carver. Life isn't either/or, yes/no, on/off. It's a round continuum. It means there are no absolutes. Nothing is completely *this* or completely *that*, but a mixture of many different elements. Instead of reducing something to its dominant feature, you should go the other way, expand it so you can see all the different parts that make it up. Trying to so rigidly define and control something just limits you. For instance, instead of seeing your current situation as trouble, try to think of it as an opportunity to get new perspectives, to open yourself to new ways of viewing your life." She added coyly, "If nothing else, you might get an idea for a new program out of it—or a new way to use what you did in your last program."

"Hmmph. I won't be able to do much of anything if I don't get this mess straightened out."

"Patience, Carver. You've done all you can for now."

"No I haven't. I've taken care of everything I needed to with Jan, but there's plenty more I could do. It's just so frustrating. It seems so far out of my control."

"Well, then, I'd suggest you try to relax a bit. Worrying won't make things happen any faster. Take it easy for today. Whether you agree with what we're trying to accomplish or not, you're our guest here for as long as you want or need to stay, so just hang out, meet people, explore the place." She winked slyly. "I've got things to do, but I bet I know someone who'd be happy to show you around."

Before Carver could say anything, a gleeful frenzy of images burst into his mind and River took his hand. Willow took the other, and together the boys pulled Carver through the field toward the woods.

"I think I'm going to take a tour," he called over his shoulder to Selene. She laughed, and Carver, somewhat to his surprise, laughed too.

SIXTEEN

After River's haphazard tour, Carver spent the remains of the day sitting with a book under a spreading magnolia tree by the lake. People kept introducing themselves, either virtually or in person, and welcoming him to the Frontier. By the time the sunlight became too dim for reading, Carver figured he'd met just about every one of the Young Pioneers.

Dinner was again a communal affair, though at most only half of the Young Pioneers were gathered at once; people trickled onto the hillside as their various schedules and activities permitted, and wandered away again at their leisure.

The confluence of people around him and in his mind had become oppressive. Over the course of the afternoon he had familiarized himself with the parameters and protocols of the Young Pioneers' System, so he knew how to eliminate the mumble of personalities from his thoughts, but he felt uncomfortable now even in the presence of these people— people who were strangers to him, yet who had shared his very thoughts. Once the night had deepened sufficiently to mask his retreat, Carver skulked away.

He had not learned to control his thoughts well enough on the fully interactive level the Pioneers generally used, so he'd kept to a buffered level that required a specific command to release his thoughts into the System. Since his thoughts were not part of the mélange, no one would notice his further withdrawal. He tuned-out altogether, shutting off the headset.

Carver walked back to the library with a bottle of merlot and took up his book again. He retired to the chair in the back corner, hoping the reading light would not be so conspicuous as to draw in any company.

After three poems, he put the book away and picked up the screen instead. His search still failed to turn up anything, and he'd now been "missing" for three full days.

Carver wondered how long he could live like this. He didn't mind the Young Pioneers for now, he decided, but knew he wouldn't want to stay at the Frontier much longer. Where else could he go, though? As he'd told himself before, his real life was in the Web. Just like his work—his art. Virtual.

But *real*.

Which meant, he realized in a sudden flash of clarity, that he could go anywhere and work. He could *live* anywhere.

Perhaps Selene was right. Perhaps he did need a change of perspective.

A woman's voice called his name, and without thinking he answered only with his thoughts before remembering he'd tuned-out.

"Carver? Hello? Is everything okay?" C.A. asked, moving into the illuminated space in front of him.

"Yeah, fine. Where's your baby?"

"Heather? Dara has babysitting duty tonight. We've got seven little tykes here under two years old, you know."

"Not all yours, I hope."

She laughed. "No, just the one. So far."

He closed the book and set it on top of the screen, obscuring the flashing images. "So, what's the data?"

She shrugged and bit back a shy smile. "I was just wondering how you were holding up. I missed you at dinner."

"I . . . needed to get away from the crowd. I've been pretty solitary for the last few months, and it's just kind of hard to adjust, I guess."

C.A. moved closer, so that her hip rested against the back of the chair. "Well, could you stand a small group?"

"How small?"

"Like, about a dozen or so?"

"Why, what's up?" He could feel C.A.'s breath stirring the air over him.

"Do you like music?"

"Yeah, I guess. I mean, sure. Who doesn't?"

She stepped around in front of him and took his hands, pulling him up from the chair. "Bring the wine." The lamp went off as they walked out into the moonlight.

Still holding his hand, C.A. led him to the water's edge. The sounds of guitars and flutes drifted on the cool breeze, and Carver saw several silhouettes sitting at the end of a short pier far down the shore. By the time he and C.A. reached the pier, he recognized most of those gathered.

Markus and Dolores scooted aside, widening the space between them for Carver and C.A. As soon as they seated themselves, bottles of stout and cider were passed to them from a cooler in the center of the group, and soon afterward, guitars.

"No thanks," Carver said. "I don't play."

"You don't have to," Markus told him.

Carver took the instrument and looked at C.A., but she was grinning across the circle at Sari, obviously engaged in conversation. He sighed and picked up his bottle.

The beer, highly carbonated and strong, danced on his tongue, fizzing all the way down his throat. An India pale ale, it was light but heavily hopped, and very bitter in both its flavor and aftertaste. Carver closed his eyes and let the beer wash the day's tensions from his body.

He opened his eyes again when he noticed the silence.

Everyone had stopped playing, and they all stared expectantly either at him or at Selene, who watched him with a bemused expression.

"What?"

Her smile became more mysterious, and she said, "With all your talent for creating realities, you never use music. Why not?"

"I use music all the time," he replied. "Sound is an integral part of any reality. I use music constantly."

"You fill your worlds with sound, and even songs, but you have yet to discover *music*. To really *use* it. Music is the rhythm, the pulsing blood and the soul of life. It has heat and electricity, and it's real. It has life and power of its own, and it can change things."

"Change things?"

"Just like you did in *The Metamorphosis*. Anything can be music if you really *feel* it. There's as much magic here in the real world as there is in the Web."

"Magic?" Against the sounds of the night, with its background of water noise and the quiet breathing of the Pioneers, Selene's rolling, syncopated speech had become hypnotic.

"Magic. You mentioned magic to your manager the other day. That was how she knew you were really you." She paused for the space of several breaths before continuing. "Magic is very important to you, isn't it?"

"In a way, it's what I do."

"It's what we do, too," she said, and began to play her recorder. The single, quavering note soon progressed and grew as more notes followed it into melody, simple and mutable. After several minutes Emily, sitting to Selene's left, began to imitate her on a guitar. Her song shifted, evolving away from Selene's, and Selene let her recorder fall silent as Emily found her own music. She, too, played alone for some minutes, then the boy on her left—someone Carver didn't recognize—took over.

The transfiguring song moved slowly around the circle. Eventually it came to Markus. He played a long, unhurried song that offered itself easily to Carver, but Carver couldn't take it.

"I don't know how to play." He felt awkward, and wondered why C.A. had brought him to this.

She took the notes for him. "Don't worry about playing." Her voice was a low whisper, attuned to the music she played. "Just do what sounds right—what feels right. That's what music is. Don't think about it. Create your own reality."

"But I don't know what will sound right. I really don't play at all."

"Don't worry about ruining it," Dolores said. "You can't ruin it if you just play what you feel inside. If you believe in what you're doing, even dissonance can be beautiful."

And with that she started a sharp counterpoint to C.A.'s song, her notes, her tempo, her beat, even her melody, in conflict to what C.A. played. And yet, Carver had to admit, it *was* beautiful. As Shade took the song from C.A., Feargal assumed Dolores's part on a flute. Soon someone else began a new melody; it joined the circle, resonating through the other music. Another voice grew, and soon another, until everyone but Carver was playing, each song distinct and yet part of the same expression. Some of them strummed their strings in a traditional manner; others plucked, or hammered with their thumbs. David T. drummed with his fingers on the body of his guitar, gently touching the strings now and then to subtly inflect the emerging tones. Ash, a younger girl with an obvious gift for music, twisted the strings of her guitar between her fingers or stroked her nails down the length of the steel-wound strings. The haunting, metallic tones reminded Carver of an Indonesian gamelan, or of whale song.

He finished his beer and took another from the cooler. Closing his eyes as he drank, he felt the music dance on his skin, a lingering not-quite-physical pressure. Hypnotic. His mind began to diffuse throughout his body, an odd, melting sensation like that of drifting off to sleep—like the sensation of his experimental workspace. He let the feeling wash over him, warm, liquid, and alive.

"Play," a voice whispered beside him.

He opened his eyes and looked at C.A., the spell broken. "I don't want to," he said harshly. "Why is it so important that I play?"

C.A. leaned away and looked down at her guitar. It was Selene who spoke.

"This is our kind of magic, Carver," she said. "We wanted to share it with you. We wanted you to share in it. I thought it might help you understand us better."

"Listen, that stuff about magic—it's just sort of a private joke. I don't really believe in magic, okay? I mean, for one thing, it's all in the Web. It's not magic, it's *program*. It has nothing to do with natural reality."

"That's not what we're talking about," Dolores said. "There is real magic, but it's not the big things you do in virtuality—like flying or turning into a sea gull. Real magic is little things like the bloom of a flower or the scent and sensation of a spring thunderstorm. Life itself is magic, all the magic we need."

"There's more magic under heaven and earth than is dreamed of in your Web," Ash giggled, beginning again to play, though softly.

Hippies, Carver thought to himself. He was already tipsy, but took another swallow anyway. "That was very deep. Sorry, but I'm not much into mystical experiences."

"It's not mysticism," Shade told him. "Call it spiritual if you want, but it has nothing to do with any kind of mystical quest. It's just the opposite, really, 'cause what we're talking about is a part of ordinary, everyday life. You just have to open yourself to the wider possibilities of what lies beyond the reality you see every day, the truth that surrounds the illusions we fool ourselves into believing."

"A change of perspective." Carver nodded and took another sip. These things were actually beginning to make a certain amount of sense to him now. A part of him said it was probably just the alcohol, but that didn't seem to matter especially. "A new way of looking at things." He drank again, emptying the bottle, and looked at Selene. "What we were talking about earlier today. Giving people a different perspective in order to change their minds. That's what I do with my programs."

Beside him, C.A. spoke again at last. "Exactly. It's not about changing reality, just the way you see it. Changing your orientation to it. If you can change that, stop centering your perception, your mind, your *world*, on yourself, you can change the quality of your perception. If you can break out beyond the narrow confines of what you've always believed— not even believed, really, but just taken for granted, without any real consideration—you can change your world. Like Dolores said, life is magic. And magic is life, if you can only experience it the right way. Openly. You need to feel the livingness of life inside you, but in your heart, not your mind. It's not mystical at all. It's completely ordinary—ordinary magic. The real world is brimming with enchantment."

"Ordinary magic. That's it exactly. That's the key." Carver smiled, even though his face was mostly numb. "That's what I do with my programs."

"You said that," C.A. whispered to him with a smile.

"No, I mean, ordinary magic, a change of perspective. Looking at things differently, approaching a problem from a new angle. That's what I did in *The Metamorphosis*."

"How's that?" C.A. asked.

Carver winked. "Ordinary magic. Programming is magic, in a way, and I used the most ordinary kind."

"I don't follow you."

"Hardware programming," Carver whispered. "That's why no one can figure it out. Everybody's trying to find it in the program, but its really part of the Web itself—it's built into the *world*."

"I'm not sure I understand what you mean," C.A. said, her husky voice soft and lilting. "Try using your headset."

Carver switched the unit on and tried to focus his thoughts. "No one will ever figure it out. No one can find any clues in *The Metamorphosis* because what I did isn't part of the program." He hoped she was getting clear images through the System; he was having trouble with words right now. "That part of it wasn't a program running in the Web. It wasn't the program running through the Fourier coil, you see—it was the Fourier coil itself. I actually reprogrammed the structure of the Fourier coil. It *can't* be detected."

"That's impossible!" David T. shouted. "You'd need to be using microcode to do something like that, and microcode won't let you do that. Even if you knew enough about system programming—"

Shade cut him off, but the damage was already done. Carver tensed, and felt his inebriation vanish in a panic-induced flood of adrenaline. He'd given away his secret—and to borderline outlaws, of all people. He stared accusingly at C.A.

He felt a flurry of conversation ripple through the System, but C.A. said nothing. Carver stood and thrust his guitar at Markus before turning and striding angrily back down the dock and into the darkness.

Footsteps raced after him, but he neither stopped nor slowed.

Carver, wait.

He shut off his headset.

"Carver!" C.A. ran to catch him, grabbing his arm. He pulled free of her grasp but stopped walking and turned to face her.

"Carver, what's wrong?"

"What do you care? You got what you wanted from me."

"What's that supposed to mean?"

"David T. is wizardly enough—he can tell you if you can't figure it out."

"So we found out. What do you think we're going to do, steal your business? Listen, Carver, we need to know how your routine operates, but our reasons have nothing to do with you, except to protect you from Captain Byrd."

"You're the ones who told me how dangerous it would be in the wrong hands."

C.A. almost smiled. "And you think we're the wrong hands?"

"I don't know what to think." The music had started again on the pier. The sound made Carver angrier. "I have no idea what or who you people are, beyond that my whole life is falling apart and you're part of it."

"We've been trying for two days to show you who we are! We've been completely open and honest with you the whole time. We never tried to hide anything at all from you or mislead you. All we wanted was your understanding, but you're just too defensive, aren't you? Why is it so hard for you to trust us? Everything we've done since you got here we did for you. Even the music tonight. *Especially* this."

She wheeled around and ran off toward the warehouses. Carver stared after her, then stormed away himself.

He stomped across a field, not caring if he trod on any melons or tomatoes or anything else. When he reached the woods, he continued on full-force, angrily slapping moon-silvered branches out of his way. He wasn't sure if he was angrier at what had happened on the pier or at the things C.A. had said, so he decided not to think about it and just be angry.

An unseen branch caught him across the face. Startled, he tried to duck and twist out of its way, but as he did so his feet slipped out from under him and he crashed to the ground. The force of his landing knocked the breath from his lungs, and while he sat there gasping for air, drunk and exhausted, his anger bled away.

It didn't matter, he decided. It had happened, and there was nothing he could do about it. He would just have to deal with the consequences as best he could. As he had with Rose's death. It would depend, he thought sarcastically, on how he looked at it. *Yin and yang*, Selene had said. Perhaps he could make something good out of this situation.

Yin and yang.

He stood, brushing leaves from his back and butt, and walked cautiously in the direction of the moon. He emerged from the woods to the cracked and weed-grown field of tarmac east of the warehouses. Some of the Young Pioneers were playing there with a luminous Frisbee. Carver walked toward the lake, keeping to the edge of the woods.

The music still belled softly against the night. Carver stared down the shoreline, but with the dark and distance, he couldn't tell if C.A. had rejoined the circle.

With a thought he triggered his headset. *C.A.?*

No reply came.

C.A., he thought again, *it's Carver. Come on, I know you're tuned-in.*

Her presence buffeted his mind, angry and hurt, but distant.

Where are you at? he asked.

What do you want?

I . . . don't know. I just . . . wanted to . . .

No words. Be like us.

Carver paused and tried to reason himself out. He felt anger, resentment, pain, frustration, helplessness—and a measure of contrition over his outburst. He soon gave up trying to separate his emotions and sent everything all at once, as confused as it was.

After several seconds he asked, *C.A.?*

She gave him a scene of herself sitting cross-legged beneath the magnolia tree at the lakeshore.

He found her still sitting in that position, like the Buddha, staring out across the lake. He sat down beside her and watched the wind blow the moonlight into a thousand shimmering ripples.

He drew a deep breath, but before he could speak, she touched a finger to his mouth and whispered, "Shhh."

He started to turn away, but she kept her hand up, her index finger resting against his lips with a barely perceptible electric pressure.

She faced him and drew her finger slowly back. It pulled him forward, and she leaned closer to him. At the last instant the finger slid away and their lips met.

The kiss lasted until C.A. raised her palm to caress his cheek. Carver pulled away then and said, "I'm sorry."

"For what?"

"I shouldn't . . ."

"Did I make you uncomfortable? Then I should apologize."

"No, not at all. It's just, I mean, well, what about, you know, Heather's father?"

"The whole village shares the privilege of raising the young'uns." She smiled sweetly. "You can, too, if you decide you want to."

"No, I meant specifically your . . . your husband, or boyfriend or whoever."

She laughed and gave him a quick kiss. "Is that what you're worried about? Carver, we try to supersede that kind of thing here. Exclusivity in personal relationships can be a very destructive thing. It can lead to jealousy and feelings of ownership and objectification. We're all one family here, everyone is, and we share everything. Of course," she added, looking Carver levelly in the eye, "that's a lot for some people to adjust to, and until they do . . ."

"So do you know who Heather's father is?"

"Not personally. I mean, her genescan's on file at the infirmary with everyone else's in case some kind of problem comes up, but it's not important to us. Like I said, we all share parenting. It's better for the kids, certainly."

"How?"

"It's just one part of giving them a more equitable world-view. Treating everyone as family, loving everyone despite their differences. If we want to change the world, Carver, we have to teach our children new values for that world. I mean, it's obvious that the old values haven't worked, but we grew up with them, and we're already hard-wired. No matter how much we change our attitudes, we're still working with— well, not instincts, but prejudices, I guess—that we may not be able to fully overcome no matter how hard we try. But the next generation can be free of them—free of gender and racial discrimination, free of all the hatreds and intolerances that mar the world today—if we actively try *not* to pass them on."

Her forehead wrinkled in thought, and then she continued, "It's like with the story of Moses. We adults can never cross into the Promised Land ourselves, but we can lead our children to the threshold. And that's enough."

She stared at Carver, her gaze deep and penetrating. "And that's what we're doing here. We want to teach our children cooperation instead of competition—instead of *combat*. We want to give our children a world of peace and love, a world without fear or hatred."

She scooted closer to him, so that her hip pressed against his, and put her hand on his shoulder. "We want you to be part of that world, too, Carver. If it's what you want. But you need to abandon all of your preconceptions."

He pushed her gently away and stood. "I don't think I can."

C.A. stood also, but Carver thrust his hands in his pockets and hunched his shoulders, and she kept her distance. "It's too much all at once," he said, backing away from her. "You're overwhelming me. Not just you, but all of you. Everyone. Everything. I—"

She raised a hand to quiet him. "It's okay. I understand. I'm sorry if I got carried away. I guess we all did tonight." She turned and started toward the warehouse. "I'm going to check on Heather and then go to bed," she called over her shoulder. "My room's just off the nursery if you want to find me later. Just ask for directions—there's always someone awake around here. Good night, Carver."

He silently watched her go, then sat down against the trees once more and watched the night. Removing the headset, he tried to keep his thoughts wandering in the realms of the meaningless. He was still drunk, the night air felt surprisingly warm, and the breeze caressed him with the scents of earth and water.

Eventually he fell asleep beneath the magnolia, alone but for the moon and the starry sky.

David T. woke him shortly after sunrise. Carver sat up and stretched stiffly, his spine cracking loudly after a night spent curled up at the base of the tree. The sun had barely risen above the warehouses.

"What time is it?" Carver asked.

"I'm sorry, man. I know it's early, but I have to talk to you."

A strain in the young man's voice made Carver look at him again. His clothes were rumpled, and dark, puffed circles beneath his eyes provided the only color to his otherwise sallow face.

"Jesus," Carver said. "You look as awful as I feel."

David T. grinned weakly. "You did drink a bit, didn't you?"

Carver groaned. "What's your excuse?"

"I've been up all night working." His expression turned serious again.

"Why does that sound ominous?"

David T. shifted from squatting to sitting and pulled a wicker basket onto his lap. "I brought you some breakfast, if you want," he said. "And coffee, too."

"Coffee?"

David T. smiled at the eagerness in Carver's voice and pulled a thermal carafe and two mugs from the basket. After filling the first cup he asked, "What do you take?"

"Coffee," Carver replied. "Just coffee."

He took the steaming mug and sipped carefully, grimacing as the coffee scorched the furriness on his teeth and tongue.

"Ugh. I need to rinse my mouth. And I need a shower." He was still wearing the same clothes he'd arrived in three days ago.

David T. set out some muffins and a sack of fruit. "Can it wait? This is really important."

Carver picked up an orange and peeled it. "Listen," he said wearily, "after last night, I decided to give up on all this. If you can figure it out, fine. If Byrd figures it out, fine. I really don't care. But I'm not going to help anyone take advantage of me, you got that?"

David T. took two deep gulps of coffee, and when he set the mug on the ground, his hands shook visibly. Carver figured the boy had been pouring caffeine into an empty stomach all night.

"I already figured your trick. What do you think kept me up all night?"

A heaviness plunged down Carver's spine and clenched at his stomach. "You had to wake me up to tell me this? Is there more to the story, or did you just feel an especial need to *really* ruin my day?"

"Please!" David T. pleaded, bouncing up and down like a frustrated child. "I'm telling you because I know what it does and you don't."

"Enough jokes, all right? I came up with the bit, you'll recall. I ought to have a reasonable grasp of how it works."

David T. refilled his mug, then leaned forward and stared intently at Carver. "I didn't say how, brother man, I said *what*. What your little creation can do is very, very *fucking* scary."

"I think you need to get some sleep," Carver told him.

"Tell me something—what were you trying for when you worked this out? Were you trying to create a subliminal effect, or were you just trying to zone folks out?"

Carver looked at him dubiously and said nothing, but David T. practically screamed, "Just tell me, man!" He clenched his fists and said more quietly, "It's important, okay? No bullshit."

"I was trying to zone *myself* out," Carver admitted, abashed by the boy's passion. "I didn't know at first that I could package any kind of message, or whatever, or that the effect lasted Outside."

David T. slumped, relief and exhaustion both evident. "That's what I figured. That's what I hoped."

"What is this all about, David?"

He seemed not to hear the question. "Getting into the Fourier coil was a bitch. We've got so many layers over it that no one ever really gets anywhere near it when they're programming anymore. We just do the program, and the system handles all the translation to hardware. It's like the tunnels under New York City, you know? It's been so long since anyone actually used them for anything that they're more legend now than anything else. I finally gave up trying to hack my way down and just felt my way in, the way you must have. That was the key, see? Anyone tech would know what you actually did is supposed to be impossible and not even try it, but you didn't know that. I was trying to tech it—like Byrd and anyone else probably is—but then it came to me that you wouldn't have been able to do it that way. You're an artist, so you approached it . . . I don't know, intuitively.

"And then once I got to the coil, I had to figure out a whole new way to work, you know, 'cause you can't just *program* it like normal. That also fucked me up until I quit trying to tech and just pretended I was you and winged it. I still can't really *do* anything, but I think I've got it figured out in principle."

His eyes had closed and he was rocking slightly back and forth. "I didn't catch it at first, 'cause I was trying to recreate how you hid your message in there. But I kept going back and forth between my workspace and the coil space, and after about an hour of that I started to notice some really odd effects."

"What effects?" Carver asked, but David T. continued to ramble, his voice so singsongy that Carver wondered if he might have fallen asleep.

"The more I concentrated on the weird shit, the more I started to think that was what the whole thing was really about. But I just couldn't figure out what it was, exactly. But then I remembered what you'd said about it, about wanting to change people's minds, and that's when it finally hit me."

Carver gripped David T.'s shoulder and shook him. "What hit you, David? What are you talking about?"

The boy opened his eyes, startled. "You said before you're not tech. Do you understand how the Fourier translation works?"

"You mean the coil? No, not really. Okay, not at all, actually."

"Put your cap on. It'll help." Carver put the headset on, and images began flooding his thoughts to accompany David T.'s explanations. "Uh, okay. Fourier transforms are a kind of calculus that can basically translate any pattern into simple wave equations. That's how holography works, translating a visual record into interference patterns on a piece of film—or in neural arrays or storage prisms, in the case of the Web—and back again. The Fourier coil was invented by medical engineers trying to develop an artificial vision system for the blind. Since the visual cortex analyzes input in terms of frequencies of wave forms, they figured the easiest thing would be to use Fourier equations to convert complex visual patterns into wave forms, then feed those waves to the vision centers of the brain by induction—that's the coil.

"But the whole brain, not just vision, is holographic and works on Fourier equations. So from that the engineers worked out a system of interfacing the human mind directly with a computer. Since the brain is analog and computers are digital, they needed lots of extra hocus-pocus to make everything compatible. But once they started applying Fourier interfaces to analog matrix systems, things worked much better. That's the system we have today—the Web.

"The Web interacts *directly* with our brain waves. That's

how come virtuality is indistinguishable from Outside—our brains experience both exactly the same way. As far as our brains are concerned, there is technically no difference.

"On a system-wide level, our thought patterns become part of the Web, and the Web becomes a part of our thought patterns."

"I guess I understand that."

"So don't you see what that means?"

Carver shook his head. "No, I don't. What?"

David T. was shaking with caffeine-driven excitement. "Your routine alters the way the coil works. You're not just programming what the user experiences, you're changing *how* he experiences it."

Carver was still confused. "But that's what directing is all about."

David T. shook his head and leapt to his feet with excitement. "No, you still don't get it. Your routine fucks with the interface between the program and the brain. The effect is created at exactly the point where the user interacts with the system. At that point, the Web and the user are functionally inseparable. This isn't subliminal—it isn't *suggestive*. Don't you see? What you've done doesn't interact with thought patterns, it interacts directly with the user's *brain*. You are literally changing people's minds! Literally. You're not programming the Web, you're programming *people*!"

Carver sat back, blinking at David T. as he tried to absorb this overwhelming influx of data. "No," he said. "That . . . no. I don't see why it should be any different. It's still the Web, it should still work the same. My routine is just more direct, so you're not necessarily aware of the process."

"It's much more direct than normal," David T. replied, "but it's not the same thing at all. The Web is a stochastic neural network system. It's all sort of guesswork. It's like if you have a stream, instead of following a straight path downhill, it curves around, turning this way and that, going around obstacles or high points, always seeking out the easiest route, the minimal-energy route. But you've bypassed all that, the stochastic process. You've taken a fucking bulldozer to the brain, man. The water isn't finding its own meandering way anymore—you've gone and carved a trench straight down the hill. It's not a stream anymore. You've turned it into a canal. Instead of leaving it all up to experience, you're creating permanent changes in neurological structure in a much more immediate way."

He sagged suddenly and rubbed his tired eyes. "What you have here," he told Carver, "isn't a subliminal program. It's a way to reengineer the human brain."

SEVENTEEN

"Well, I guess it really is a good thing we took you in," Selene said after David T. had explained the nature of his discovery to the Young Pioneers. "There's no telling what would have happened if Byrd had found this out." She sat beside Carver, the only other Pioneer besides David T. physically present for the discussion.

He still could as long as Carver's alive.

Carver grokked the identity underlying that thought; it came from an older man named Kurmiya, one of the few Pioneers he hadn't met.

And David T., for that matter.

Selene accompanied her question, *So what do you propose we do?* with an image of Carver and David T. hanging from gallows.

Laughter rippled through the System.

The past already is. Jenny's thought carried resolution rather than resignation. *We should accept that and move on, optimize instead of pessimize.*

Agreement and uncertainty blossomed across the System, surging against one another with greater or lesser force as the argument progressed, each emotion tagged with the vaguest hint of the individual's personality. After only a few seconds the uncertainty evaporated. Carver, however, kept his thoughts to himself. He still felt like an outsider here, and his mistrust of the Young Pioneers had increased since they gained access to the awesome power of his program.

Well then, Selene thought, *the question now is how do we optimize?* She cast out conflicting possibilities: maintaining their secret, to keep from anyone else the chance to unlock it, butted against the advantages of spreading Carver's routine throughout the Web; while between these two oppositions she left the question of using it only in emergency situations. Carver was so fascinated by her ability to convey so much in wordless thought that he missed the substance of the question she directed at David T. and him.

David T. did not speak, but Carver could see his eyes flit back and forth across Newnan's Lake as he sent his thoughts into the System: *The only thing I'm sure of right now is that any effect will take repeated exposure. We're not going to change the world with one Disney. But it is pretty fucking amazing . . . Memories are too holographic to change them without scrambling the whole wetware. Other than that, it's pretty wide open, I think.*

Carver felt a query brush at his mind, but he ignored it, and David T. continued without pausing.

The more specific or complex you want to get, the less effective it'll be, and anything real specific—like, I don't know, making someone touch their nose every time they hear the word "bucket"—will take a lot of exposure. But something fairly general and not too involved ought to kick ass. Something like giving folks a general predisposition to our ideals, just like Carver did. Yeah. What do you think, Carver, man?

"I think this is a dangerous conversation to be having. If what David T. says is true, this could be used not only to create nifty programs or to teach, but also to *control.* It's not just the FCA who would be dangerous with that sort of power. I mean, we're talking about possibly altering someone's thoughts, the way they think. Their personality. We're talking about arbitrarily changing *who* someone is. What right do you have to do that?"

Only an indistinct wondering flowed through the System until Feargal speared at Carver a thought that was painfully clear. *What right did you have to do it in The Metamorphosis?*

It was the question Quadie had asked him in the medieval pub. "That was different. I was—" He stopped abruptly. What *had* he been doing? Making an artistic statement? The Young Pioneers wouldn't accept that as an answer. Carver was no longer sure if he could accept it. He thought back to his conversation with Quadie, but he could only recall his friend's arguments. His own rationalizations were gone. *I'm not trying to change the world. Just the way people experience it.* Did art really give him that right? Not anymore. It sounded too grandiose, too pompous, and at its heart it was a purely subjective stance. After all, the Young Pioneers thought what they wanted was best for humanity, too.

Maybe they were right.

It's not as much a matter of what's best for humanity— Panic flooded Carver's mind, squelching the end of Selene's thought. Hints of amusement swam to him through the System, but Selene fed him reassuring calm. "It didn't really feel like you'd meant to share all that," she told him aloud, "but it's okay. You'll learn to control that soon enough." *But getting back to our discussion, I really do think your routine could significantly ease the transition.*

"What transition?"

Western society has always been very rational and logical, always wanting to understand everything, needing to explain. But this is a sociological dead end. Viewing the world only in terms of the rational, limits you to understanding things only in terms of what is currently known—and if those base assumptions turn out to be wrong, you're up a tree without a paddle.

"Up a tree . . . ?"

Look at the Copernican revolution. Heliocentrism was a far better, simpler, more elegant theory than what they had before, but it wasn't rational—after all, we can see the sun move across the sky, while the earth seems pretty fucking rooted in place. Heliocentrism challenged all the accepted, most basic assumptions about the world, and that scares people. It's very disruptive, psychically. Most people are addicted to their beliefs, and go through withdrawal if they try to change them. So even though heliocentrism was a better theory—it was right, for chrissakes!—people fought it tooth and nail. People were killed over it. Any kind of major paradigm shift like that is bound to cause a lot of conflict and suffering.

While Selene chattered in his mind, Carver poured himself another cup of coffee and took a large bite out of a muffin. Although he wore his headset and was tuned-in to the System, he was still uncomfortable with the new mode of communication and did not take advantage of it. He chewed the muffin slowly and swallowed, following it with a sip of coffee. When his mouth was clear, he said aloud, "I understand that. Is there a relevant point?"

Our concept of reality isn't fashioned only by our physical experience, but also by our societally influenced interpretation of what reality is.

Shade took over with an image of a Native American spirit dance. *For instance, if someone eats psychedelic mushrooms or peyote or something like that, she'll have visions. Native tribes, shamanistic cultures, view these experiences as revelations from gods or communion with natural spirits. Mescalito and so forth. By accepting them as real—not necessarily a part of the physical world, but real nonetheless—they can use those experiences therapeutically, learn from them, apply them to the problems of daily life.*

But Western society, grounded as it is in the material world, dismisses these experiences as hallucinations, illusions. The spirits in Carver's mind popped like bubbles, and the dancer abruptly turned into Sigmund Freud, lying on a leather couch playing with his beard. *It downgrades their importance, denies their power on the psyche by saying they're not real.*

And it treats the Web exactly the same way.

"The Web is our culture now," David T., beside Carver,

said. "It's here to stay unless *everything* falls apart. But society's going to fall apart if it doesn't rewire its logic. Three-quarters of the people on this Continent work in the Web, did you know that? And almost everyone spends more waking hours in the Web than they do Outside. A major paradigm shift is on its way, and this society is going to have to change or die. That transition is going to bring a fuck of a lot of conflict with it. A lot of people won't survive—like your wife."

C.A.'s thoughts eased gently into Carver's mind. *Your program could save a lot of suffering, Carver. You could help a lot of people, make everything better. Help people accept the changes that are coming, make them better able to deal with the new paradigms. Isn't that what you want? Isn't that why you create programs, to help people see the world differently?*

"Yes, but . . . I don't know. I need to think about it. I feel like I'm being railroaded here."

"Take all the time you need," Selene told him. "I'm sorry if we're going too fast, but this is the kind of opportunity we've been looking for for many years. But realize that if we decide this is something we need to do, we'll use it whether you approve or not. I don't mean to seem threatening, but that's how it is."

Yes, Carver thought to himself, *that's how it is*. His entire life was out of control—had been for the last two months. And now control was being taken from him. The Young Pioneers wanted to take the routine he had tried so hard to keep as his own and use it for their own purposes.

Purposes which were, as C.A. had pointed out, very close to his own. So why fight the inevitable? If he worked with them, he would at least stand a chance of maintaining some control over the situation.

No, I don't need any time. I'm with you.

A hard edge of excitement thrilled through the System.

But only if you consult me before doing anything.

Of course. Everyone shares in decisions here.

The meeting ended, Carver stood and wandered to the Webworld. "Let's go to One twelve," he told God when he tuned-in. "I need to leave Quadie and Jan a note."

Carver manifested in Network 112. As he stepped away from the entrance field and started down the hill, he noticed his appearance. His warrior's accoutrements were the same as those he'd worn on his first visit—a standardized default image, he decided. Using that image was begging the same kind of unwanted attention he'd attracted the last time, so in spite of David T.'s warning against incurring special charges, Carver requested the Network's main menu.

He withdrew the ornate vellum scroll that manifested in his pack. Scanning the list, he read aloud, "Personal Effects." The menu vanished in a flash of gold magic, replaced by a new listing. Carver quickly selected a charcoal robe with a matching separate hood, tooled leather boots, and a wide sash of woven silk. Satisfied with the cheap ensemble's anonymity, he clicked to the Jerusalem. He hoped none of the pub's denizens would recognize his face.

Mistress Quickly's patrons all watched Carver as he walked in, but quickly returned to their conversations. Only one brawny reveler scrutinized Carver with any interest, but an imperious magical gesture from Carver convinced the man that his ale was more worthy of consideration.

Carver walked to the stone wall. Withdrawing a coin from his purse, he switched off the signal modulation to reveal his ID pattern and asked, "Has anyone left a message for me?"

The coin vanished from between his fingers, and Quadie's voice spoke from the wall.

"Mate, I hope this is what you meant, and I hope you get this. You don't know how fucking worried Jan and I are about you right now. I'll check here once a day, so please let us know what's your data. If there are any developments on this side of the law, we'll let you know. Goddammit, Carv, I'm supposed to be the fuck-up, not you. Be careful, okay?"

Carver took out another coin. "Private message."

"*Speak.*"

"I'm fine, Quadie and Jan, so there's no reason to worry. If it weren't for the FCA, I'd be perfect. Jan, see what you can do about them, but don't believe a word they say. They want something of mine that I've just found out would be extremely dangerous in their hands. I can't let them get it, but they won't leave me alone until they do. It would be much too valuable to them. I've got some help, uh, here on my side, but please see what you guys can do legally, okay? I'll try to leave you updates every day, but don't panic if I miss a time or two. I love you both. End message."

He attached both Quadie's and Jan's addresses to his message and then he tuned-out.

Selene was waiting for him, sitting cross-legged on the adjacent set. Though she wore a calm expression, her eyes betrayed a certain discord.

"What's the data?" he asked.

She handed him his headset. "News of the world."

They both stood and walked outside. "What news?"

"You. Word of your disappearance is out. It's hit every 'board. Big story. There are conflicting reports as to whether the FCA has you in custody or not, but everybody knows they're involved." She cracked a smile. "Except for those tabs that say you've really been kidnapped by UFOs or Bigfoots and the FCA thing is just a cover-up."

"Has the Agency said anything?"

"Oh, you bet. Officially, you're wanted for the Network Thirty-seven hack."

"That's ridiculous!"

"Of course it is, but only you and the FCA and whoever really hacked it knows that. The people who did it aren't exactly going to come forward, so it's your word against the Agency's. And this way, they don't have to let anyone else know about your toy."

"So the only way I can really defend myself is to reveal the truth behind my routine, show that I couldn't have used it to hack—which they know full well I don't want to do."

"Exactly. They've got you, and they know it."

He stumbled over to the wall and sagged against it. He bumped his head back against the cinder blocks, closing his eyes against the blinding warmth of the sun. "So where does *that* leave me?"

Selene took his hand in hers and squeezed reassuringly. "That leaves you right here with us, Carver, for as long as you need to stay—or as long as you want to."

Carver opened his eyes. "Thank you." He tried to smile, but failed, so he just started walking again, still without direction. "Thank you."

Selene released his hand and instead slapped him on the back. "You are welcome to stay here with us, but not as a guest. As long as you stay, it will be as one of us. You'll have your say in our affairs, but you'll also be expected to pull your own weight."

"I don't think there's much I can do, but I'll gladly do whatever you want me to. It's only fair."

"You'll do whatever *you* want to do. And I can think of at least one thing you can do better than anyone else here," she said, a sly grin lighting her face. "But if you're not careful, you just might find yourself enjoying it."

Prepackaged emotions and state-of-consciousness routines had been some of the first private programs available in the Web, and their use remained widespread. They were of little value by themselves, but usually ran as background routines, coloring the user's perceptions while he or she tuned-in a Network or specific major program. A user could be happy or excited or madly in love or terrified or angry at whim. They were cheap, simple, and usually very effective.

Usually. Now, though, Quadie's anger was too deep and strong to be glossed over by his relaxer. Anger was an unhealthy emotion in the Web unless it had a context within a program—anything that interfered with clear thought processes diminished one's effectiveness—but right now Quadie couldn't help himself. He felt incredibly stupid and foolish and betrayed—all emotions that led quite easily to anger.

He burst into TJ's and scanned immediately for Var, but didn't find the boy. Quadie sat down at the nearest table, exasperated. What had he been thinking when he hired a hacker? They were criminals, and they couldn't be trusted. They didn't even trust each other. He hadn't even gotten the kid's ID.

"What's the data, sweetie?" a pleasant baritone asked. "I'm getting some *bad* vibes from you today."

Quadie turned to see Willie standing behind him. "I really am not in the mood."

TJ quickly took Willie's place and sat down across from Quadie. "What is it?"

"I need to find that weasel Var. You have his ID?"

TJ leaned back and put her hands up before her. "Whoa, Quadie. You know I can't do that. All business here is strictly confidential. I never get involved in my customers' business, you know that. That's why I have the reputation I do, and I don't risk that for *anyone*."

"The little fucker just sold me out, TJ."

"You accepted the risks when you made the deal, babe. You should have known that. Var is my friend. You used to be. I wouldn't touch this one even if I could." She shook her head and stood, morphing back into Willie as she did so. "You've been away too long, Quadie. You just don't belong here anymore."

Quadie watched Willie go in silence. It was true—he didn't belong here. How had everything changed so much? The Web was supposed to be what you made of it, but it all seemed way out of his control now. One twelve had a different protocol, he didn't belong at TJ's anymore, TJ had changed—even his best friend had changed drastically.

Or was it he who was changing?

"Why the hell am I thinking about this?" Quadie asked himself aloud. "I'm going as loopy as Carver. What the hell is wrong with me?"

He stood up to leave, but as he approached the door, a tall, heavily scarred black man dressed in camouflage fatigues fell into step beside him. Thick dreadlocks sprouted from beneath his camouflage cap.

"You looking for Var, brah?" he asked in a thick Jamaican accent.

Quadie looked at the man. "Cute image. Sorry, mate, but I've had all the bullshit I can take for one day."

"Hey, no gigo, man. You want the ID, I got it. Simple enough."

"You have his ID?" Quadie stopped. "All right, what do you want for it?"

The mercenary laughed. "Simple, like I say. Half a K not hurt you too much, nah?"

Quadie thought quickly. Five hundred dollars wasn't exactly petty change, even to a millionaire. But it was a small price to pay to find Var, and it was a better option than waiting for God knew how long at TJ's for the motherfucker to show up.

"How do I know you're not just scamming me?"

The man threw his head back and laughed so loudly that everyone in TJ's turned to look. "Look at me, brah," he said, his speech rolling with syncopated cadence. "I'm a mercenary, nah? A trader. Buy and sell, man. I screw you, word get around, nobody deal with me no more. Screw you, I screw myself. It all reputation. You understand reputation, nah?"

"All right, then," Quadie said. "But you fuck with me and I'll make sure *everybody* knows it."

The mercenary laughed again and held out his hand. "That's a deal, brah."

Quadie shook the man's hand and data transferred

between them—Var's ID address from the mercenary to Quadie, and five hundred dollars from Quadie's account to the mercenary's.

"You need anything else, you just ask for me, brah, Soldier Ras."

"Thanks."

"My pleasure, brah. Blaze your trail."

"Whatever," Quadie said as he left TJ's.

Once outside in the Network proper, Quadie accessed Var's ID and clicked. After a brief pause he appeared in a small, fairly plain interface manifesting as a cube only a few meters on a side, each face a video screen displaying something different. Var floated in the center. His head was swollen and distorted to sport three faces, each of which watched one of the screens.

"Well, well. It's Mr. Big-time. You found me—good hack."

"Cut the shit, you son of a bitch. I thought we had a deal."

Var's three faces merged into one as he turned his attention fully on Quadie. "We do. What the fuck's your problem?"

"I told you that data about Carver was confidential. Now suddenly it's all over the Web. How much did you get for it?"

"Get for what? I didn't leak to nobody. Calm your fucking ass *down*, man."

"I didn't let it out, and neither did Jan. No one else knew except you and the FCA—and they sure as hell don't have a security problem." Quadie approached Var, his fists balled up and ready to strike. "That only leaves you."

"Hey, hold on, man." Var held his ground and froze Quadie's image, halting his advance. "I'm telling you I haven't done anything, no fuck. I mean, I've been working for you, yeah fuck, but I haven't blabbed."

"Then how did this data get out?"

"How should I know? Maybe Blervaque's friends. Maybe Blervaque." He manifested a leather motorcycle jacket and shrugged into it, turning the collar up for extra effect. "Maybe someone just found out. He is kind of well-known, you know. People are going to want to know about anything he does, you know? It was bound to get out, especially after *Metamorphosis* got fuzzed." A clove cigarette appeared in his mouth. He inhaled deeply, then blew a perfect smoke ring. "Listen, Newman, I'll be honest. Your deal is worth way more to me than what I could get spec'ing tips to 'boards. Yeah fuck, I'm working for you, honest and straight up."

Quadie faltered. "Yeah? Maybe you're right. I don't know. Hey, I'm sorry, Var. I guess I overreacted. But when I found out, you know . . . ?"

"Ah, don't worry about it. So we're still working together, right?"

Quadie looked at Var, then around the interface. It was rudimentary enough to prove that Var's resources were limited. Still, it was fairly imaginative for its scope—especially the image modification—and Quadie recalled that Var had been the only pirate at TJ's who'd been able to hack him. He didn't doubt that Var had promise. If the kid was still somewhat new to the game, he wouldn't be well-known—which could be an asset. Yes, it would definitely be an advantage to keep Var on retainer.

"Yeah," Quadie said at last. "Yeah, we're still working together. I want you to keep a low profile about this, but if you find anything out, you let me know right away. Understand?"

Var smiled. "Sure. You got it. Whatever you say. But hey—what about the other side?"

"I'll make it worth your time," Quadie promised.

"Good. How?"

"I'll let you know when you find something out."

Carver began his new occupation the next day. He was not overly fond of children—a fact that had fostered untold arguments with Rose, who'd wanted a large family—and he'd never taught before, but after a few days he warmed to his job teaching programming fundamentals.

He still had no intention of staying at the Frontier indefinitely, so he didn't bother to plan a course of instruction. Instead he retired to his set at the Webworld after breakfast each day and tutored anyone who tuned-in. Of the thirty-eight children living at the Frontier, thirty showed up every day. River, of course, was foremost among them.

In the end Carver learned more from the children than he taught them. Just as the Web had always been a part of his life, these kids had grown up in the System. But where he'd learned to use the Web as a tool to expedite or enhance reality, these children thought of their System as an integral component of natural reality—a separate-but-equal flipside, an internal analog that had no effect on the Outside except through interfaced mechanisms such as the motors and solenoids on doors.

Through his work with the children he also learned more of the Young Pioneers' jargon. He had thought it mere slang until Shade explained it to him.

"Language and culture are intertwined," Shade told him one evening as they sat together on the dock drinking beer and watching the sun set. "If we want to build a new society, we need a new language to go with it."

"Why?"

"Well, for instance, the Hopi Indians didn't view time as a continuous flow of events. That's actually a fairly modern development, courtesy of Western science. Because of their cultural outlook, the Hopis didn't have words for concepts like past, present, and future, or anything like that. Now, if you met a Hopi and wanted to explain to him how time works—excuse me, how *you* think time works—how would you do it? See, there literally aren't words for the very fundamental concepts you want to describe to him. And because of the way our minds work, it's hard to fully understand something you can't describe. At least, it is in Western societies.

"Now, think of what we're doing here. Our System is functionally no different from the Web, yet we grok. Why isn't that done in the Web? All your virtual communication in the Web is verbal—well, *conceptually* verbal. You know what I mean. Now, why is that?"

Either despite or because of two large bottles of the Young Pioneers' home-brewed ale, Carver understood. "Because we don't have the components in the English language to express those concepts?"

"Exactly! And if you can't express, you can't comprehend. The kids here grow up grokking, so it makes sense to call it something simple like 'grokking' instead of 'direct mind-to-mind communication of emotion and complex nonverbal conceptualization' or whatever. Instead of using all those semantical gymnastics to describe new concepts or nuances of old ones, we just come up with a new word. It makes things a lot easier."

Carver had many such conversations as the days slipped by. In the afternoons he helped out in the gardens, the rough, physical labor and the feel of loam on his skin bringing to his mind a clarity long absent. There, he learned practical skills and discussed practical matters, but once night fell, the talk became more lighthearted. Gradually Carver began to relax and accept the Young Pioneers, as they accepted him.

On his sixth night at the Frontier, C.A. stole into his bed just as he was falling asleep. This time he did not turn her away.

He checked the 'boards several times every day, and traded messages with Jan and Quadie. It seemed that everyone on the Continent was looking for him, half trying to save him, the rest convinced of his guilt in any number of plots and schemes, believable or not. Jan was working with lawyers, while Quadie had hinted that he was exploring certain other avenues, but the monolithic bureaucracy of the FCA reacted far more slowly than the forces of speculative journalism.

One day in the gardens, an upsetting thought occurred to Carver. According to the Young Pioneers, Captain Byrd's Security Research Project was headquartered in Atlanta. Yet Byrd had arrived at his house within minutes of the report of the burglary. This was, of course, simply not possible—unless Byrd had for some reason already been in Gainesville.

But what could that reason be? Carver had a terrible suspicion he knew.

Byrd had seemed much too interested in the *Metamorphosis* routine. He'd said it was his job to make sure nothing threatened the Web or the country. Had Byrd, then, been the one to pirate his matrix, and when nothing useful turned up there, driven to Gainesville and committed the burglary? Any other explanation relied too much on coincidence. Why else would Byrd himself come so far just to investigate a routine burglary?

Determined to investigate this further, Carver took to exploring the Web and the Young Pioneers' System, looking for any data that might prove or disprove his theory. He was not so naive, of course, to think that he might find some evidence to directly implicate Captain Byrd and the FCA, but he did hope to find news that the FCA had leads or perhaps even real suspects in the piracy.

They did not—at least, not that Carver could determine on the sly. However, through his wanderings across the System and the Web, he found dozens of other groups of the Young Pioneers all across the Continent. He tuned people in several of these groups; through them, and through his own snooping into the System, he became acquainted with a wide variety of people on the fringes of technological society—Freeks, hacks, and others whose activities could not so easily be categorized.

At first his tunes were little more than random attempts at human contact, a way to keep in touch, however peripherally, with the world from which he'd been cut off. But gradually, as he learned his way around and met more people, Carver began to work with a purpose, and he directed his explorations toward the gathering of data—data he kept in a private workspace within the set he used. He told no one of his work, not even C.A. And especially not Selene.

Carver fell inevitably into routine as February warmed into March. To fill his idle moments, he took to browsing through the library. One day, shortly after lunch, his reading was disturbed by an especially raucous game on the tarmac. He tried to ignore the noise, but it was too much, so he gave up on his book and went out to watch the game.

The children were kicking a soccer ball around, but Carver soon saw that they were playing an altogether different game. There were no goals, and there seemed to be only one team.

Some sort of noncompetitive game, Carver decided after a few minutes. Typical of the Young Pioneers. He watched fascinated as the game progressed. After certain maneuvers, generally requiring a high degree of cooperation from a number of players, everyone would cheer.

It quickly became evident that much of the game was being played virtually. Carver dipped into the System area encompassing the game and tried to make sense of it.

Apparently, six or eight players at a time were chosen at random to be "it." These players closed their eyes and tried to guide the ball through a virtual obstacle course, guided only by the visual input from the others. Cooperation was essential, not only among the players who were "it," but also among the remainder who became their guiding senses. The continual shouting from the constantly moving field of players, Carver discovered when he closed his own eyes and grokked the game, served to disorient the blinded players—in effect, making the game more challenging.

Keeping his eyes closed, Carver became engrossed. As

game tasks were completed, new players were chosen to be "it," and new maneuvers were required. With each change, the sensory gestalt morphed, evolving to reflect the new situation. At first these switches unnerved Carver, but he soon learned to anticipate them, and even became reasonably successful at predicting the new arrangement. It almost felt like he was watching the same scene through a variety of viewpoints, through a different person's eyes—or rather, through a different person's *experience*.

Fingers tickled at the bare scalp around the edges of Carver's headset. He opened his eyes and saw Selene and River.

"Having fun?"

"Hi, Seli. Hey, Riv. I'm just watching the game and . . . thinking."

"Thinking?" Seli tried to hide a smile. "Uh-oh. I don't like how that sounds. It's put a strange look in your eye. Just what are you thinking about?"

Carver ignored her and looked instead at the boy. "How are you enjoying programming class, River?"

The boy beamed, setting off fireworks of enthusiasm in Carver's thoughts.

"Think you're ready to start trying some *real* work? I need an assistant for something."

River nodded vigorously, a thread of uncertainty barely dimming his excitement.

"What are you up to?" Selene asked

Carver stood beside her. "Promise you won't tell anyone?"

She laughed and rubbed her headset. "Oh, sure. Not a soul."

He leaned close and said in a stage whisper loud enough for River to hear, "I think it's time for me to start work on a new program."

PART 3

EIGHTEEN

Jan turned her interference suppressor up four more points. She felt no pain—the set blocked all somatic input—but her headache had interfered with her concentration, making it hard to think, and that effect did carry over into the Web.

She manifested in a distant corner of Quadie's expansive interface, colorbursts of diaphanous fractal data eddying softly in the air around her.

"Quadie? Are you here?"

"Hold on." The fractals froze, their colors solidifying, then the shapes began to recede, collapsing toward the center of the room. The data shrunk down to a globe two meters in diameter, at which point it disappeared, revealing Quadie standing at the eye of the storm.

"How are you, Jan?"

"Oh, I'm fine," she said automatically, but she paused, then said, "No, I'm not. That's why I'm here. What was all that?"

"My new program. Remember that Impressionist experiment from a few weeks ago?"

"Uh-huh." That had been the day Carver disappeared. How could she possibly forget it?

"It's about two-thirds done now." A pair of chaise lounges

manifested, and Quadie motioned for her to sit. "I was just correlating some data tracks and locking down the hyperstructure before I add all the little niggly details and stuff."

Jan did not recline, but sat nervously on the edge of the couch. "I see. When do you expect to have it finished?"

Quadie shrugged. "Today. A couple more hours. My target release date is next Saturday—the first of April."

Jan nodded solemnly, steepling her fingers. "Well, good luck with it. Too bad your timing is so unfortunate."

"What, April Fool's Day? That's the whole point! You see, I've got this—"

"That's not what I meant."

"What, then?"

"Competition."

"Competition? What competition?"

"*Faces.*"

"New program? Who by?"

She looked down at the gray marble floor, then took a deep breath and fixed a riveting look on Quadie. "Carver."

"What? A new program? Little bite or full-length?"

"Full-length."

"He hasn't said anything about it."

"No, he didn't tell me, either. Apparently he's only been working on it for the last couple weeks or so. He started it after he . . . disappeared."

"A couple of weeks? That overachieving workaholic."

"I don't know that he's had much else to do with his time."

Quadie rolled onto his back. "Point. Wait a minute. Where did he make it? How did he get access to a set? I thought he only had headset access through his Freek friends."

"I don't know, Quadie, but it's definitely Carver's work."

"What's it like?"

"You'll see for yourself when you tune it."

"Where is it?"

"In my office. He hid it there sometime last night, I guess.
I don't have a clue how. It was just *there* when I tuned-in
today, coded only to you and me. My agent didn't even
know it was there!"

"So is there anything . . . weird about this one?"

Jan stood and walked to the edge of the floor. Beyond,
dinosaurs and mythical sea beasts swam through a luminous
green sea, occasionally munching on kelp, or fish, or one
another.

"I don't know. I mean, yes, it's got something like what he
did in *The Metamorphosis*, but, well, I don't know."

"Are you all right, Jan?"

She laughed, a short, cynical bark. "I don't know that,
either. I can't explain it, Quadie. You just . . . you have to
tune it yourself."

"Okay. Let me take care of my body first, then I'll see you
in your office."

Quadie stood on a cobbled street, the gently rounded stones
glistening with the slick of a recent rain, his breath steaming
in the cold, damp air. He drew the collar of his heavy wool
frock coat close about his unprotected throat and inspected
his surroundings.

The shops along either side of the narrow street were all
closed, dark and empty. Rising above the storefronts, tower-
ing over the street and all but blocking out his view of the
leaden sky that hung low overhead, half-timbered upper stories offered no hint of occupation.

Quadie searched, but found no manipulation of his emotions; his reaction to this utter solitude—relief, excitement,
with a background note of sinister—was wholly his own.

He laughed out loud, the sound thudding dully along the
avenue, dying away before the clammy stones could thrust
back any echo. This program began so differently from *The*

Metamorphosis. He had expected another tricky start-up, a breath-taking punch in the gut to immediately submerge the user in the program, but instead—nothing.

And yet, Quadie knew Carver too well, and knew his style. Carver rarely went Disney, but his programs always packed a punch, even without that shit he'd done in *Metamorphosis.* This was too simple. It had to be a setup for some big surprise later on. Had to be, judging by Jan's reaction.

One end of the street opened on what appeared to be a large plaza, perhaps the center of Carver's town. At the other end the cobblestones passed beneath a high stone arch to a crossing avenue. Quadie walked toward the latter, his hob-nailed boots clattering over the road.

He turned left under the arch onto what was in fact only an alleyway. Here the stone walls rose without mitigation to the upper story, where thick rough-hewn beams, grayed from age and weather, rose like prison bars through cracked whitewashed daub to meet the peaked thatch roofs. Overhead, the clouds mottled, thinned, and a pale shaft of sunlight broke through, setting fires within the puddles in the street but lending no warmth to the day.

The air carried the scents of a downpour too early to be called spring rain. Quadie sucked in a deep breath, icy enough to make his lungs hurt, but ozone masked any odors that might have given him a clue to his location—seaside, farm land, deep forest, moors. The architecture looked distinctly European, probably English, of three or four centuries past, but that really meant nothing. Aside from his footsteps and the rustling of his clothes as he walked, there was no sound. Judging from the angle and quality of the light, Quadie assumed it was early morning. The alley offered no more clues than these.

As he neared the end of the alleyway, a shape detached from the corner of the building, resolving out of shadow into human form. Quadie's first thought was to pump this person for data about the program, but he quickly changed his mind.

He could see now that it was an old woman, plump and raggedly dressed. She sat on the curb at the street corner, doubled over, her forearms resting on her thighs, her face buried in her hands. At first Quadie thought she might be sobbing, but within the unwashed black sack dress her body shook only to the steady rhythms of regular breathing. Occasionally a sigh, weary and forlorn, escaped from the hidden face.

Whatever Carver intended with this woman, Quadie did not want to test that experience now. He was worried about Carver, and Jan's reaction to this program had done anything but put him at ease. The last thing he wanted right now was a hassle with some beggar woman.

He kept his silence and slowed, walking carefully to keep his footsteps quiet. But the alley was too still and sullen in its emptiness. It captured the clop of his boots on the stones and threw the noise out at the walls, oppressively high and close, so that the clattering bounced back and forth between them, echoing down the alley toward the old woman.

Quadie stopped dead in his tracks, horror rooting him where he stood, for when the woman straightened abruptly, startled by his approach, she sat up quickly, too quickly, before her face could withdraw from the bowl of her palms.

Quadie stood staring at the hollow mask her head left behind, iridescent ridges of personality carved into the inside of that orphaned face.

The woman stood, her ancient joints popping audibly from the effort. Quadie fought to keep his gaze fixed on that terrible sight cupped in the outstretched hands like an alms bowl, for in spite of his revulsion, the thought of seeing that head stripped free of its face terrified him so much more.

But she began to move toward him, her body swaying

with each shuffling step, and some inner force of morbid fascination tugged at his eyes, twitching them up to meet the faceless head.

For an agonizing, infinite instant it held his attention captive, the marbled red and gray surface glistening, bloodless and devoid of any recognizable human feature except for the gaping, lipless mouth, a silent flailing tongue visible occasionally within the dark cavity. Then, with an indescribable effort, Quadie forced his body into motion.

He took one step backward, away from the flayed head and its separate face, but his heel caught on the uneven stones of the street and he stumbled, falling against the wall. Rough stone and mortar scraped the skin from his palm. His hand stung from grit and water. When he looked up, the old woman was there before him, reaching out, her empty, hollow face held like a mask, pressing forward to his own. He tried again to run, but the wall held him against escape.

The woman slipped her face over his, and Quadie screamed.

Sal screamed and backed away toward the open street. The man had scared her, sneaking up from the alley like that, but his stealth hadn't been half as bad as the sight of him. It weren't his size, nor even his hair, short and white and standing up like a madman's, but a flash of lightning that streaked across the left side of his face. No painted or tattooed design, the bolt flickered with an evil blue-white burn, causing demon-runes to star his pupils, deep and black as hell itself. Sal waved a hasty sign of protection as she hobbled out into Redburn Street.

She wouldn't dare a look back for fear of magic, but something about the stranger troubled her far deeper than his threatening appearance. He looked familiar to her somehow, and she had a feeling she should know him. Even his name sat at the tip of her tongue.

She forced the thought from her mind. She'd have no acquaintance with anyone who knew as much magic. Moving along the edge of traffic, she let the scents and sounds enfold her in the familiarity of a day's normal business.

Sal wiped her nose on her grimy sleeve and ran her fingers through her hair, then like a cat licked the sides of her hands and pawed at her face, hoping to rub away the worst of the dirt. If she were lucky, it might also pull a bit of color into her cheeks.

She drifted from person to person as she wandered down the street, but each and every soul studiously avoided her pleading gaze. She was at an awkward age for a beggar woman, was Sal—the beauty of her youth had long since fled her face and figure, but she wasn't yet time-ravaged enough for pity alone to bring her money for bread and beer.

"Could you spare a few pennies for a poor old woman?" she asked time and again, but never received more of an answer than a mumbled "Sorry" as her quarry shouldered away from her through the crowd. She'd gone without breakfast that day, and would go without her supper to boot if she didn't improve her take.

How much easier it all was when I were a young, pretty girl, Sal mused bitterly. She'd wanted for nothing then, nor could she even have dreamed of any fancy, any chimera, but some young buck would promise it for her. In those days there'd always been a man to buy her dinner, to buy her drinks or dresses, to keep her in a small though very posh flat. And if not all her nights were spent there—nor all her nights there spent alone—well, the gentlemen weren't the only ones who took their pleasures from it.

She caught herself smiling at the memories, but once she realized this, her smile disappeared. They'd been happy times, sure, but that happiness was gone now, shriveled as her beauty, and her present situation only magnified the bitterness.

The crowd at Morrisey's was thin, usually a good time for Sal, but before she'd even shuffled through the door, the portly old butcher was threatening her with his bloody cleaver, and the woman nearest the entrance quickly shoved the door closed, very nearly bashing Sal's forehead. She almost spat on the glass, but turned away instead. She'd wasted enough of herself on that lout, and pride would let her spend no more. In middle years, when her waning charms had forced her to be less discriminating in her choices, she'd briefly befriended the man, already with a stomach that strained against his apron though he was still but his father's assistant then, and with the drooping eyelid gained in a childhood fall, but with money enough for her. His father found out, though, and after two weeks the young butcher left her with no more thanks for her kindnesses but the itch.

She'd had charms, for sure, but while they brought her much admiring from men, she'd received only jealousy from other girls. Lies and rumors against her they'd all spread, whispering poisons to the men so that in the end though any man would have her for a night or a week or a month, none would have her for a wife.

And now her bewitchment had died away, never to return, and what had once been given to her freely she now groveled for, and instead of a rich bed with a satin canopy, she slept in alleyways or beside hedgerows. And though the whole town knew of her, none knew her anymore, or cared. The only magic she had ever had was gone, and now out of spite the world beat her down with its own magic—its wild and ungovernable magic, which she hated.

A tattoo of hooves on stone and the rattling of carriage wheels and harness drew her back to the street. Echoes disguised its direction, but she thought it more likely that a coach would travel Atkins Road then Crowsbeak Lane, so she rushed forward as fast as she could. Anyone riding here in a coach was likely to be a visitor to town, and therefore more inclined than locals to throw a few coins to a poor old woman living her last days in husbandless poverty. Sal was a long while from her end, but if she tied her straggly hair into a bun and stooped her shoulders just a bit more . . .

Her instincts proved true. She reached the wide street while the carriage was still a block away. The crowd parted before the horses, and Sal easily pushed her way through. Hunching herself over, she gathered her ratty shawl about herself with one hand and stepped out from the edge of the crowd, cupping the other hand in front of her.

The driver shook the reins to spur his team past her. Undaunted, Sal took another step toward the carriage's path, hoping to attract the occupant's notice. But the driver raised his whip, swiveling his shoulders in her direction as he prepared to strike.

Pressed forward by the crowd, unable to move away, Sal watched the driver flick his wrist. She uttered a foul curse, and in the instant before the whip struck her, she caught and held the driver's gaze . . .

The old architect bowed low as his patron retreated back into the carriage. Though his back trembled with the effort, he held his bow until the horses moved beyond his hearing—limited though that range was now.

He shambled across the piazza, the bright midday sun pleasantly hot over his black cassock and scholar's bonnet. Gathered near the fountain, a knot of young libertine students argued philosophy with clever words and broad, dashing gestures—designed, no doubt, to attract the ladies, who these days drew their bodices so tight they practically pushed their bosoms out of those embroidered puffed-and-slashed gowns. The architect ignored them all, as he did everyone else in the piazza, from the extravagant church officials and nobility to the lower classes huddled in the shadowy alleys. On any other day he would at least have appreciated the ladies, despite his age. But not today.

His thoughts today had room for only one person—his patron. His very generous patron.

It was, the architect knew, the last commission he would receive in this life. Therefore, he would make it his greatest work ever—his grandest, his loftiest, and his most subtle.

His patron's commission was rich indeed, unequaled in its generosity, assuring the old architect great comfort for his remaining years—and yet the price would not be unearned. The proposition was highly unusual, almost bizarre in concept, and so potentially difficult that both men knew that of all the artists known to the world, only one could ever realize such a work.

The old architect hefted his newly filled purse as he climbed the stairs to his garret. His knees and feet cracked aloud with every rising step, but he barely noticed. His mind was too much full of unfolding geometries to worry about the mundane.

He threw open the windows, letting light in. His apartments were small, but comfortable enough for one old man. When he looked up from his drawing table, he could behold Saint Mark's Canal, and beyond that, almost lost to his aged eyes even on a clear day, the site where one day would stand his masterpiece.

His patron, a man of extraordinary vision even for these enlightened times, would build a Temple to Music.

Not a cathedral where liturgical music would glorify God, not a hall for the performance of opera and other secular music, nor even a shrine to Euterpe, the Muse of music, but an edifice constructed to glorify the spirit of the sacred force that was Music.

The proper design of buildings was all a matter of proportions. Even so seemingly inconsequential an element as the entablature of a column glorified proportion, the division of its parts corresponding to the proportions of the human face.

Music, too, was a study of proportion, for harmony arose from sounds that stood in proper relation to one another.

But to discern the underlying proportions, those ratios—those rational relationships—that produced the *concept* of music, and then to apply them to architecture, to the design of a building: therein lay the mystery that only he could illuminate.

The old architect poured himself a glass of anisette and unrolled a fresh, crisp sheet of vellum across his desk. Tasting the liqueur's sweet, stringent burn in his mouth, he held the tiny glass up to the window and watched the thick swirls of clear liquid as he contemplated where and how to begin.

He sighed and took another sip. He had no idea how to reconcile music with architecture.

Taking one last sip, he set the glass on the windowsill. He fitted a new drawing lead to his compass and began where geometry always began. Unity.

He drew a large circle in the center of the parchment. Within, and having their centers on the horizontal diameter, he inscribed two circles of half the original radius, so that they were tangent to the large circle and tangent also to one another at its center.

He paused in his work and regarded the figure he'd drawn. He had always found this figure curious. The inner circles, each having half the diameter of the outer circle, had half its circumference, and a fourth part of its area. Taken together, then, the two had the same total circumference of the one but only half its area. In a way, the curiosity disturbed him. It contradicted intuition. It was not rational.

Afternoon sunshine flooded into the room through the open window, but the architect's eyes, aged and weary as they were, played tricks on him nonetheless. The lines blurred and faded as he stared at them. The bottom half of one inner circle disappeared altogether, as did the upper half of its neighbor, so that the outer circle seemed to be divided in two by a single wavy line. The strange word *yin-yang* came unbidden into his thoughts, but it was a word without meaning for him. Instead, he saw in the two regions bounded by the circle a pair of fish following after one another—Pisces.

Pisces, twelfth and final sign of the zodiac, a sign encompassing the powers of the other eleven—a sign encompassing all else. The most mystical zodiacal sign, Pisces symbolized a coalescence of the theoretical into the actual. Just as did the sacred geometrical process of Squaring the Circle. And in the Squaring of the Circle, the next step was to draw the vesica—one of the Piscean symbols.

The old architect smiled as he bent once more over his desk. It was indeed all coming together. As he had known it would.

Pushing out of his mind the lingering echo of *yin-yang*, he drew the vesica. From the point where the vertical diameter intersected the bottom of the large circle he drew an arc tangent to the upper surfaces of the inner circles. A similar arc swung down from the upper diameter to cradle the inner circles. These two arcs joined one another outside the large circle, along the line of the horizontal diameter.

The region thus formed—the vesica, the union of two overlapping circles—resembled, he realized, the shape of a vibrating string on a musical instrument. He was getting closer.

The points where the upper arc and the vertical diameter intersected the large circle formed three vertices of a pentagon. The architect drew these sides, then to create the rest of the pentagon, he centered his compass on the lower extreme of the vertical diameter and scribed an arc tangent to the lower curves of the smaller circles. Between the two points where this arc cut the outer circle he drew a horizontal line, then the two remaining sides of a perfect pentagon.

Five was the number of Man, with his five fingers and five toes and five senses. And the ratio of side and diagonal in the pentagon produced the Greeks' famous golden mean—the governing principle of classical architecture, and of all beauty.

From the golden mean, a geometric proportion, one could produce both the arithmetic and harmonic proportions, which were the bases for the fundamental divisions of the musical scale.

So the golden mean truly did govern all beauty—visual and musical. The only proportional division possible with just two terms—where the ratio of the smaller term to the larger term equaled the ratio of the larger term to the sum of the two terms—the golden mean also accounted for the fundamental proportions of the human body.

But what did it all mean? The old architect rubbed his eyes. *Yin-yang* still resonated through his thoughts, distracting his concentration. He needed another drink. Another drink would help.

As he reached for his glass, a small pearl-white flower fluttered through the window and fell into the anisette. As it broke the surface tension and sank into the liqueur, the architect noticed that the flower had five petals.

He looked out the window until he saw the tree from which the flower had come. Planted an easy stone's throw from his window he saw an almond tree in full bloom, resplendent with thousands of delicate five-petaled flowers.

He rushed to his sideboard. There, decorating a bowl of oranges, a branch from an orange tree sported several pale flowers, each with five petals. On the opposite wall a painting of idealized agricultural life showed both olive and apricot trees with their quinate flowers.

All plants that bore fruit edible to Man showed flowers

based on the pentagon, on the number five. That could not be mere coincidence. Was the fivefold flower some kind of divine signal to Man, marking his proper foods, or was there some deeper meaning, a more mystical connection between geometry and life?

He looked at his glass. The flower had somehow dissolved. It formed a thick white blob in the clear anisette, the pollen from its center creating a similar but yellow globule. The architect shook the glass, watching the white and yellow swirl into a Piscean shape, spiraling into one another without mixing into the liquid.

Yin-yang, his mind said again, and as he watched the white and yellow chase after one another, meld and separate, it all came clear to him in a lightning flash of insight. Just as the colors of this Piscean *yin-yang* became one another while remaining separate, so was everything connected by the golden mean. That one simple proportion governed art, architecture, music, the human form. It governed all creation. This, his sudden illumination told him, was the secret of the universe—that through the fundamentals of geometry, everything in the universe was connected. All was One. The golden mean was the key to Creation, it was the sublime; it was God. It was magic.

Magic.

The philosophers' stone, alchemy. His heart thudded with the enormity of his discovery. He had to tell someone—he could not contain this knowledge. Without stopping to don his hat, he rushed out of his garret and down the stairs to the piazza.

The students still dominated the fountain. The old architect broke into their circle, babbling in his excitement. The students began to laugh, but he grabbed one young man by the shoulders and shook him as hard as he could. The smile vanished from the philosopher's face as the architect stared into his eyes and began to speak . . .

*   *   *

Minerva rose, and the man slipped out of her, murmuring with pleasure but otherwise lying still; spent, exhausted. Minerva laughed aloud and ran out of the hut into the moonlight.

The night air was cool on her bare, sweaty skin, the man's fluid a warm tickle on her thigh. She laughed again and danced naked under the moon, feeling in the caress of that soft and gentle light the power of the magic within her—the magic that she was.

The scent of flowers wafted sweetly to her nose, the rainbow of colors muted in the dim silver moonglow. Grass, slick with dew, slid by underfoot as she ran.

She could feel the magic of her self growing. The twins she carried kicked and curled about one another. On her left the flowers budded under the moonlight; on her right they withered and died, returning to the earth in their recurrent dance. Ahead of her the world bloomed with the richness of primal life, the force of magic.

A breath of wind chased her heels, ran up her slender legs to her back, colder than the night warranted.

Minerva stopped and turned in time to see winter's dormancy transmute quickly into vibrant summer. Still from behind, the cold breathed on her.

She laughed and twirled about in circles, trying to turn fast enough to catch the magic that lay behind. Lifting her arms away from her sides, she threw her head back and spun faster, faster. Light from moon and stars swirled against darkness like two fish chasing one another in the everlasting dance of eternal creation.

Dizzy, she fell, stretching out full on her back in the snow. Laughing still, she sat up, gasping from her exertions.

In front of her lay a river, its frozen surface dusted velvet with snow. When the world stopped spinning and tilting around her, she stood. She walked to the ice, the freezing air and ground stimulating but causing no discomfort.

Shadow moved beneath her feet. She knelt and brushed snow from the ice with wide sweeps of her forearms.

In the quicksilver pale of the night, through the clear ice, Minerva saw a man lying beneath her in the river. The ice distorted his image so that she could not see more than his general form, though where his face pressed against the undersurface of the ice she could discern blurred features. The river flowed sluggishly past the man, and he moved against it. He was alive.

His mouth gaped open as though he spoke to her, but she could hear nothing more than the river sliding against the ice. She leaned closer to him, and closer still until her breath fogged the ice.

Still she could not hear him or see his eyes, but he was alive, a living part of the living universe, and she loved him as she loved herself and the twins stirring inside her and the frozen river and the dark sky above. She bent farther, until her lips touched the ice above his. She kissed through to him with the love that was her life, true magic, and in that instant she saw deep into his eyes and recognized all that he was . . .

Above, through the ice, Quadie saw only a bleary moon and refracted stars. The icy river flowed all about his naked body, flowed into his mouth and nose, deep into his lungs. He clawed frantically at the ice, but it was too hard for his numb, frozen fingers. He tried to call out for help, but his lungs were filled with water and he could make no sound.

Then everything came back to him.

He screamed with the shock of what had happened to him, but his scream died soundlessly in ice water.

He remembered them all now: crazy Sal, Herbert the chauffeur, his Grace the Archbishop, the old architect, the philosopher Peter, Goren the mystic, Minerva. He remembered them all, remembered living their lives. He recalled clearly the entirety of his experience in Carver's program, and yet he also remembered with exacting clarity the experience of being *only* old Sal, with her resentment and fear of the uncontrollable world around her; of being *only* Minerva, perfectly happy and at peace with the natural force of life. And he recalled each individual along his journey, and knew that throughout the program he had been entirely the individual person within each section—had been only that man or woman in Carver's program. His own self-knowledge had somehow been suspended. He, Quadie, had ceased to be. Carver had stolen his self away.

Before, in *The Metamorphosis*, Carver had subdued the self, laid the user's conscious mind asleep. That in itself had been startling—and unsettling—enough. But now he'd gone so far beyond that. He had created new personalities—not just personae, parts the user played in the program, but new and independent *people*. And most disturbing of all, Carver had forced those personalities onto him, Quadie knew, making him become those other people, with not even a vestige of his real self remaining. It was too much, too much . . .

"Well, what did you think?"

Quadie lurched forward, his image fluttering on the edge of an emergency Escape, but Jan caught him in her arms. She held him tightly and said, "It's okay. It's over. You can relax now. Relax."

His image stabilized. He felt her solidify in his embrace. He squeezed tighter, then let her go and collapsed on the couch.

"Drink," he pleaded.

A Red Mars manifested in his left hand. He drank it down in one draught.

Jan sat beside him and put her hand on his shoulder. "You survived?" she asked.

Quadie nodded. "I'll let you know in a few days."

Jan tilted her head back and stared at the faraway cloud-bank ceiling, letting her body slump down on the couch. Her hand fell from Quadie's shoulder onto her lap. "So it wasn't just me. I was afraid of that. What did he do?"

"Same thing as he did in *The Metamorphosis*, I guess." Quadie drained his glass a second time, then dropped it, letting Marissa demanifest it. "The only difference is that this time he put down a new personality—several of them—over the one he, I don't know, subdued, removed, put to sleep. Whatever."

"I don't know. This one fucked me up a lot more than the sea gull sequence."

Quadie sat forward and buried his face in his hands to massage his brow, but when he realized what he was doing, the similarity to old Sal, he jumped to his feet and crossed his arms over his chest, keeping his hands very deliberately pressed against his body. "I think it's just because of those other people. You know, just the effect of being so wholly under a different personality, and coming back and having to deal with all of them at once. I think that's all it is. I don't think he used the other routine. I mean, he could have, and it'll take a little while before I can tell, but I really didn't—"

"What are you talking about, Quadie?"

"The subconscious part."

Jan stared blankly at him. "What are you talking about, Quadie?"

"The . . . holy shit." Quadie's eyes grew wide. "He never told you, did he?"

Jan crossed her arms across her chest in vexation. "Told me *what*?"

"Oh, shit. Okay. In *The Metamorphosis*, Carver used the sea gull thing to disguise . . . I don't know what, but he implanted ideas with it somehow. Didn't you notice any changes in your attitudes about the Web after you tuned it a few times?"

She shook her head. "No. But I only tuned it once."

"Oh. Well, he was messing around with our thoughts somehow. Not just our interfaces, but our real thoughts. He did some kind of subliminal thing, I think, to make us think of the Web as real."

"But everyone thinks of the Web as real already," Jan protested. "That's the whole point, isn't it?"

"No, you don't get it. Experience in the Web seems real, but deep down we know it really isn't. Carver was changing *attitudes*, not just surface thoughts. And it was subconscious— you wouldn't notice the change, but it was there all the same. It happens without you realizing. And the effect doesn't end with tune-out, and it gets stronger the more you tune."

Jan swore under her breath. "No wonder everybody wanted it."

"Maybe. I'm not sure how many other people know about it. It's really subtle. I only knew about it 'cause I saw it when I beta-tested the program. Speaking of which . . ."

"Yes?"

"What do we tell Carver about this one? I mean, it's a great fucking program, and I can't find any real flaws in it, but do we tell him it's okay or not?"

Jan stood and looked directly into Quadie's eyes, her face rigidly serious. "It doesn't matter. This wasn't a beta-test."

"It wasn't?"

She shook her head. "I'm not the only person who got a copy last night. The message he attached said installations are going out all over the public Networks."

"What? Unannounced, no promo? Wait a minute—how's he going to route the charges? I thought FCA had locked his accounts."

"They have, but it doesn't matter. He's not charging."

"He's not? Why?"

Jan shrugged. "He said he wants everyone to be able to tune *Faces*. That's why he's putting it on the publics only."

"Shit."

"What?"

"Carver doesn't need the publicity or the exposure."

She almost laughed. "No, he certainly does not."

"So why would he be so concerned about letting as many people as possible tune it, unless . . ."

"Oh my God. Unless he is playing with our thoughts in this one, too."

Quadie nodded grimly.

"Oh, Quadie, I don't like this at all. It scares me. Is Carver all right? I mean, with everything that's happened lately, do you think he might . . . might have . . . followed Rose around the bend?"

She gazed into his eyes, searching for reassurance, but Quadie could only stare back helplessly.

Jan looked down at her hands fumbling in her lap. "Quadie, I'm worried. I think Carver needs help. You know, *psychological* help. I don't know what he's trying to do, but—"

"I know. We've got to find him and get him some help." Quadie put his arms around Jan and held her to him. "And if we can't help him, we've got to stop him."

NINETEEN

Sweat glistened on Carver's dark skin, running muddy
rivulets down his arms in the immodest heat of late
March. He crept on his knees through the soybean green-
house, the rich, moist loam cool against his legs and feet as
he worked his way down the row, snapping green pods from
their runners. After a solid hour of labor his reed basket was
still not half full. Three weeks had not cultivated in him the
knack for this sort of work. His hands were cramped and his
knees and back ached.

Even so, he enjoyed the task. As much as he liked plants,
he had never really gardened before—Rose, not he, had pos-
sessed the green thumb, and he had quite happily left all the
landscaping work to her—but now he found it an excellent
way to free his mind of work, worry, and other extraneous
matters. In spite of the discomfort, concentrating on the
mindless repetition of his task allowed him to relax utterly.
"Zen and the art of bean-picking," Providence, the head gar-
dener, called it. Carver preferred to think of it as "Zen and
the art of getting dirty."

He finished the row and stood, arching his stiff back and
flexing his hands. Before he could bend to the next row, an
explosion of noise caromed down the alley, followed closely
by a gaggle of children. Carver took several long swallows

from the large jug of pear juice he had with him and watched the children play, glad of the excuse to take a break.

He knew all of these kids, though not well. None of them ever tuned his "classes," and there was a widening exclusivity between his students and the other Pioneer children. More and more, those kids who tuned-in to study with Carver— now numbering eleven, with the youngest a mere seven and the eldest almost twenty—were maintaining their own clique. A few adults had noticed this fact and commented on it, but so far without any real concern. It was generally assumed that the common experience and knowledge was fostering a natural bond between them.

Carver, of course, knew the real reason behind this behavior. He'd been studying what the Young Pioneers had termed his "neuro-adaptive routine," and unbeknownst to anyone, he downloaded it to the children's patchspaces during class.

While Carver's experiments were primarily intended to test his routine, he did at the same time engage in a little subterfuge. The more time he spent at the Frontier, the less comfortable he became with the Young Pioneers' agenda. With the help of his routine, though, he stood a chance of mitigating their influence on the children.

He had wrestled with his decision for the better part of a week, fully aware of the inherent dangers. And he used extreme care when he programmed the worm, making sure it created precisely the effect he wanted and nothing more. The routine seemed to have the greatest effect on the youngest children, but no one entirely escaped its influence.

He knew Selene and the others would be livid if they discovered his activities, and he sometimes worried about this— and about the ethicality of his actions in general. He told himself that he was doing no more with the neuro-adaptive routine than what they wanted to do with it, but he knew that was no justification.

In the end, Carver resorted to a more philosophical rationalization. The Young Pioneers raised their children as they did because they wanted to instill certain values and attitudes in them. It was nothing more than all parents—and, to an extent, society—did. In a sense, his neuro-adaptive routine was merely a much more effective means of imprinting. And he had as much right as anyone to do what he thought was best for these children.

A Frisbee flew into the warehouse and landed among the soybeans. Carver walked down the rows and picked it up just as a six-year-old girl named Rainsong ran haltingly up to the edge of the tilled earth.

"Here you go," he said, tossing the disk gently to the child.

She caught the Frisbee and smiled shyly at him, then ran a few steps back to her playmates. She planted her feet firmly on the ground and, holding the Frisbee in both hands, screwed her body around and threw her arms outward.

The Frisbee landed in almost the same spot in the dirt. Carver again picked it up and returned it to Rainsong, and again the girl flung it clumsily away. This time the Frisbee hit the outer wall of the warehouse and dropped to the ground, rolling in a lazy spiral back toward the girl.

She scowled at the disk and scolded it as she picked it up.

Carver smiled. "Here, Rain, let me help you." He knelt behind her. "Just hold it with one hand—yeah, like that." He reached around and put his hand on hers. "Now hold it like this. No, put your fingers here. Yes, that's good. Now pull it toward you this way and hold it *there*, and when you throw, do it like this." He guided her arm through the motion several times, then took his hand away. "Try it now."

Rain still twisted her body around, but this time the throw was more controlled, and the Frisbee wobbled over to where her companions waited impatiently for their game to continue.

"Good," Carver said. "Much better."

Rain grinned broadly at him, showing her teeth, then rushed out to rejoin the game. Carver stood, groaning aloud with the effort and the ache of sore muscles.

"That was very sweet. You're really good with kids."

Carver turned to see C.A. approaching. She held Heather snuggled tightly to her breast, and she carried a drinking skin in one hand.

When she reached him, she gave him a kiss and offered the skin. "I brought you some mineral water," she said. "Nothing like it for beating the heat."

"Thanks." He took a small sip of the water, then put the skin down beside the jug of juice. "What's the data?"

"I just wanted to see how you were doing. I tried to grok you, but you're out of the System."

Carver wiped a hand over his bare, smooth head, then shook away the perspiration. "Too hot for the hat," he told her.

"Well, can I hang out?"

"You can help!" Carver laughed.

"I would, but I've already got my hands full."

"So I see."

The children had moved down the alley, but an errant throw sent the Frisbee sailing toward Carver and C.A. Carver snatched it out of the air and sent it back.

"They're so cute," C.A. said. "You should grok one of their games sometime. It's fascinating."

"I have," Carver told her. "Where do you think *Faces* came from?"

"Oh, right."

They continued to watch as the game moved farther away. When it had disappeared around the corner, C.A. said, "I can't wait until Heather's old enough to use a headset."

Carver stared at her, concern darkening his features. "Really?"

"Oh, yeah! Why not?"

"I don't know. How long have you been at the Frontier?"

"Three years." She blushed and said sheepishly, "I came to U.F. for grad school, but after I started hanging out with the Pioneers, I dropped out and moved in here."

"What were you studying?"

"Anthropology. I figured that I'd rather help create a new culture than just study old ones."

Carver stared into the far recesses of the warehouse. "I've been doing a lot of studying of human cultures myself lately."

"You mean us?" she asked with a smile.

"Not just the Pioneers. You wouldn't believe some of the people I've been talking to. Not just other Pioneer communes around the Continent. I've been doing some personal research, which has led me to all sorts of fringe folk. I even ran across someone who was—so she said—very peripherally involved with the big Network Thirty-seven hack last fall."

"The one you're being accused of?"

"Exactly the one."

"And what did this person have to say about that?"

"She said it was a big help having someone else take the heat." Carver smiled. "But she did say she was sorry they'd picked me. Anyway, some of these people I've been talking to are engaged in experiments similar to the Frontier. Some are much less ambitious, some are a lot more so. Some even seem to be very aggressively trying to supplant society."

"Well, it takes all types," C.A. said evenly.

"I suppose so. Come here."

Carver led her into the warehouse and sat her down against the cool of the cinder-block wall. "What brought you to the Pioneers over anyone else?"

"I don't know. The Young Pioneers were the first ones I met."

"So if you'd met some other group first, you would have thrown your lot in with them?"

"Maybe." She shrugged. "If they weren't too weird."

"Haven't you even looked around at some of the others?"

"Why would I want to?"

"C.A., some of these people are so fascinating. I never even knew about half the ideas they subscribe to—probably never would have if I hadn't been brought here."

She smiled at him, but he shook it off. "In a way, I guess I'm glad I was brought here, but this isn't where I want to *end up*," he said.

"You still expect to get clear with the FCA, don't you?" C.A. asked.

"Well, sure. But even if I don't and I have to spend the rest of my life hiding, I won't do it here."

"Don't you like us anymore?"

C.A.'s pout was jesting, but Carver sensed some real hurt beneath it. He leaned over and kissed her.

"It has nothing to do with the people."

C.A. was about to say something, but she stopped herself. Her head cocked to the side and her eyes flitted back and forth. "Sel's trying to find you. Better put your cap on."

"Tell her it's too hot."

"I think it's serious, Carver."

"All right, tell her to hold on." Carver reached over for his headset and put it on. It squished slightly against the perspiration as it affixed itself to his scalp, a singularly unpleasant sensation. "Yuck," he said. "What's the data, Selene?"

David T. tells me you've been tuning the Web a lot lately.

"Well, you know. I've had a lot to do."

Seli sent disapproval. *You've been doing too much. It's dangerous, Carver. For all of us.*

"I'm paying for it all myself, from legitimate accounts. Not traceable to me. Shade helped me set that up."

That's great, but it's not the problem. As long as you're in the

Web, there's a possibility you'll get cracked—by the Feds or anyone else who might be after you. And every time you tune-in, it gets more likely someone will bust you.

"David T. keeps updating the security—"

Selene hit him with a sense of disapproval at David's misspent time. *Can't you just work within the System? Do you have to hit the Web so much?*

"Yes. It's what I do, Sel. The FCA keeps deleting *Faces*, so I have to keep putting out new installations. And I need to stay in touch with Jan, to find out the data on her side of things. And I've been going back and forth with a bunch of your contacts."

Oh?

"As long as I'm going to have to work like a Freek, I might as well learn how to do it myself." His attitude was almost challenging. "So David T. can get on with more important things."

Yeah, well, as long as you're working from here, I think you should limit your Webtime to no more than half an hour a day. If you get busted, we all do. It's not fair of you to put us in that kind of position.

"Really? I should think bootlegging copies of *Faces* for private systems would attract more notice."

A synthesis of fear and alarm ran into Carver's thoughts before Selene recovered. *So you know, huh?*

"I did kind of wonder why you were all so eager to help tweak an autorep for it."

Oh, come on. It wasn't premeditated, Carver, you know that. She stopped short, then grokked with an edge in her thought, *Does it bother you?*

"Not really, I guess. I'm not charging for usage, so it's not like you're stealing from me or something. But I do think it's a little dishonest all the same. Tell me—was this just your idea, or did everybody get a say first?"

C.A. squeezed his arm. *I didn't know about it, Carver.*

A touch of rebuke bled into Carver's awareness as Selene grokked to C.A. a desire for confidentiality with Carver, and of C.A.'s exclusion.

"She's sitting right next to me," Carver said. "Besides, she can listen in if she wants. After all, you do share everything here, don't you? No matter where it comes from?"

It's not for personal gain, Sel told him. *We're spreading the credit around to all the Young Pioneers on the Continent, so we can all be ready for the next big step.*

"And in all the excitement, it never occurred to anyone to ask me if I wanted my money supporting that?"

Beside him, C.A. said, "You really don't feel comfortable here, do you?" She spoke aloud, and kept her thoughts out of the System.

What's bothering you, Carver? We can't help you if we don't know what's wrong.

Carver dug his hand into the soil. He pulled up a handful and compacted it tightly in his fist. "Why am I working in here?" he asked.

C.A. looked at him quizzically. "I thought you liked it."

You don't have to, you know, Selene thought. *You can do anything else if you'd rather.*

"No, that's not what I mean. I meant, why am I working *in here?*" He grokked a picture of the soybean warehouse, imbuing it with a sense of cold claustrophobia. To drive his point home, he followed that with the freedom and joy of the outdoor "gardens," then switched it off, returning to the former image and redoubling the sterility of his grok.

We need to grow things inside during the winters. And since soybeans grow here during the winter, it makes sense to keep growing them here the rest of the year. I don't see why you're so concerned about it.

"I'm not concerned about it, I'm just making a point. Everyone here makes such a big thing about their ideals, but the more I see, the more hypocritical it all looks. You talk about letting things grow naturally, about letting nature take care of itself, and on the surface it all seem wonderful and rosy. The garden flourishes, and no one has to do any real work aside from picking their fruits and vegetables. But then there's this place, and the others, as backup—all indoors, shut away, protected from nature, cultivated." He crumbled the clod in his hand and let it fall back to mingle with the rest of the soil.

C.A. shifted uncomfortably. "We have to eat, Carver."

I don't see what this has to do with what we were talking about, Carver.

"It has everything to do with it, don't you see? It isn't just agriculture I'm talking about. It's everything. Everyone is so committed to the ideals, but only as long as they're convenient. If they don't work, you fall back on the old way of doing things—*but no one admits it.* You still give lip service to the ideals, even as you're abandoning them. You accept ideas without ever thinking about them. The Young Pioneers are no different than the rest of world. You're as self-deceived as the society you so mistrust."

We don't mistrust society.

"No? Perhaps not." Carver reached over to stroke Heather's head. "But your children certainly will."

A forceful questioning, tempered with challenge and defiance, buffeted Carver.

"Because of how they're being raised." Carver paused for more juice. "I don't understand the need for your philosophy here. You keep talking about how Western society is terminal, how it's going to fall apart any day now, and how you're preparing for that. You've got these kids growing up expecting the whole Continent to explode at any second. Is this a good thing? Aren't you making them pessimistic?"

No, it's making them realistic. We're preparing them for the next step—

"In human evolution, yeah, I know. But they're so cut off

from outsiders, they'll never really be able to make a place for themselves in the grand New World Order. And I don't mean cut off just physically. When they do have contact with outsiders, which isn't often, they have trouble communicating. Try *talking* to River sometime—his English hardly makes any sense."

That's the whole point, Carver, if you haven't figured it out yet. Language is too limiting to communication, so we try to move beyond it.

"But then they can *only* communicate through the System, and only with someone else who can grok."

"But as more and more people learn the concept, that will change," C.A. protested. She was frowning heavily, obviously troubled by what Carver was saying, but she did seem to be thinking about it.

"Granted. But until more people learn to grok, it's limiting. Speaking of learning, it's about time for today's lesson, so if you'll excuse me . . ."

Wait, Carver. That's something else I want to talk to you about.

He kept the tone of the query he sent neutral.

We decided you don't have to keep teaching anymore if you don't want.

"That's okay. I kind of enjoy it, actually."

Well, put it this way—we don't want you to teach anymore.

He sent a thought that was half demand, half accusation. C.A. privately sent him a wave of shock at this turn of events, and an affirmation that she herself had not known of this. Carver squeezed her hand absently and waited for Selene to respond.

We'd just prefer to have someone who's truly one of us teaching our kids, that's all.

"So it's ideological? I'm only teaching programming."

Please don't get defensive, Carver. You don't fully understand how things work with us yet, so we're not sure that you're the proper influence for the kids.

He formed a picture of himself dressed in a toga and drinking a bowl of hemlock.

Dammit, Carver, it's your own fault. Look at River—he's changed completely since you got here. He doesn't do his chores, he's argumentative, he goes around telling the other children that none of the adults really understand anything, he causes trouble in every class but yours. Your presence here has caused a lot of disruption.

"River idolizes me. He wants to be just like me and now he's got the chance. You certainly can't expect that he'll go back to acting like he always did before if you take that chance away from him. It's not my fault. He's a little boy— that's just how little boys are. You can't expect to change two million years of evolution just like that, no matter how right you think your new world order is."

Why can't we change it? You seem to be doing well enough.

Carver squared off. "Meaning?"

River's presence spilled a teasing impatience into Carver's thoughts with a reminder that the students were assembled for class. Carver let them know that the class was canceled; he let both his brusque thought and the children's subsequent disappointment bleed over into his conversation with Selene.

She waited until the boy tuned-out to ask, *Have you been using it on them all along, or didn't you think of that right away?*

"What's she talking about, Carver?" C.A. asked.

He's been using his little trick on our kids.

"You don't know what you're talking about." His voice was gruff, but he couldn't meet C.A.'s eyes.

Bullshit.

"Why, Carver? What have you been doing?"

"I've just been enculturing them," he told C.A. "I'm not trying to get them to abandon your ideals or anything." To Seli he added, "Have you even asked the kids about it?"

The effect is too subtle, too confusing. They can't explain it.

"Then don't explain. Just grok."

Carver caught what might have been contempt. *That still won't work.*

Before Selene could send any more, C.A. said, "We adults can use the System, but we can't truly grok, even though we say we do. Remember what I told you about not being able to completely free ourselves of preconceptions? How the only real hope we have for changing things lies in bringing up the next generation with different attitudes right from the start? Well, it works the same for grokking."

She shifted her weight and bounced Heather lightly a few times before continuing. "To us, grokking is sort of like a second language—no matter how good we might get at it, no matter how 'fluent', it will never be completely natural. But it can be for our kids, who grow up grokking *and* talking. And since grokking will be so natural for them, when they raise their kids they can go one step farther."

Carver scratched his shoulder. "But why is it so important? Tell me that."

You don't realize? Selene seemed shocked. *It's perfect communication. When we can all grok without having to use any language at all—any artificial language—then there won't be any miscommunication, and so no misunderstanding. And that's the key to the next step in human evolution.*

In his mind, Carver created a short narrative continuum illustrating River losing his headset. The boy slowly faded away as the rest of the Young Pioneers ignored him due to his absence from the System—his inability to communicate.

As soon as River had completely disappeared from both scene and thought, the Webworld vanished in a puff of smoke; Carver synthesized confusion and fear, total isolation, even a certain sensory deprivation, all leading to mindless panic as the Young Pioneers, having made themselves wholly dependent upon an artificial means of communication, found themselves abandoned by their technology, and so able only to babble and gesticulate incomprehensibly at one another without hope of understanding. Specific languages might be artificial implementations of a natural system, Carver posited, but the reliance of grokking upon an external technology made it an artificial *system*.

His years as a director standing him in good stead, Carver formulated his whole argument within seconds and let it loose into the System with a resolute mental shove.

He felt a momentary shock from Selene at having to assimilate so much all at once, but she quickly regained control of herself and squelched any further reaction.

Sitting beside Carver, C.A. frowned. "But as society moves toward that, it would develop ways to deal with any—"

"Exactly! Society needs to evolve toward something like this, not have it forced upon it. The concept behind grokking is good, I'll grant you that. But there's no reason to load it up with all that other crap. When grokking enhances communication between enough people, attitudes will start to change by general consensus—if they need to be changed. When everyone understands each other better, they'll naturally get along better, according to your philosophy, right?"

He felt a sense of wary affirmation from Selene.

"I understand what Carver's saying," C.A. said. "The new society should be left to change their own attitudes, come up with their own philosophy. Since we can't ever reach the Promised Land, so to speak, that also means we can't fully understand the ethics that will apply to such a society. The new system you're trying to instill in them might be no better than the one you're replacing. So why make things more difficult than they need to be?"

Carver hugged her. "I think you should let those who are going to live in your new world develop its codes. All I'm doing with the routine is trying to give them that chance."

You don't have the right to make that decision.

"I think he has as much right as any of us do," C.A. told Selene.

A bitter silence fell between them. Finally, Carver stood and walked out into the sunshine. His churning emotions were a mélange of anger, disappointment, hurt, and betrayal. He tried for a while to separate them and force them down, but he could not. In the end he wrapped them in a picture of himself floating through the air away from the Frontier, leaving behind the Young Pioneers and their world. He added to this his desire for this scene to be reality, and sent it out through the System to all the Young Pioneers. A bevy of reactions from disappointment to stern approval raced back to him.

As Carver walked on down to the lake, C.A. ran to catch up with him. "You don't have to go alone. Perhaps its time for *us* to move on."

Perhaps it is. Of course, you know enough about us that it could be a real problem.

"And you know about my neuro-adaptive routine. Which I'm not exactly thrilled about."

So. I guess we'll just have to trust each other.

"Why not?" Carver said sarcastically as he shut down his patchspace, shunting himself out of the System. "It's worked well so far."

TWENTY

Var had just destroyed three other players with a single maneuver, catapulting him solidly to the top of the ratings, when the notice blossomed in his thoughts. Normally he would have resented any interruptions during a campaign—especially in the midst of battle—but this was a hi-pri override, and he knew what it meant. Not even *Star Force Patrol* could keep him from this. He notified his force commander of his withdrawal and tuned-out before she could start yelling at him. Rega had been one of his best friends for over a year—ever since he'd started playing *SFP*— but she was the hardest of hard-asses to play under.

A gray bloodhound squatted before the main attention screen in Var's cubical interface. Behind the dog the screen glowed with schematic data.

"Ho, snooper," Var greeted the routine. "What's your data?"

"Ho, Var. Nonprotocol-queue system activity current, public Network Four twenty."

The dog lifted a paw, which morphed into a human hand, and pointed at the screen. The data displayed there looked vaguely like something from a high-energy physics program Var had kifed once.

"Isolate the protocol queue and dehance related subdata."

Most of the data grayed and faded, leaving behind some

random flickering—and a sizable pocket of roiling zigzags, subtle, barely noticeable unless he looked away and caught it in his peripheral vision.

"Correlation?"

"Ninety-three percent," the dog replied.

"Yeah fuck! Can you get a trace?"

Data sprang to life on the right-side wall. Var's head automatically distended to sprout another face. He could handle six different inputs this way, keeping all the data separate or superimposing any or all for comparison or processing. Imagination and intuitive programming skill helped him make up for his lack of resources.

The second screen displayed a green map. Var was pretty sure it was North America. Yes, there was a dot for his address about in the middle of it all, right where Minneapolis probably ought to be. In the upper right blob of the Continent a white cross flashed an identifier for Network 420. A couple of dashed yellow lines zipped out from the cross, ending in faint blue circles. One of these lines became solid and bright white, its terminus also turning white. The other lines from the Network's cross disappeared, replaced by a new array of possible transmission nodes emanating from the white circle.

"Randomized cross-transfer link," the snooper explained.

"Um, cross correlate with priors. See if you can get a handle on the algorithm. That might make it easier to weed out the diversions."

The dog flickered for an instant. "Current processor resources insufficient for multitasking trace and correlation. Prioritize or task switch?"

Var watched as the trace verified another node. He was so close to making it. If he could only find the origin of these *Faces* installations.

"How's for multitasking with total resources?" he asked.

"Resources adequate."

"Cool. Shut everything down and put it all into tracing that signal. Flash me if anything happens."

Outside, Var scrunched out from under the coil, feeling the set's aluminum frame sway under his shifting weight. He walked to the kitchenette and yanked open the fridge. One quick glance at the barren interior dashed his hopes.

"No beer?"

"Sorry, dude," his roommate Larry called out from his room. "I'm broke till Tuesday. You're too young to drink anyway."

"Fuck you. I'm old enough to emancipate from my parents, I'm old enough to have a job, I should be old enough to drink a fucking beer. I can do it in the Web, so why not Outside? Fucking Congress."

"If you hadn't quit school, you know, you'd be certified to vote by now, and you could maybe do something about it." Larry was three years older than Var, a sophomore in economics at U.Minn, and he was way too civic-minded for Var's taste. Not that Var had much choice where roommates were concerned—between his job and Larry's aid package, they could barely afford even their tiny apartment.

"I'm not going to spend another year in school just so I can fucking *vote*."

"Yeah, who needs a diploma anyway, eh? After all, you like slinging falafel, right?"

Var shut the fridge and brushed his shaggy blond hair back from his face. "No, dude, I want to go to college and major in econ. That's where the mega cash is."

Larry laughed cynically. "Oh, you got that data true. Speaking of which, are you through with the set? I've got homework to do."

"I'm kind of in the middle of something real important. Can't you go to the lab on campus or something?"

"You know those sets are even worse than ours."

Var heard the set beep. "Look, I'll be out soon, dude," he shouted as he ran back into the living room. "Promise."

Before Larry could protest, Var scooted his head under the coil and dropped his hand on the safety switch. When the default interface sprang up before him, he said his password.

"What did you get?" he asked the snooper routine as soon as his own interface manifested.

"Origin node detected and confirmed."

Var stared at the pulsing cross hairs on the map. "Motherfuck," he said, a wide smile spreading over his face. "Tune Quadie Newman right now. Top pri."

Ariel paused in mid-massage. "Tune for you, Quadie. It's from Var and it's urgent."

Quadie demanifested the massage table and dressed in loose green slacks and a bone-white sculpted vest. "Let's have it."

Ariel vanished discreetly just as Var's simple image manifested. The boy wore a smug grin that seemed about to split his face in two.

"Ho, Newman."

"Var."

Var looked all around, taking in the full luxe expanse of Quadie's interface. "Nice job."

"Thanks. What's your data?"

Var's smile broadened, a feat that would have been impossible Outside. "I was just wondering if you were ready to negotiate your end of our bargain."

Quadie's eyes went wide. "No way! You found Carver?"

Var nodded.

"Where is he?"

"We deal first, Mr. Big-time. Remember?"

Quadie tensed momentarily, but Ariel booted a relaxer. "What do you want?"

"Well, you see, I've been thinking lately I might want to go to college. I'm in a dead end right now, but everybody says I got talent. Even you." He stretched his arms out to his sides and spun in slow, lazy circles. "But see, I never got through high school. I can't afford to go back—and I really don't want to, 'cause, you know, it's just so much bullshit. But I was thinking if I signed up for one of those virtual equivalency courses, I could get certified without having to quit my job. Of course, VEC's aren't cheap, either, really . . ."

"How much?"

Var looked pleadingly at Quadie. "Five thousand?"

"Do you have a definite address?"

Var hesitated. "I'm not sure. Sort of. I traced back to where the *Faces* installations are coming from, see, and if it's not him doing it, it's got to be whoever he's with."

Quadie thought this over for several seconds. "Three thousand," he said.

"Three thousand, and a recommendation for my university admissions? A rec from you, nobody could turn me down."

Quadie laughed. "Now that's a deal. Where is he?"

"Right where he started—Gainesville."

Var paused only long enough to verify Quadie's credit transfer before retrieving the address he'd been keeping on file. Var desperately needed credit, and the reward for locating Blervaque would definitely set him up. But he didn't care about the credit as much as he did about the director's promise of help. Newman's fame, and his help on top of that, would be very useful; anything would be possible. Of course, Var knew that Newman would nuke out if he learned he was selling this data, but the hotline was guaranteed confidential. Newman would never know a thing, and he won both ways.

Var tuned the address. The space he manifested in was drab and functional, stereotypical government programming style.

"You have reached the data hotline of the Federal Communications Agency. Your address and identifier have already been recorded," an authoritative male voice announced.

"Under terms of the Data Privacy Act, your confidentiality is assured and an encrypted code number has been downloaded to your interface. Only this code number will appear in all official datawork. If you know the case number pertaining to your data, please give it now, or state the subject of your data."

Var took a deep breath. "Carver Blervaque."

"Please wait while the appropriate file is located."

Var waited for several seconds, which became many seconds and eventually minutes. Light diffused from above, leaving the circular room with no apparent ceiling. The wall and floor were both entirely featureless and colored a dull blue-gray. Only his breathing broke the otherwise perfect silence. In that vacuum, the sound quickly swelled in intensity, rasping in and out and then dying against the government surfaces, returning no echo. Var deleted the noise from his image, but his nervous claustrophobia grew. He tried pacing, but the room was too small. It made him feel like he was spinning around, caught in some sort of whirlpool. He forced himself to stand still in the center of the room. Something was up—this was taking way too long.

Just when he couldn't stand another second, the voice broke in again. "File located. Please record your data now."

The moment finally at hand, Var panicked. Without uttering a single word or transferring any other data, he tuned-out.

Once returned to his interface, Var held his head in his hands and permitted himself a moan. "Oh, fuck me."

"Fuck you is right, little man."

Var spun toward the undulating voice. "The *fuck*?"

The fatigue-clad Rastafarian laughed. "Var, brah. You been a *bad* boy today. Who you been tuning just now, eh?"

"Who the fuck are you? How did you hack my interface?"

"Question is, what *you* been hacking?"

"I've seen you before—I've seen you at Willie's."

The black man nodded and laughed again. "That's right.

You seen me, and I seen you. We been watching you a long time now. You a good hack, but you stupid, neh? What you fucking with, you don't know, but it much bigger than you. It going to eat you up, little man."

"You don't know anything about it."

"But I do, I do. Like I say, we been watching you, Var."

"We?"

"That's right. See, you the one don't know anything. We know *every*thing, Var. You found Blervaque, you sold him to Newman. We would have stopped you if we knew in time, but that's okay, we don't mind. It's a free market, nah? And we not worried about Newman. We can handle him, sure. But then you go to FCA. What you tell them, brah?"

"How did you—"

"You think the Man going to give you a big reward and say, 'Thank you very much,' neh?"

"Fuck off."

"Think what you doing, boy." The Rastafarian's dreadlocks were swaying sinuously about his head, heightening the hypnotic effect of his syncopated speech. "You nobody, Var. What is to keep the Man from just taking your data, eh? What you going to say when they ask how you got it?"

Before Var could think of an answer, his visitor continued. "You even stop to think why the FCA want Carver so bad?"

Var snorted, gaining some bravado. "That's obvious to me."

"Is it? Then why don't they just say, 'Please, Mr. Carver, tell us how you do that'? Carver got some folks trying to kidnap him, steal what he got. Maybe FCA want to do the same, eh? Maybe there's something *special* Carver does they want—something makes their job easier, yours and mine harder. Something they don't want no one else knowing jack about. *No one*."

Var's confidence evaporated as quickly as it had crystallized. "Sounds like none of this is *maybe* to you."

"I told you, Var. We know everything. You want to take

your chance that I'm wrong, that the Man going to be nice to you? Agency got *that* reputation, neh?"

The man's dreadlocks had ceased their movement, and he stared silently at Var, his eyes wide, doubting.

"What do you want from me?" Var asked meekly.

The Rastafarian seemed to relax. "You a good hack, Var. You're new, but you got much talent, neh? We can give you a chance to get better. Tech, resources, training. We make you *world-class* if you come with us."

"Why? Why should you care?"

"We don't want the Man to find Carver. Simple as that."

"Why not?"

"You find that out if you come with us."

Some strange impulse within him almost made Var accept, but rationality took over at the last moment. "I need some time to think about it."

"Time something you don't have, Var. As soon as your data gets through to a human in the Agency, they'll come after your ass. You got to decide *now*, brah."

"What about my credit? I just made—"

"We got that for you already, brah." The man laughed. "No worries."

Var quickly checked his account. Zero.

"We cleaned your set, too. Everything but your interface randomizing right now. Don't want the Man digging out the data for himself."

Again Var checked his set. "Fuck."

"See, Var, you got nothing now. So what you going to do?"

Var felt a warning tickle from his set. His heart rate was dangerously high, his breathing quick and shallow. He was panicking. "I don't know."

"You got to decide, brah. You should have thought of this a long time ago, when you started working for Mr. Newman. This situation is your own making, Var. Time now to reap what you sow."

Var shook his head. He couldn't think.

"Okay, brah, I give you this. You in Minneapolis, neh? Get your ass down to Nicolet. Go to the fountain. Some brothers and sisters there, all wearing headsets. They be easy to spy. You go to them, say you're a friend of mine, Soldier Ras. They'll be expecting you. They'll be there one hour, brah, no longer. You got that much time to make up your mind. But do it Outside, eh, brah? You tuned-in when the Man comes looking, that'll be the end of you. You understand that, brah?"

"Yeah, I understand."

"Good boy. Think about what you going to do, but do it quick." The Rastafarian held up a clenched fist in farewell. "I like you, Var. I hope to see you again. I really do. Blaze your trail, Var."

Soldier Ras demanifested. Var watched the space where he'd been, then swore and tuned-out.

He lay on his set staring up at the ceiling for twenty minutes. Whoever Soldier Ras really was, he'd hacked him over mega bad. He was good, but was he right? Probably, Var had to admit. Ras definitely knew far more than he did, so chances were Ras hadn't been after his data. And even with Quadie's three K, his credit wasn't worth this kind of effort just to steal. Besides, if it had been simple theft or piracy, Ras wouldn't have stuck around to chat. No, Soldier Ras was almost assuredly telling the truth.

But could he be trusted?

Probably no more than the FCA.

The set beeped, and the coil began to move into position. Var yelped and rolled free of the set. He stood, shaking as he backed away from it. That shouldn't have happened. He bumped against the wall and flattened himself against it, staring at the set as though it were some kind of monster. The control panel lit up—something had taken over the set and was running through what remained of its data.

Var ran to his bedroom. Snatching his backpack from the floor, he stuffed a few shirts and some underwear into it, then headed for the front door.

"You going out, Var?" Larry called from his room.

"Uh, yeah."

"I'm gonna tune-in for a while then, okay?"

Var stopped in the open doorway. "Um, you better not, Lar. Set's acting weird—fritzing again. Gave me a headache. I'd stay away from it if I were you."

"Ah, fuck. Well, I guess it's off to the lab for me. I'll probably be really late. How 'bout you, dude? When you gonna be back?"

"I really couldn't tell you."

"I'm sorry, Mr. Newman, but Ms. Tarrega isn't in at the moment."

Quadie thrust his hands deep into the pockets of his crimson unisuit in order to contain their nervous fluttering. "Can you page her, Marissa?"

"If you could wait a moment, I'll see if I can locate her."

"Sure."

He started pacing around Jan's small reception space, his eyes darting impatiently at everything in sight. He was much too agitated to think straight right now. As soon as he talked to Jan, he should tune-out and take something to calm himself down.

"I believe Ms. Tarrega is asleep."

"Could you wake her up, then? Please? This is really incredibly important."

"Just a moment."

Seconds later Jan's disembodied voice said sleepily, "Quadie? What's the data? Marissa says you're acting very nervous."

"I've found Carver."

"What? How? Where is he?"

"I . . . I'm not going to tell you."

"What? Hold on—I'm coming In."

"No," Quadie told her. "Don't bother. I can't talk long. I'm on the plane right now."

"You're *what*?" Jan's voice had risen in both volume and pitch each time she spoke, until now she was practically screeching.

"Calm down," Quadie said. "I figured that it might make more of an impression if I talked to him in person." He smiled. "Actually, I'm kind of looking forward to it. I've never actually met Carver in the real before. We've known each other for twelve years, but it's all been virtual."

This time Jan's voice came very quiet, controlled. "Quadie, where is Carver?"

"Jan, I'm not going to tell you. I can't. Nobody knows I've found him, so no one will suspect anything if I go on a little trip, but if we both suddenly took off for the same place, everybody in the world would know something was going down. I don't want anyone else after Carver. I don't want to make things any worse for him than they already are."

"Quadie, please tell me. You have to tell me. I promise I won't go after him. I'll stay—"

"Oh, that's bullshit and we both know it, Jan. You'd be on the next flight out just like I was. Besides, it's not only dangerous for Carver—it could be dangerous for me, too. So I certainly don't want you getting involved."

"What, you don't think I could handle it?"

"Oh, I know you could handle it, Jan. It's just . . ."

"Yes?"

"Well, I just don't want anything to happen to you."

"Oh."

They both fell silent until Quadie said, "Look, I have to go, okay? But I'll keep in touch. Promise."

"All right. Goodbye, Quadie. Quadie?"

"Yes, Jan?"

"Take care of yourself, all right? I wouldn't want anything to happen to you, either."

Shade poked his head into the room Carver had taken for his own, far back in an isolated corner of the warehouse. "Got a minute?"

Carver didn't even look up from the book he was reading. "I didn't realize the High Council was still speaking to me. I thought I was still persona non grata."

"Carver, this is serious."

"Not again. What's the data?"

"We just found out some bad news."

"What's that?"

"Someone traced you here."

Carver shut the book and looked up at Shade. "Oh, God. Who?"

Shade ventured into the cubicle. "It's not as bad as it sounds," he said, sitting beside Carver on the futon. "Our friends managed to keep the data from the Feds."

"They don't know? Who was it, then?"

"Some neohack, if you can believe that. Apparently, your friend Quadie hired him a while ago to find you. Not sure why. Fortunately, the kid's on our side now, although somewhat reluctantly." He smiled. "Kind of like you."

"You're sure no one else found out?"

"Positive. The problem is, the kid tried to sell his data to the FCA. Our people got to him before he actually told them anything, but he did make contact, and we're pretty sure the Feds know you've been found."

Carver rubbed the stubble where his hair was growing out. He'd stopped wearing the headset after his fight with Seli. "Do they know this kid told Quadie?"

"Probably not. Our people are pretty thorough."

"Well then, we should be fine, right? I mean, all they know is some kid says he found me, then *he* disappeared.

Even if they think it's some kind of conspiracy, there's nothing they can do."

"But they'll be on the alert now."

"So what?" Carver shrugged. "I've been staying out of the Web altogether, so as long as Quadie doesn't do anything stupid with the data—"

"You mean like hop a plane down here?"

Carver stared, dumbfounded. "He didn't."

Shade nodded grimly.

"Oh, shit."

"Var—that's the hack—only got the address of our university node. Still, if your friend starts snooping around, you know Byrd's flunkies—and probably some other folks—will be following his trace." Shade stared pointedly at Carver. "Carver, you know our situation here. We'll help you if we can, but you know we'll do whatever we have to keep anyone from getting out here."

Carver looked down at the floor. "Of course. How long do we have until Quadie gets here?"

"His plane lands at Ocala International in a couple hours. I assume he'll rent a car and drive right to Gainesville."

"That's not enough time to do anything. Still, we've got a few hours yet. Hmmm." Carver tapped the spine of the book against his chin while he thought. "Okay," he said, standing. "I've got an idea. But I'm going to need your help on it. Is that all right?"

"I'll do whatever I can to keep Byrd out of here. What's the plan?"

Carver smiled. "Let's get everybody into the System. Conference time in five minutes."

He walked out of the room. "Where are you going?" Shade asked.

"To the e-lab," Carver called back. "I'm going to need my headset for this one.

TWENTY-ONE

Quadie turned the windscreen as dark as it would go. Just cresting a hill, he'd found the dawn sun hitting him directly in the face. He tried to concentrate on driving, to keep his thoughts from the whole ridiculous situation. Once again he checked the traffic computer, even though he knew he stayed on I–75 until he came to Route 26 in Gainesville. That would take him to University Avenue and the Marriott, where Ariel had booked him a room. The hotel was just a kilometer or so west of the campus—where, hopefully, he would find some answers.

The address Var had given him was assigned to the main library on campus. Quadie figured it was an automated data line that someone had taken over without anyone's knowledge and redirected to give Carver's Freeks unhindered and undetectable access. This was a common tactic, and most organizations monitored their data lines to prevent this. But he knew that if someone with legitimate access to the library's systems was involved, an override would be easy enough—especially for Freeks.

Finding the line and tracing its true source would be impossible, but someone would have to know about it and be maintaining it for the Freeks. Probably one of the gang who worked there, Quadie speculated. The trick would be asking the right questions and finding that person without arousing anyone else's suspicions.

Quadie reached the exit and drove east until he reached the hotel. He parked the rental car and headed inside to register.

Once in his room, he'd only just begun to unpack his suitcase when he heard a knock at the door. When he opened it, the hallway was deserted, but he found a scrap of paper on the floor just inside his room. Whoever knocked must have slipped it under the door. He locked the door again and looked at the paper.

It bore a simple map, the destination unlabeled, marked only with an X. Below the map was written, *Memorize and destroy. Come now. Bring headset.* —C.

Quadie committed the map to memory while he donned his headset, then tore the paper into pieces and flushed it down the toilet.

Apparently, this was going to be easier than he'd thought.

The car sped south on Interstate 75 toward Gainesville, the whine of its motors lost beneath the road noise of the tires. Captain Byrd stared out the window at the trees rushing past.

"Newman's leaving the hotel, sir," Thiele said from the back seat.

Byrd pressed the accelerator closer to the floor. "Keep a track on him. Hopefully he's just going to the university."

"ETA to Gainesville is approximately seventeen minutes," Hills announced.

"I doubt he can do much damage at the university," Byrd thought aloud. "But if he actually goes looking for Blervaque, if he screws anything up, we're going to crucify that bastard."

"It looks like the university is a negative, sir," Thiele told Byrd. "Newman just made the turn onto four forty-one. It looks like he's going to the house."

"Dammit!" Byrd clenched his teeth and sped even faster. "That doesn't make sense. Why would he go there instead of to the university? The data we reconstructed traced the signal to the university complex. Newman has no reason to go to the house first." An idea occurred to him. "Unless he's been told to go there—unless he's had contact."

"Our security at the house is good," Morgan said. "No one's in."

"It doesn't matter. Blervaque is there—I can feel it. We've got the bastard now."

Carver shook his head sadly as he surveyed the wreckage. Furniture was overturned or broken, books littered the floor, paintings hung crookedly—the room bore all the classic, cliché signs of a ransacking. Byrd's people had certainly done a good job here.

The bedroom looked just as bad as the living room, as did the bathroom. Every room in the house had been wrecked except for the workroom. Byrd had cleared that room entirely of everything it once contained—both sets of shelves had been removed, and even the carpet.

Carver turned away. None of that mattered now. He walked into the kitchen and opened the doors onto the deck to let in fresh air. The smell of rotting food permeated the kitchen, lingering in every breath. The refrigerator stood open, and the house's power had been shut off.

This last fact, Carver realized, had worked to his advantage. The security sensors Byrd's team had installed all ran from their own cells. Had the monitors been hardwired or inductively coupled into household power, they would have been much trickier for Shade and Feargal to bypass. As it was, however, the two had rewired the front door in less than ten minutes, and the French doors in the kitchen in half that time. Carver hoped he wouldn't need to use the back way out, but he'd prepared for the worst just in case.

The box of household papers was missing from its customary shelf in the living room. He was annoyed at their confiscation, having wanted to turn them over to Jan, but told himself it didn't matter much in the end.

Other things were more important. It took a few minutes of searching through the ruins of the bedroom before Carver found the photo album and the silver Victorian bracelet that had been Rose's favorite. Slipping the bracelet into his pocket, where it clinked against the data prism, he sat on the bed to leaf through the photographs.

Pictures from school, his graduation, their wedding. Rose's first gallery exhibition. Their house in progress, and the finished product. The vacation to Hawaii. Holidays, birthdays, and any days.

It all seemed so long ago. So distant. It had all changed. Even the pain was now lost in a faraway, very different past.

A blip of warning flashed into his thoughts. Someone was coming. Carver shut the album and left it on the bed.

From the living room he peered out through the front window, keeping himself hidden behind the draperies. Soon, a single car drove up, with a single occupant. Carver watched the driveway for a few seconds more, but no one followed. As the driver hefted himself from the car, Carver moved to the front door.

The driver, dressed in rumpled khaki slacks and a denim shirt with the sleeves rolled up, was a huge man. He stood almost two meters tall and weighed at least 150 kilos. Carver laughed aloud as he opened the door and said, "My God, Quadie, I never knew you were *fat*."

Quadie stopped dead and stared dumbfounded. "Carver? Holy fuck, mate, what are you doing here?"

"It's my house. Get your ass inside before Byrd shows up."

Quadie lumbered up the porch steps and enveloped Carver in a crushing bear hug. "You really do look like your image. Oh my God, it's good to see you, Carv."

"You too, Porky."

Quadie laughed and stepped back. "What can I say? When

you spend sixteen hours a day tuned-in, you don't have much chance to exercise." He wiped a hand across his dripping forehead and tugged the sweat-damp shirt away from his stomach. "Though I just might sweat it all off down here."

"Welcome to the Florida summer."

"Summer? It's only April."

"We start early down here." Carver motioned his friend inside and shut the door.

"Gee, I love what you've done with the place," Quadie said as he looked around at the chaos.

"I'm not sure who my decorator was. Probably Byrd."

"Who is this Byrd person?"

"FCA."

"Carver, what's been going on? I know there were people after you, but why haven't you just turned yourself in to the FCA? I mean, Christ, if anyone can help you with something like this, it's going to be them."

"Boy, you've sure changed! When we first met, you never would've said something like that."

"And you never would've done anything like what you've been doing."

Carver peeked out the window again. "Byrd's no regular Thompson, Quadie. He's head of a secret branch called Security Research. He wants to take my neuro-adaptive routine and use it for Web security."

"Your what?"

"The routine from *The Metamorphosis*."

"So let him. Hell, you can probably get more selling it to the government than anywhere else. You know how they love spending money."

Carver shook his head. "He doesn't want to pay for it, he just wants to take it. He's already tried once—he's the one who broke in here back in February, I'm almost sure of it."

"Carver, they just last week busted some people at RadTech for that."

"No, no. I grokked that story. That was just for the piracy. I think Byrd used that as an excuse to come down and break in the next day. Then he used that to try to scare me into talking. Fortunately, he never got anything, though. Government's the last ones I'd want to get this technology. It'd be too dangerous."

"Dangerous? It's unusual, sure, but dangerous?" Quadie sat on the couch and stretched his legs out in front of him. "Listen, I know what you've been doing with it, but I think you're taking this a bit too seriously."

"That's because you don't know what it really does. But you will when you tune this." He withdrew the data prism from his pocket and tossed it to Quadie.

Quadie looked at the prism, then at Carver. "What's this?"

"Insurance." Carver sat next to Quadie. "The people I've been staying with cracked the routine, but only partially. They haven't perfected it. But they do have it. And I don't know if that's a good thing. I don't like a lot of the things these people are trying to accomplish with my routine, and I know I wouldn't like what Byrd would do with it. But chances are they'll all figure it out soon enough. I've got a lot of the younger kids on my side for now, but that could change when they get older, so I'm the only one who would definitely try to set things right if they ever get out of control. And if anything ever happens to me . . ."

"I don't understand what you're saying."

"You will. The prism will explain everything. It's all there—how the routine works, what its real effects are, how to make it. Everything."

"Wait a minute." Quadie shifted uncomfortably. "You're giving me—"

Carver nodded. "I can't risk keeping it to myself anymore. And you're the only person I can trust."

"Listen, mate, obviously I don't understand everything that's going on, but are you absolutely sure you want to do this?"

"I really don't have a choice anymore, Quadie. But I'm not

too worried. I'm betting you'll change your mind at least partially once you've been through that prism. And even if you don't . . . well, shit, Quadie, you're my closest friend. I trust your judgment."

Quadie stared at Carver, amusement sparkling in his eyes. "You certainly *have* changed, haven't you? I do believe that's the first time I've ever heard you use profanity."

Carver laughed. "I've picked up a lot of bad habits lately. And they said *I* was a bad influence." The warning spiked into his thoughts once more, crushing his levity. "Shit."

"What's wrong?"

"They're coming."

"Who's coming?"

"FCA. They followed you."

Quadie scrambled to his feet. "What? How could they? They didn't even know."

Carver nodded somberly. "Oh yes they did. The neohack you hired went right to them when he was through with you."

"Fuck, fuck, fuck! I trusted that little bastard." Quadie stopped, suddenly realizing the situation. "You've got to get out of here, Carver."

"It's okay. I've got things taken care of. My friends will keep Byrd busy long enough for me to get away."

"Jesus Christ, Carv, why did you even come here if you knew they'd show up?"

"I knew you would have exposed everything if you started snooping. You're too good, and you never give up—it's that competitive streak in you. I knew Byrd would follow you, and I couldn't let you lead Byrd to the Frontier. I do owe those people a lot, no matter what they've done, and besides, Byrd would get too many clues to the routine from them. And I wanted to get that prism to you. No one else knows about that, no one at all. So you don't have to worry about anyone coming after you."

Quadie stared at the prism in his hand, then shoved it into his pocket. "What are you going to do now?"

Carver shrugged and smiled. "I'll figure something out. I've been making lots of new friends lately, and I've got plenty of places I can go now. You'd be surprised how extensive and organized the technological underground is. Those people are everywhere. Whatever happens, though, I'll keep in touch. Either through the wall, or maybe in person. Some people I know can get me a new ID, and between them and the *Metamorphosis* routine, I can change my pattern enough that no one will ever be able to detect me as *me*."

"This is ridiculous, Carver. What are you going to do, be a fugitive for the rest of your life?"

"Who can say? Others have done it—Salman Rushdie and Taslima Nasran both spent part of their careers in hiding but still put work out. In any case, I won't be alone—a few of the people I've been staying with are coming with me. You just take care of that prism, mate. I don't mean to be dramatic, but the future may depend on it."

Quadie forced a smile. "This is absolutely insane, you know?"

"Oh, indubitably," Carver answered, clapping his friend on the shoulder. "But there's nothing wrong with that. Insanity is just a different way of looking at reality, that's all. A new perspective. Reality is all in the mind, after all. Each of us creates his own."

He paused, then said, "Sometimes you can even create someone else's. Get the door, would you?"

Quadie opened the front door to see three men and a woman wearing dark suits, dark glasses, and government-issue headsets rushing toward him. The man in front had already drawn a gun.

"Carver, run!" Quadie tried to slam the door, but the men were already upon him. They shoved him back and spilled into the foyer. The leader pushed Quadie up against a wall and waved his gun at him.

"Where is he?" the man growled:

"Leave him alone, Byrd."

Byrd and the others whirled, Byrd swinging his pistol around to point in the direction of Carver's voice.

"Mr. Bler—"

"Drop it, Byrd, or I'll drop you."

Quadie strained his eyes to see into the darkness at the end of the hallway. There, in the doorway to the bedroom, Carver stood with a revolver leveled at Byrd's chest.

"All right, Mr. Blervaque, just take it—"

"Put it *away*, asshole. Now!"

Very slowly, with exaggerated and careful movements, Byrd opened his coat and returned the gun to its shoulder holster. "It's gone," he said in a soothing voice. "Calm down. Nobody wants to hurt you. Put your gun down and we can talk about this. Nobody has to get hurt."

"I want you out of my house right now."

"Carver, what are you doing?" Quadie asked. This was not at all like Carver, neither the actions nor his speech—he sounded like a character out of a bad adventure program.

"You shut up," Byrd ordered. "You're in enough trouble already. As are you, Blervaque, and this isn't helping your case."

"No, I don't suppose it is."

Quadie felt strangely detached as he watched the confrontation play out. The entire situation seemed too surreal. Something about it just plain did not ring true.

"Come on, Blervaque. Be reasonable. What do you think this is going to accomplish?"

Byrd took a step forward, holding his hands slightly away from his body. Carver made no response, and Byrd took another step.

Why was Carver doing this? Quadie wondered. He'd said he had it all taken care of. He couldn't have meant *this*.

He'd said his friends would help him get away. Where were they?

Movement distracted Quadie. One of the Thompsons, standing where Carver's sight of him would be blocked by Byrd, had begun to reach into his coat. Quadie realized with sudden horror that the whole team had been coordinating their actions virtually, through their headsets, all along.

"Carver, look out!" he shouted.

Two of the Thompsons threw themselves against Quadie to restrain him. In the same instant, Byrd leapt to the side, flattening himself against the wall as the other man drew his pistol and fired at Carver.

Carver did not react. The man fired again, as did Byrd, two more explosive pops shattering the air. Quadie knew they couldn't have missed at such short range, but none of the darts had any effect. Carver neither fell nor fired his own gun.

Everyone froze for a second, and Carver said, "See, Quadie, this is what I've been trying to tell you all along. It makes no difference. True reality, virtual or natural, is all in the mind."

He raised the gun to his head.

With a scream, Byrd dropped his pistol and rushed down the hall, leaping the last two meters to tackle Carver.

He landed on the floor alone.

Carver had vanished.

There was another second or two of stunned silence. Byrd rolled to a sitting position and looked back and forth between the bedroom and the hallway. "Where did he go?"

The three others took off to search the house; Byrd retrieved his gun and approached Quadie. "What just happened?" he asked, a threatening edge in his voice.

Nonplussed, Quadie just shook his head and shrugged.

Byrd seemed about to say something more, but turned abruptly and looked through the living room.

"Shit," he said. With his gun he motioned Quadie ahead of him. "Move. No tricks."

They walked through the living room and into the kitchen. French doors stood wide open to a deck overlooking the woods. One of the Thompsons stood at the top of the stairs that led down to the ground.

"He's gone, sir," the man said without turning, still staring out to the trees. .

Byrd grabbed Quadie's collar. "How long ago?"

"He was here. He was. I touched him. It must have been right when you got here. He told me to open the door. I—"

"It's been three or four minutes, sir. He could be anywhere out there."

"Shit!" Byrd let go of Quadie's shirt and reholstered his gun.

It's all in your mind. Quadie heard Carver's voice ring in his head. Judging by the man's reaction, Quadie figured Byrd heard it as well. *That's what magic is all about.*

"Oh, fuck this. He doesn't know any more than we do."

"What have I been trying to tell you for the last hour?" Quadie shouted in exasperation.

"All right," Byrd snapped. "Get the fuck out of my sight. Go back to your hotel. You want to go back home—or anywhere else—I'd better hear about it first. This isn't even close to being over."

Quadie drove back to the hotel. He left the car there and started walking. It was mid-afternoon now, too hot and muggy, and he was unaccustomed to the exercise, but he was too antsy to just sit in his room. He needed to move.

He came eventually to the campus. Across the street he saw shops of all kinds. He'd passed by here on his way to and from Carver's but he had been too preoccupied to notice any of it then. Now he noticed, but did not care.

He continued on along the campus wall, moving through a crowd of students without paying them any attention. He rounded the corner and kept walking until he came to the entrance gate.

Quadie half expected Byrd had prohibited his access to the university, but the guard at the gate let him through without a hassle. With his headset he accessed the university information system and found a map to the library.

Quadie reached the building and walked up to the doors, but hesitated before going in. What was the point of his being here? he asked himself. He'd found Carver, and lost him again, perhaps for good. In any case, he knew it would be pointless to try to track down the Freeks who'd had been helping Carver.

A huge lawn, planted with magnolias and sprawling with students, spread out before the library. Quadie wandered out into the sunshine and with an awkward effort sat down on the grass. He shut off his headset and just sat there watching the people around him, trying not to think about anything at all.

Something tapped him on the head. He looked behind him. A little boy stood there, dressed in ragged clothing and a heavily decorated headset. He held a stick in one hand. He grinned down at Quadie and said, "Abracadabra."

Quadie smiled perfunctorily and stood. He was in no mood to be bothered right now. As he walked away, the boy laughed and called after him, "This magic wand. You grok *magic*, neh, mister?"

Magic. Quadie froze. His hand crept into his pocket and found the data prism Carver had given him. *I've got a lot of the younger kids on my side*, he had said.

The young boy's eyes glazed and he cocked his head as though listening to someone. He nodded, then stepped close to Quadie.

"Quadie," the boy said solemnly. "I meant what I said back at the house. We can work anywhere—physical location is not a constraint."

The boy stumbled over the words, and Quadie knew they

weren't his, that he was only repeating them as they appeared in his thoughts.

"There are *no* constraints at all anymore. That's what Byrd is so afraid of."

"In the Web, maybe," Quadie said to the little boy.

The child shook his head vehemently. "No, Quadie, no constraints *at all*. Virtual or natural. It doesn't matter now, 'cause reality is all in your mind. Reality is phenomenal. We can change it all. I can change it."

Quadie stared. "With your program?"

"Yes."

From across the way someone called out, "Hey, Riv, let's go! It's time to hit the road, if we don't want to miss the caravan."

"Don't worry, Quadie," the little boy told him. "I'll be in touch soon. Somehow."

The boy touched him with the stick again and laughed. "Blaze your trail."

Quadie watched as the boy ran away toward a group of kids, some college age, some much younger, but all dressed like the little boy, and all wearing headsets.

Those people are everywhere, Carver had said. *We can work anywhere.*

When the little boy reached the group, they all walked off around the far side of the library. Quadie watched them go, a strange sinking feeling developing in his stomach. He continued to stare for a long time after they disappeared from view, then abruptly turned and strode hurriedly away toward the main gate. He suddenly wanted to be very far away from this place.

The prism will explain everything. The future may depend on it.

Quadie clenched the prism tightly in his fist all the way back to the hotel, afraid to let go.